Black Angel

First of the Shikarath

by

Charlotte Lester

To Jean & Harry,

Best wishes,

Charlotte Lester

ISBN: 1-4140-6398-9 (e-book)
ISBN: 1-4140-6399-7 (Paperback)

This book is printed on acid free paper.

Cover art by Adam Beckett

1st Books - rev. 03/10/04

Acknowledgements:

Firstly a huge thank-you to my best friend Charlotte Merton, for all those hours you spent, and things you do that make me honoured to know you. I would like to thank my much-loved inspiration, a.k.a. my very dear mates Fish, Charlotte W, Hayley, Zoe, and Toby, for their unwavering friendship throughout the years. Thank you to my friend Ricky, without whose caring empathy I would be lost. A big hello to all the faithful minions at my Creative Writing Club; I deeply appreciate all your enthusiasm and support. I would also like to thank my Nan, who devotedly kept my book a secret and always had faith in me; I treasure the times, all too few now, that we have chance to sit and talk. Thank you to Adam Beckett, who kindly took care of the front cover for me, and lastly many thanks to my wonderful parents and brother, Jon, who have guided me during my life.

I love you all.

This book is dedicated to

Charlotte 'Bozza' Merton

For her enthusiasm, ideas, encouragement, devotion, and loyalty.

She is the enemy of procrastination, my muse, and my mind's twin.

You, my dear Charlotte, not only seem to share my very thoughts, but also are in my heart.

One chance, vile spawn, to save your life;
Nip the flower whilst in the bud,
For he will come with an angel in strife,
Your path, not mine, lies drenched in blood.

Erendiir the Wanderer

Prologue

"It is done, my mistress," whispered Eskiros as he bowed low before the throne. He kept his eyes fixed upon the floor as the figure on the throne spoke back.

"Were you seen?" asked the woman in a cold, polished tone. She stood lithely and paced to the far end of the vast cavern where she stood, staring questioningly at the now crouching figure by the marble throne. She was dressed in black, with a dark cloth concealing most of her face. Below the low sable robes the faint glimmer of a golden hem betrayed the importance of her position.

"There was no one there," replied Eskiros in his hissing drawl, "And the guards were easily dealt with. Gold tightens even the loosest tongues," he added, with a satisfied smirk fleetingly lighting his otherwise impassive face. At the robed figure's nod he stood up with an easy grace, and lounged against one of the six marble pillars supporting the roof. Looking around the cavern, he saw rich furnishings overlaid on cracking marble, and knew he was working for a very wealthy person. He had never been told his mistress' name, so was trying to get an idea of her identity by the power she possessed. He waited for a while, then finally parted his lips to ask the question. "Who is to be the next?" he rasped, his black gloved hands twitching with anticipation as he strove to conceal his excitement.

The dark figure at the end of the cavern gave a low, throaty chuckle. "Come, Tsumetai Ka, " she said, using the mock rank of the hungrily waiting warrior. "The poison needs four doses to work. The next 'casualty' will be decided only when the Kaji Tioni is… let us say, permanently out of breath."

When he would normally have asked for dismissal, Eskiros lingered. "What is to be done with the traitor Luellor? You should have had done with him long ago. I could make a few exceptions today and find time to make him regret every minuscule detail he had ever told the Kajarito…" he rasped, with a demonically eager expression.

"You forget yourself. No one tells *me* what to do! You are only a Tsumetai, whereas I will be the Kai of all Bakarn. Without me, you would have been executed long ago." She nodded once, dismissing the Tsumetai, and he strolled gracefully to the door. "And Eskiros…"

"Yes, O future Kai?"

"If you even think about betraying me, then…" she made a quick gesture with her fingers. Eskiros gave a wicked smirk, and loped stealthily away down the corridor.

When she was sure he had gone, the woman once more crossed the cavern and draped her sinuous self upon the pillar stump that served as a makeshift throne. She made a harsh noise in the back of her throat, and a blue-black raven dropped from one of the rafters and alighted upon the arm of the throne. Its head was a black that seemed to shine purple in the low light, and its plumage caught a beautiful, shiny, opalescent tinge. And it was knee high on any man.

"Amenis, my faithful companion," the figure said, her voice changing to a loving, distorted croon as she addressed the bird. "Go and fetch Imcarr and the prisoner."

With a grating call, the raven spread its iridescent wings and swooped out of the door. Moments later a dark-haired young guard entered, leading a large, balding man on a chain. Both men bowed low to the woman, then the younger pushed the prisoner to his knees. The cloaked woman dismissed the dark-haired Imcarr, and looked at the fat captive trembling fitfully on the floor as if he was no more than a repulsive maggot.

"So, Luellor," she spat, in a proud tone filled with loathing, "You thought you could try to sell me to the Kajarito? Did you not realise what punishment you would get when you were stopped, traitor?"

"I b-beg you, m-merciful lady, not...not...no, p-please, n-not that...show mercy, m-my Mistress!" He tried to reach for her shoe, his breath coming in harsh sobs.

She contemptuously kicked his hand out of the way, her eyes blazing. "You thought that I would spare you, that you would not have to endure a punishment? *No-one* gets away with treachery here," and now she chuckled maliciously, "we have certain punishments."

She paused, and called softly, sweetly, "Amenis! Come, my darling, I need your advice!" She turned back to Luellor, and smiled slyly beneath her veil. "But, as usual, you get a second judgement." Amenis glided in to perch again upon the throne, his wings just clipping Luellor's shaven head. He ducked, passing a hand over his sweat soaked brow. The woman stroked the raven's head gently, then took out a thin pack of large cards from her pocket. She laid them face downwards on a small table to the side of where she sat. Amenis cocked his head to one side, surveying the pitiful captive with his beady eyes. He then turned to his Mistress and jerked his head.

"Treachery to me," she said, as if answering an unspoken question. The raven bobbed his head once, and then scrutinised the cards with his beady, intelligent eyes. Nine of them lay upon the table, each one predicting a different fate for the victims of the lady. After staring at the cards for what seemed to Luellor to be an eternity, Amenis dipped his head and picked up one, then dropped it into the lap of the cloaked woman.

Slowly her hand reached down, and picked it up. Turning it over, she laughed mockingly, caressing the head of her creature with her other hand. She held up the card for Luellor to see, and he blanched with fear. The words at the bottom of the card read, 'The Changing'.

"A fate worse than death for you, traitor Luellor!" the woman crowed. She reached behind her improvised throne and drew out a blue crystal with a single feather trapped inside the middle of the rock. The crystal was blue in itself, but acted as a prism, throwing out the colours of the spectrum in a myriad of different shades to bathe the cavern in its breathtaking light. She fondly stroked the crystal, and the colours writhed and changed around the cavern, illuminating her dark eyes to make them shine like diamonds.

She closed her blazing eyes and held the wonderful crystal in both hands until she seemed to shine, with the same dazzling colours twisting and enveloping her body in glistening strands of raw power. She slowly brought up one hand to point at Luellor and he struggled wildly against his chains, pleading and praying to the last. She opened her eyes; there was a blinding flash, and a drawn-out scream of agony.

And then silence.

*   *   *

Far above, on a wild, snow-capped mountain, a huge bird stood watch over her eggs. The snow still fell, threatening to cover the precious objects, but the exhausted mother spread her vast wings and shielded her unborn children with her body. She lay there, slowly disappearing as the dirty white slush rose to her wingtips. Every now and then she would struggle free of the enveloping white blanket and flap her wings to clear them.

The shikara could smell the storm in the air, and could sense that it would go on for at least another two suns. Though the cold was taking its toll, she was glad that her children were safely inside their warm vessels until they hatched, which should be in about four suns.

She stood again awkwardly, crying out in exertion against the keening wind as she freed her enormous wings and beat them fiercely in the air. She was mighty and fierce, a queen of her race. She stood over three times as high as any man with a wingspan of over fifteen metres. She was the last adult of her clan, massive, compassionate, beautiful birds similar to enormous eagles which had long since been considered a myth by the people of Bakarn. The gold markings on her back were faded with exhaustion, the white plumage on her breast was dirty and grey with ill health, and the once keen and shining talons were blunt and dull. Yet she still covered her clutch of nineteen mottled eggs with fierce motherly adoration, calling softly to them with messages of hope and love.

She tried to shake her wings again, shivering as she felt the snow trickle down between the strong layer of protective feathers and touch like a frozen kiss against her skin. Then she felt fear. The snow had trapped her wings by her and was sealing them into the ice; she could not free herself! Her thoughts of panic and desperation unsettled her unborn offspring in their eggs, and she briefly felt the reassuring touch of their minds flicker with alarm and unease. She had to be strong, she had to fight for her life and those of her children! With a shrill scream of effort, she clenched her muscles, then drove upward and erupted out of the pile of building snow. Standing there she shrilled her challenge to the fury of the blizzard. Then with a start she turned.

Her precious eggs were lost under the snow!

Immediately the shikara hopped to the area and began feverishly gouging at the area with her talons. The tip of an egg came into view; one, then another, then another until she had uncovered all but one. Throwing herself over the nest, she again spread her wings and shielded them with her body, yearning with all her heart for the storm to stop. She turned her head to stare desperately out of the cave mouth, and the bitter wind roared its cruel mockery of her challenge. Numb with horror and fatigue, she could only stare back.

A sudden cracking sound reached her through the noise of the wind, and with sudden dread she whirled around back to her nest. To her horror, she saw that one egg was opening. She stared in terrified shock. This was not right! They should not be hatching for a long time yet! How many would hatch into the freezing white nightmare? This was all wrong! This was evil! She had no way to stop her chicks from venturing out into the deadly storm without other shikarath to aid her.

She watched as the newborn hatchling pushed its way out of the dripping eggshell and stood, glistening and cold, on the rim of the nest. She called to it, worriedly at first, and then frenziedly. She could sense its confusion. Where were the people to Link with? Where were their future life partners? It called out, searchingly, then awkwardly stumbled out into the blizzard.

By now, other hatchlings had emerged and clumsily started to follow their brother into the storm's pitiless lure, crying piteously for the humans that should be there, that had always been there before. Their mother, frozen near to death, watched helplessly as her children stumbled out to their deaths in the bitter cold. She gave one last, piercing scream which echoed the anguish and torment in her heart, and with almost closed eyes saw her last child walk out into the wrath of the blizzard.

Only it was not the last. Inside one last egg, hidden in a cocoon of snow, one single chick slumbered peacefully, not knowing how important he was to be in events to come. Outside the storm raged on, and the snow settled on the stiff body of the once mighty queen. Her expression was one of terrible loss and her face was streaked with frozen tears.

Chapter 1

-The cool breeze gently blew a couple of glistening brown leaves along the floor of the courtyard. They tumbled and blew about, here and there, dancing on the wind. As the wind dropped they skittered to a halt at the feet of the third youngest Kaji, Destinariae. The young woman's hair swirled about as the breeze returned, and she paused in her contemplation to push a few of the erring silky black strands back behind her ear. People had often told her she was beautiful, but she was indifferent because it meant nothing to her.

She turned her concentration back to the fountain on which she leaned. It had been a gift from her father, the Ka of Bakarn, to her younger sister, Kaji Faitan. It had seven bronze turtles, representing the age of the Kaji on that birthday, balancing a golden fish on their shells. An elegant stream of water constantly rose from the fish's mouth and trickled down the heads of the turtles to land with a pretty tinkling in the large dish below. It was a beautiful piece, and had cost thousands of gold eagles to forge and buy.

She smiled. It had been her late mother's idea to call the new money after birds. There were the gold eagles, the silver hawks and the bronze wrens. Both her father and stepmother were mad about money, though, she thought. Because of his immense wealth, the Ka had always tried to exceed himself on rich gifts for his wife and seven daughters. He had promised to give Faitan a gold and pearl life-size statue of herself for her eighth birthday. It was not for love of his children, she knew, but for showing off the wealth of the royal family. But he was very fond of his girls. Destinariae knew that whatever she asked for, he would give it to her without hesitation.

She crossed the courtyard, her satin shoes making slight scuffing sounds on the stone floor. Destinariae pulled a face. The shoes were like most things in her life, ridiculously expensive but terribly impractical. She looked down at them, and turned one foot on its side to get a better look. The movement uncovered a small imperfection in the stone of the courtyard, and the Kaji leaned down to get a closer look.

Running her fingers over the rough surface, Destinariae at once knew what it was. The small dent had been made by the tip of an arrow. The very same arrow that...

A sudden breath of chilling wind swept over her, making her shiver involuntarily. She looked up, and saw the empty battlements rearing tall against the grey sky. The battlements where a lone bowman had once stood, poised to fire...fire at the very spot she was kneeling at. She looked back at the indentation in the stone and saw her mother's still form lying there, transfixed by an arrow that went the full way through her slender body and yet still had the power left to chip the flagstone. The sudden image had such terrible clarity that Destinariae could have almost been there at the scene; even though she had been a baby scarcely out of the womb when the murder of Isete was committed. For a moment she remained deathly still, kneeling on the cold stone floor while the unsettling breeze whispered to her with faint echoes of her mother's gentle voice.

The sound of bawling cut through the eerie silence of the courtyard, reminding Destinariae of her little baby sister Efaerin. With an abrupt toss of her head, like a spirited mare, Destinariae stood and dusted herself off, concentrating on the matter in hand. Six sisters! Now what was she meant to do with six sisters? Kaji Rieda was to be the next Kai, and Destinariae and all her other sisters were as useful as a sparrow chick in a vulture's nest. Why couldn't she have been an only child, or a boy? A Kajo would take precedence over any Kaji to be heir. Hearing her name, she stood, and walked into the nursery, ignoring the pompous servant waiting to announce her.

As she waited to be admitted by her stepmother, Destinariae wondered about the tradition. It seemed slightly strange to her that it was the eldest child who inherited the throne, and not the most fit for the position. Tradition, she shrugged, mentally spitting the word. It never did to argue about it, especially as that was the dominating focus of the Royal family's life. Her life seemed to be so much more complicated because

3

of being a girl. Not that it didn't have its advantages as well, though. Multi-tasking, for one thing.

"It's what separates the men from the women," she murmured to herself with a slight smile. "That and intelligence."

Thinking of her stepmother, she impatiently tapped her foot. If there was one thing which really annoyed her, it was being kept waiting. These meetings with the Kai were all the same. Wait, wait, wait, could you do this, I thought I told you to do that and of course the old favourite have you chosen a husband yet. At the guard's signal, she raised a slender hand and opened the heavy oak door.

Kai Tifiert was seated on a red velvet, padded chair with a small, squirming, wriggling baby in her silk-wrapped arms. She was clothed in a low-cut gown of shimmering gold which, Destinariae had to admit, blatantly showed her mesmerising, if a little too obvious, beauty. Her face was angled towards the tiny baby girl, but her mind seemed to be elsewhere. She looked up and smiled haughtily as she saw Destinariae, and laid Efaerin gently in the ornate cradle by her side.

"Hello, Kaji Destinariae," she said in a tone as sweet as honey, yet poisonous as a serpent's kiss.

"Greetings, Kai Tifiert," replied Destinariae with a tight-lipped smile, trying to turn a tired sigh into a bright greeting as she curtseyed elegantly. "I await your pleasure, your highness." Although being so respectful to her stepmother, the woman who so casually had slipped in and replaced Destinariae's mother, felt disloyal and hurt deeply, the Kaji knew that as far as her father was concerned Tifiert was the new Kai, and should be treated like it. End of story.

Tifiert nodded graciously, then beckoned Destinariae to rise, with a self-satisfied smile adorning those perfect lips. "You seem to be spending your time well," she added superciliously, her elegantly plucked eyebrow arching amusedly as she viewed the slightly dusty patches on the dress over Destinariae's knees.

Destinariae gritted her teeth to retain her pleasant smile. "I've already been to my poetry and reading tutor, and I fed the salamanders last week. They only eat raw meat now, you know, it could be quite dangerous if one of them escaped." The only criticism I dare offer, she thought bitterly.

Tifiert stood and put on her most winsome expression, pouting her lips and widening her eyes theatrically. "Now, you know that isn't fair. They were my birthday gift, if you remember rightly. My husband bought them for me, he insisted that he would, and it would have been very discourteous of me to refuse. And, while we're talking of discourtesy to your betters, don't take that tone with me!"

To the casual, naïve eavesdropper, Destinariae observed, Tifiert was a beautiful, delicate angel, and a protective mother. Every word she said was calculated for maximum congeniality to the eavesdropping audience, and ultimate condescension to the person she was addressing. 'If you remember rightly' was Tifiert's way of asserting her own authority and forcing her own point of view. 'My husband' was a way of reminding the young Kaji that while Destinariae was the one of the many daughters of the most powerful

5

man in Bakarn, Tifiert was his beloved wife and so was eminent over others. And of course the 'don't take that tone with me' was a threat, concealed in the guise of a loving reprimand from a concerned parent.

But Destinariae was wise to the tricks of courtly speech, and knew that anyone listening would discredit the 'loving overprotective parent' scheme, for they all knew that Destinariae was the daughter of the late Kai Isete. Also, thought Destinariae wryly, that facial expression might have a truly devastating effect of my father, but it certainly will not win me over.

Tifiert obviously realised that she had not quite cut deep enough yet, so she quickly donned her most angelic and innocent face, and crooned gently, "Desti, I only want to know if you've, you know, chosen anyone yet. I mean, you have less than a year now before your sister takes centre stage and you become unattractive as a wife..."

Typical, Destinariae thought, lowering her eyes to hide the anger that shone from them, she's trying to pit us all against each other. It wouldn't work though, she considered sardonically. Rieda's always had centre stage, and nothing I do now will alter that. And 'Desti'. She was sure that Tifiert only called her these things to annoy her. No doubt *'daughter'* would come up soon, too.

But two could play at that game. "No, *Tiffi*. I want freedom to control my own life, not sit around playing the obedient dumb wife." At the malicious gleam that entered Tifiert's eyes as she opened her mouth to interject, Destinariae pushed on. "I'm not just a thing to be traded for gold and to be bartered like an object. I'm a human, with human emotions and human needs. And one of those needs is *not* a rich snooty husband!"

"Listen, *daughter*," hissed Tifiert, drawing back in a swirl of golden skirts, her face distorted with malice. "I'm… your parent and you must obey your parents, remember? I've given you a choice of six Lords, haven't I? *I* say that you get married, and you shall be married by next Winter Solstice whether you choose and come willingly or I tell your father…"

"I've told you every single time and I will tell you again, *mother,* I am *not* getting married off to some pot-bellied, pig-headed, arrogant, snivelling weasel of a Lord so that you can demand tax off him to add to your overflowing treasure rooms!" she replied, through clenched teeth. She fought to keep from shouting, but knew with a sickening feeling in her stomach that she had already gone too far.

"How the hell are we meant to find a new home for you when you get older if you cannot even begin to see sense and insist on insulting every half decent man who comes here?" shouted the Kai. "We only care about your safety, in the hands of a lord!" Her tone spat venom at the young Kaji. "And I hope your husband gives you a sound thrashing, brat, for it's more than you deserve!"

"Oh, finally you drop the act, Tifiert! You only care about your money from the hands of a lord, you greedy hag!" snarled Destinariae.

Tifiert's face hardened, and with the speed of a striking snake her jewelled hand shot out and slapped Destinariae hard around the face.

The Kaji's head turned back slowly, her face marked in angry red where the heavy rings had bitten into her skin. Her dark eyes gleamed with frustrated loathing, and she fought to keep herself from lashing back at the arrogant bitch.

"You shouldn't have done that, Tifiert," she warned in a low, threatening voice. "You really shouldn't have done that."

"What are you going to do about it, little girl?" taunted the Kai, though her eyes gleamed with panic for a second. "Tell daddy? Well who do you think he's going to believe, his wife, or his little child?" She smiled viciously.

Destinariae heard the ring of truth in her stepmother's words, and bit back a scathing retort. "Oh never fear, mother mine, I shan't tell a soul. But some day an evil will fall on you, and on that day you will remember my words and regret the spite you have visited on me, you hateful creature. Goodbye, bitch."

With a last look of pure hatred, Destinariae turned, and struggling to hold back tears she left the room. The acknowledgement of her own failure of self control bit as sharply as the sound of her baby sister's crying, echoing in her ears.

The aviary was huge. Mossy branches littered the ground and vine leaves had been skilfully looped through the mesh at the top of the massive area. It could have comfortably housed one hundred peacocks, but only a medium number of assorted birds sat hunched around the perches. Destinariae clucked coaxingly to them through the mesh, but they made no move to come closer to her. A shabby looking venya-stork stared balefully at her, and an old chaffinch croaked fearfully from a safe distance away. Destinariae tried once more without success, then hearing footsteps behind her, she turned.

"Oh, hello Chova!" she said brightly.

"Destinariae." Chova gently inclined her head. "Where did that weird…stork…thing come from?"

"Another present from our wonderful father. Shame he could only get this old wreck, though," replied Destinariae, with a black look directed towards the offending bird.

"Don't say that. He always tries his best for us, though you seem unable to see that. He loves us dearly, you know," scolded Chova with a mildly worried look on her face.

Destinariae frowned. "I know he is fond of us. He owns us, though. We are like the pieces on a Gijau board. Wherever he deigns to place us, we must do our best to keep him winning the game."

"Loose talk like that in front of somebody could be considered treason. You should be careful," warned Chova. "I've heard there was an attempt on Kaji Rieda's life today. The Kajaritoka wanted to question us all, but our father protested that loyalty was so strong within our family that there was no need for *us* to have the ordeal of questioning. Talk like that and you'll find yourself talking to the Kajarito!"

"Don't be ridiculous," scoffed Destinariae. She continued in a singsong, mocking voice. "The Kajarito serve the Ka and the royal family. *We* are the royal family. That means that *they* serve *us*. That's why they are called the *Ka*-jarito!" she added scornfully. "Anyway, tell *daddy* that I want a proper creature of my own, not a shabby old bird!"

Kaji Chova purpled, then stalked off. Destinariae watched her moody sister as she headed for the steep stairs leading down to the 'questioning room', as the Ka so liked to call it. Everywhere else it was called the torture chamber. She thought for a moment of following Chova to make sure the task was carried out, but decided against it.

Looking back, she might have been a little harsh on her sister. After all, Chova was going through a difficult time in her life; the teenage years. As her older sister, Destinariae could understand that being a member of the royal family during this time *could* be hard. But then again, she had managed it- and done quite well by herself, all things considered. So Chova had no reason to be so moody, walking around with a face like…well, something unmentionable. It really got on her nerves, though she tried to stay calm and pleasant. The protective walls of the palace seemed to be shrinking daily, becoming confining. Couldn't they see she needed her air? Why, oh why, did she have to have six sisters?

She heard a gasp from behind her, and a clang. She turned swiftly to see her personal servant, Kethar, stooping to pick up a bucket and sponge.

"I'm so sorry, your highness," he apologised, his face red. He stood, then remembered himself and bowed, the jerking movements causing his thick black hair to flop over his eyes.

"Please stand up, Kethar, you're making me feel seasick with all that bobbing," she said. Kethar smiled, knowing by experience that the slightly sharp words belied a kind thought for him. He knew how she hated being 'bowed and scraped' to.

"Yes, my lady. Thank you, my lady," he said, standing upright.

"What are you doing here, Kethar?" she asked, a pleasant smile gracing those bright lips. He tried not to stare at them.

"I've just come to clean your aviary, my lady. I can come back later, if you'd rather be alone with the birds." He stood, ready to be dismissed.

She shook her head prettily. "No, please go ahead." He nodded to her and removed the key from his pocket, unlocking and pushing open the small side door. She could not see him for a moment; then he emerged behind the grimy window, hauling a bucket of soapy water over to it. He wiped sweat from his forehead, smiled at her, and began to clean it carefully.

Destinariae gazed at him through the glass, knowing he was not just putting on a show of industry for her benefit. Often she watched from her window and saw him energetically scrubbing the walls, his mouth moving as if he talked to himself. She really must get round to asking him about that.

Kethar tried not to look out at his gentle mistress, feeling her gaze fall upon him. He tried to look bright and enthusiastic, though he groaned inwardly as his sponge made small circles on the glass. He wished he did not have to do this monotonous chore so often.

Twice a week! Each time it was the same; wash, scrub, clean, then come back a few days later and it was exactly as it was before he had started. Birds were such messy creatures. He'd be lucky if he escaped without at least one bird dropping on his clothes. Usually he was covered in them. Cleaning day was one of the few times when he really appreciated a bath.

As he scrubbed at the dirty window, some birds perching on the branch above the window felt the need to relieve themselves. Swearing at them profusely, he once again washed out the yellow marks. "Mangy old birds. You had to pick just there, didn't you?" he muttered, squinting up at them.

"Who are you talking to?" enquired Destinariae from outside. Kethar froze for a second; had she thought he was talking to her? If he had dared speak to her, there was no way 'mangy old bird' would have been his choice of words. Then he looked outside and saw a look of amused interest on her flawless face.

"Just to the birds, your highness," he replied, trying not to blush. He shook his head. The birds always seemed to dislike him cleaning their cage. They didn't have a problem with him being there, but as soon as they saw his cleaning things...

He had always had the honour, albeit a dubious one, of cleaning out the Kaji's beloved birds. Not that he saw it as much of an honour. It wasn't the birds, they were all right, more or less. It was just the constant cycle of dirt. There had to be something better he could do with his life rather than just being, well, a cleaner. But as a servant, he was lucky he didn't get a worse job, like cleaning the bedpans.

"If you don't clean us out better than last time, our mistress said she'd make you clean out the privies." A lilting voice fluted out from the safety of a large bush.

"I always clean it until it's spotless!" he answered tolerantly.

"Was that to the birds again?" called Destinariae with a charming laugh.

"Yes, my lady," he replied. "It's nice to talk to them. They talk back to me, sometimes," he added, moving on to the next panel.

"I wish sometimes they'd talk to me," she confided with a sigh.

"No you don't, begging your pardon my lady, for they can be rude little buggers sometimes!" he laughed, then bit his lip as he realised what he had said. Then he relaxed as he heard her laugh outside. Why on earth did he complain about his chores, when he had such a kind, tolerant mistress? Such a beautiful mistress, he thought, forcing himself not to look out at her.

"If you don't mind, Kethar, I think I will go to my chambers now. I will look forward to seeing you soon."

"I look forward to seeing you too, my lady," he answered, hearing her light footsteps crunch over the gravelled path. He put all thoughts of her out of his head as he tried to concentrate on the task in hand. Otherwise I'll never get this finished, he thought to himself.

As he moved round to the next part to be washed, Kethar groaned inwardly. This was the worst part. They were always especially protective of their nesting area. It had been suggested that this part was left alone, but the Kaji was adamant that the *entire* cage was pristine to provide the best possible level of comfort for her treasured pets.

"If you miss even the tiniest little spot our mistress will have your head!" This time a harsher voice croaked the warning, and Kethar suspected that it belonged to the Kaji's greenwing, an evil-minded bird.

"If I die she'll just send in somebody else," said Kethar calmly. "Not that I'd be executed anyway. You obviously don't know your own mistress. Why don't you try talking to her once in a while?" he asked persuasively, trying to repay some of his debt towards the lady he...ai, he loved.

"We try, we try, but she will not hear us!" came an echoing reply. Kethar got back to work, contemplating the remark, until another birdcall broke his concentration.

"I've got a really good idea, why don't you not clean us out, ever, then the mistress will cut your head off and we can live in peace in our own cage!" chattered a speckled yellow bird that Kethar did not recognise.

"Stop being so nasty to him- he's nicer than the others we had!" a golden fantail cooed sympathetically. An argument broke out.

"Look, will you just let me get on with my job now? You might want to have my head chopped off, but I don't!" exclaimed Kethar, slightly impatiently. They soon fell silent again, but only for a matter of seconds.

"Clean it properly, properly, will you?" echoed a preening blackback, rocking forwards on his perch. "I am not eating no treats off a dirty floor, dirty floor!"

"If I have missed even the smallest spot of dirt, I swear I will use all of my money to buy you premium quality bird treats."

"Okay mate, you're on!"

Some of them were quite impressive birds, Kethar noticed, sweeping the floor of dead leaves. The Ka spared no expense for his daughters' benefit, especially when they asked for certain items that they desired. The birds were, he thought to himself, rather too spoiled. It's a good job we like each other, he thought wryly to himself. Or else I'd be attacked every time I tried to clean them out. He knew this for a fact, because all of the other cleaners who had been tried had come out far more injured than he did.

It was strange, he mused. Maybe it was because they sensed that he quite liked them. Not that they talked to him very much. Sometimes that offended him, when he said something and they did not answer. But, after all, they were only birds. How much could he expect of them?

He turned around, satisfied that he had done a good job, and surveyed the aviary. It was not bad, if you thought about it. Actually, it was impressive. It gave the birds a lot of room to fly, and they had toys to play with. Aside from that, it was pleasant to look at, with its finely structured beams and ornamental arches. The green was a welcome relief from the rich, overbearing colours of the palace.

Turning his face to gaze out of the window, he saw the brown path winding down to the stables, with its neatly pruned borders of flowers. The Ka loved neatness. A worried looking servant hurried past the birdcage, hardly sparing Kethar a glance when he waved in greeting. Idly, he wondered what errand he was on. Something had gone wrong, by the look of things. Well, that was no concern of his. Back to business.

Walking over to the small, dark room at the back of the aviary, Kethar picked up the basket of birdseed and slowly wandered to each feeding point, scooping handfuls of grain into the bowls. The birds did not start feeding until he had walked away.

"What happened to premium bird food, friend?" chattered a Garoan hookbill, tipping back it's head to swallow.

"This is more like what low class people feed their birds," agreed the fantail.

"We demand to see the manager!" Raucous laughter greeted this comment, ringing out from the surrounding branches and perches.

"Look, I only give you what I'm told to, like a good little boy," said Kethar, smiling.

"Little? You're a bit on the podgy side if you ask me!" More laughter ensued. As he replaced the grain, carefully so as not to waste a single seed or nut, he wondered if birds were ever polite to anyone. They never seemed to be the least bit civil to him. Maybe it was just part of their nature. He had resigned himself, years ago, to the fact that no matter what task he had, someone was going to look down on him and insult him. The birds were certainly good at that. Actually, he thought with a fleeting grin, it was quite refreshing to be insulted by his inferiors. Though to be sure, the birds were probably the only living creatures in his life that could be counted as his inferiors.

Taking the broom from where he had left it leaning against the wall, he started to sweep up the newly scattered food debris from the floor. Kethar seethed inwardly as he watched the acrobatic performance of a hyperactive Cular-finch. It was causing all sorts of things to fall to the floor. Birds were such messy creatures!

He turned to leave, but stopped as a storm of noisy chattering broke out among the birds. "Shut up!" he shouted, waving the broom handle enthusiastically. "I will be back tomorrow. Remember, though, the promise of premium seed doesn't count for the mess that's been made since I finished cleaning." He put the cleaning things away and locked the cupboard.

As he walked through the door, a small, annoying voice squeaked unhelpfully, "You missed a bit." He slammed the door shut and walked off without a backward glance, highly irritated by the birds' lack of gratitude toward him. Feathered wretches, he thought sourly.

* * *

In the flat plains of Kanako a village was burning. The old wooden huts blazed like a bonfire and the meeting hall was a raging inferno. Timbers cracked and gave way, and hit the ground with showers of flying sparks. The houses creaked and groaned ominously, and every now and then another twig would catch light and fly from one roof to another. The whole village was ablaze, and the fiery smudge in the night sky could be seen clearly in the exposed area. Dotted about here and there were the blackened or still burning corpses of the late inhabitants. A few of them were still alive, and the terrible smell of scorched flesh filled the air.

Khalla awoke to an intensity of pain on her face. She tried to raise a hand to probe the agonising area but found that she could not. Only then did she feel the weight of the heavy, charred beam across her back. She rolled slightly on her side and felt the wood shift. Trying to wriggle forwards, she dislodged the beam even more. With mounting hope she tried again, and felt the heavy bar shift again. Eventually, with a combination of rolling and wriggling out, she managed to get clear of it. Around her, buildings disintegrated and people screamed, but she could hardly think at all.

She jumped backwards as another huge piece of burning wood crashed down, and ducked as ash and sparks went everywhere. Limping forward, she narrowly missed being impaled by a jagged spar of broken metal, and staggered on again. She tried to shriek in terror as another roof fell in beside her, but her smoke-dried throat could only let out a choked gasp. Finally stumbling out of the scene of carnage, she dropped to the ground. Numb with pain, terror, and disbelief, she watched with horror-filled eyes as her birthplace, her home of happy memories, was eaten by the fire's insatiable lust. A grey smog filled the air, and with a lurch Khalla hit the ground and blacked out.

Woken by the burning agony of back, lungs and heart, Khalla coughed agonisingly, and her pain-filled gaze took in the appalling scene. All that remained of the catastrophe was a smoking skeleton of the village. Khalla stood up shakily, and took a few tottering steps forward before finding some reserves of inner strength. She walked slowly through the awful scene of carnage, towards the place where her hut had once stood, and looked with slowly filling eyes at the bodies of her parents. Both lay crumpled on the floor; their bodies contorted into grotesque shapes beside the blackened stones of the fireplace. The agony they had suffered was shown clearly in their faces; mouths twisted open with terror, eyes wide and glassy, and…Khalla had to look away. There were two other bodies there, both hideously maimed beyond recognition, and she knew that one must have been her beloved sister. With tears dripping down her bloody face, she started to pick up the corpses to lay her family to rest.

Two hours later, Khalla stood, dry eyed, silently watching the corpses she had found burn. Passed beyond the point of emotional and physical pain, she had no tears left to cry. She had been through the ruins of the village, taking bodies out and placing them on the wood that remained of her home. She had wept every time she uncovered a familiar face- Hurai the blacksmith, Naraia the nurse, her friends Toria and Yaelon, and Araquin the stable boy, who had been her closest companion. Now, watching the funeral pyre,

19

she was immune to all feeling and could only stare into the fire.

She thought of her mother, once warm and vibrant, now cold and still. She thought of her father, outwardly brisk and gruff, inside caring and loving, now just a fond memory to think of in troubled times. She thought of her sister, her lovely, joyful, happy, beautiful, wonderful sister, now just another dead body in the dying land. She would never see or embrace or be with any of them again. And it was all *his* fault, she thought, wrath bubbling up inside her. All this, it was *him* that had done it. *He* was responsible for the death of her family, her friends, her whole *life*.

Something inside her mind snapped. She would find him, aye, and kill him. She would avenge the deaths of everyone she had ever known and loved.

With that thought, she stood up, and walked purposefully to the pile of blackened belongings she had gathered from the wreckage. She had already found a warm cloak, a loaf of charred bread, a few turnips and a carrysack, so she should be fine for a day or so. She rummaged through the pile, and examined several of the items. She'd need a knife...oh no, that one wouldn't do. It was far too heavy. What about that one? The pommel stone was grimy and thick with ash, but she could see its amber hue. No, she thought, very unbalanced, she wouldn't be able to throw it.

She caught herself thinking just as she was about to toss the knife aside, and stopped, shaking. Here she was, Khalla, an inexperienced village girl with only a few training sessions to prepare her, planning to find and kill a skilled, trained assassin, and discarding a beautiful knife because it would be unsuitable for killing or maiming another living creature. She sank down onto the scorched grass, and shut her eyes tight. How could she even think of killing and murdering?

Because *he* had done it, and to her family and friends. If she did nothing, who knows how many other families would be murdered, and how many other people would be wondering whether to give chase and kill, or mope pitifully and just leave it to someone else? With a new determination, Khalla went back to her scrutiny of the pile. She shifted aside a charred box, and her gaze was immediately drawn to a dusty, ash-covered, curved sabre. She slowly extended her hand and picked it up, and tested her finger along the edge of the blade. She lifted her hand to her face, and saw that the grime on her fingers was washed away by a trickle of dark blood. She smiled with grim satisfaction, turned on her heel, and stalked away into the night.

Chapter 2

"Kaji Destinariae! Come quickly! Kaji Chova is dying!"

Destinariae whirled around, shock written all over her usually smiling face. "What?"

"She was found just a few minutes ago...and... his Imperial Majesty the Ka summons you to appear at the council chamber with all haste. He begs you to come speedily. Please!"

Destinariae took one look at the servant, and set off at a run for the council chamber. There could be no mistake, the swift glance at the servant's trembling face had told her all the proof she needed. But Chova... dead? She descended the flight of stairs three steps at a time, and burst into the chamber to stand directly at her father's side. The Ka was gracious enough to look desperately worried, she noticed acerbically, and wondered if her normally impassive father had some emotions in his body after all that were not directed towards gold.

"What happened, my lord Ka?" asked Destinariae with a gasp as she looked at the limp form lying on a bier in front of the Ka. She saw just how worried her father must be in the number of the expensively paid priests and healers gathered around the prone body.

"She fell down the stairs down to the torture chamber. An ominous injury, apparently."

Destinariae swept past the moaning healers and chanting priests, pushing them over each other as she knelt at her sister's side. "You idiotic fools," she spat at the cringing people, "Can't you see she's dead? She's got a broken neck, a fatal injury! Get out of my sight! You can do nothing for her now!"

The assembled throng scattered and several people were trampled in their undignified sprint for the door. "Kaji Destinariae, that was uncalled for," reprimanded her father.

"Maybe so," replied Destinariae angrily, "but I know more than that load of idiots put together. They care more about their own money than about my sister! Can't they see that Chova is... is..." and she broke down and wept.

"Destinariae," started the Ka slowly after some time had elapsed, "You're quite quick. Do you suppose that this wasn't an..."

"Accident?" interrupted Destinariae, raising her tear-stained face. The startled flash on the Ka's face told her that she had correctly interpreted her father's thoughts. "Well, she is a member of the royal family, so that makes her a perfect target."

"A target for whom, daughter?" mused the Ka, drumming his fingers on the arm of his chair.

"Somebody with a motive...I can't talk about this now!" sobbed Destinariae, running from the room. The Ka watched her go, beckoning to the servants to remove the body. He understood, though. Chova's death must make Destinariae feel emotionally fragile and terrified for her own life. He frowned, then went to carry the news to his wife.

* * *

"I never knew a Kaji could weigh so much," complained Sanniah on the way back from the palace. "Lifting a horse would have been easier." She smiled a wicked little smile, flicking her mousy blonde hair back with a work-wrinkled hand.

Bheffor chuckled spitefully. "Well, she was kind of...how can I put it? A little bloated. Slightly on the tubby side, maybe." He gave another giggle. "Cheer up Kethar, you look so miserable. A good servant with a nice meal every day shouldn't be sad. And with such a *nice* mistress too. I never did find out how you got the Kaji Destinariae. I'm stuck with Efaerin, bawling baby of Bakarn."

Kethar shrugged, trying to push the thought of the beauty of his mistress' smile to the back of his mind. "I dunno why, but I feel kind of unsatisfied with, well, everything. I feel like there's something missing, something important."

"Well we know who that is, don't we guys?" smirked Sanniah. "The lovely Opias, jewel of Bakarn.

That's who he's missing, right Kethar?" She elbowed him in the ribs and made a knowing face at Bheffor.

Kethar shot her a withering look. "Oh shut up, just 'cos Bheffor likes her, along with almost every man in the servant village, I have to as well? Give me a break."

He sighed. It was always like this. Just because he hadn't indicated an interest in girls in *that* way, people were always teasing him, seeming to feel that he really did like them but just didn't show it. Although Opias really was quite pretty, there were far too many jokes and jibes aimed at him for him to do anything about it, Kethar thought sourly. Besides, he assured himself stubbornly, I have no time whatsoever for that sort of thing. He sighed again, remembering the emotions that raged in him whenever he looked at Destinariae's serene face. Why didn't I say anything to her then, he thought, his mind full of regret.

Because you're only a servant, and she's one of the nine most important people in Bakarn, he thought bitterly. Even if she did like you, nothing could ever happen...not that she does like you...why, she hardly even looks at you!

Sometimes, Kethar thought acrimoniously, I absolutely hate myself. Then he blinked a couple of times, as he noticed he had been ignoring the conversation between his two friends. A grin spread over his face when he realised they were still talking about Opias.

"Well, I think that I'm quite justified in liking her, if you know what I mean," sniggered Bheffor, grinning inanely and making crudely obvious hand motions.

"Hey!" shouted Sanniah, in mock outrage, "I don't particularly want to hear about her, thank you. Anyway, let's change the subject. What did you have to do today, both of you?"

Bheffor, still foolishly smiling, gave no answer, so Kethar felt that it was his time to talk.

"I had to make the Kaji Destinariae's breakfast, clean her rooms, then clear out the bird cage."

A sympathetic groan greeted this piece of intelligence.

"Gods, Kethar, you've had to do that for weeks. What did you do that's bad enough to be punished by cleaning the death-cage for a month?" asked Bheffor, his mouth twisted in frank disgust.

Kethar shrugged. "It's not a punishment. I just get on better with the birds."

Sanniah nodded, her mousy hair loosening from its untidy bob at the back of her head. "Rather you than me. Last time I came to clean 'em out, that huge great one with a whopping big beak attacked me! I only just escaped with my life!"

Bheffor snorted. "Well, I'm glad it could make up its mind about what to do. Most creatures that see you don't know whether to attack you or run away!"

"*Bheffor!*" Sanniah screeched, smacking him on the arm, "They do not! That's more the situation with you, and every person you meet!" Her quite plain, quite pretty face turned vicious as she launched into a argument.

Kethar listened mildly to the blazing row, noting how short a time it had been until an argument had developed. Sanniah and Bheffor yelled and squealed, gesticulating wildly, as they tried to defend themselves and send scathing retorts to the other. Sanniah, he noted, for all her intelligence and shrewdness, could simply not bear that she was wrong. Nor could she even try to make herself see anyone else's point of view.

She made up for this in other ways though, Kethar considered. For one thing she kept Bheffor in his place. He matched, even outdid Sanniah in his attempts to be condescending and arrogant. When he really tried, he crossed the line and descended into downright rudeness.

A chance arm waving caught Kethar in the face; he slapped it off and returned to his contemplation of the pair. Although essentially a nice person, Bheffor tried Kethar's patience to its limits with his crude attempts to be witty. For Bheffor was constantly showing off. This made him incredibly popular with the female half of the population, for some strange, unknown reason.

The argument carried on for quite a while, until Kethar finally intervened, with an abrupt, "Stop yelling and return to the real world, you two."

At this point the others focused their full attention on Kethar, each shouting their own point of view until, when they could talk no more, they subsided into a sullen silence. Kethar shook his head wryly. It was always like this; even the smallest conversations developed into a blazing row. Shrewd, shrill Sanniah and blundering braggart Bheffor, they made a good pair and made some good arguments. But enough was enough.

Stepping in between the scowling duo, Kethar held a palm up to each of them. " Look, you guys, that's enough. Neither of you two repel others, and as for the…" he raised his first two fingers from each hand in the well known 'sarcastic quotation' sign, " 'huge great one with a whopping big beak', attacking all other birds is a good trait for continuing its survival." He paused, contemplating his last point. "Well, looking at it from the huge one's view instead of the pathetic little pile of feathers on the floor."

Bheffor laughed, his broad face stretching into its usual good-humoured grin, and turned back to talk to Sanniah. Seeing the situation was resolved, Kethar went back to his thoughts. He hardly ever joined in arguments, but still liked to have some fun. But then, he was rather quiet compared with the others. My main goal in life, Kethar reminded himself, is to move up in the world; after all, being a servant is about as low down as one can go. I'm a person who takes life seriously, but knows how to have a good time as well. He sighed. Not everyone had the same opinion of him. Others see me as more of a reclusive, sensible lad, he mused mournfully. He sighed again, thinking of Opias.

Then he cheered up again. With regards to leading and making plans with my friends, I definitely have the upper hand, he asserted, his face brightening. I'm the only one who can prevent arguments from breaking out… or at least stop them from continuing for more than a few minutes. He tried boosting his self-confidence again, something it seemed only he tried to do. People respect me, he thought proudly. Then he deflated slightly. Admittedly, the respect was chiefly due to the fact that everyone grew uncomfortable under his amused stare. It was best if he didn't dwell on such matters, he considered.

"Look everybody, I can see the gateway already. If we hurry, we can get back before they start serving the food." The others increased their pace, as latecomers were just served the scanty, cold leftovers from the evening meal. It was like most aspects of the servants' life; unfair.

He could still remember Eredeth, the village where he had been born. He could remember his parents turning away, not even bothering to wave as their first-born child was taken away forever. And he had only been a toddler then. What he had not known back then was that the villagers, all being poor, had embraced the chance of tax-free shelter on the condition that they produced children to be menial workers around all Bakarn. He had been lucky though. He'd been chosen for a servant. But that was not all that much to rejoice about. After all, they only just give us enough to live on.

Servant, he thought bitterly, as the trio reached the rough gate, why don't they just call it a slave?

* * *

The carriage rattled down the bumpy road, the white horses at full gallop. Their manes and tails streamed in the wind, and the harness jangled as it bounced around. Inside the carriage, the one occupant stirred from his slumber, and forced himself to think. Where was he going again? Lyriv...Lyvir...oh yes, that was it, Lyvilan. Why in the name of Destiny was he going there? His sleep-befuddled brain took a while to realise that he had been sent for by the Ka. On 'important business', apparently. He watched the glowing moon in the night sky as it reappeared from behind a cloud.

Suddenly there was a muffled thump from the top of the carriage. Lord Onguet immediately tensed, and moved to the far side of the enclosed space he was in. It was probably the coachman, he thought. Who could it have been besides the coachman? No, that's not a good question, he mentally reprimanded himself. It had to be the coachman. Obviously it was the coachman. The coachman. Yes.

A moment later the coachman's blood-covered body flashed past the window.

Onguet wished he knew some prayers that he could now utter. He had thought he was safe here, even in bandit country, when he had paid the bandits a fortune to leave him alone. All of a sudden the roof crashed open and splinters flew everywhere as a dark cloaked figure dropped into the cabin. In one hand there was a dully gleaming sabre, and in the other a throwing dagger. With a despairing shout, Onguet flung himself past the lithe person and out of the door. The figure in the cabin smiled grimly, and threw the dagger. The weapon left the hand like chain lightning, and buried itself in the back of the still running lord. Onguet dropped without a sound.

Khalla straightened up, and jumped through the open door, twisting in mid-jump to land gripping onto the outside rails of the carriage. She tensed; then did a double backflip, flipping her leg over the top rail to land in a crouch on the roof. Luck be praised that I made him train me while he was there, she thought thankfully.

"Sorry about that, your lordship," she murmured respectfully, "but I can't see you lending me your carriage otherwise. And I have no wish to end up with a price on my head." The carriage horses snorted warily, sensing the brooding, changing, volatile aura around their new mistress, and sidestepped uneasily. Khalla took up the reins, and the horses laid back their ears and plunged forward into the darkness.

A thunder of hoofs awoke Khalla from her slumber. She lifted her head just in time to hear a voice shout "Yer a terrible, terrible boy! Get outta here, you piece of filth!" She scrambled up, grabbed her sabre, and rolled into the dense bushes opposite her. From there she saw the wheels and dust of a quickly retreating carriage, and a prone body lying sprawled by the side of the track. She picked up her weapon and rushed over to it. At once, she saw that the boy was unconscious, having hit his head on a rock on the road. She tried to lift the body then, after several attempts, rolled the stiff boy to the bushes where she had slept.

After several minutes of cleaning the wound on the boy's head, Khalla noticed her patient's eyelids moving. She squatted by his side, and lay her sabre on the floor. The boy's eyelids flickered once more, then fully opened. On seeing Khalla, his eyes widened and he moved away, gabbling in a rough, untutored tone, "I didn't kill 'er! Honest! Please believe me! It was a…a…a… accident, I swear. Jus', jus', don' hurt me!"'

Khalla grabbed the boy's arms, and said soothingly, "I believe you, but…who are you?"

The sandy haired youngster wrenched his arms out of Khalla's soothing grip. "I'm a terrible boy. Tha'ss what 'e says. Filth. Scum. Take yer pick."

"Who cares what that awful man said? What is your name?"

He shook his head, his shaggy hair tossing like a grubby mop.

She tried again, putting what she hoped was a caring look on her face along with a beseeching tone to her voice. "Please?"

"I…I'm called…um…" The boy seemed to be having trouble remembering. She smiled, trying to rob him of his obvious shyness. It seemed to do the trick. "Yeh jus' call me…um…Shoy. Yep, that's ma name. Shoy. Right. Now, any chance o' some grub?" Impertinently, the boy sprang up and started to rummage through Khalla's pack. She clipped him with the back of her hand and he sat down hard, scowling.

"You're a cheeky little urchin, aren't you?" Khalla asked, her darkly pretty face creasing into a bemused smile. She looked into her pack, and took out a loaf of hard bread. She twisted it in half, then tossed a piece back carelessly. When she turned around, Shoy had finished and was eyeing her bread hungrily. With a sigh, she passed the other piece of bread to him. She studied the boy's face carefully. Was it her, or did he seem to be thinking deeply about something? She shook her head, wisps of her dark brown hair flying around. The boy was harmless. A bit stupid, and rough perhaps, but not devious.

A moment later, Shoy spoke again. To her, his voice seemed to have lost the uncertainty and fear that it had carried before. "Thanks, I should pay yeh back some'ow. How 'bouts I come wiv' yeh, an' I can like, go ahead to see whass' comin'? Yep, I'll scout ahead of yeh."

And that was that.

* * *

Destinariae swept through the palace corridors, her black mourning robes fluttering out at the edges. She passed the silent guards with tosses of her head, and paused only to nod to other mourners. After all, she thought, anybody who has the decency to come and weep for my sister has to at least be acknowledged. She strode past the slow moving line of people and pushed open the doors. To her surprise there was nothing inside except the mourners; no priest, bier, or anything. She marched up to the front and looked through the door into the ready room, where she expected to find the official who would conduct the ceremony. To her relief she found the Master of Ceremonies, an important enough person for the occasion.

"Why is the Kaji's body not here?" she queried, arching a beautifully plucked eyebrow at him.

The man stuttered and stammered, turning his embroidered maroon cap around and around in his trembling, clammy hands. "Um…the…the Ka decreed that it would be unsanitary to have a dead body in with so many pe…people, m-most of whom could not afford a…a…doctor." He squeaked as she shot him a frosty look, then strode out.

As she walked down the steps to the Royal Crypt, she thought angrily to herself, well, at least *I* will pay my sister the proper respect that she deserves. As she entered the cold stone rooms, she looked behind her and saw a figure in black following at a distance. She paused, then called out, "I can see you, Eskiros, you're not invisible."

"I just wanted to make sure that you were safely where you wanted to be, *Kaji*," he said in a sneering tone.

Destinariae watched him retreat, and wondered why he was in the crypt. As a Tsumetai, if that was really true, he had earned the right to be inside, but he should really be doing his job, she thought. Unaccompanied journeys around the Royal crypt were certainly not authorised. She should by all means tell the Kajarito. That would serve him right, for she had borne many insinuated slights from him, and wanted to see him punished. She had the power to do so, but did not for two reasons. Firstly, he would just tell the Kajarito that he was there to mourn and thought they were assembling in the Crypt, or some other such nonsense to weasel out of it, and secondly, she knew that he was hiding something, and this intrigued her. Who knows, he might turn out to be a greater asset than she had first thought. She went back to the task in hand, and knelt at her sister's temporary resting-place.

After all, it would not be very long before she was moved to an outside grave in the palace gardens.

Try as she might, she could not totally focus on what she was doing. Instead, her attention wandered to the peculiar conversation with her father. She vividly remembered him saying, "Do you suppose that this wasn't an..." and her own answer-"Accident?" If this was true, then there could be more of a threat than they thought. But worrying right now was stupid. Or was it, she mused. Thinking of the threat now might save a life. But there was little anyone could do for now. She smiled despite herself. They were all so helpless to face this new, unknown danger, despite the mighty Ka and all his companies of trained soldiers. She had a feeling that *they* would not get to the bottom of it. She smiled again, a pretty gesture of her lips, but full of secrets. She smiled because she had a plan.

* * *

I hope I have not called you from any extremely momentous tasks, my brothers and sisters.

No, Eternity, and I think I speak on behalf of all.

Is my sister Chance correct in this?

Yes, she is.

Good, then let us proceed. I have called you to council because I believe we should review the situation of our enemies. The future's events are clouded, and I sense that there is much chaos and bloodshed to come.

I have not noticed any in particular other than the two we are currently monitoring.

Yes, and we do not even know the name of one of them.

That is not our fault, Fortune. We cannot see past the royal-killer's treachery to his or her identity.

So are there others that pose a threat?

Not as far as I can see.

How irksome these humans are. I do not know why they were created, except to provide a mild irritation. I do not give them a second thought, save the ones that pose a threat. I, too, cannot see anyone to bother with except the killer and the assassin. What say you, Destiny?

I am only interested in the future of one other, but she is not an enemy.

I think I know of whom you speak, sister.

Yes, Ashikra?

The girl Khalla.

We should help her.

What, is Fate, keeper of ice and a million souls, concerned in the fate of one individual?

Do not mock, Luck. Of course I am concerned. But chiefly because her interests may be similar to our own.

Explain.

She is bent on killing the enemy who we have the identity of. Therefore, we help her, and help ourselves.

Why cannot we just kill the man ourselves?

Have you forgotten the ancient laws? Can the mighty Chance, Lady of the earth, not remember that to kill one who is not yet draining our power is forbidden?

How then, Fate, do you propose we help her?

We can change her. Morph her into an unstoppable machine. She will better be able to carry on with a shape built for hunting, deadliness, and speed.

The idea has merit. I am with Fate.

Are we all in favour?

Surely she will reject our influence if it is laid on her so suddenly, and without consent. Should we not prepare her somehow?

Fortune's perception is great. Khalla must be altered first, gently bent to our will so subtly that she cannot perceive it.

I have it. We must change her views, her inner emotions and attitudes, so slowly she becomes what we want her to be.

When could this take effect?

We could set it in motion immediately. She will find herself doing things she would not before have dreamed of, and they will not trouble her.

In other words, we will remove her innocence, the characteristic that so hinders true strength.

Indeed.

You have already begun it, have you not, Destiny?

I see there is no fooling you, Eternity. Yes, it is begun. She has begun to lose her humanity, and already commits acts without a second thought that she once would be horrified at.

Enough bragging, Destiny. We must prepare for the Changing. Who will perform the deed?

Let Fate. He is used to making powerful creatures.

Chance is right, though her choice of insult is far from subtle. I will undertake this. Agreed?

It is agreed.

Chapter 3

In the snowy cave, high up the mountain, the egg rocked. Only a little, just that once, but it definitely moved. Soon it would rock again, and again, and the young creature within would start to peck at the restricting lining and inner shell of the egg, but for now, it just rocked.

* * *

It was all Bheffor's idea. On the Spring Equinox, when they were excused from working for the whole day, they would try and climb to the peak of Skyria, the highest mountain in Central Bakarn. Both Kethar and Sanniah met the idea with enthusiasm, and when the day arrived Kethar was tremulous with excitement.

"Nobody's ever done anything like this before," he grinned to his friends as he bounded up a steep slope. "They'll give us awards or something when we tell them."

"That's if we don't die in the attempt," puffed the stout Bheffor, bringing up the rear. "Holy finger of Fortune, what's that?" he swore.

Kethar followed his gaze. Hanging from a nearby twisted tree was a body, whipped and scarred out of recognition. But Kethar knew exactly who it was, or rather, had been.

"Yeah, I can't believe they executed old Mocrin."

"They execute people. They slaughter animals like him," sniffed Sanniah disdainfully.

Kethar kicked at a stone lying beside the rough track. "He wasn't too bad really. I liked him."

"He murdered his sister!"

"But they never proved him guilty, did they?" protested Kethar. "They just assumed he was, didn't even look at the evidence. Just killed him."

Bheffor shrugged. "He looked guilty enough to me. Blood on the floor, dead sister lying there, him standing there with a lamp in his hand, staring at her...you don't need to be a genius to work it out." He said this in the voice of one spoiling for an argument. Kethar saw the danger signs immediately. He cast his eyes to the sky, and prepared for the shouting to begin.

"I can't believe you seriously think that he was anything other than a complete monster, Kethar! He was inhuman, a savage, a beast in a man's body!" Sanniah screeched, turning her furious gaze on Kethar.

"I disagree completely, but let's not get ourselves too heated up about it," Kethar said calmly, eyeing her flushed face worriedly. "Anyway, it's not exactly important now that he's dead, is it?"

Sanniah looked as though she was going to retort, but closed her mouth again when she caught Bheffor's warning glance. He knew when it was better not to push Kethar too far.

As they progressed through the foothills of the mountain, their wandering minds focused on the rotting tree stumps littered around. They were not pretty, with patches of damp mould and fungi sprouting out from every crevice and rift. Looking at the blackened, shrivelled shapes, Sanniah could not help giving a revolted shudder. "How on earth did they get up here on the mountain?" she asked, pointing to a clump.

"I heard that there used to be a forest up here, many years ago. At least, there was a forest until the lord whose responsibility it was fell into disfavour with the Ka. He had the forest and its villages burnt, and the lord was executed."

"I wish I hadn't asked, now you've told me that, brainy Bheffor. Oh well, that explains why the remains are charred. Still, it shows that our Ka's not one to cross." Each of them gave a patriotic agreement, but bowed their heads as they walked on, as much in tribute to the dead as to avert their eyes from the sight.

Trees were not the only things that they came across. Boulders of all sizes dominated the landscape, some large, weatherworn ones with deep grooves running through, some smaller, dotted all over with curiously shaped growths of yellow lichen. Each separate rock was fitted snugly into a shallow hole in the ground where it had lain there for so many years. They looked impossible to move.

Every now and then a rock would come hurtling down the side of the mountain at an impossible speed, bringing other debris down with it and causing a miniature landslide. Each time this happened the trio jumped aside into the nearest cave to take cover. Soon they found they had to both keep their eyes on the ground lest they miss their footing, but also scan the slope ahead in case of any possible avalanches.

It was all so empty, thought Kethar. Though he knew that it was full of objects, and plenty of insects, it seemed to emanate an aura of desolation. Even with his friends beside him, he felt suddenly aching inside, like something was missing. It weighed down on his mind, so to stave away the depression, he tried to make conversation.

"It's a shame we have to go back to work as normal tomorrow," he said wistfully, "I always feel so lethargic on the morning after each free day."

"Probably because you've just had a day of doing nothing."

"You call walking up the side of the largest mountain in Bakarn *nothing?*"

"Well, no, but you chose to do this, Sanniah. It's not as if you had to do it."

"Anyway, I'm still not looking forward to going back. Not that we'll get back for a while."

"Don't think about that. Concentrate on getting to the top of this mountain."

Looking slightly to the left, they noticed a small cave with a wide opening, just past a sheer drop. Though not very deep, it looked large enough to hold all three of them.

"Let's stop for some food. Look, we can rest in that cave over there," said Kethar, pointing. He pressed his back against the cliff, and edged cautiously past the yawning gulf, trying to think light thoughts. As he reached the cave, he slumped wearily against the wall, turning on shaking legs to see Sanniah, then Bheffor, round the bend and enter the cave. They walked over and wearily sat down near him.

"My feet hurt already," Sanniah complained, massaging her feet gently. "I'm so glad you suggested this break, Kethar, if you hadn't, I would have sat down and refused to go any further until you saw sense."

"Yeah, Kethar, you're the sensible one," said Bheffor, with a slight grin as he pretended not to notice Kethar's annoyed face.

Sanniah joined in, her face bland. "Mmm, sensible and boring, that's our Kethar!"

Though Kethar knew they were just trying to wind him up, he could not help but respond. "Boring? How am I boring? I'm not boring!" he returned indignantly. This was exactly the reputation he wanted to avoid, the kind of remarks that made him doubt his own worth and sink into depression. And his friends knew that, which made it all the more infuriating when they deliberately taunted him.

"No, you're right, you're not boring," replied Sanniah with a few slow nods of her tousled head. Her mouth twitched. "You're as daredevil as they come!"

Bheffor snorted with laughter, then turned it into a slight cough as Kethar's head snapped back round to look at him. "She's right. I'd like to catch you doing something boring, a servant like you. Why, you...you wash dishes in the face of danger!" He started sniggering.

"And you clean bedpans to spite fear!" Sanniah screeched with glee. They fell over on the floor, screaming with laughter.

Kethar watched them laugh at his expense, his jaw clenched. Though the pair were, undoubtedly, his best friends, at times like this he could have cheerfully pushed them over the cliff.

"If you've quite finished," he said tightly, trying not to lose his temper. "I'm going to start eating. Keep laughing if you want." He took off his carrysack and removed the rations. They stopped laughing immediately.

"Well, bread and cheese isn't exactly a feast, but I guess it'll do," Bheffor murmured to himself as he hungrily bit into his food.

Kethar had to laugh at him; his stocky friend was always hungry. As soon as they were rested, they started walking again, making sure to keep up a brisk pace. They had spent more time than expected on their break, and they still had a long way to go.

"Remind me again why I'm doing this," "Whose idea was this anyway?" and "This was such a bad idea," all seemed to be exceptionally popular comments among them as the journey became more of a chore than an adventure. There never seemed to be an answer for any of them; except, of course, they all blamed Bheffor for suggesting it. All of a sudden spending the day in the village celebrating with the others didn't seem like such a bad idea. The minds of the three young people constantly pictured the long trestle tables packed with food, the dances and music-making, the lighting of the ceremonial bonfires, and the wildflowers that lay in wreaths upon doors, tables, and the heads of pretty maidens.

Although they tried to keep cheerful, one can only look at so many dead trees without becoming slightly bored. Travel games were not a success. After the fourth 'R for rock' there were more arguments and then silence once more.

When they were about half the way up, Sanniah and Bheffor began to complain.

"I'm hungry."

"I'm thirsty."

"My feet hurt."

"My feet hurt more."

"They couldn't possibly."

"They most certainly could!"

"Don't start arguing now, we're almost there."

"I don't want to be almost there, I want to be home, with a nice bed."

"And a chair with a cushion."

"And food."

"And *ale!*"

They walked on for a while. Every now and then one of them would look towards the sun, their frowns becoming more and more worried as the fiery orb of the sun traversed its route across the sky. Each one of them was privately wondering how they could possibly make it to the top and back again before the morning, and all were mentally preparing their various excuses. Yet none wanted to suggest turning back in case their idea was spurned along with themselves.

As they grew slightly closer to the top of the mountain, frost started to crunch beneath their feet, and icicles glittered in the many crevices and holes. Ahead, the unspoiled white snow was painted all of the rich hues of a sunset on a cloudless night. They watched in speechless wonder as the icy landscape before them was transformed into a flickering myriad of colours. They trudged on up the treacherous white slope, giving each other as much support as possible for the ice was slippery, and if one of them fell, the injuries could be fatal.

As they hauled themselves onto a reasonably flat ledge, Sanniah's voice, sounding small and alone in the icy wilderness said, "Well, he was definitely guilty."

A chorus of groans greeted this remark. " Look, we finished that argument ages ago. Let's not start it up again." said Kethar.

It was now dusk, and the moon glittered almost overhead while the trio half-heartedly argued on.

"So anyway, he was not proved guilty, and so could have been innocent. End of story."

"Except that he definitely was guilty, and so executing him was totally correct...hey, what's this?" asked Bheffor, stooping to pick up a small white fragment from the snow-covered ground. When it became clear that his numb fingers couldn't find the edges, he started to brush away the snow from around the edges. The other two joined him, their work eventually showing them that the fragment was part of a huge bird skull.

"Wow," breathed Bheffor, lifting it awkwardly in his arms and panting under the weight "I would love to see a live one of these. We could get so much money for this. We'd be as rich as the Ka himself! I mean, look at the beak on this thing!"

"Faith, Bheffor, that must be awful heavy!" said Sanniah, her eyes wide with admiration for both the boy and the skull.

"The skull itself doesn't actually weigh that much. It's this vicious beak which is so damned heavy!" Bheffor put his hand in the empty eye socket that he could reach, and pushed in his arm until, by moving his wrist, he could open and close the lethal hooked beak. Sanniah laughed gleefully as Bheffor conversed with the skull, trying to look like a puppeteer, pretending the skull was really speaking the words. Kethar felt ashamed and angry that such a mockery was being made of an unknown creature's magnificent head. Just as he stepped forwards to try to put an end to it, he heard another noise besides the laughter of Sanniah and the silly noises of Bheffor. It was an angry, piercing scream, growing louder by the second. Suddenly, as the eerie noise reached a point where Kethar felt his head was on fire, a large creature crashed not four metres away from them, and the noise changed to a shrill screech, then stopped.

Facing them was a shoulder-high, black, powerful-looking, almost hawk-like bird. There was an unmistakable feeling of anger emanating from it, and the whirling crimson eyes radiated an intense hatred. Kethar could see that, though the young one was wobbly on its feet, it would be deadly when it grew. And its obvious youth did nothing to discourage the terrible fear that welled up inside him. It did not seem to be looking at him, though. Instead, with a harsh cry, it launched itself at Bheffor, still holding the skull. What happened next happened too quickly for him to see, but when it was finished Bheffor was lying on the floor, his neck broken.

So great was his shock, Kethar did not even try to stop Sanniah from shrieking hysterically and hurling rocks at it, or the creature from delivering an almighty blow of its beak to the back of her head. Sanniah crumpled to the floor without another sound. Kethar stood still, sweating, and watched fearfully as it swivelled its head around to look directly at him. Instantly the air of wrath vanished.

Kethar stared into its eyes, lost in delight as the bird's thoughts and emotions flooded into his own. They would always be together, looking out for each other, through the seasons, through the years. Whenever Kethar needed help, his winged defender would be at his side! They would be as one mind and share everything with one another. He would never again lack a soulmate, a friend that instantly knew his every thought and wish and desire! They stood still, their souls binding for all eternity. Kethar found himself suffused with an almighty joy, a glorious, intense happiness that he wished would just go on and on. He felt as though his heart would burst with love. He had lost himself in the wonderful shades of his soulmate's shining golden eyes, and hugged tightly to him the creature that had just killed his friends.

That hurt, Kethar! The voice seemed to talk directly into his head. Instantly he released his hold on the bird.

I didn't say don't hug! You always a person of extremes?

"I don't know…what should I call you? Do you have a name?"

The gleaming jet black bird looked proudly up at his new soulmate, and instantly knew. He gazed at his human link with shining eyes and said, *I am Zakrivath!*

Overcome with the wonder of the events that had passed ('it all happened so quickly!' Kethar thought amusedly), he gazed at his sleeping new-found friend and murmured "Zakrivath…"

Looking closely at his friend, which was hard in the cold starlight, Kethar noticed as if for the first time the sheer size of him, and he was just a hatchling! Although, he reflected, there would be some rather big problems to overcome in that particular area. How to feed him, for one thing. He sat for a minute considering the prospects of this, until he suddenly thought in astonishment; what am I doing sitting here wondering about this thing? I don't know what it is, where it came from, what it does, and if it's the only one or not.

Then he corrected himself. Zakrivath was not an it; he was Kethar's soulmate. However, there were still more immediate problems to be faced. Then, out of the blue, a thought hit him, causing rivers of sorrow to run through his veins. His two best friends were dead! Killed by...his friend. Another wave of grief hit him then, but he quickly suppressed it for the youngster's sake. After all, the huge bird had just hatched, and Bheffor and Sanniah had been making fun of the bones of what was, presumably, another one of his kind. His Zakrivath could not be a wanton killer.

That was another thing. Zakrivath, although an impressive name, was a bit too...Kethar's fatigued mind took a moment to locate the right words...long and formal for such a clumsy chick. He'd call his friend Zak, or Zaki as his 'pet' name.

Kethar yawned tiredly and rubbed his eyes. It had been a long day. Long and eventful. He glanced up at the night sky, the gentle whisper of the wind soothing him into a half doze. Dreamily, he wondered what time it was. It had been dark for some time. Letting his head rest gently on his chest, bathed in the silvery light of the moon, he slept.

Kethar woke in the small hours of the morning. He was surprised to find that he was not in his solitary rug on the floor of his hut. He sat up slowly, trying to avoid the buzzing and light-headedness that sitting up quickly usually provoked. As he did so he felt the area of ground around him. It was not rock like he had expected, but straw. As his hands slowly explored the area around which he was sitting, he found a large, smooth, light object with a serrated edge along it. Further fumbling ascertained that the object was not unlike a large, misshapen sphere, and the serrated edge was all around one part, like a rim or lip.

As he sat in the dark, guessing wildly at the name of this object, his hand brushed against something soft and warm. His blood ran cold. Whatever it was, it was large, close, and alive. His ears strained to catch any noise it made, but he could hear nothing. All of a sudden there was a peculiar noise. *Wrrr wrrr wrrr wneeee wrrr wrrr wrrr wneeee.* Kethar yelled and ran to where he hoped the exit was. Instead he ran into a solid wall of rock, and promptly collapsed in a quivering heap.

Kethar? asked a voice sleepily, *Is that you? You woke me up. Zak need sleep. No wakey early for Zaki. 'Kay?*

Suddenly the previous day's events flooded back to Kethar, and he untangled himself and walked back over to the dozing bird. Before he could speak, the strange noise started again. *Blub blub blub wrrrr blub blub blub wwrrrr.* It took a moment of terror before his sleep-befuddled mind identified it. He immediately fell to the floor laughing, partly at his friend's snoring, partly at his own terror. The echoes of the laughter woke Zakrivath again. *Now whassup?* grumbled the creature, putting on an air of mock outrage. Kethar could not tell if he was really grumpy or just joking, so with great difficulty ceased his laughter.

"It was your snoring, you loud sleeper! It sounded pathetic!"

With great dignity, the bird pulled himself up to his full height. *I don't snore, you dithering thing. You noisy one! This is second time in minutes you woke me up! Me snore, indeed!* he added, in a hurt tone.

Kethar burst out laughing again. From Zaki's direction he heard a disgruntled *Huh!*, and that provoked him to new heights of merriment.

Well, when you've quite finished! huffed the bird, standing tall and proud and scowling at Kethar. Immediately, Kethar saw that he had offended his friend and put an arm around him. Zak blinked solemnly back at him, his hurt forgotten. *I had strange dream,* he remarked, his voice carrying a trace of uncertainty. *Mother came to me, said things to me, but can't remember what all of them were.*

Kethar urged him to continue.

She said...that I had properly aven...avenge ...avenged her. She was important, I remember that. Very important. And she said I would be too.

"Anything else?"

That I was the last shikara.

The friends paused, contemplating the information. After a while they stumbled outside, and slumped down together to watch the sunrise. When it came, it was breathtaking. First the dark maroon of dried blood, followed by the lush scarlet of a whore's lips, the light red of cheap watered wine, then a magnificent tawny orange that would not have looked out of place in the mane of an emperor of lions. The distant golden sun at the horizon flooded the sky with yellows and creams, transforming blind darkness into a breathtaking orgy of colour and splendour.

Kethar was bitter, though. He was feeling angry at himself. The new morning had awakened his mind from the dreamlike stupor he had been in the previous night, when he had Linked with Zakrivath. Why, he had befriended, no, given his soul to a creature that killed the little that remained of his already lonely lifestyle. He turned, his heart cold, preparing to confront the creature savagely. But then he saw the sunlight reflecting in the shikara's eyes, felt the overwhelming love, trust, happiness and almost worship that emanated from him, and broke down in tears.

Zakrivath craned around his head until he could see Kethar's face. *What wrong?* he asked, his voice loving, betraying deep consternation. *You're upset. I have upset you? I'm sorry!*

Kethar felt the drip of new tears upon his bare arm. He felt irredeemably guilty that he had made his friend take the blame, and also felt that he needed to allay his friend's fears. "No, Zaki, I was just...very overwhelmed, that's all."

Overwhelmed as in happy or sad? came the forlorn little voice, this time carrying an undercurrent of hope.

"Happy! Oh Zaki, you could never make me sad." Yet even as he said these words he realised that his world had changed. He could not go back to the Palace, he'd be executed as the killer of Sanniah and Bheffor. Yet he could not regret that now. He had Zakrivath. He sat with his arm around his friend and worried. How am I going to feed us? What does he eat? Where will we live? What will we do? The questions ran in circles in his mind, making his head spin.

"Oh Zaki," he said softly, leaning his head against the soft chest feathers, "What are we going to do?"

Zakrivath looked at him lovingly. Being young, he did not understand his human counterpart's worry. After all, it was now that was important, wasn't it?

Don't worry, Kethar. Everything will be all right. I have you and you me, and that's all that matters. As long as we're together nothing can happen. And you can always be sure that I will never, ever leave you.

Chapter 4

"So, Shoy. Where did you come from, anyway? I mean, I don't want to pry or anything, but you didn't tell me. Any skeletons in your closet?" They were walking along a narrow road, empty except for the two travellers. "You don't have to tell me everything if you don't want to, but it would be nice to know something about my companion."

"Sure," he said easily, laughing, "I like food, ale and walking in the sunshine with beau'iful girls. How 'bout you?"

"Aren't you a little young for all of that?" Khalla asked curiously.

"Aren't you a liddle' bit young to be walking alone, armed wiv' a sabre and an unknown destination?"

"Excuse *me*, I'm almost seventeen!"

"Ooh, yeah, four years makes *such* a difference," he said sarcastically.

Laughing, Khalla held up her hands in defence. "All right, all right, I admit defeat. You've got me there. But you have to admit that it is stranger for a twelve year old to be walking the world alone other than for a sixteen year old; even if the difference is only a few years."

For a few minutes they walked on in companionable silence, watching the birds fly around the trees. At one point a spider fell from an overhanging branch down the back of Shoy's tunic, causing him to wriggle and squirm like a hooked fish. Khalla collapsed at the roadside with hysterical laughter, and Shoy's exclamations of righteous indignation just made it worse. As her laughter was so infectious, he could not help joining in, and they both ended up on the floor, clutching their sides, tears of laughter streaming down their faces.

"You must be glad that you've got me with you, for protection, I mean," said Khalla, grinning at the chirpy youngster.

He shot her a pugnacious look. "I'm more brave than yeh, but tha'ss not sayin' much," he sniggered.

"Except when it comes to spiders," grinned Khalla, getting her own back.

Some time afterwards, wiping the tears from her face, Khalla commented that if this was going to happen often, then they wouldn't get anywhere. Shoy soon reassured her this had never happened before.

They walked along the same road almost all day, only stopping once for some food and a short rest. One thing that puzzled Shoy was that Khalla seemed to have absolutely no idea of where they were going, though she continued unhesitatingly in the same direction, as if drawn on an invisible thread.

She just told him that she needed to find someone, she had 'unfinished business'. Similarly, he had no idea of what her past was, as she always seemed to evade his questions. He shrugged off the thought, after all, that wasn't exactly important for his purpose. She was at least easy to get along with. For her part, Khalla found Shoy to be the perfect travelling companion; his witty, though sometimes rude comments never failed to make her laugh. Their light-hearted banter made easy conversation, and they soon felt perfectly at ease with each other.

The day passed quickly, the hours seeming to fly past. As the sky began to darken, they made camp. They were lucky it was not raining, for they had light clothes and little shelter available. But they made the most of their limited resources, and soon were sitting at the side of a small fire, facing each other.

"When's supper gonna' be ready, Khalla?"

"Soon, soon enough."

"Make sure you take it out in time, 'cos I didn't take hours catchin' that rabbit for nuffin'."

"Okay, it's ready." Khalla took the meat out of the fire, and neatly slit it in half with her sabre. Tossing half to Shoy, she set upon hers like a tiger. Halfway through a mouthful, she asked Shoy, "So what do you think? I cooked it fine. And if I'd listened to you it would've been half raw."

Making a face, Shoy continued to eat, replying through a mouthful of meat, "S'okay, I s'pose. Had better though."

"Me too. My mother used to prepare the best rabbit soup you've ever..." her voice trailed off. "Doesn't matter."

Shoy leaned forward, his eyes bright with the question he was to ask. "But where's yer family? And where yeh from? You haven't said a single thing about your past. I tell yeh, yeh look as if you need to get it all outta yer system. I won't tell, promise."

Khalla leaned back, discarding the last bones on the floor. She knew he was right; she would have to tell somebody sometime or other. But she vowed that nobody but herself would ever know the full story. "Okay, I'll tell you. As long as you don't question me any more afterwards. You see, it happened like this..."

*   *   *

The Royal Dining room was huge and ornate. Even the table was breathtaking, with intricately wrought silver chalices and shining bronze plates. Where there was not red velvet, there was marble, where there was not marble there was silk. Large tapestries adorned the walls, and satin hangings were artistically draped over rails and beautiful furniture. A crystal drop chandelier, with hundreds of painstakingly lit candles, was suspended above the great mahogany table at which the Royal family sat. Crystal ropes hung down from the main frame, tinkling prettily against each other. It looked as if the Royal designer was fond of anything expensive, and rich in both colour and texture.

The food was rich and wonderfully presented, but, as the Kaji Destinariae mused, not awfully filling. She speared a quail's egg on her fork, and chewed the oily morsel delicately while she thought. That was the trouble with all of these riches, they were impressive enough to display, but really they were cold and unsatisfying. Taking another egg from the ornamental platter as she signalled to a waiting servant, she studied the other guests at the table.

At the head, almost opposite to her, sat her father the Ka. He looked suitably impressive in his splendid robes of dark green and gold. His heavy black brows were cocked, giving an impression of polite interest as he listened to their guest, Lord Atisato of Rhaleon. However, he glanced down the table and met her eyes, and then raised his own dark ones upwards in a gesture that told her only too well that he was not in the least bit interested. She smiled back, remembering all too vividly the dreadful conversations she had had on occasion with Atisato. His conversational skills were every bit as good as a...a...she couldn't even think of a word to describe how dire and uninteresting their guest's speech was.

Her eyes moved onwards down the table. Kai Tifiert was also pretending to listen, but she made a far better job of the act. Destinariae paused in her scrutiny, surprised for a moment. Her stepmother was actually absorbed! The Kai was dressed in a low cut crimson gown, the better to expose and accentuate her creamy skin. Her face was not long, but more rounded, with a pretty turned-up nose and a neat little mouth. Her skin was almost flawless, and she was far less than double Destinariae's age. She had given birth to Tioni at just under sixteen years of age, Chova at nineteen, and Faitan at twenty-one. Efaerin had been born when Tifiert was twenty-eight. At twenty-nine, the Kai still had the looks and the baby to stop the Ka from choosing a different wife. She was the Ka's second wife, and also blonde like Isete. The Ka's fondness for blondes was something of a legend. Even after three children, Tifiert was still slim and enticing, but would this weigh up against the fact that the Ka wanted a son, a male heir?

The ash blonde hair of which she was immensely proud was in a new style, having been recently cut. It had been cut short, shorter than the nape-o-the-neck style which she had once worn, so that it now reached just down behind her ears. It gave her head a round, slightly spherical look, Destinariae thought wickedly, rather like a ball. She stifled a catty giggle; with her stepmother's softly triangular hairstyle from the front, and her long smooth neck, she looked rather like a giant mushroom. She often teased her stepmother about the haircut, but would never win, as the favourite retort would always come out. It was either "I'm the Kai, I like it, whether you like it is immaterial." Or the fact would come up that the people of central Bakarn were so loyal, or imbecilic, Destinariae thought, that the women would immediately go out and have their hair cut in the same style of the Kai. That is, the ones who could afford it. This held its own problems for Tifiert, as she would no sooner have had her hair cut in an exciting and new style, then everyone would have it.

So the Kai had taken to wearing her style for at least a week before allowing anyone to glimpse it.

On the Ka's left sat Verda, looking pale and wan in the soft light cast by the scores of candles. She, like almost all of the daughters of the current Ka and the late Kai had inherited her mother's blonde locks and creamy skin. She had her mother's beauty, and none of the harshness of her father's face. Her hair, however, was shoulder length, and held back from her face by two golden dragonfly shaped clips. Her eyes were hazel and beguiling; one flutter of the long eyelashes would send Destinariae's suitors hurrying to attend on Verda. Not that Destinariae minded, though. In fact, she made sure that Verda was with her whenever her suitors approached.

She turned her attention away from her older sibling, and looked down at her empty plate. She must have had, what, at least twenty different delicacies that evening, but they were small and unfilling, rather like party food one would serve politely so that the guests would not get overfull. Her stepmother was very strict, though, and insisted that a young Kaji 'must not stuff herself like a pig, she must eat lightly to preserve a flat stomach'. She smiled, her mouth unconsciously framing the words typical of Tifiert.

Destinariae's stomach was growling, so to distract herself, she glanced at the others present at the table. Next to Verda sat Tioni, Destinariae's favourite half-sister, lovely in a pale green, silk gown. Her blonde hair was longer and slightly darker than Verda's, and it reached almost down to her hips. However, tonight she wore it up, coiled tightly into an intricate bun, set high up on the back of the head. A water lily provided it with a soft counterpart, blending with the light hair and delicate gown. Tioni's face was slightly harsher than Verda's, taking more after her father with a larger nose and darker brows, but her smile was gentle, and she had a beautiful voice.

Meeting Destinariae's eyes quickly, Tioni smiled at her, then turned back to her conversation with Verda. There was nobody sitting at the head of their end of the table, and Destinariae was quite relieved at that because it put Faitan further away from herself. Admittedly the little brat was seated opposite her, but as the long mahogany table was over three metres wide, this was no real problem, as table etiquette prevented either of them from shouting the distance. Talking to a guest was different, but the Royal family had to keep with tradition. Tradition mattered little to Faitan, though, as did anything not connected to her. Besides, the eight-year-old was perfectly capable of raising her voice so it could be heard three miles away, let alone three puny metres.

Destinariae looked on in distaste as her half-sister proceeded to grab food and stuff it into her mouth, then chew with her mouth open. Anything that tasted bad was spat onto her plate. Some of her short dark hair swung loose in an untidy fringe; the rest was done in two high plaits. This, combined with the red, whiney face, gave an impression of a pig. Her bad-fitting dress was stretched over a bloated stomach, the buttons missing in places where they would not hold. The dress itself was not tasteful, with far too much lace, pearls and gold thread. It was gaudy and very expensive. But Faitan had wanted it, and what Faitan wanted, Faitan got. She made sure of that by a careful routine of screaming and tantrums. Yes, Destinariae thought, she's a brat.

She glanced once at the empty chair, remembering Chova, then quickly swept her gaze across to her left. There sat the Kaji Rieda, the Kai-to-be, and the only one (the other Kajis felt) that the Ka really cared about. Despite this, Rieda did not behave in a spoiled manner, and Destinariae often went to her when she had a problem. Rieda looked beautiful in a lilac and silver gown, with puffed sleeves and a tight bodice. Rieda was the only one at this private dinner, apart from the Ka and Kai of course, allowed to wear her crown. It was silver, a wide band around her head with amethysts and opals that sparkled brightly under the dancing candle flames. Her golden blonde plait swung low, its end brushing the floor. Rieda's eyes were focused on Lord Atisato, yet her face reflected deep thought. Her red lips pursed as she tried to think of a clever remark to display her intelligence. A servant girl came forward to offer their guest some more food; he waved her away. Another servant came to him with a heavy platter of foreign food-he narrowed his eyes, sending the woman scurrying back.

"Oh, Lord Atisato, won't you have some more squid rings?" asked Verda anxiously, fiddling with her napkin. Destinariae frowned, for Verda had been overly attentive to the man that evening.

"No, no thank you, Kaji," replied the copper haired Lord, with a slight grimace. He picked at the food on his plate, obviously full up.

Verda persisted. "Are you sure you won't have any more jellied sandfish eggs? They were brought especially from Garoa."

"I'm full, thank you, I do not desire any more food" returned the Lord, slightly impolitely. He frowned, his thick ginger eyebrows meeting as he did so.

The Kaji Rieda chose this moment to say "Another mint and cucumber biscuit?" Her calculating, sly expression belied her innocent tone.

The Ka and Kai burst out laughing. "You timed that...just right!" wheezed the Ka. After a few seconds Lord Atisato joined in, somewhat unenthusiastically at first. Soon, the whole table was laughing.

Almost.

Destinariae watched, silently remonstrating them in her head. It wasn't fair! Rieda was obviously the favourite. If she, Destinariae, had said that one remark she would have almost certainly been scolded for 'annoying and bothering the poor man'. But when Rieda said it, Destinariae mentally spat the name, it was a hilarious joke! And what in the name of Fortune was so funny anyway?

When the laughter subsided, Destinariae went back to her original task; watching Lord Atisato. As one of the most powerful of the Lords, he was a possible suspect for the...well, the possible murder. She was meant to have been watching him more carefully, but her mind had wandered. In fact, having thought this, he had not shown any slip, any peculiar sign of weakness when she had been watching him. Maybe...she should spur things on a bit, ask him a question. In the next interval in the conversation, she leaned forwards and opened her mouth.

At that moment, Tioni started to cough. It did not sound normal, and for a second Destinariae thought that Tioni was just trying to interrupt her. When it continued for a while, it became evident that something was wrong. When Tioni was asked this, she held up her hand, as if to warn them away. Verda thumped her on the back; still she continued choking. By now the room was eerily quiet, except for the frantic coughing. Glasses of water were offered, and denied, servants stood, dully immobile as their mistress choked. The moment went on, suspended in time...and then it was all over. Slowly, oh so slowly, Tioni's still body toppled to the floor.

Destinariae paced around her room, frustrated. How dare he confine them to their rooms! Could he not see that poison did not have any less effect when consumed in the palace, in the market, in a prison? Whatever was he thinking? She knew that her father was both clever and shrewd, so she could not understand why he had effectively imprisoned them. And the Kajarito guards standing outside the door served to both prevent people from entering...and to stop them from leaving.

Maybe it was Tifiert's idea, she thought, seating herself on the edge of her bed. Her skirts swirled around her feet, setting in the perfect modest fan that she had become so accustomed to. If it were the Kai who had suggested it, that would be more acceptable, well, the idea rather than the current situation. She threw herself back on the freshly made sheets, but her head hit the metal headboard rather than the pillow. It jarred her head, and tears of pain came to her eyes.

When the agony receded to a dull ache, she was able to think clearly. The Ka had called her to his work-chamber, and had conferred with her about Tioni's death. He had told her that his fears were not in the food, which Tioni had taken from several different platters as she wished, but in the drink. They had summoned a servant, and ordered him to drink from the glass that Tioni had been drinking from. He had drained the glass, and been fine for the next day, and the next. But Destinariae *knew* that there had to have been poison in that glass and she suspected that her father knew, too. Knowing his mental need to discover everything that might be a threat to him or to his family, she was also certain that he would do something about it. But that was not her concern...or was it? Her father did not mix with peasants and commoners, but what if the answer lay with them? The Ka would almost certainly seek out a mage or a wise person skilled in the use of drugs and herbs. He might miss out the commoners...she could not take the risk. But what to do, what to do?

On impulse she looked out of the stained glass window at the gleaming city below. It's like an egg, really, she thought, leaning her elbows on the windowsill. It's white, smooth and so beautifully simple on the outside, but on the inside it is a mess of complicated matters, a dark place we don't have a chance of understanding. But she was trapped inside the palace; the city was a different world. Unless...she swung her legs off the bed, and reached for the window catch. It was stuck firmly in place. Pulling it towards her as hard as she could, she used her free hand to rap sharply on the nail that held it in place. To her surprise, the catch came off in her hand. Reaching out, she pushed the window open.

As she was preparing to climb out, the edge of her heavy skirt caught on the frame, and a small tear appeared in the rich fabric. Cursing her thoughtlessness, she struggled to remove the offending garment and heavy petticoats, and tossed them carelessly on to the bed. Leafing quickly through one of her large, oak wardrobes, she drew out a dark cloak, a pair of stretchy black leggings and a navy tunic. Pulling them on, she removed her jewellery and placed it on the dressing table. Taking a look at herself in the floor-length mirror, she frowned. Even with the hood down she was recognisable. What could she use to disguise herself further? A thought hit her. Crossing the room, she opened a large ivory chest at the foot of the bed. Inside were all the clothes she had worn at Chova's funeral. Rummaging through them, she came across a black gauze veil. Fastening it behind her head, she surveyed herself again in the mirror. I could pass for a commoner, she thought, grinning. Or a minor noble's head steward, she corrected herself as her carefully tutored royal pride kicked in.

Returning to the lazily creaking window, she swung her leg over the sill, and brought her foot down on a stone ledge a foot or so down the wall. Using the many decorations in the masonry to speed her descent, she made good progress, and reached the foot of the palace wall in a minute or so. Not bad for a palace-bred Kaji, she congratulated herself, stopping to take a breath.

Suddenly she noticed a company of Kajarito heading towards the main gate, the entrance to the palace itself. Throwing herself into the cover of some nearby bushes, she watched them proceed. When she was certain that they had gone, she stood up and brushed herself down. She then ran towards a small iron wall-gate, leaping over plants and shrubs with minimal difficulty. Only slightly out of breath, she ran her nimble fingers over the simple mechanism which kept the door locked. Pulling one lever upwards, she slid the bolt back, and pushed hard. The well-oiled hinges allowed the iron door to swing open with hardly a creak.

Stepping out of the dark alley, Destinariae entered a different world. The smells of exotic spices assailed her, and she breathed the delicious aroma in deeply. The cries of merchants eager to sell their wares, the colours and voices of the huge crowds of people, the air of busyness and excitement...she moved forwards, entranced. When passing through before, she had never had much time to experience the peasants' everyday atmosphere, but had appreciated that it was strange and thrilling. But now it was different. No standards to meet, no rules to keep to, she wandered around, her original mission forgotten. Though she had just exited the palace, nobody seemed to be looking at her. Nobody stared, bowed, grovelled or trembled. It was a real sensation. Here she could be a nobody too. Though of course, she was far better acquainted with palace life. Lost in a myriad of scenes, sounds, aromas, and a whirlwind of thoughts, she continued dreamily down the bustling street.

*   *   *

Lady Poricala of Thermone paced around her over-elaborate solar, her large feet thudding down onto the warm wooden floor. Her dark eyebrows were drawn together into a fierce scowl, showing the grim nature of her thoughts. As she paced around the room, her black cloak swirled around her feet. Suddenly she stopped in front of a full-length mirror, and stared at herself. Slowly, she drew up the deep cowl, and peered out from the depths to see her reflection. Despite her heavy-set frame, she made an imposing, no, mysterious figure, she thought.

She stood for a while in front of the glass, pondering on her appearance. The way she lived her life, it was very important how she appeared in other people's eyes. Well, she thought, smiling grimly from the beneath folds of the dark robe, it certainly seemed to work. People saw her drawn up imperiously, hidden from view beneath a voluptuous, flowing cloak, and to their easily led minds she was a dark sorceress, someone to be served, respected, and mostly feared. And that was exactly the way things should be, she thought to herself with bleak satisfaction.

Still, it has been a mistake, using so much magic, Poricala told herself. It was impressive, yes, and therefore very useful in getting people to do what she wanted. Fear was a wonderful ally, she thought with a cruel smile. But she couldn't risk annoying the Gods this early. No, she had so much to do, to get caught now would just be a dismal failure - and she abhorred failure. She was a winner. She'd be the first in line. A power-hungry, goal orientated *winner*!

And she needed all of her energy just to deal with all of those pesky, uppity lords. The Lady of Thermone turned away from the mirror, throwing off her robe in anger. It pooled upon the floor like a stagnant black tarn. Her frown grew deeper as she thought of their endless tirade against her. Just because she was a woman! Men can never admit that a woman could command more respect than they could, she thought maliciously, but quite truthfully. It would be quite unthinkable for the lords to have a woman doing a man's job, and totally preposterous the idea that a woman could do it more efficiently than they ever could.

It made her absolutely furious, but she would show them. She was above their pathetic attempts to thwart her; she had power beyond their imaginings, and more importantly the will to use it. Yes, she might even be able to get rid of Thambar soon. Her face contorted with a mixture of scorn and revulsion as she thought of her poor, weak half-brother. He had helped, though, in his feeble, unknowing way. Without him she would never have got where she was now.

Some of them are definitely more troublesome than others, she thought, directing all of her fury to the lords once more. Some of them actually have brains, pea-sized though they may be. But then again, they were easily dealt with using tiny amounts of magic.

So easily manipulated, controlled just as I will one day control the empire.

Poricala laughed, throwing off her dismal mood as she pictured their blustering, disbelieving faces. They thought they were so clever, so powerful, these arrogant men. And yet they were so easily manipulated, so blinded by their self-importance that they couldn't see what was right in front of their noses. Well, she would show them. When she was the Kai, they would pay for the anger and toil that their arrogance, clumsy manoeuvring, and unwitting obstacles had cost her. She could have them killed. Yes, a public execution would strike exactly the right balance between humiliation, torture and death. The perfect revenge, in fact. But for now she must concentrate on the present.

Yet the past still occupied much of her mind; thoughts of Isete plagued her night and day, reminding her of her intense loathing of her old rival, of her vow to kill off the children of her most hated adversary, albeit a dead one. It had been so satisfying, so beautifully fulfilling, receiving the message that declared the death of the Kai. It was such a pity that she hadn't deemed it wise to go and witness the event herself. The sound of the crossbow bolt thudding into her chest must have been quite musical.

Also, the triumph she had felt at the funeral was indescribable. Behind the ebony mask with a grieving countenance etched upon it, she had been silently laughing. Which was why, in part, she was also going to assassinate all Isete's daughters, one by every last one. She would once again feel that surge of triumph and be inundated with power, and she would make sure that every trace of her nemesis was obliterated from the face of the earth.

The only problem was which to kill first. It would be most gratifying to kill the eldest first, Rieda. After all, no daughter of Isete's was going to be Kai. Not while she was alive. But killing the heir could prove to be risky, and getting caught now was just unthinkable. Yet the youngest – it just wouldn't give her the same feeling of pleasure. So the middle one, then. Destinariae, yes, Destinariae was annoying. She had her mother's innocent – 'I'm just so perfect, my people all love me' expression. And now she could be a martyr, Poricala smiled wolfishly. Yet the real question was: how to do it?

It would be difficult, with all of these new safety restrictions in place. Less times that the Kajis were allowed out, less places they were allowed to go, more guards to evade. Maybe the best way would be to just hire an assassin to watch her, and then the second she was allowed out, she would be face-to-face with death. And to make doubly sure that there was no implication of her own involvement in the assassination, afterwards she could just dispose of the assassin. That had the added bonus of saving financial resources as well. After all, she'd have to employ only the most skilled of assassins, and their services didn't come cheaply. Lady Poricala was very sensible with her money, knowing all too keenly what a lack of it could do to her plans.

With the middle daughter of the late Kai out of the way, it would make it all the easier to get at all the others, the eldest especially. Of course, the crowning glory would come soon after. How she hungered to see the look or crushing realisation on the Ka's face when he cowered before her, watching as she took his empire from his twitching hands and crushed the life out of his feeble form.

A timid knocking came from the heavy panelled door. Irritated, Lady Poricala swung the cloak once more around her sturdy form, then drawing back into the shadow of the cowl, she bade the apprehensive servant enter. A clearly petrified messenger trembled his way towards her, and then, unnerved by the silent figure before him, he prostrated himself on the floor before her. From within the depths of her cloak, Lady Poricala smiled a terrible smile of cruel pleasure.

Summoning her most arcane and commanding voice, the ambitious lady ordered the quivering man to speak, her lip curling in a contemptuous sneer. When she ruled, such pathetic males as he would be enslaved, or better, dead. She smiled the toothy smile of a shark circling a sinking boat, in fervent anticipation of what was to come. Still, if all was to proceed as planned then there was still much to do. People to see, Kajis to kill. Such a demanding life she led these days.

And there was still the tiresome ruling of the province. And people thought that Thambar could deal with it by himself! Senile old fool, he couldn't deal with eating a banana without drooling in imbecilic, inane and incontrollable terror. But he must be one of the last to go, she thought to herself. Without him as the figurehead she would have no power, nor authority; a woman could not rule in her own right in this chauvinistic land. But that would all change. With Thambar gone she would no longer have to concern herself with the meaningless concerns of merely one petty estate. No, rather the ruling of the entire empire. The splendour, the gloriousness, the *power* of it...

Suddenly she realised that the servant was speaking to her, in his wavering, uncertain voice. With an audible sigh she brought herself back from the glorious future to the tiresome present.

"My lady, his lordship desires your presence. He says you are to come at once..." his voice trailed off, and he quailed under her awesome glare.

Lady Poricala turned around and drew a deep breath, attempting to calm herself. "Tell his *lordship*," she said, the words seeming to freeze the very air, so cold was her expression, "that I will see him when I am ready. You may leave."

She whirled around, sniffing suspiciously. She glared furiously at the cowering servant, her hooked nose reddening along with her cheeks, and slowly took one menacing step forward. Her voice sounded malevolently from between her painted red lips.

"When, you foul creature of the despicable sewage system, did you last take a bath?" When there was no answer to her question other than a terrified whimpering, she continued contemptuously with her interrogation.

"Did you not imagine the possibility, anywhere in your enormous, thick-skulled, yet completely empty head, that entering my presence required at least some degree of cleanliness?" she roared, any semblance of calm leaving her contorted red face in an instant.

She advanced upon the mortified servant, pointing at him with her left arm, and muttering arcane words under her breath. The hapless man cringed, curling instinctively into a shuddering ball, and awaiting the agony that was his Mistress' sorcery to fall upon him. Suddenly the chanting stopped. Lady Poricala opened her hand, and a fat block of tallow soap materialised in her palm.

She flung it at the bemused servant with unerring accuracy and hissed, "Get out of her, you spawn of horse-refuse collectors, and so not return until you have robbed yourself of that appalling stench of decaying corruption!"

The traumatised man ran from the room, just remembering to bow before he made what he felt was a lucky escape.

When the servant had gone, Lady Poricala sank down onto her knitted bed coverlet. She really should not have lost her temper this time. Inflicting pain on others with magic was one thing, just making their bodily organs stop working to bring terrible agony, but using her magic to create matter was quite another. Well, creating would honestly be the wrong word. Converting would be more suited to the magic she had just cast.

She shook her head, staring down at her hands. She saw that the smooth, delicate skin of her childhood and early adulthood had been replaces with brownish red tough skin like old leather. No wrinkles as yet, she was pleased to see, but her knuckles were too callused and her palms too rough to be innocent of sorcery. Poricala was not pleased with herself; she had almost forgotten one of the first rules. Matter could not be created; it had to be converted from one thing to another. She didn't know what it was that had provided the particles that were probably being rubbed into a lather against the servant's body about now. She shuddered at this image. Being dirty was despicable, and worse...common.

She made herself concentrate on the matter at hand, this debasing summons from her supposed superior. The audacity of it! How dare he treat her in this way, she who had done so much for Thermone! It was unthinkable; somewhere in his senile, deranged mind he truly seemed to believe that he was in control over her as well as his estate, let alone his own body. Well, she thought deliberately to calm her anger, it will make the farce seem more believable to the other lords.

She crossed the room and poured herself a generous helping of rich Garoan red wine. Throwing back her head, she downed it in one swallow. It was, she noted with some pleasure, a distinctly superior vintage. She ran a still tingling finger around the rim of the fine glass, absently observing the smooth texture.

She really should stop dithering and go and see her half-brother. He'd probably got a stomach-ache from actually eating something for a change, and was claiming that he'd been poisoned. But she ought to visit him, in case he really did have a problem, unlikely though it seemed. In addition, she had to arrange little Kaji Destinariae's assassination as quickly as possible, if all was to run smoothly.

Poricala sighed, then walked purposefully out of her chamber, along the corridor that led to Lord Thambar. Her black robe contrasted sharply with the pale pink carpet and pastel tapestries that her late mother had chosen personally. Leicette had had, she thought, shuddering at the excess of frilly feminine decoration, dreadful taste. Maybe one day she would get around to redecorating, but for now she must just grit her teeth and endure.

She reached the door of Thambar's suite, and was admitted by yet another quivering servant, this time a maid, who dropped a belated curtsy. Poricala ignored her and stormed into the room, her eyes glittering coldly as she prepared to put her weak half-brother in his place. Thambar was lying in his large, four-poster bed, his aged and wrinkled body swamped by the huge furs covered him. He tossed and turned, moaning, his face an ashen grey colour.

She walked over to the bed, frowning. She knelt beside him in a false expression of respect, and forced her voice to soften. "What is wrong, my lord? Does something ail you?" she queried, her voice that of a concerned admirer. Indeed, she was truly concerned, for if he died prematurely then the limited power she held would be immediately severed. The lords would not accept her leadership without him, more fool they.

Thambar made no answer save a low groan. Lady Poricala impatiently beckoned the waiting apothecary. He hurried over to her, and bowed deeply.

"What is wrong with him?" she demanded harshly, gesturing over to the twitching lord in the four-poster bed, who was now in the grip of a terrible seizure. The apothecary looked a little worried, but said nothing. He cleared his throat nervously.

"Are you so unskilled at your trade that you cannot offer even an obvious diagnosis?" she sneered mockingly, "Or are you just so pathetic that you cannot even answer a simple question? I ask you again – what ails him? Answer quickly, or I will have you flogged." The man gulped in trepidation at her menacing warning.

"I...I'm not sure, my lady. He has a fever, and is suffering from continuous seizures, but his other symptoms don't match. If I may make so bold, your ladyship, I think it may just be old age catching up with him." The apothecary looked shocked at his own daring, and he paled noticeably.

"I see. Well, don't let it catch up. Make him rest. Get him the best medicine available. I'm not asking much of you, you know," she snapped, noticing his legs trembling as fitfully as Thambar's, "I'm not asking for you to perform any miracles such as returning to him his sanity or curing him so that he can dance around the room." Or even put him in control of his own saliva, she thought waspishly. She glared through magic-reddened eyes at the quaking apothecary, and delivered a final warning, "If he is not at least peacefully free of severe symptoms within a month then you will suffer the consequences. Dire consequences!"

And with this dreadful ultimatum she left, slamming the door behind her and leaving yet another traumatised servant in her wake.

Chapter 5

Two solitary figures walked along a dusty lane. Night had just fallen and they were looking for a place to rest. The long grass at the side of the road waved gently in the breeze, brushing softly against their legs. After they had walked for some time, they moved off of the road and stopped in a thicket. The smaller figure went off on his own to gather firewood, while the other laid out their cloaks and took the food out of their packs.

Soon, the boy returned from the woods and placed a small bundle next to the young woman. Once the fire had been established, they sat down and shared out a hunk of cheese.

"We're going to have to be especially careful with the rations now, Shoy," the young woman warned quietly, "this is almost everything we have."

"Don't worry Khalla," breezed Shoy, trying to reassure his friend, "We can easily get more food in the next village. We have to, anyway, it's the last before the Kanakoan desert."

"And just how to you intend to do that? With no money and no means of making any, we're a bit, well, stuck."

"I'm sure we'll think of something when the time comes." Seeing her still doubtful expression, he grinned cheerfully. "We'll cross that bridge when we come to it."

Khalla smiled wanly and lay down, leaving Shoy to put out the fire. She could not help worrying about the lack of money. It was an urgent problem. There was no point in thinking about it now anyway, as Shoy had rightly said.

Shoy… there was something not quite right there. He seemed so evasive at times, and it almost seemed like she was talking to a locked door. She frowned, just exploring a new train of thought. She knew it was none of her business, but it really was curious the way he managed to change the subject whenever she talked of his family, or of his background, or anything to do with his history. Not that he had been sullen or angry, but he had always just said a clever remark or made a joke that made her forget it. In fact, she realised, he managed to manipulate the conversation so skilfully she had only just noticed the omission of his past details.

It was not as if she was putting too much pressure on the matter, all things considered. After all, she had told the whole story of her old life. 'Only a few weeks and I already think of it as my old life,' she thought dreamily as she drifted off into sleep.

The next day, they reached the village in the late morning. When Khalla raised the question of how they were going to raise the money to by food, Shoy simply grinned mischievously and said to leave it to him. She was going to ask him about that, a worried frown creasing her face, but he disappeared without saying a word.

It was a very small village, with only a few houses dotted around. There was, however, a shop and an inn. She decided not to go into either of them before she had any money. It was a strange feeling, she decided, not knowing what to do with her time. She had always been a busy person, always on the go. She wandered around, looking at her surroundings, at peace with herself, and, for the moment, the world.

Meanwhile, Shoy had found the busiest part of the village. At the sight of all of those people, most of them with pouches on their belt, the flat of a small, sharp knife blade pressed onto the inside of his palm. 'Its crowds like this that make my heart beat faster,' he thought to himself, as he helped himself to the fattest purse. Belonging, he noticed, to the fattest man.

It's not stealing, he thought piously, it's redistributing the wealth of the empire to those who need it most. The contents of the purse, however, were mostly disappointing. A few hawks, but mainly wrens. He sighed. It had looked *so* promising, as well. He looked disgustedly after the man he had robbed. The fellow was obviously too worried about what everyone thought of him.

Looking around for the focus of the crowd, he saw a bookmaker and several rats in cages. Glancing at the coins in his hand and then back at the rats, he smiled.

At noon, Shoy found Khalla sitting on a fence, staring into space. "Look Khalla, look what I got!" he shouted, running over to her. He threw the coins at her feet. Snapping out of her reverie, she stared in astonishment at the small amount of money.

"Where did you get those?" she asked shrewdly, "In somebody's purse? Their pocket?"

"Yes! I mean, no! I mean…Oh, you've gone and confused me now!"

"I'll bet I have!" she scolded, her face irate. "Who did you steal it from?"

"It's not stealing! It's redistribution of the empire's wealth!"

Khalla grimaced, then started to laugh at the earnest expression on his freckled face. "Oh honestly, Shoy! Have you not got any morals?"

"Not many, no. What's a moral again? I might have stolen one once."

Khalla shook her head, her rich laughter filling the air. It was so hard to stay angry with him. He had, she noticed, an utterly innocent little boy grin. And, she admitted to herself, they did need the money, and the child hadn't stolen much. "Well, at least you weren't gambling. That is one thing I can't stand." She said as she watched him scoop up all of the coins into a small leather bag.

"But…" he said slowly, "I met some people and I promised them I'd meet them on the green." Again he was off before she could say a word. 'That could get really annoying,' she thought before heading towards the village centre.

A few hours later, Shoy returned to her with still more coins. "Oh, Shoy. You haven't stolen that, have you?" Khalla said with more than a touch of exasperation in her tone.

"Well, not exactly..." he replied, looking slightly uneasy.

"What do you mean 'not exactly' you've either stolen it or you haven't. Its not as though it's a difficult question to answer." This time there was definitely a hint of anger in her voice.

"Well, I know you'll be angry 'cos you said you didn't like it but there were these rats and this man and really good odds and all these people said that the sleek one was gonna win and I thought that the fat one would because it had more energy and it ran real fast and it won and I won us lots of money," he burbled, dashing out all his information in one gigantuan sentence. "See?" He held up the bulging money pouch.

This time she was not amused. She had just told him of her total disgust for gambling. They had, for the first time, a real argument, and after a while she simply refused to speak to him, storming off to buy some supplies. She was sick of hearing his pathetic excuses and wheedling attempts to win her favour back again.

By the time she reached the shop, her anger had faded. He was only a small boy, probably with no family to teach him what was right and wrong. It wasn't his fault. In addition, she admitted to herself, she had overreacted a little bit.

She was not the only one in the shop. A middle-aged woman was gossiping with the shopkeeper, a basket in her hands. "So I 'eard from my cousin, who's come to stay all the way from Bakarn, that there's some kinda kerfuffle with the Royal family over there."

Khalla listened in surreptitiously. She and Shoy might be heading into Bakarn, and if there was some kind of trouble, she wanted to know so that she could take care to avoid that area.

"Oh yeah?" replied the shopkeeper, clearly interested. "Their king not in any more trouble, is 'e?"

"It's Ka, not king, or so my cousin tole' me," the woman corrected proudly. "I dunno what the trouble is, but it's a right ole' mess! But," she warned, leaning in conspiratorially, "I did hear word that there was some-"

The woman's next words were drowned out by another woman, conversing with a friend, both waiting in line to be served.

"I do declare, it's about time some real action was taken 'bout that Pravar. T'ain't right to let some young juvenile d'linquent run around setting traps for people, killin' and strippin' them of all their earthly goods. T'ain't natural, I tell ya."

"D'ya know I heard that he has a group of boys like him, all under his command, that help him. It's a good job those wanted posters are up."

Khalla frowned and tried to lip-read the shopkeeper. She caught random words like "the stairs", "panicked", and drew in her breath sharply when she thought she saw the word "murdered" appear. She tried to block out the words of the women behind her, but their voices were loud enough to drown out the all-important conversation.

"Aye, but if 'e don't get caught, and soon, there's gonna be trouble, you mark my words."

"Remind me what 'e looks like again. Just so as I have a clear picture in my mind."

"Well, he's...he's...hard to say, really, I've only seen his poster once or twice. But I'm sure 'e must look summink awful. I do know that 'e's a tricky lout, and roofless and 'ard 'earted."

Just then the storekeeper noticed Khalla, who was grimacing at her countrywoman's atrocious accent. "Well, 'ello young lady. What can I do fer yeh? Don't think I've seen yeh 'round 'ere before."

Being a cautious person by nature, Khalla gave nothing away of her identity. She got the items that she needed and left quickly, trying to piece together the fragments of information about Bakarn in her mind.

* * *

The murderer sat on her marble throne, her hands tightening convulsively around the cold stone of the armrests. Unseen behind her heavy veil, a smile played across her face, one of satisfied complacence.

She's dead, the Kaji's gone, crowed her mind, and the killer mentally rejoiced. At last, the poison had done its work. It had been an exceptional scheme, using such a weak dose, until so much of the poison had absorbed into Tioni's blood. And that last dose, supplied at a never more perfect time...she sighed in gratification. When all the Royal Family, and the most powerful of the Lords were present, there could be no better time to kill off the Kaji. Now, fear and mistrust were rife in the minds of all. And dark, twisted schemes were what she dealt best in.

She ran her gloved fingers lazily up and down the intricately carved patterns along the ends of the armrests. But her thoughts turned from exultation to malaise. How much did the Ka suspect? After years of observation, she had come to see that he was an extremely powerful adversary, both in cunning and hegemony. If the Ka was to find out the nature and details of the plot, he might hazard a guess. And knowing the almost infallible accuracy of the Ka's guesses, that was a position she would much rather avoid being in. So, how to stop the investigations? She pored over the possibilities. What she should do depended on the Ka's course of action. And she could easily find that out.

"Eskiros!" she called, her voice echoing harshly throughout the dimly lit cavern. A moment later, her underling strolled casually in. He bowed low, the stood and lounged by a pillar at an irritable wave of her hand. As she watched him, he smiled thinly, and raised his eyebrows the merest fraction. She had no time for his games, however. "Eskiros, report on the most recent orders of the Ka and the latest movements of the Kajarito." At her nod, Eskiros came forward and once more prostrated himself before the makeshift throne.

"My mistress, the Ka has lately given no orders, save that the Kajarito are to guard every door of the Royal Family, moving on no orders but his own." At the irritated hiss from the woman before him, he knew she had been expecting something else. When her voice next came, it was low and thoughtful.

"But were there any other…tasks, journeys he sent his soldiers on?"

Eskiros wrinkled his brow and pursed his lips, though he had had an answer ready from the moment he was summoned. He would keep her waiting, though; he had borne many slights and subtle indignities from her, and could remember every one. "Let me see, I think there was something. Oh yes, a squad of the Ka's Kajarito, 4th squad, I think, left the palace…about two minutes ago. They were told to head for a Damelin."

The woman raised herself up slightly. "A Damelin? Are you sure?"

"Positive, Mistress. I heard it myself."

Leaping to her feat, the black clad female gave him a slight push with her booted foot. "Why didn't you tell me earlier, you ape? He's sharper than I thought! Get the men to follow them, and get rid of them once out of Central Bakarn. Get to it. Now!"

"Get rid of them?"

"Kill them all, you fool!"

Eskiros stored the kick and the insult in his mind for future reference, and headed for the door. "We have very few soldiers, Mistress. Are you sure-?"

"Of course! This is of vital importance! Go with them yourself if you must!"

Eskiros bowed quickly, and hurried out of the doorway. So, the woman thought, settling herself back into her seat, slightly insubordinate, is he? She did not miss his deliberate stalling, or his slight scowl every time she goaded him. Well, she would see about that, even if he was a Tsumetai. And the Ka had sent his squad to a Damelin, one of the poisons specialists who could do just about anything with a potion. Or find out anything about a potion, she reminded herself mentally. But if Lady Luck continued to smile down on her, all would be well. She smiled suddenly. She had an insubordinate subordinate, and with any luck, the Ka would never know what happened to his toy soldiers.

*   *   *

It was midday, and the brilliant sun shone lazily over the snow-capped mountain. Two figures were making their way down the side, one pacing slowly, the other by his side hopping forwards in an ungainly manner. The youth's hair was black, and his green eyes shone in his tanned face. The other was a huge bird, ebony and shining with the glare from the sun.

"So, Zaki, what are we doing?" Kethar asked, jumping over a patch of slippery ice.

Looking for water so we can drink and I can wash, replied Zakrivath in a patient tone.

Scowling playfully at his friend, Kethar retorted, "You know I didn't mean that. I meant, what are we going to do next?"

Zakrivath smiled cheekily back, then replied in a vacant voice, *I imagine we'll eat, sleep, drink…*a buffet from Kethar's elbow sent him into a fit of chuckles.

"When you've quite finished!" said Kethar, his stern voice slightly spoilt by the small snigger that escaped him. "No, seriously, we have to really think about this. We can't go home, I'll be branded a criminal and you a freak!"

Well, replied the shikara matter-of-factly, *we'll just have to go elsewhere, won't we?*

"Well duh!" remonstrated Kethar, conscious for once of his friend's youth and immaturity. Why, Zaki was only two days out of the egg! But they shared thoughts and mental pathways, so Zak was listening to him right now...he hung his head. "I'm sorry. I... forgot how clever you are. Why," he tried to lighten the mood and repair the damage, "when I was two days old, I couldn't even recognise what anything was, let alone hold conversations and walk...hop down a mountain."

Zak pulled up short. *What, you couldn't...when could you start actually doing things?*

Kethar shrugged. "I could walk unsupported about half a year after I was two years old, and say quite a few words." He turned, hands on hips, at his soulmate's laughter. "What's so funny?"

You took your time learning, didn't you? You were really stupid! And slow!

"Well I'm older now, and can walk properly and talk properly. Huh! *Stupid!*" he muttered rebelliously, then slipped over on a patch of ice. This prompted further laughter from the gigantic black hatchling.

Walk properly? You call that properly?!"

"Yes yes, fine," replied Kethar, though he laughed ruefully at himself. "Okay, you win. Now, can we go back to our talk?"

Well, all right. So isn't there another village we can go to? Or do we really need to go to a village? We've got everything we want, right here.

"Actually, I've been meaning to ask you, what *do* you eat?"

Zak tried to shrug, then looked at his wings, surprised when he couldn't. *Well, if it helps, I haven't felt hungry when looking at anything we've passed so far. And did you know, that white stuff is really cold!* He gestured with a talon at the melting snow. *It tastes like water!*

"It would, it's made out of it!" laughed Kethar. Then a thought occurred to him. "Water, running water, that's what we need. And if we buy some stuff from a village, you can try some and decide if you like it!" He stood up, ready to go again.

But which village will we go to? Surely all the ones around here will have note of your going?

"No, they won't know yet. I'm property," he spat the word, "of one of the Kajis." At his friend's quizzical gaze he explained, "Kajis are the daughters of the Ka. They're...like princesses. Very high up important people who have lots of servants to order around. My mistress was the nicest, though. But she won't let a description of me get to the surrounding areas until some time has gone by. She'll probably get word of our expedition on the Equinox, and then circulate a poster." He paused, reflecting. "If she can be bothered. After all, I was only a servant." He smiled at being able to use the past tense when referring to his old, lowly status. Now, he was a free man.

So we have some time to gather supplies and things? asked Zakrivath, cocking his head on one side. At

Kethar's nod he continued, *Oh good! I'm really hungry! But there's a stream or something down there, and my wings are dirty from trailing in the cold slush. Come on!* He raced ahead of Kethar, who started to charge after him. He found the massive bird sitting at the edge of the water.

"Well go on then! You wanted to wash, go ahead!"

It's cold, came the forlorn little voice. With a laugh, Kethar ran towards the dark shape hunched at the water's edge, and pushed him into the stream. As Zak fell, his wing reached out, and buffeted Kethar in too. Soon they were splashing each other and laughing, the shikara using his short, cumbersome wings to sweep water at his friend. When the fun had worn off, however, they clambered out, using the strong bulrushes to aid them. Kethar helped to dry his young companion with his shirt, and some soft moss. Being only a young hatchling, his Zakrivath required constant attention. When both were dry, Kethar noticed his friend staring into the stream.

"Zaki? What is it?"

There's things in there! squeaked Zak excitedly. *Big silver things, all wiggling round!*

Joining the shikara at the bank, Kethar tousled the jet-black bird's head plumage. "Well done, Zaki! You've found supper!" Seeing Zak's still vacant expression, he clarified further. "They're fish."

He went to find a pole to construct a rod, and heard Zak try the new word. *Feesh, fee-ish, fi-ish. Fish! Hello fishes!*

"They can't talk. And the plural is fish too," explained Kethar patiently. *Is it?* he wondered silently. Then he shrugged, and went back to examining sticks.

When he returned with a stout switch, he saw Zak, proudly sitting by a pile of glistening silver bodies. *See!* shouted the triumphant bird, *I got fish! I catched them all!*

Seeing Zaki's pleasure and triumph, Kethar forbore to mention the grammatical error. Instead he hugged his friend, already so adept at catching fish. "Well done, Zaki!" he congratulated, "It would have taken me hours to catch all those!"

Zakrivath swelled with pride. *Do we eat them now? I'm so hungry!*

Kethar used his rod to light a small fire. "Well, I'm going to cook mine. But you're welcome to try one if you're so hungry."

It became evident that Zakrivath was quite happy with raw fish. In fact, he liked them so much that Kethar had to hide his own two to save them for himself. But Zak didn't seem to mind, though he did comment, *I don't know how a little thin person like you can eat two whole fishes!*

"Well, I'm taller than you, and you've eaten eleven!" joked Kethar, licking the last juices off his fingers. When the fire had burned down, the sky was almost black, and the pair felt that it was time to get some rest. They finally fell asleep, with Kethar tucked firmly under Zaki's sable wing.

*　*　*

The sheer walls of the gorge were made of solid ice. They were like this always; frozen, year in, year out. The sunshine that touched them was hazy, and rarely seen in this remote place. In between the cliffs lay a deep valley, covered as always in a blanket of snow. From the tops of the precipices, the isolated villages looked like small patches of muddy ice. In a snowfall, you would not be able to see them at all.

Far up in the heights, a snow-hawk soared, its sharp eyes picking out the antediluvian dwellings. The sights were of marginal interest to it; it folded its wings to its sides and dropped downwards for a mile, spreading its wings again to catch an up draught. From here it could see each individual being, wandering across the snow in their fur coats and many layers. It knew by some instinct at the back of its mind that it should not go too close; these beings were primitive, and desperate. But it could not help its natural curiosity. Besides, there might be prey here.

Noticing one human with a long stick, it wheeled around and hovered overhead. A shiny thing was put with the stick, and held by the human. Interest overcame caution; the bird swooped closer to better see the strange device. Instantly the bright thing seemed to be flying towards it, and took the snow-hawk through the wing. With a startled cry it tumbled to the earth, the ragged hole in its wing making it impossible to navigate the swirling air currents.

The girl moved across the snow to the fallen creature, every step light so as to avoid breaking the snow. She was naturally graceful anyway; there was hardly a crunch as her booted feet smoothly came down. When she reached the bird, it was dead, the extreme cold having penetrated its feathers and broken wing. She picked up the carcass with a fur-gloved hand, and looked sadly at the body. Even though killing was necessary for her own survival, birds had always seemed so beautiful to her, wild and free. Especially hawks. They were such beautiful creatures, fiercely independent, lethal with deadly grace. She stroked the proud head, murmuring a silent tribute as the poor thing stared back at her with glazed, dead eyes. Then, with a sigh, she carried it into her own, dilapidated hut. Her mother stood there, staring vacantly out of the window. The woman looked around, acknowledged her daughter with a smile, and then cried out with joy when she saw the kill.

"Oh you brilliant girl!" she sang, kissing her daughter on the cheek. "Fresh meat! You know how scarce it is with the new mouths to feed. Oh, you clever thing, Ionté!" She snatched the carcass and immediately began to pluck it, regardless of the arrow still sticking from it.

"Mother, shall I…" asked Ionté, indicating the arrow.

"Oh yes, right," her mother replied, still overcome with excitement. When the girl had finished she went back to preparing the carrion, chatting all the while. "You know, I am *so* glad you brought this. I'm beginning to worry about your father; he's been gone on the hunt such an awfully long time. I do hope he's okay."

Ionté patted her mother on the arm, trying to reassure her. "It's alright, he's with the other men. And besides, he's not an amateur at hunting elk." The men of the tribe all went out together, leaving the just as fierce women to guard the village. The men all hunted from the largest herd near them, as it could spare the most losses. They had to be skilled in a number of ways, the least of which was knowing how many to take to avoid the extinction of the main food source. But food had been so scarce lately that the council elders had come up with a new plan.

"Yes, and it's not as if he has to even kill one this time," she continued, as her mother bustled around. "They just have to herd the animals back here, and we've finished building the pen already." She smiled at her busy parent. "Then you won't need to worry about food anymore. We'll have it right outside our door."

"It's not that that I'm particularly worrying about," continued her mother, with a slight frown. "But we can talk about that later. I notice young Kieso is hunting with the adult men now." She turned a naturally pale face to her daughter and winked. "He's old enough to get his own house, start a family..." she left the sentence dangling.

"Come, mother, I'm fifteen. Not old enough to marry." Especially not Kieso, she added, in the privacy of her own head. Why, the lad was barely old enough to use a bow and arrow, let alone be a dependable husband. She giggled softly.

Her mother, mistaking the origin of her giggle, beamed at her. "Nonsense! I married your father at fourteen!"

Ionté giggled again. "More fool you!" Sindarre laughed too, and then went back to preparing the dinner. As she worked, she glanced at her daughter. The lass had grown up beautiful, with a delicate, crystalline bone structure and almost ethereal features. She was slim and agile, quick-witted and friendly. She was intelligent, and skilled with the bow and knife. And it helped that she was only a half-blood albino, too. With an albino mother and a darker skinned father she had white-blonde hair, with pale golden streaks. Her eyes were a brilliant green contrasting with her pale face, and were often marvelled at by the white skinned, red-eyed folk who comprised the population in all of their country.

As the two women sat down to eat, Ionté tried to start up the earlier conversation. "So what were you particularly worrying about?" she asked, between mouthfuls. Sindarre sighed, and laid down her wooden spoon. She knew she would have to tell her daughter sooner or later. Looking straight at the finely-etched face in front of her, she began, "Love, I don't want to alarm you, but a group of...other men were seen not far from Treulle."

Ionté sat back, surprised. "Why would that alarm me? Men from other villages pass here fairly often."

"No, Ionté. Dark people."

Instead of concern, a small squeal of excitement escaped her daughter. "Really? Real dirty skinned folk? Oh, how exciting! Did anyone talk to them?"

Reaching out, Sindarre grasped her daughter's arm. "No, Ionté! They killed the men of Treulle, and killed some of the women! The surviving women and children were carried away in cloth bags! Don't you see?" At the way Ionté's face crumpled in horror, Sindarre felt guilty at the blunt way in which she had divulged the news. Moving round next to the sobbing girl, she gathered Ionté's frail body to her, and rocked her comfortingly back and forward. "Shh, it's okay," she whispered, and touched the beautiful, tear-stained face gently. "I'm sorry. Don't cry, sweetheart."

When she was in a sufficient state to talk, Ionté whispered softly, "Was nobody left?" At her mother's denial she blinked back more tears. "What about Papa? He'll be okay, won't he?" Her gentle face stared hopefully at Sindarre, longing to hear more comforting words.

But Sindarre could not lie to her. Instead, she clasped her daughter to her tightly, and murmured, "I don't know, love. I don't know."

Chapter 6

As much to reassure herself as to comfort Shoy, Khalla put her arm around him. "I'm sure there's nothing to be scared of. It *is* a little creepy here, but at least it isn't likely that there will be many people. Or bandits. After all, there's practically nothing to hide behind."

He shrugged her arm off, slightly roughly as if embarrassed. "I'm not scared. If anybody is, then it's you. But you're wrong. There'll be more bandits here in the desert than anywhere else, because it's so far from towns n' stuff that there's nobody to arrest 'em. Also, they'll most likely get travellers in small groups, and tired ones, I'll bet."

"I suppose you have a point," she agreed. "We should be on our guard. But this place is so bare that few people would willingly stay here for longer than necessary."

Shoy agreed reluctantly. He felt slightly put out with her worrying over whether he was scared. They carried on walking, each privately still convinced that their point of view was correct. This time their journey was rather duller. Their surroundings were desolate, unchanging, and neither of them were in the mood for laughter.

Shoy had been preoccupied of late, Khalla noticed. She had several times caught him looking at her strangely. She shook her head abruptly; she was just imagining things. The atmosphere of the place was making her imagination go into overdrive. It was strange how the place itself could influence one's own mood.

Her thoughts came back one more to Shoy. He had been very insistent that they search for coins at the roadside during their journey. She had thought he was joking at first, after all, what was there to buy in the desert? He'd said something back about making sure they had at least some money. She had to admit it had been a productive idea. And they could definitely use the money. Not that Shoy had been much help, though. Once she had noticed this, Khalla had insisted that they work on a 'finder's keeper's' basis, as her travelling companion had so delightfully put it. Added to what was left over from the money from the village, which hadn't been much, she had a fairly heavy money pouch, though it was mainly rusting wrens. But quite satisfying, all things considered.

That was another thing. She had noticed him eyeing her sabre with a rapt expression. He had already told her how much he admired it, although Khalla had already told him of its origins. He appeared to have no weapons of his own, so it was only natural that he craved one. Still, he was completely tactless, looking at it with blatant envy in his eyes, but it did make her feel as if she had the upper hand.

The cacti cast eerie shadows over the sand dunes. In the half-light, the two travellers thought they could make out strange shapes in them, but ignored the growing feeling. They were sure that it was, once again, down to their imaginations. The air was crisp, and the dull thuds of their footfalls in the sand echoed around the empty dunes. Although it was hot during the daytime, at night the temperature dropped drastically.

Drawing her thoughts back to Shoy, Khalla remembered something strange that had happened earlier in the day. In fact, it had happened a couple of times before, just after they had left the village. He had gone over to a post at the roadside, telling her that he would catch her up in a few minutes. The first time she had thought nothing of it and had just continued down the road without a backward glance. Then, today, she had turned her head discreetly round, watching him out of the corner of her eye. He had taken some things out of his pack and buried them. It was most peculiar.

"Did you hear something just then?" asked Shoy quietly, bringing her out of her reverie, "because I could have sworn that I heard some people whispering back there." Khalla had no time to reply, because at that moment two men sprang out from behind an abundant cactus, swords drawn.

They rushed straight for them, all the while shouting to each other to "Get the girl, get the money!" For a short moment the prospective victims stood still with shock. Then it sank in. Khalla drew her sabre, yelling a wordless challenge at the two would-be killers. She did not lose control, but merely expressed her anger at the audacious fools in a violent way. The first, not expecting any resistance from a young girl and a small child, died immediately as Khalla's sabre slid easily through his torso. She pulled it out with some disgust at the arterial gore that she had expected, but nevertheless gave her a slight shock with the large amount of blood.

Shoy also proved himself to be more resourceful than Khalla would have thought. He *was* armed, contrary to her previous opinion. He held a small knife, not as well made as it could have been, but in very good condition. Khalla approved of this. Shoy slew the second robber with a quick jump and thrust technique, slicing his throat neatly. Khalla was more than a little impressed.

They walked a short distance away from the scene of bloodshed after wiping the dirt and gore from their weapons on the corpses' shirts, now stained red with blood. They glanced at each other briefly, but looked away again timidly. There was nothing like seeing a friend kill somebody to create suspicion. It seemed to each of them that they had just met once again, for the first time. The pair continued with their journey for a while, neither of them mentioning the assassination attempt just a few minutes earlier.

They set up camp when they were a good distance away. While Shoy laid out the bedrolls, Khalla cleaned her sabre reverentially on a scrap of cloth. When it had been restored to its usual, gleaming brightness, she lay down with it hugged to her chest.

It had been a long day, and they finally fell asleep watching a small rodent scurry around on its nocturnal wanderings.

Khalla woke up in the small hours of the morning, whilst it was still dark. Wondering what had awoken her, she lay looking at the unfeeling stars, staring at her with customary coldness from the dark blanket of the night sky. Hearing a noise, she turned her head slightly to the side. It was probably just the wind. Or Shoy snoring, she mentally added. But just to be sure, she scanned over the surrounding area.

Everything seemed calm and quiet...but something about a cluster of shadows did not look quite right. Narrowing her eyes, she could just make out three figures huddled close together, discussing something in excited whispers and pointing occasionally in the direction of their camp.

Alert at once, Khalla patted at Shoy's bedroll, to wake him. When her hand encountered no resistance, she was immediately concerned. Where had the little senseless idiot gone? She dared not call out for him, for fear of alerting the watchers that she was awake, or getting Shoy into danger. Maybe he had sensed the danger and slipped out. Yes, she reassured herself, that would be like him. He was probably eavesdropping on the watchers right now. No doubt he would warn her if the observers were to advance.

Putting her head back down on the makeshift pillow, she pretended to sleep. In the privacy of her own head she could see that everything would be fine. Shoy would tell her all about it in the morning, and he would have probably worked out their identities.

They would decide what to do about them together tomorrow. Despite herself, she found her eyes closing. Tomorrow...

With this comforting thought in mind, she drifted back to sleep.

* * *

Well, once again we are gathered here together, all seven of us. What do you want this time?

Luck, we do not gather the Circle of Gods unless it is needed.

Our brother Eternity is right. So why has the Circle of Gods been called?

We need to further discuss the servant Khalla. Though she seems to be unaware, as yet, of the dark changes that have blossomed in her mind, body and soul, we need to bring forward the rest of our plans. When is the Change to be laid upon her?

We must discuss this further before we decide on time, Fortune. There might be deeper problems that we have not yet discussed.

I think I perceive brother Fate's meaning.

Go on, Ashikra.

Firstly, there is the boy. His youthful influence counteracts the dark powers we are laying upon her. He must be removed.

The boy will soon not be a problem.

And how is that, Eternity?

Do not dare spurn my knowledge, Fortune! I have Seen it.

There us another problem.

Yes?

Well, she is strong of mind and character, and may reject the Change. And there is no telling what she could do if she found later that we were behind it, knowing her rejection of the Gods.

We could just leave her as a Changed-being, so she would never be able to think it was us, with an animal mind.

That idea seems to be favoured. But no, there must be a loophole in the action. The old laws must be respected.

Ah, Chance, always the peacemaker.

She is right. We could make it so that she could only return to her original state if she were to see something.

Something to the contrary of what she has always believed? After all, how is that to happen?

Luck is right, for once. Now, only the time has to be decided.

Well, an exact time cannot be chosen yet, but I vote that we should monitor her, and Change her only when she may not totally register it.

For example, when anger clouds her mind?

Yes. That would be excellent. Anger would take her over, and we could unleash the beast.

* * *

The fire licked hungrily at the dry logs, a beacon in the night. But this was no problem for the men siting casually around it, as they were the sort that would go and investigate this open a fire, and woe betide them that lit it. Shakna stared into it, his thoughts lost amid the flickering intensity of the flames. This was his last night here, and he was having second thoughts about leaving as he surveyed the other members of the mercenary group, and thought back to days gone by.

There was Black Sye, their self-appointed leader, the near-winner of countless conflicts who had the scars to prove it, sitting alone at the edge of the circle. Untya and Ghiron sat together, sharing a chipped tankard of ale as they joked and laughed raucously. The former had once been the partner of Black Sye, but they had drifted apart when they had formed the group. It was just as well, mused Shakna idly, their personalities were totally different. Ghiron's was much more suited to Untya's.

He caught himself before he could go any further. Shakna, he told himself sternly, you're a mercenary worrying about *personalities?* That's why I have to leave the band, he thought gloomily. He had not been brought up to do this, he was sure, although it had been fun at times. He remembered the time they robbed a merchant who turned out to have too much gold than was good for him. They had gone into town with the loot, and went to a fine tavern and spent all night getting drunk...ah, yes, he was going to miss it.

And the band was so...interlinked. One had killed someone's brother, another had unknowingly saved this one's life, one had been secretly seeing another's wife...they were all practically family. But Shakna, although made to feel as welcome as any of the others, had never really seen anything other than rob, burn, pillage, and rape. He knew that there was another world out there...and he wanted to see it. Let the others have their crimes until judgement day, he thought wryly, I'll have none of it. Well, he relented slightly, maybe I do enjoy this life, but I can at least see what other choices there are.

He was roused from his thoughts by an elbow in the ribs. He looked up, and the men he was playing cards with eyed him expectantly. "My turn *again?*" he sighed. He selected one from his hand without much thought, and put it down. It did not seem to bode ill or well for him, so he started to study the faces of his intent opponents. Sitting cross-legged on his left was One-eyed Em, his face swarthy and mean in the firelight, and his red eyepatch cast into shadow by his hooked nose. Nobody knew anyone's real name, just their show-names, except Shakna's. Untya got his from 'hunt you', Black Sye from 'blacks eye'...and Em had earned his by the 'M' shaped brand mark on his shoulder blade. Many of the band called him Emmy, but none to his face. He placed a card on the pile, and looked at Shakna with a shrug.

Next to Em sat Mad-Red, the ginger haired fighter from Cular. He had once killed a grizzly with his bare hands. Directly opposite Shakna sat Hound, as always attended by his parade of dogs. Hound had received his name through his curious affinity with the creatures. He was said to talk telepathically to them, but when asked just shrugged and went back to his canines. Hound's chestnut hair was tied back by a red cloth band. He winked back at Shakna and patted his favourite mongrel, Nyip.

Next to Hound knelt Desert, the dark skinned stranger from beyond the Garoan Mountains. He spoke rather bad Bakarnian, but was not faltering in his speech. He was totally ruthless in all matters, and usually won at games of strength. On his left and Shakna's right lay Vine, the poison specialist who had a deep and dark knowledge of plants and their uses, with his green-dyed hair and nimble hands. Vine's eyes moved shiftily from side to side, and he laid down all his cards saying matter-of-factly, "Triple void, and two comets. I win." All the other players threw down their cards with regretful sighs, some looking accusingly at the intelligent Vine, as he was well capable of cheating. But for once, Vine had played a fair game of void.

At that moment, the most beneficial of their number bustled up to them, bearing a tray of cooked meat and ale. With hearty cheers the men ran at her, and one kissed her soundly while another divested her of the tray. When they had sat down to eat and drink, their cook let out a chuckle. She came up next to Shakna, and sat silently by his side. Looking at her, young and pure amidst a den of murderers and thieves, Shakna wondered what on earth had possessed her to join them on that fateful day.

He remembered it vividly, the bright flames, the screams of the women trapped in their wooden houses, the yells of the men cut down by the mercenaries, and the acrid smell of burning meat. The two women they had found outside the houses were tied and bound, the mercenaries despite their orders aghast at the thought of drawing their blades across a woman's throat. There had been more than a slight reluctance to undertake the job at all, on not just his part. He was uncomfortable with the fact that a Tsumetai had paid them for the total annihilation of the village. Otherwise they certainly would not have done it.

They had then found this girl, trying to reach another beneath a fallen beam. She had not screamed when they dragged her away. When Mad-Red came to take his pleasure with her, she had grinned at him and punched him hard in the face, breaking his nose.

She had then run off. When they returned to their camp, they had found her sitting by the fire, cooking a wild boar that she had just killed. They had tried to scare her, and were bewildered when she told them brightly that she wanted to remain with them. Soon, the adventurous lass had settled in to the rhythm of the crew, and was adopted into their number.

"You do like to mother us, don't you Kad?" he teased her gently.

Her young, proud face lit up with an impish grin. "Mother you?" she laughed. "You're all older than me!"

"Me and Vine are the youngest, though. And Hound." He fondly reached out, and brushed back a lock of her hair. Immediately he felt her tense, and asked despairingly, "Why do you always flinch away from us? Is it because of your village?"

Her head bowed; he knew he had the answer.

"But then, those guys just kissed you, and when I just stop your hair from going in your eyes, you back away! Is it me then?" Reaching out again, he brought her face up so he could look at her properly.

Kadira smiled. "No, not you. And I would've punched those guys, but I had my hands full! How would you feel if you cooked a good meal, and then chucked it straight on the floor? Use your head, Shakna." Knocking his hand away with a sweep of her arm, she stood up, and walked slowly away, receiving the whistles and catcalls with a gracious wave of her hand. He tilted his head to watch her go, noting the trim waist and curve of her hips as he did so. She suddenly swung around and noticed him looking.

Scowling playfully, she blew him a kiss, then slunk off.

'How can one be that pretty and useful and yet so lonesome?' Shakna mused. Kadira did everything gracefully, her every movement a tempting promise to any man, yet she flinched from all human contact, save those few she really trusted. He remembered with a gleeful smile the time when a very drunk Ghiron had leaned forward to kiss her, and she had smiled sweetly at him, spat a mouthful of ale in his face, then leapt up and hammered a flying kick into his chest. Shakna himself, along with the rest of the group, had often thought longingly of Kadira, but she was nobody's but her own. He continued to dream of her for a while.

At last, when the fire was guttering and the men had fallen into a contented silence, he felt that it was time to make his move. Using Vine's head to pull himself up, he approached the dying flames. Turning to face the others, he called out, "I have a confession to make." Seeing that he had their attention, he thought how best to phrase the oncoming statement. He decided that bluntness was to be his approach. "I will be making this my last meal with you all. What I am saying is that I must be leaving tonight. You see, I cannot…accept that this will be all there is to life, so I am to study other…methods of living." His voice cracked at their expressions. For a ruthless band of killers, they had all a strong bond to each other, almost like brothers. But he could still scarcely believe that they would be this troubled at him leaving.

Untya was the first to rouse himself from his stupor. "Where will you go?" he asked, wide eyed.

Shakna shrugged. "Wherever I must, to experience everything."

"But you have the best of life with us! Things can only get worse if you leave!" That was Mad-Red. Other shouts backed up his statement.

"You stay with your life; I need to see another."

A third voice rang out above the disquiet; Em was standing up. "How are you going to manage without us all?" Many agreed with him; Shakna had always been seen as the young one, the new breath of life. And everyone helped him and looked out for him. Shakna did not begrudge this, however.

"I don't know," he whispered quietly, "I don't know."

He wandered off to his trodden down patch of grass at the edge of the group and lay down, sprawling himself over it. In the background he could hear the gang talking in low voices, though he could not quite make out the words. It would be so much easier if he could just stay with them! But he had decided resolutely that he would go. And he had no right to ask them to accompany him; they had their own lives to live, and seemed contented enough. He had no right at all to change all that, yet he was sure they would not come if he asked. After all, how strong a bond could there be?

"Shakna." The name was stated, not asked. He turned around, ready to gently but firmly stop any protest about his leaving. Black Sye came forward; it was he who had spoken.

113

"Shakna, let me say this to you. You have been an apt member of our group, and we would not stop your purpose for anything. But we have unanimously decided," here he glanced abruptly at Vine, standing a little way off, "to come with you." Regardless of Shakna's shocked expression, he continued, "You are the youngest of us all, and have a sound aim in mind. We have also not become this way of choice, so now that we have a choice, we will take a better path. As long as we can still have some fun along the way!" he added with a grin. As Shakna started to protest, Kadira bounded up to him.

"What, you didn't think we were going to leave you on your own, did you?" she laughed. "I mean, you could do without that lot," here she waved a hand at the beaming men, "but without me, you'd starve! You know his cooking!" she added as an aside to the others. To Shakna's surprise she gave him a quick hug, then let the others get to him. She was glad that the others had been in favour of the plan; she would have been sorry to see Shakna gone. He was the only one she could be really sure of, one who had morals of a sort, whose heart was not really in the killing and plundering. Seating herself at the fireside, she started to feed it some twigs, so she could cook some more lamb. Men were always hungry after doing any serious thinking, she considered thoughtfully. Then she chuckled cattily. It was probably something to do with their tiny brains.

* * *

The palace loomed over the city, huge but elegant against the comparative dirtiness of the sprawling cluster of buildings. From the highest room in the castle, a small room in the turret of the highest tower, you could see everything for miles, spreading out below in a breathtaking patchwork quilt. A sea of green was the palace gardens, a pool of blue was the ornamental lake...from here you could be above everything and apart from the world.

However; today it was empty. The sights stayed unseen, the beauty clandestine. But it did not really matter, for if there had been a watcher from the window, they would not have made out the small dark figure approach the castle, coming down the main street.

Destinariae strolled past the sedulous people, her legs moving at a pendulum gait. It was doing her good to get out of the palace, far more good than staying under the watchful eyes of the Ka, and the Kajarito. Poor fools, they had no idea that the room they were guarding was empty. She would have loved to go strolling up to the front of the sentries, to see their puzzlement at her coming into the room when they believed that she was already in there, but she knew that that would restrict her comings and goings even more.

Letting herself in at the wall-gate with the small iron key that she had recently commissioned to be made, she slunk across the grounds, jumping the shrubs with practised ease. Indeed, she had practised many times this trot across the gardens. How many times had she been on her excursions? Five, or was

115

it six times? She reached the base of the stone wall, shining pinkish in the falling levels of light, and started the climb to the top. It was made easier by the leather gloves she was wearing. Reaching her own balcony, she swung herself up onto it and opened the window, shutting it behind her as she entered. Walking across her bedroom, she was pulling off her gloves when she froze.

Verda was sitting on the four-poster bed, regarding her with a worried expression. On seeing her sister's shock, she calmly said, "Well, you didn't expect to keep your little trips secret for long, did you?"

Destinariae rushed forward to the bed, and grasped her sister's arm urgently. "Verda, does anyone else know? Who have you told?"

Verda smiled prettily. "You don't know me at all, do you? I haven't told anyone. I for one know the restrictions of this life."

Destinariae breathed a sigh of relief. She hugged her sister gratefully, and sank down beside her. "But how did you get in here?" A wave of suspicion washed over her. "You didn't sneak in too, did you?"

Verda dissolved into pretty peals of laughter that would quite easily have called over a score of lords and nobles to attend upon her. "Oh you mistrusting Royal! That's your arena, by the looks of things. I just said that I was here to visit you. My escort returned to my door as soon as I arrived here. Yours are still here, though." She gestured toward the door.

"So why are you here then?"

"To tell you to be more cautious with your voyages."

Destinariae shrugged. "I need to get some fresh air! In here it's so confining and repressive, I just need to be able to get out and relax a bit."

Verda looked uncertain for a minute, as if weighing something up. Then she said in a low whisper, "I know what you mean. Our father seems to have gone out of his head. And...I need some fresh air too."

Destinariae grasped her older sibling's hand. "You could come with me, if you wanted."

Verda shook her head. "I have other plans." At her sister's eager and enquiring look, she shook her head again. "No. It's best if you do not know. We don't know who else might be listening." She gestured toward the door again. "And then you can act more naturally surprised." With those words she stood, and walked to the door. On a sudden impulse, she ran back and hugged Destinariae tightly. Then she ran out of the door, much to the astonishment of the eavesdropping Kajarito guards.

*   *   *

It was so nice to have some time to oneself, the young Kaji reflected, as she ambled around the neat borders of the small Palace Lake. Although it *was* wonderful to have so much attention lavished on her at home. She giggled wickedly; she could wrangle absolutely anything out of her parents in the light of the new family crisis. She didn't dare question it, but she supposed it must have something to do with the deaths of her sisters; she had almost forgotten their names already. It was not important now that they were dead, though, was it? Anyway, even if they were in mourning, that was no reason for Faitan not to enjoy herself.

The evening air was crisp, and ice crunched beneath her boots as she made her way over to the small jetty with the boats. Her progress was slow, as she did not want to fall on the slippery path. It would not do to embarrass herself. Her breath smoked in the wintry air. Tiring slightly, she sat on an ornate bench. Dreamily, Faitan ran her small, podgy fingers over the intricate engraving. This particular bench portrayed a bird rising up from a fire. Not to her taste, but she had plenty of her own that were.

Idly, she made a mental list of possessions that she had acquired since the first Royal death. There was the whole new wardrobe of pink and red lacy dresses, the life-size model of herself made from pure sugar, and the…of course, the bird-bath.

But there was one thing she had forgotten to ask for. She had seen the most wonderful toy. Although, she usually shunned toys; after all, she was every bit of eight years old. This particular one, however, was special. It played delightful, tinkly music, and when you flipped the switch a hundred different animals, all handcrafted and made out of the purest white gold, paraded around the jewel encrusted platform. The animals all made the right noises, as well! The person who had designed it must have been an inspired genius, and the person who actually made it was surely a master craftsman. It was one of a kind, and therefore was the perfect toy for a Kaji- the most important Kaji, too.

It was, of course, slightly possible that she would be refused. But this was not likely, as she would make them sorry if she did not have her way. First she would sulk and refuse to speak. If that didn't work then she would scream, scream, scream some more and throw several tantrums. That usually worked- few people could bear to be subjected to the high pitched shrieking of Kaji Faitan once she was started. Also, it tore at Tifiert's heart to see her cherished daughter bawling her eyes out. As a last resort- and only as a last resort- she would go down on her knees and plead. Although it was degrading for one of the Royal line to have to beg. She had never done it before, so she shouldn't need to do it now. It was beyond her why they bothered to deny her in the first place, as she always got her way in the end.

Having regained her strength, she carried on with her walk, trundling along like a tubby, pampered pet. Living in the palace was living in luxury, so she was not in the best physical condition. Her hatred of exercise was well known among the Palace staff, though Faitan did not know it. She did know, however, that she was given everything she wanted, and knew she was probably referred to as 'spoilt'. After all, she did not have any friends beyond the daughters of lords, who had been told to play with her. Well, if they didn't need her, then she didn't need them. She shrugged indifferently. Less people she would have to share her fortune with.

Bored of contemplating her lifestyle, Faitan quickened her step. She reached her destination, and sat down on the edge of the jetty, staring down into the icy water. Glancing over her shoulder wanly, she looked around. She had a vague suspicion that someone was watching her. Annoyance flared. No outsider could get through the heavy guards, so it must be someone from the palace. How dare they! She was a Kaji, and that demanded respect far beyond being spied upon by an indiscreet...but there was nobody there. Strange, she thought she had seen somebody.

Taking her thoughts back to her family, Faitan felt suddenly angry. Rieda was getting all of the attention lately. Just because she was the heir to the throne. What about *me*, she thought sulkily. After all, I'm the most important one. It's not as if any of the others even looked right. In her own opinion, Faitan was perfect.

When she was younger, the knowledge that she had many other siblings had seemed but a minor inconvenience. She had assumed that as so much attention was paid to her, she would go on living in her perfect dream world forever. However, as she grew older she began to realise that she would never be the ruler of Bakarn. She would be married off to some ugly boy and be only second best. Yet after many unhelpful tantrums and a lot of contemplation, it had been almost perfectly bearable until The Brat, alias Efaerin, had been born. Although Rieda had always been the Ka's favourite, the Kai had positively doted on Faitan, as the youngest. Now all of her attention was focused on the baby. Why did everybody always dote on ugly, bawling, crying podgy babies? The spoilt Royal was insanely jealous of her eldest and youngest siblings.

Her thoughts continued to dwell on this unfortunate subject, regardless of the fact that she was surrounded by unmistakable natural beauty. The water was frozen, and the waterfalls connecting the different levels had formed delicate white patterns. The tiny white icicles seemed so fragile that they were almost too insubstantial to exist. She thought it slightly odd that it had been cold enough for ice, as it should be spring already. But the weather had been changeable lately, and odd climate changes were now more common than the expected temperature. Standing on the edge to take a closer look at the glistening white wonders, Faitan leant out over the glacial water, squinting at the patterns. Maybe she could catch one, and show it off to her sisters. As she leant further and further away from the jetty, her slippered feet lost their grip on the frosty surface, and she slipped over, clumsily trying to catch hold of something, anything...

Finally she fell, her overweight body splintering through the thin ice and splashing into the sub-zero water. Struggling for breath, she kicked furiously, frantically trying to break the surface. Gulping down gallons of water, she rose, her robes inflating, gasping. She pumped her arms in a desperate effort to stay afloat, her eyes wildly searched for the jetty. It seemed to be getting further and further away.

She felt herself getting closer to unconsciousness as the cold penetrated her body, clouding her mind. As her concentration slipped, her head ducked once more beneath the surface. The Kaji's eyes stared blearily at a face that obscured the light. It seemed somehow familiar...

A black gloved hand grasped her face; at first she thought that she was going to be rescued. But no, instead Faitan was forced cruelly down, down into the dark, unknown depths of the lake. I'm dying, she thought in astonishment as she met still more arctic water.

Her fat, stiff body sank down to meet death, enveloped by the sodden, voluminous robes that filled with water and dragged her down. Faitan's final thought was one of shock, and of outrage. The wintry water at last swallowed her life, and a silvery, cruel laugh danced through the crystalline air.

Chapter 7

Outside his Mistress' chamber, a man slouched in sullen silence. He had decided not to go with his men on the mission; he had work of his own to do. The cold stone passageways were empty; and he did not have to look around to ascertain his solitude, as the lightest footstep made an echo that you could hear for miles along the tunnels. He needed some time alone to think. After all, he did not just possess physical strength.

Reaching into his tunic pocket, Eskiros drew forth a whetstone and ran it up and down his favourite blade as he reflected. He had sent the men off at the Mistress' whim, and had stayed to find out something that would no doubt be of use to him- his employer's identity. At the moment he had not much to go on, just a flash of gold edging, the proud stance, the correct voice and commanding tone she used. Oh and that, too: she was female. He knew she could not be common-born; so much was obvious. But for the minute he could just presume she was a landholder, or a noble's wife. Some lord's daughter, perhaps.

It would make it easier if he knew her age. But the only parts of her he could see were her eyes- dark, brooding, pensive, *dangerous*. Some said that eyes were the windows to the soul...if he believed that, then he was lucky to escape with his life. Luckily for him, he avoided superstition and rumour, and concentrated on real things, like gold, victims, and employers.

How to find the identity of the woman, he mused to himself. He could follow her back one night...but there were risks that way, and the result was uncertain. Eskiros didn't like to take risks; he liked to know he was going to come out on top before he went in. So that plan was off. He could try and find out more from her associates, but that had two faults- he did not know of any other associates, and they would be hard to bribe information from.

He tucked the sharpened blade back into its sheath, in the black velvet sash that he wore around his shoulders. The other knives, machetes, daggers, throwing stars, light maces and short swords gleamed as they were exposed to the low levels of light. Okay, Eskiros thought, I definitely need a plan. He clicked his tongue; he always liked to be ready. To soothe his rising frustration, he decided to punch someone, whilst he started to walk back towards the city.

*   *   *

"Let's aim for that one," said Kethar, pointing towards a brown splodge in the green patchwork of fields.

Seems a good a village as any, remarked Zak. They had been travelling for a few hours in the darkness, and the first pale streaks of dawn were just appearing over the horizon. *But, can I just ask, what is wrong with that one?* He jabbed his hooked beak in the direction of a much closer village.

"Too close to Central Bakarn," answered Kethar, excavating the contents of a fingernail. "If and when they send out rewards and descriptions, that'll be one of the first places they come to. If we'd already been there, somebody would be bound to tell them everything they know." Picking up a flat stone, he carelessly skimmed it across the surface of the stream they had stopped at.

As they started to walk again, Zaki gave an exclamation of delight. Kethar, mistaking the origin of the excited squeak, said, "Zak, we've not time to catch fish now."

No, Kethar, not fish. Little Zakis! Look at them! They're so tiny! Zak was hopping excitedly from claw to claw, staring at two blackbirds who were staring impassively back. *Hello, little Zaki! Can you talk?* He squeaked in joy as they chattered back to him. *They talk! But I can't understand what they're saying.* His head feathers twitched as if he was furrowing his brow.

Kethar was growing slightly impatient. "Come on Zak! Or else there'll be no supper!" he coaxed, knowing his friend's major weakness. With a downcast expression, Zakrivath allowed himself to be led away from the 'little Zakis'. Only then did Kethar realise that he hadn't been able to understand the birds either.

The two friends made good progress, Kethar helping the young bird over large rocks and piles of scree. By the late afternoon they were about a mile away from their destination, and had acquired a few bronze wrens thanks to Zaki's sharp eyesight. The shikara wanted to stop for a meal, but Kethar was adamant that they should reach the safety of the village before nightfall. In another hour or so they reached the small town.

"Okay, Zak, you stay behind me, and wait while I go into shops." He heard with a smile his friend's rebellious muttering behind him, like the vexatious tantrums of a moody teenager. The streets were almost deserted, but many lights were on, and the sound of raucous singing filtered out from a local tavern. The first shop the pair came to was a grocer's store. With a pleased smile, Kethar walked inside.

"Hello, young sir. And what can I get for you, then?" the man behind the counter greeted him.

Kethar's eyes scanned the crowded shelves. "Er, just a loaf of bread, and two apples, please. Oh, and a small water flask."

The man nodded, and reached up to select the items the customer wanted. Laying them on the counter, he said without hesitation, "That'll be seven wrens, please." With a grateful sigh, Kethar handed over the coins and took his goods. Stepping outside, he noticed a butcher's, and purchased a large ham. His money almost spent, he looked around for Zak. He finally spotted him halfway down the street, peering with interest into the window of the tavern. When Kethar reached him, the shikara pointed inside, and cocked his head questioningly.

"Tavern. Pub. Where you buy drinks from."

Zakrivath preened his wing thoughtfully. *But you can get water for free everywhere!*

Kethar grinned. "Not…water, but ale. Alcohol. Makes your head spin and you feel lousy when you wake up the next morning, but when you're drinking it…" he sighed rapturously, remembering his limited experiences of ale. At the last Midwinter feast he and Bheffor, too young to be counted as adults, had swiped a tankard of ale from one of the tables. They had taken turns at sipping it, sitting behind the kitchen screen, while Sanniah tried one mouthful and moaned about the taste all evening. Kethar blinked back sudden tears, turning to face Zak again.

I want ale, affirmed Zaki. *Let's go and get some!*

"You wait here," Kethar said, and walked into the tavern. The night was in full swing, with drunks singing and shouting uproariously, and lush serving girls flirting and bringing out ale by the barrel-full. Kethar breathed in the sweet aroma, and walked up to the bar. He had just ordered two tankards of ale, when suddenly there was silence. Turning around, Kethar's mouth went very dry. Standing in the doorway was his Zak, surveying the occupants with interest.

"What does it want?" gasped a fellow, dropping his pipe.

I want ale, came Zaki's eager voice. Looking around, Kethar realised that he was the only one to have heard the voice.

"A devil has come for us!" screamed a barmaid, hiding under a table in fright.

The men murmured amongst themselves, casting fearful and angry glances at the huge black bird in the doorway. Hoping to resolve the situation, Kethar stepped forwards and placed a hand placatingly on the shikara's head. " It's okay, he's with me," he called out.

Immediately the mob erupted, throwing tankards at the pair in the doorway. Cries of, "He's a devil!" and, "Kill the demons!" echoed all around. Kethar and Zak ran out into the street, pursued by a vengeful mob and a barrage of hard objects.

When they reached a crossroads, Kethar stood and faced them. Unsure of what the 'devil' was going to do, the rabble stood back and whispered fearfully. "We have not done anything to you!" cried Kethar, spreading his arms wide in a gesture of acceptance and peace. "We were just hoping to stay here in peace for a few weeks. Why are you attacking us?"

A woman holding a rolling pin stepped forwards. "I'll tell you why," she screamed, "It's 'cos you'll lie, and then murder us all in our beds, and burn the village down, you and your demon! We've seen your type of murderer before! Kill them!"

With a roar, the crowd ran forwards again. Kethar ran as fast as he could and then noticed that Zak was not beside him. Looking back, he saw the crowd descend upon the screaming bird, hitting him with heavy blunt tankards and fists. Kethar ran back towards his friend, and scooped him up off the ground. He ran, encumbered by the bleeding form of his friend, and reached the outskirts of the village. He looked back and saw the pursuers stop and ready bows. With a cry of despair, he launched himself up the slope of a hill, and crashed to the ground. He recovered himself, and leapt up the hill, reaching the cover of the trees just as the first arrow whizzed into the ground by his foot.

When they had got a little way into the forest, Kethar laid the young creature on the ground, and studied his wounds. Luckily, they were not serious, and the blood that showed had already dried. Looking at the legs and feet of his friend, he could quite clearly see that they were not built for running long distances, but mainly for walking and hopping. And tearing, he thought, looking at the already long talons. He was puzzled though; if Zakrivath was not built for speed on the ground, and his wings were too short and hindering for flight, what was his friend good for? Swimming? No, he could fish, and bathe, but otherwise did not enjoy going in water. Kethar shrugged. That did not matter at the moment. There were more immediate problems to be solved.

* * *

Lord Maxirant of Eldron looked out of the wide window pensive, his gaze following delicate snowflakes as they made their descent from the heavens. How odd, he thought, that the snow should have continued this far into the year. Could he have lost track of time? No, the trees knew the season, and obviously resented the difference, as the few new leaves and buds that showed on the twigs of Maxirant's private plants were furled tight with the bitter cold. The animals felt the change too, as Eldron's best stud bucks and stallions were fierce-tempered and uneasy as spring approached. However, winter still held the land in its frozen embrace, and the landscape beyond the safe walls of the chateau was a plain of unbroken snow. It had fallen over night, and none had yet ventured out to leave their footprints on the snow.

With and almost melancholy sigh, he turned his back on the bleak view. Yet another Kaji had died. The news had come yesterday, and it seemed that Faitan had drowned. Although, shadows of doubt as to whether the death was natural seemed to lurk behind every sentence in the carefully official letter. Hiding beneath the seemingly confident words, an underlying sense of fear seemed to leap from the page, and alarm emanated from beneath the formal greetings that began the official proclamation. And if the normally controlled and taciturn Ka was worried, there was cause for him to worry.

He rested his head on his hand, and recalled the past few months. An athletic, good-looking man in his late twenties, Maxirant was in his prime, and it had surprised many that knew him that he had not yet taken a wife. He did not believe in marrying for love. He wanted an attractive, young wife with an enormous dowry. So he had been trying to attract the attentions of the lovely Kaji Verda, the most beautiful of the daughters of the Ka. She did not seem to be showing much interest, though, past a few demure smiles and fluttering of her eyelashes.

Blondes have to be the best, Maxirant considered, scratching an itch on his arm. He sighed deeply, inhaling the crisp air. Though he had no wife, he had an illegitimate son. The mother, Aryss, had died in childbirth. But at least Maxirant had an heir, even if the boy was a bit too free with his father's money. But a rich, pretty bride would be just the thing for him at this time.

All of a sudden the thought hit him; he was not setting his sights high enough! The next in line for the throne of Bakarn was...the Kaji Rieda. He started to pace, not caring that his new bullock-hide calf length boots were damaging the expensive material of the elliptical carpet. Rieda was to be the next Kai, and the one who married her was to be...and he stopped himself just in time. He had to be sure that the plan would work before setting it into motion and indulging in wild fantasies. Why, that dowry was certainly large enough to satisfy even him!

But he was no fool, and he knew that the Ka would only permit the best possible suitor to marry the heir to the throne. That basically meant the one with the most suitable age, and with the most land. That counted out Lord Thambar, who was eighty-three, bed-ridden and toothless. The other major landholders were himself, Lord Andrade of Gianesa, and Lord Atisato of Rhaleon. Of the three, Andrade was married with several grown children, but Atisato...yes, Atisato would be a problem. He was unmarried, and of a possible age. His estate was of roughly the same size, as Eldron, too.

But wait, he thought, the near penniless Lord Ontua has put up ten acres of forestland for sale. If Atisato were to buy it, then he would have the largest estate, and I would be out of the running! But it all depended on two things; who Atisato was aiming to marry, and if he had bought the land. Well, one of those could be decided soon!

Calling to his servants, Maxirant slipped on an emerald velour riding cloak, and fastened it swiftly with an ornamental brooch in the shape of a stag. He flung the door open, and bellowed to his servants again. Striding down the corridor, he burst out of the carved doors and summoned his carriage. It was ready promptly, wheeled in front of him and the horses' bridles checked. As he mounted the folding steps to the coach, Maxirant noticed with satisfaction that the accompanying soldiers filed into ranks quickly and efficiently. Twenty were to ride before the coach, to scout out the land, twenty to surround the coach, and another ten to ride behind as backup. With a retinue like that, who would dare oppose him? Being the joint second most powerful lord, Maxirant was no stranger to assassins. Settling himself upon the padded seat, he stuck his head back out of the door and shouted, "We ride to Rhaleon!"

The carriage was soon moving at a fine speed, and he felt slightly queasy as the wheels hit the potholes on the rough dirt track. However, time was of the essence, and so he bellowed to the coachman to increase the pace. He heard the whip crack, and the driver's increased encouragement to the horses. He could also hear the thunder of the hoofs on the muddy ground, and smiled grimly, for he had a plan.

As the carriage drew up at the gates to the Rhaleon Palace, a squad of scarlet-garbed soldiers marched to meet the lord and his retinue. Twitching the heavy curtain aside, Lord Maxirant peered out to see one of his captains, Captain Tansden, in conversation with the squad leader of Lord Atisato's soldiers. After a minute Tansden wheeled his mount and trotted up to the carriage.

"Your Lordship, I have been informed that you are permitted to enter, but only twenty of your guard are allowed to accompany you."

Maxirant nodded slowly, trying to keep his voice level. "Take twenty of your finest and most obedient. Leave orders for the others to wait here." Tansden relayed his master's acceptance to the waiting militia. The black iron gates swung smoothly open. As the carriage resumed movement up the gravelled path, the lord's usually controlled face was livid. Twenty soldiers. Twenty! That was the bare minimum when asking a guest to enter your residence! Only a minor nobleman would bring that few! The insult reminded him painfully of the state of relations between Rhaleon and Eldron.

The landau drew up at the entrance to the Rhaleon Castle. Lord Maxirant stepped out unusually gracefully, for a man, and almost lost his temper again. Instead of being there personally to greet his guest, that...swine Atisato had just sent his head steward! He stopped briefly to let his personal guard form up in their square around him, and then proceeded to the middle-aged man standing just in front of five guards. The steward bowed deeply, and then spoke in a quiet but unwavering voice.

"Lord Maxirant, it is an honour to see you here today. Lord Atisato of Rhaleon presents his compliments, and requests that you join him in the Blue Drawing Room."

Maxirant nodded curtly as a reply, and followed the older man along a few corridors. He noticed the hangings and tapestries, and approved of the slight finery, but his sharp eye was drawn to some cracks in the plaster on the walls, and fading patches in the rug beneath his boots. So, the wily lord thought, intrigued, he has either not the time or the money to see to all the little details. He smiled thinly. Any information about Atisato, no matter how seemingly insignificant, he could put to a good use.

"Lord Maxirant of Eldron," announced the herald. Accompanied by his alert retinue, Maxirant entered the Blue Drawing Room.

The room was obviously better looked after than the other few glimpses Maxirant had seen of slight disrepair. So, he thought amusedly, he wants to impress the guests, and deafen them to the obvious cry for help from his corridors?

But he could not help but admire the finery in the room before him. The walls were hung with gauzes and linens of all the beautiful shades of green and blue in a peacock's tail. A roaring log fire stood at one end, casting the shadows of the dancing flames across the luxuriant ocean-blue hearthrug. The rug depicted a sea serpent undulating wildly as it tried to battle with a man with a trident and a net. The furniture of the room, many low-backed sapphire blue divans, were arranged in almost a circle on a slightly raised elliptical podium, with a gap facing the fire.

On one of the couches sat Lord Atisato of Rhaleon. Every detail, from his new doeskin riding boots, through his elegant navy blue tunic and shimmering grey cloak, to his elegantly styled coppery hair, exuded confidence and power. Upon seeing Maxirant, Atisato stood gracefully, and bowed his head slightly, as one would to an equal. Returning the compliment, Lord Maxirant snapped his fingers, and his retinue marched behind to stand in position by the door.

"Perhaps your men would like to refresh themselves at the mess hall. If they would follow my Captain?" Atisato inquired, his tone turning the inquiry into almost a direct order. Maxirant glanced over at Captain Tansden, and nodded very slightly. After a moment the troops of both Atisato and Maxirant had vacated the room.

As soon as the lords were alone, the latter sat down on the divan facing his rival, and said bluntly, "I have an urgent business proposition."

Removing his booted feet from the glass table that was serving as his footstool, Atisato brought his legs down to the floor with an audible thump. "Go on, Maxirant."

The lord of Eldron quickly outlined his offer. "I would but know which Kaji you seek to procure. I have here," and he reached into his tunic and drew out a roll of parchment, "the deeds to the ten acres of forestland that lies between our own lands. If you would but tell me, then it is yours, with my compliments."

"How would you know if I desired one of the Kajis?" asked Atisato, in his mellifluous voice, while toying with his rings.

Maxirant snorted, smiling thinly. "Come now, Atisato. We are not to believe that you spent all those hours at the Palace to play Gijau with the Ka?"

He waited, marvelling at the plan that he had so quickly wrought. If Atisato were not aiming for Rieda, then he would hand over the worthless warrant and buy the land from Lord Ontua forthwith. The document was a fake, and would count for nothing. If Rieda were the object of Atisato's attentions, then he would still win, by buying the land from Ontua. And Atisato would gain nothing either way! The thought that the copper-haired lord might lie did not present itself to him.

"What if we both seek to marry the same Royal lady?" asked lord Atisato, a sceptical look on his handsome face.

Maxirant put the parchment on the small table between them, and answered, "Whether we are competitors for the same Kaji or not, the land is yours. An answer is all the payment I need. You win, either way." He smiled slyly, and almost laughed. This was as easy as putting on a shoe!

"Fine, Maxirant, fine," nodded Atisato, his voice sounding convinced at last. "I aim to marry… the Kaji Destinariae!"

*   *   *

Hooded and veiled, the killer of the Kajis made her way down the corridors of her underground lair. There was nobody around; she was not sure if she was thankful or not for that. It meant that she did not have to be as careful and wary, but it did also mean that she had nobody to carry out her tasks as she wished.

She was about to call for her aide when she realised his absence. He must have decided to go with the soldiers after all, she mused. It was annoying to have nobody on hand to obey her orders, especially when she had so much for them to do. Well, that was just her luck. No doubt they'd all be around when she really wanted solitude.

Yes, there was a problem here, but it was easily solvable; she needed more soldiers. Actually, not soldiers, for they usually had some morals. What she really needed was a good number of hired blades; assassins, thieves, mercenaries. They would serve any employer with the money. More precisely, any employer with the most money for the easiest tasks. But that presented her with another problem. There was no shortage of jobs for extra men right now, with the sudden decline of the Royal Family. Everybody wanted to be up to military strength, just in case they could get a slice of the action, or there was to be a vacancy in the line that had been strong...well, forever.

But if she created a job shortage, then they would come flocking to her. It would work even better if she could actually speak to the men, rouse them a bit with the promise of easy money. And that would serve to lessen the threat from any contenders to the throne and raise her army, so it would be easier for her to claim and keep the honoured place. Indeed, she would see that there was no vacancy to be filled.

Smiling grimly to herself, she continued her walk, her mind relieved at the new plan.

* * *

In a remote village in the valley always covered by snow, the days were usually hard, but quiet due to the closeness of the small community. The snow would be crisp, and fresh, marked in places where a booted foot had come down. Occasional track-marks would be seen, and few people were ever outside at one time; such was the extreme cold.

But today it was different. Today, villagers swarmed around, all heading for the largest hut in the village. Actually, to call it a hut would be technically incorrect; the word 'yurt' or 'roundhouse' would be a better summary of it. The ceiling was twice the height of a man, the diameter similar to that of a number of the huts in the village put together. Banks of crude wooden benches were around the walls; but mainly the seats were just barrels and hay-bales. Many were already seated, and as the latecomers drifted in a middle-aged yet white-haired man stepped into the centre of the ring, onto a raised wooden platform. He stood silently, not wanting to impose his will by silencing them.

After a while an authoritative voice rang out from one of the benches. "Quiet, now! Dyrebus speaks!"

With a nod of thanks in the man's direction, the Speaker began.

"Good people of Garoto, we now face a new dilemma. During the night, a number of dark people came in from the south. They ransacked the village of Darea, and were last seen heading in two different directions." He paused, knowing that the news of their closest neighbour's fall would cause considerable upheaval. He was not wrong. When the shouts of alarm had subsided, he continued with a grave face. "Half of them headed back to the south, with many captives in chains or on poles. The other half," and here he sighed deeply, passing his hand over his brow, "headed due north. Yes, they are coming almost directly to us."

The wave of panic and despair affected everyone. Women and children cried, as did some men, many got to their feet and shouted questions at the speaker, and some just sat back, incredulous. Again Dyrebus waited for silence. When he had it, he continued softly, "So we now need a decision." He looked up at the panic stricken people, his face resolute and his voice hardening. "We have two choices: to stay and hope they will pass us by, or to leave and find shelter in the mountain caves. Either path bears danger, so we will vote for the outcome. Firstly, I will try to answer your questions."

A wiry man stood up in the second row. "We have children and babes to carry. How will they make it through the snow, if we were to leave?" A chorus of voices backed his statement.

The Speaker nodded at the reasonable question. "We would take the sledges, and try to shelter where we could. There is a risk to the children, and more to the babes, but we must try to save all we can."

Another man stood up, his hair also white and shining, though not with age. His red eyes gleamed as he proclaimed, "I vote we leave. Look at the effects to those who stayed within their villages!" Again, a group of people backed him.

Dyrebus nodded curtly, agreeing but reluctant to seem totally decided on this idea. After all, he thought, it has to be the people's decision, not just mine.

A woman stood up, cradling a babe in her arms. "But what about the men? My husband is out in the blizzard, trying to secure food to last us all winter. He will come back to an empty village and a host of enemies!" This time the statement was met with a roar of approval.

The Speaker looked sad. "Of course we would try to meet up with the others on the way, but if something happens to them, we must try to ensure the survival of the rest."

As the woman sat down amidst a crowd of mumbling dissenters, an exquisitely featured young woman stood up gracefully, despite another, older woman desperately trying to pull her back into her seat. "My father fights the famine, yet I would feel more comfortable leaving the village. Cannot those who wish to wait for the others stay, and those who would leave go?" The clamour of agreement was unanimous.

Dyrebus bowed his head. He had feared that this point would come up. He tried to explain, to show the crowd that there were not enough men to guard two separate parties, that, if split up, there would most certainly be many casualties, but the mob would not listen. The vote turned swiftly from a decision of what to do, to a name taking of who would stay and who would go. In the end, the only thing for the Speaker to organise was the time of departure. He arranged it for as soon as possible: now.

As the crowd dispersed, some to start the preparations for hiding the village, some to gather their essentials, Ionté stared at her little hut. She was proud of herself for resolving the debate, yet sad to leave her childhood home. She had been relieved beyond all measure when her mother had unwillingly decided to accompany her. She was one of the eleven people who had decided to leave, not counting the council member who had been the Speaker at the meeting. Thinking of which, she mentally added, here he comes now.

"You should really be getting your things together, Ionté. We're leaving in a matter of minutes." The albino's face was stern, his red eyes fierce for some unknown reason. Ionté was slightly worried.

"I have not done anything to offend you, have I?" she asked, frowning slightly as she struggled to recall the last hour.

"In the meeting… you shouldn't have…you could've…oh, it doesn't matter. Now, go and pack, and only bring the essentials. Go on!"

Dyrebus stood watching as she sped away, like an arrow from a bow. He had badly wanted to reprimand her, but saw her childlike confusion at her interference. She had not known she was making the situation worse. He gave a short, barking laugh. She had probably thought she was helping him. He went to check the sledges, and saw with approval that the sure-footed shaggy ponies were being harnessed up.

The two large sledges were well constructed, and already one was half full of packs of food and belongings. A small number of people stood around, stamping their feet for warmth, despite having been brought up in these sub-zero temperatures. Soon, the pitifully small number of villagers was ready to set off. The sledge carrying donated food and possessions had been led off by the ponies, and the other, carrying a mother and baby, a woman, and a child, was being waved off by the majority of the villagers.

At first Ionté was excited. She and her mother were evading being captured by real dark-skinned people, by sneaking out from right under their noses! She looked sideways at her mother, meaning to share her enthusiasm. But she saw Sindarre's gentle face gazing sadly into the distance, and the crystal tears that adorned her white cheeks like glistening diamonds. Ionté turned back, feeling guilty for her lack of immediate understanding.

Slowly, as the group struggled on, their steps becoming shorter and shorter as they strove valiantly against the treacherous snow, the thrill of the escape began to pall. Ionté concentrated on putting one foot in front of another, and tried to ignore the biting wind that chilled her with its frozen kiss. If she had not spoken out, they may be back in the village now. The dirty-skinned folk may not be aware of Garoto's whereabouts, and miss it entirely. But, she thought reassuringly to herself, at least this way there was a chance for at least some of the albinos to survive. If the slavers did not locate Garoto, then the small group of escapees could find their way back. But even if the worst happened, some people at least would be left to restore the village, and start again.

The day wore on, the conditions becoming more and more inhospitable. The small band made slow progress through the howling gale and the heavy snow. It was not just the usual thick drift of gentle flakes, but a brutal blizzard with piercing sleet. The baby was close to death, its tiny heart bewitched by the icy breath of the blizzard. The mother was already wallowing in grief, hugging her precious burden tightly to her. As if this was not bad enough, when the council member ran ahead to check their with the driver on one of the ponies, they discovered that there was a hole in the first sledge, out of which had dropped their only bags of food. They then decided to stop for the night, turning one sledge upside-down to provide shelter.

Ionté, huddled up under the scant protection of the sledge, felt the cold seeping through her fur-lined clothing. She knew that not all others would have as thick layers as she, and her gentle mind numbed with horror at the realisation that she could be one of the only ones alive the next morning. Without food, without proper shelter, without hope, the pitiful group had little chance of surviving the night.

But what can I do, wondered Ionté? I can hardly conjure up warm shelters to shield us from the cold for a night! However...she felt the thought flood her mind with energy as she thought of a possibility for their survival that both warmed and chilled her at once. But what if she was to fail? Sindarre would be heartbroken, and may well give up the will to live. Ionté glanced

143

sideways at her mother, who was sleeping silently in the chilling embrace of a snowdrift. For a second the girl panicked; then she made out the slight mist that every now and then appeared in the icy air just in front of her mother's lips. The sight strengthened her resolve, and she crawled forward to speak to Dyrebus.

He gave her a weary nod of recognition as she reached him, and she saw the deep creases of strain and anguish in his face that seemed to have appeared during the endless day. If Ionté was racked with helpless sorrow for the inevitable fate of the group, then what was he feeling, he who had put forward the idea and led them? She saw the haunted, torn look in his glazed eyes and wept inwardly for his torment. Pausing, not certain how to begin, the slender girl tried out several sentences in her head.

"I could go back," she said finally, "to find the dropped food, or to get more from the village."

He was just as direct. "No, you can't." he said hollowly, dismissing her. "You're too young, you'd never make it." She saw his face suddenly turn thoughtful, and her blood turned cold as the falling snow when she saw his thoughts as if written plainly across his face.

"No," she whispered urgently, realising she had planted the idea in his head. Dyrebus began to shake his head; she rushed on, ruthlessly qualifying her idea. "You can't go, we'd be lost without you! You're needed here, you have a purpose, whereas I..." she shrugged helplessly, trying to convey what she was loath to say. When he looked at her curiously, she cursed inwardly, then continued. "I'm just a waste of rations. There's no need for me here, so if I don't make it there'll be one less for you to worry about." Her throat closed up briefly, and she blinked back tears. "Please. I have to try." She looked at him pleadingly, green eyes wide and beseeching.

Suddenly there was another voice from behind her. The driver of the first sled, a heavyset albino named Macharra, whispered, "Dyrebus, listen to her. We need the food. I don't need to tell you exactly how much we need it. Give her a chance. She can do this, she's a keen tracker and an expert pathfinder in these frozen wastes. C'mon, she's our only hope now." He looked at Ionté, and flashed her a fleeting smile.

With a heavy heart, Dyrebus nodded slowly. Stripping off his thick furred scarf, he handed it carefully to her, closing her hands around it when she protested. In the frozen world that they inhabited, making a gift of an item of warm clothing was an honour indeed. He nodded once more, saying, "May the Gods protect you."

Ionté nodded back, wrapping the scarf around her neck. Then on a sudden impulse, she threw her arms around the fatherly man and hugged him, feeling him return the pressure. Then with a deep breath, she ducked out of the shelter of the cart into the face of the blizzard.

The freezing air hit her like a solid wall of ice. Ionté began to walk, trying not to think of the numbness seeping already through her clothes. With her keen eyes she could dimly make out the shadowy spire of the great ice mountain that loomed up behind Garoto. As long as she walked back that way, she would locate it. She walked briskly for a while, then the lack of mental stimulation meant that she started to feel the cold once more, penetrating her many layers. With the realisation that *she* was the group's only hope, she broke into a trot, then a run.

The falling snow now totally obscured the mountain and her path, so Ionté had no hope of finding the fallen packs. Running blind, she struggled to move as she had been taught, with feet flat so she did not sink into the snow. She gritted her teeth. Her legs and face were chilled to the bone; still she kept going. One of her gloves slipped off of a stiff, numb hand; she did not turn to pick it up.

Oh, the cold, the terrible, merciless cold! Her limbs were so freezing they burned, and she flinched back from every shard of sleet as it trailed a path of white-hot ice down her skin. Through her tortured, pain-filled eyes fire and snow met; the sky was bathed in red, orange, silver and white as she struggled on through deep snowdrifts. She was running no longer; her feet were leaden and weighed down by snow. The snowflakes brushed her cheeks, clinging to her eyelashes and making it hard to keep her eyes open. It would be so easy, so easy just to shut her eyes and sleep; to get away from the pain. So easy...

With a start, Ionté realised she had fallen over and was lying in a pile of wet, freezing slush. The shock jerked her mind back to reality, and with an anguished wail she pushed herself upright, despite the legs that treacherously buckled underneath her. Gritting her teeth, the girl started to walk. Every step was torture; her head spun and she struggled to lift one foot at a time out of the snow. I will do this, she thought determinedly, feeling her strength slipping away. I will do it, I, I can do it! Oh Gods, I have to do this!

But the going was too hard, and Ionté sank to her knees with a choked cry of despair. She reached out her stinging, blue-tinged hands to pray, and felt a hard, rough surface. The cold, hard rock of a stout wall. She'd found the village!

Her breath rasped in her throat, and she cried in relief for her unbelievable luck. Putting her hand out again, hesitantly, she ran her palm over the stone, feeling its coarse, sharp nodules with an unbelieving smile of pure happiness. She took a few seconds to convince herself she wasn't hallucinating, then stood up slowly on shaking legs. Someone approached her, and she raised an arm in greeting. When she had regained her breath, the person was closer, and she called out, "We've been having problems, and we're out of food. There's nine people left, and they're all about a mile and a half Northwest of here. They need help!"

Only when he reached her did Ionté notice the complexion of the man. As she stepped back in shock, the dark-skinned person reached out and pinned her unresisting arms behind her back.

"Do they now?" the slaver smirked, "In that case, then, we'll have to…help them!"

Chapter 8

"Oh my feet hurt and I'm soaked with sweat
And my shoes almost worn through
But I'll be okay when I'm on my way
Travelling along with you!"

Khalla smiled despite her hunger and extreme thirst. Shoy was always entertaining, if nothing else. For the few hours he had told stories, made jokes, and taught her simple ditties, mostly rude ones. The current song isn't that bad, if only for a 'make-it-up-as-you-go-along' song, she thought...well, at least it rhymes. Badly.

Khalla coughed and smiled. She had decided to ration their water that morning, as they only had one canteen left. They had already eaten the last of the supplies that they bought in the village. She could not see how they were going to last in the extreme heat of the Kanakoan desert; indeed she was sure that, if they could not find water in the next few hours, they'd be goners. She was about to tell Shoy to conserve his energy, but decided against it. I mean, she thought morosely, how many more happy times are there going to be? Instead she listened to the second verse.

> "There's a pack upon my sweaty back
> And my water's runnin' out
> But there's no sense in bein' miserable
> So I need to sing and shout!"

Khalla's smile faded. She knew that she had to ruin the mood by asking the boy about the meeting a few nights before. When he had failed to tell her anything about it, she had started to feel a niggling doubt at the back of her mind. She had been putting it off, but it could be more serious than she had first thought. Though Shoy had probably been spying on the meeting, when she had seen those boys talking to each other in those hushed, fast voices, she knew that something was amiss. Did he overhear something he did not want her to know? She turned and looked at Shoy; he seemed simple and harmless enough. Though maybe he was just trying to stop her worrying. Very well, she would not address the matter for a while yet. She gasped involuntarily as she saw a twisted, warped spire of rock come into view. It was the oddest looking natural formation she had ever seen. The slumped pillar undulated, looping around itself, its surface a mass of seething coils and puckered caves. With her eyes fastened on the amazing sight, Khalla listened to the third verse. She frowned as she heard a subtle change creep into her companion's voice.

> "We are coming to a pile of rock
> I wonder who is there
> Hey lads I've got a traveller
> We've caught her in our snare!"

He immediately bounded away from her and stood, grinning wickedly, as a dozen boys of the ages eleven to seventeen ran out from behind a rocky spire and circled her. "Shoy, who are these boys?" asked Khalla, a note of anxiety creeping into her tone.

The boys laughed, and one said "Shoy? Ashikra's balls, Pravar, couldn't you come up with something better?" Another tossed Shoy a knife as he resumed his song.

> "I've played you for the fool you are
> For once I'm speaking true
> We bring the travellers here to die
> And take all their stuff too!"

All the boys cheered, and a dark-haired youngster called out, "Come on lads, lets get 'er!"

Khalla gasped. A sunken memory of disjointed fragments of conversation resurfaced. What was it those women from the village had said?

"...I do declare, it's about time some real action was taken 'bout that Pravar"..."D'ya know I heard that he has a group of boys like him, all under his command, that help him..."

A sudden thought formed in her mind. "Those things that you got, from the roadside...the things I saw you bury...?"

"Well, I couldn't have yeh guessin' my liddle plan before we got 'ere, could I?"

Abruptly she knew, and cursed herself for not realising sooner.

"'Wanted' posters!"

The youngster grinned, that oh-so-adorable little boy smile. "Well, yeh weren't that likely to accomp'ny me if yeh saw me mug up on a post, wiv' *fifty 'awks dead or alive* writ underneath!"

"C'mon Pravar, let's get on with it!" yelled one of the boys, impatient for action.

Shoy started to speak, and the boys fell silent. Hope flared in Khalla, she *knew* it had been a joke all along. But he just shouted, "Yeah, kill 'er, but I get her sword!"

A harsh voice rooted him to the spot for a second. "Then come and get it, you little scumbags!" cried Khalla, drawing her sabre. The boys advanced slowly, each wanting to appear braver than the others but none wanting to meet the flashing weapon first. So Khalla ran forward to meet them. "Last chance!" she said, staring around at them, "I don't want to hurt anyone!"

Only a thrown knife answered her. Jumping quickly aside with the resolution not to seriously injure any of them, she brought the sabre around in a flashing arc that went streaking out to sting the thrower's hand. One approached from behind, the thump of his sandals clearly audible on the rocky floor. Khalla she spun on her heel, shouted defiance into his teeth, and scored a bloody line down his leg with the needle-point of her light sabre. She was turning back into the guard

151

position when suddenly Pravar called out. The boys retreated to a safer distance on an outcrop of rock.

"Khalla, we were only playing." Khalla looked up at him suspiciously, and he said, "It's me, it's Shoy, your friend. Your buddy. Come on, believe me. We was just jokin', honest!" He smiled disarmingly, and dropped his knife. A swift kick sent it to her feet. "Look, I'm unarmed, so you return the favour." Khalla stretched out her sword arm, and considered for a moment. She hated killing normally, had no wish to be known as a child killer, and it made sense that they wouldn't want to die…she dropped the sabre.

An audible expulsion of breath greeted her action, and reassured, she kicked the weapon to Shoy's feet. He smiled, then picked up the sabre. His small hands turned it over and over as he inspected it proudly. Then…"KILL HER!" he screamed, brandishing his new weapon. The boys rushed down toward her.

For Khalla, time seemed to move sluggishly. She saw Shoy…Pravar's deceit, his lies laid bare, the horrible truth uncovered. She had been betrayed again. She saw the screaming boys draw closer slowly, saw them change and warp, looking more like snarling monsters than people. She felt rather than heard the roar of anger and defiance emanate from herself, and looked upwards. She heard a roaring noise, not unlike sea crashing on the rocks, and realised it was like a whisper coming from afar, but amazingly loud. It flooded her with a surge of energy, and before the rage seized her made out the one word echoing throughout her head and body: **Change.**

She felt her nails lengthen out into claws, her teeth grow to razor spikes, her mind drift into oblivion, her sight focus on the charging monsters; and she ran snarling to meet them. Her jagged claws sliced open one's belly, her teeth came down to catch a flailing sword. Freeing her claws from the corpse, she slashed at another's head, he went down screaming. She felt the sting of a knife slice her shoulder, and screamed; an unearthly, feral sound. Her jaws savagely punctured her attacker's chest, and she tasted blood. With amazing speed her talons slashed out left and right, tearing and gouging, cutting and slashing. Her jaws were everywhere, biting down on sweet flesh. She had to fight, had to kill, had to rid herself of the demons that clung to her back! Suddenly, there was silence. The beast-Khalla stood in a circle of maimed corpses, the red mist in front of her eyes staying despite the lack of enemies. She stood alone, her wild eyes not focusing on the carnage, or the insects that were already burrowing into the bodies. She lifted her head and howled, a torn sound full of pain, grief, and vengeance. Some distance away, Pravar shivered at the eerie noise. He was alone now, with only a sabre to guard him. His head told him that he would be all right, he had a weapon, but his heart told him that a mere sword would be no protection from the beast's wrath.

* * *

The forest was lush and green, the leafy treetops swaying gently in the morning breeze. A stream wound around the forest floor, like a silver snake slithering with a persistent hiss. Several large trout flicked their tails idly, swimming lazily against the weak current. Their fish minds did not recognise the threat of a shadow on the surface. Suddenly, a black beak plunged into the water and skewered one of the trout, flicking the writhing body onto the bank.

That's fifteen, Kethar. Shall I get any more? asked Zak, eager to please. At the negative answer he received, he used his talons and beak to ferry the fish to the place where Kethar was sitting, dabbing carefully at a shallow cut in his arm. As the encumbered bird approached, Kethar set down the strip of cloth he was using as a swab, and stood up to caress Zak's soft head lovingly.

"Excellent, Zaki. We'll eat well today!" he congratulated, relieving his friend of some of the trout and placing them in the shade of a tree-stump. Zak followed suit, and soon they had a neat cache. But Kethar's expression turned to one of concern. "I have only a little bread, and no fruit. How are we going to get by?"

Zakrivath looked thoughtful. *Well, I like fishes, so I don't need bread or fruit. And we can get fruit from bushes and things. But you need some bread, to make you grow bigger.*

Kethar smiled to himself as he surveyed his soulmate. Zaki had grown amazingly quickly, and now was over a foot taller than Kethar. His feathers were losing their infant fluffiness, and strong pinions were growing in place of downy tufts. For a month old, he was amazing! But again Kethar's thoughts turned to the bread shortage. He had been strict, eating only a little every day, but it had been used up to the last dry stale end. And he needed to eat bread, for...here his knowledge wavered a little...special *things* in it that he needed.

It's not even as if I could go and buy some in the village, he thought dourly. Why, Zaki and I would be under risk of death, returning there! But...if the villagers here would not serve us, then other, further-away villages would most certainly not. So we've tried paying, and being friendly...

Zakrivath interjected into Kethar's thoughts with an eager tone. *So maybe we try...being unfriendly?*

Kethar thought it over. There really seemed to be no other way. But they had tried the proper way first and been rejected, and almost killed...so they'd have to be doubly careful. Zakrivath's beautiful eyes gleamed an unusual yellow with an excitement similar to his own. Well, if Zakrivath was all for it, he certainly was!

Zak caught the confirmation in Kethar's thoughts. *Let's go! But...should we hide our fishes? Anyone could eat them!*

Kethar agreed, and bade the shikara help him move the fish inside the hollow log on which he sat. When they were safely tucked away, Kethar trod the charred remains of the fire well into the ground and hooked his arms through the straps of his carrysack. "Okay Zak," he declared, "We've got to be quiet and fast. Let's go!"

Ducking and weaving through the lush vegetation of the forest, they made good progress to the outskirts of the village. The morning sun swam lazily into view from behind the distant peak of Skyria, and the team crouched lower as they considered their main objectives.

'Just bread, then,' reminded Kethar mentally, knowing they had to be quiet. 'As much as we can carry.'

Zak looked wistfully at his friend, and said, *Can we get some other meat? Fishes can get tedious after a while.*

Kethar prodded his friend none too gently, thinking loudly for Zaki's benefit, 'You can catch your own.' Then he looked deeply into the glowing golden eyes of his friend and sighed. 'Oh all right, we'll try to get some meat if we can. But mainly bread, d'you hear?'

At Zak's enthusiastic affirmation, Kethar grinned, and motioned for them to continue. They crept quietly in, wary of being spotted, but the streets were almost deserted. They reached the small shop that Kethar had visited first, and he rattled the handle. It was tightly locked. 'Okay Zaki, do the honours please', thought Kethar. One swift stroke of the heavy black beak and the window dissolved into a shower of flying glass. Kethar froze, staring at the mess; then a surge of power overrode his old panic on seeing something broken. Quickly, they hopped in and began loading themselves down with bread. As they exited, however, people had begun to awaken, roused by the sound of the smashed glass. With a strangled cry, an elderly man pointed at them, and shook his stick. The pair could do nothing but run, before the streets erupted with vengeful people.

To their surprise, they reached their campsite with no pursuers. "We lost 'em!" shouted Kethar, whooping with mirth. Zakrivath laid down his loaves beside the fish, and then looked reprovingly at his exuberant friend.

We didn't get my meat, he protested, looking sadly at the huge pile of bread they had stolen.

Kethar ceased his jubilation immediately, and walked over to comfort his companion. "Well, to make up for it, let's go and get some tomorrow!" he exclaimed, his pride bloated with their success. "Or why not now?"

Zak's eyes gleamed with glee and titillation. *Now! Let's go!*

They returned almost an hour later, carrying between them a gigantic joint of ham. Kethar's voice, had there been anyone listening, would have sounded peculiarly alone as he conversed with the shikara.

"Did you see that old woman? She almost passed out when she saw you!" grinned Kethar, laughing exuberantly.

I think the young woman passed out when she saw you! returned Zak, his mental tone full of unbridled hilarity.

"Why thank you, my good shikara!" replied Kethar, dropping the ham and running a hand jocularly through his shaggy black hair. "You allude, of course, to the way I can't contain my stunning good looks, and how I ooze charm!"

No, I mean one look at your face and she wanted to scream! replied Zakrivath mischievously. *And I don't think I'd talk about oozing at all, if I were you!*

The good-natured banter was cut short by the shikara's gargantuan yawn, closely followed by Kethar's.

"Shall we have a nap before lunch, my dear friend?" asked Kethar.

By all means, the bird replied. *The morning's efforts must have worn you out. Though I'm not against having a little sleep myself.*

Kethar chuckled, his mind as always attuned to that of his soulmate. Zakrivath was drowsy with the hot sun, and as Kethar reached right up and stoked the soft head-feathers, Zaki's eyes turned a vibrant orange-gold with contentment, bliss, and love.

Shortly, the birds perched in the canopy of treetops came down to peck at the fresh bread, lulled by the snores of the slumbering pair.

* * *

The winds howl and wail around an old, stone building. The surrounding area is desolate, and the courtyard walls are overgrown. Inside, the smooth marble floors and stark stone pillars give no trace of friendliness or warmth; just a cold echo of once majestic splendour.

A solitary candle faintly illuminates two figures. One sits on a piece of loose masonry while the other kneels on the floor, propped against one of the pillars. The sitting figure speaks in a cracked, elderly voice.

"Why have you journeyed here, my son?"

The kneeling figure turns his face towards the first and answers in a young, faltering tone, as if unused to speaking much. "I seek knowledge and understanding. I was told of your wisdom, so I came."

The first feels that there is something that has been left out of the answer, but does not comment on this. Instead he says, "You are indeed young to be wandering the barren marshes of Jaharon alone. Did you come armed?" At the nod from the youth, he says, " Here, let me see the blade." He stretches out his hands and receives the worn knife. The blade is heavy with rust, the scabbard grimy and well used. The pommel-stone is thick with grime and there are traces of cobweb up the frayed rope binding.

The youth looks up, perhaps noticing the slightly sceptical look on the other's face, and says with a hint of defiance, "It is my father's, and a more sturdy blade you would have to look far to find." With a slight frown he reaches out his hand for the knife. He yelps in surprise as his hand is sharply smacked with the flat of the blade.

"Is that so?" asks the elder, referring to the aforementioned remarks. He lifts his hand, sights along the weapon, then throws it accurately at one of the pillars. As the knife hits the stone, it shatters into many jagged pieces. When the elder next speaks, it carries a trace of patronisation. "I am from a peaceful order of brothers. To carry a blade is to betray the trust of our society. And remember," he says, his voice sinking back into peace and lethargy, "Hardly anything is as it seems."

The youth looks down, his face humble. "I …did not realise. I ask forgiveness."

The old man smiles sadly at the white haired boy. "Do not worry. There are more dreadful sins than ignorance. Do not blame yourself for this, when many evil men think nothing of terrible deeds. However, it is wise to know some humility." The monk's face turns grave. "Are you sure you would give up everything for this knowledge, your freedom, your family, your life? Are you certain that this is the right choice?"

The youth looks up, his red eyes shining in his pale face. "I am willing to do whatever it takes to learn the truth."

The old man sighs. "I feared it would be so. Very well, I will teach you. But only if you make a promise to me."

"Very well, name your terms," speaks the lad, sounding older and more refined than before.

The other closes his eyes, and speaks as if reciting from a book. "You will not handle a weapon again, not to give one, pick one up, or merely touch one. Under no circumstances must you injure another living thing. You must never, ever, kill another person, and animals can be killed only if the food is the only way to escape death. You must obey your Master in all things, and stay in his service until he judges you fit enough to continue alone. Swear this, in your own name!"

"I, Sirenthe son of Theyron, swear to honour this agreement. Now, when does my training start?"

The old man smiles. "Right now, if you want." At the boy's eager nod he begins.

"The Gods of this world are the main influences on life. They control the planet, but have very little to do with us individually. Occasionally, they will reward a faithful follower, but their main duty is to control the magic of the world."

"Magic?" interrupts the youth excitedly.

The older man shoots him a look, then continues. "Yes magic. It is natural, raw, energy. The Gods use this to keep the forces on this world balanced, so everything can continue in its right place. But it is a tradition that those of royal blood are permitted a little of this. Most cannot or do not use it, save as a reminder to their people that *they* are the rightful ruler. But occasionally, one comes along who wants more power, and knows how to get it. You see, a lot depends on names. Recite to me the names of the seven Gods."

"Eternity, Fate, Destiny, Fortune, Luck..." he pauses, considering. "Er...Chance...and, um...aren't there six?"

"SIX! My son, you have much to learn. The seventh God has no earthly name, so in the elder tongue He is called Ashikra, and is sometimes thought of as the most important of them all. Each God controls or is responsible for an element of the planet: Eternity alone knows the future of souls, Fate controls the element of ice, Destiny oversees the changing of time and the seasons, Fortune watches over the water, Luck manipulates fire, Chance is Lady of the earth, and Ashikra dominates all that is in the air."

"So how do people get more magic and power? And what's this to do with names?"

"Well, the Gods have magic and power because they have these names." As he sees the boy's puzzled look he explains further. "For example, if you were writing out a list of who gets what amount of magic you would write that Chance has a seventh of all magic. So, answering your questions, the power-seeker has to make their name more like the name of the God, and so receive some of the power meant for that God. The closer the name is, the more of the God's share they will receive."

"Ahh, I see. So the God is losing His or Her magic while the person is gaining it. Doesn't this bother them at all?"

"Of course it does. If the person who tries to claim more power is just a commoner, not Royal, then the God will just reclaim the power by killing them. Of course, with a commoner, the magic would almost certainly be unable to be used, but still, the indignity of a commoner impersonating a God..." His voice trails off.

The youth nods understandingly, then asks, "But what if the person who changes their name is Royalty?"

The other continues. "Well, it really depends on how serious the situation really is. Sometimes a queen will call her child a vaguely God-like name, and providing it stays like this, the Gods will not act upon it. Similarly, if a normal name is changed to something that only gets a minuscule amount of magic, that is generally allowed, though frowned upon. But if a Royal name, normal or vaguely God-like, is changed to something that takes up a quite a large amount of a God's magic, the God in question is forced to combat the by now very powerful sorcerer and kill him...in the main."

"In the main?" queries the lad.

"Yes. One time in a million, a sorcerer will be so strong that the God is reluctant to combat him for fear of losing...and being cast out of the circle of Gods to wander the endless abyss of empty space. So the sorcerer would continue to drain the magic of the God."

The boy runs a hand through his snow-white hair thoughtfully. "So it's not really that bad for anyone except the God, is it? I mean, it doesn't really affect anybody else but the sorcerer, and he doesn't really come off too badly, does he?"

"Foolish boy!" snaps the man. "It would affect everybody! As I said earlier, the Gods harness magic to keep control of the different elements, and keep everything in the unique balance required to ensure the future of all the different species. If one God did not have sufficient magic to run His or Her responsibility, then the elements would be unbalanced and all hell would break loose. Just think, if Fortune was bettered then the planet might be...flooded by water and everything drowned. If Luck was beaten or sucked dry of magic, the world might be consumed by fire and become a torture pit! Can you really be so blind as to not see the effects this might have? And if Destiny or...Eternity was...oh, by the bird of Ashikra, I would not want to be alive to see the effects of that!" He turns pale and mutters darkly to himself for some minutes.

After a while the boy speaks hesitantly. "I...am still confused. If it is so terrible, why are...why are we here now?" He cringes, expecting a verbal lashing.

When the old man speaks again, he is curiously subdued. "It has not happened yet. I speak not from experience, but from Seeing the future. You see, I am of the Farseers, and I have Seen that this will happen. I cannot be exactly sure of when, but I do know that such a thing is a certainty." To the boy, the elder man's face takes on the weariness of his voice. "My son, there will always be those that seek power beyond their control. They, in their complacence, will assume that they are great enough to wield the power of the Gods. Alas, their overwhelming arrogance will not only be their undoing, but the end of everything."

"But surely there could be some mistake in your Seeing? Some error in your calculations? Are we all doomed, as you say?"

The old man shrugs and shakes his head. "I wish it could be so, my son. The main of the Seeing will come to this planet some day. But there may be some slight change in the events to come, something that has escaped me. But take some comfort in the fact that you will probably not be here to see it."

"But what of those who will be there? Can they not prevent the disaster from striking?"

"My son," the old man smiles bitterly, "we are but mortals. The affairs of Gods and royalty are beyond our comprehension. We cannot stop them, weak, magicless, pathetic humans that we are; mortals cannot even begin to comprehend the thoughts and wishes of the supreme deities."

The boy pauses to consider for a moment, then asks, "You say that we cannot stop them; we have no magic. Could then sorcerers stop the disaster?"

"No mortal, with magic or without, can afford to meddle in the affairs of the Gods. That is, if they do not want to be destroyed in unimaginably horrible ways. But yet, boy, you have given me the glimmerings of an idea. Come, let us research it." So saying he beckons the boy to follow him, and leads the way down a carved flight of narrow stone steps, spiralling sharply downwards. So unexpectedly nimble are the monk's steps that the boy is forced to jog to keep up, worrying about the fate of the candle in his left hand. Mercifully though, it does not blow out, but some of the hot liquid wax spills from the small well of wax around the wick and dribbles slowly down to touch the youth's pale hand. With a start he drops the candle and is plunged into darkness.

He hears the light patter of the old man's footsteps recede and calls out. Immediately a pale light shines from below him and he watches in amazement as the old man climbs back up, a warm light outlining his figure. "Yes boy, I am a mage," he says simply. "Did you not guess? Even when I told you I am a Farseer, one of the Orders most notorious for turning out mages?" He chuckles, then leads the way into a huge library.

The youth watches with wide red eyes as they pass row after row of dusty bookcases filled with thousands of volumes. Some of the shelves have given way, and many books lie on the ground, coated by dust and plaster. After a while they reach a bookcase that, to the boy, looks like all the others. But the old mage seems to know exactly what he is doing, and reaches out a hand to pull out a large, old volume. He opens it and sneezes when a flurry of dust arises from the old pages. He carefully turns the dry, brittle parchment, careful to the extremity, but still a couple of pages fall out. He seems to find what he is looking for, and starts to read aloud.

"At once there was hatred and jealousy among those divine powers known as the Gods, and they each wanted the others' share of that energy that we call *Magick*. Each used their own Magick to manufacture entities common to that which they watched over. Eternity had the *Emathai*, Fortune had the *Ishel*, large water-swimming creatures, Fate had the *Mantifel*, ice beasts of great power, Luck made *Findaena*, huge fiery golems, Chance had wood *Nyaphim*, the essence of the plants, Destiny had the *Urgroth*, poison-toothed flesh-eating lizards, and Ashikra had a huge bird born of thunder and lightning torn from his own substance to rule the skies."

"What was this bird? This guardian of the skies?" asks the albino boy, his face alight with wonder.

The old mage smiles. "It was a Shikara."

Chapter 9

A group of travel-worn men reached the gates of Lower Lyvilan, and hauled themselves with considerable vigour into the nearest tavern. A few moments later, a young woman entered the same building, and spotted the travellers at a table in the furthest corner. Schooling her features into a non-committal expression, she sauntered over to them. They leered up at her, each one smiling suspiciously. The woman then spoke in a simple country voice.

"Lawks, excuse me gennelmen, but could Ai possibly join yew for a mug or two? That is, if yew're not too busy?"

The men shifted aside to offer her a seat, and she took it primly, twitching her skirts back to a more modest angle. She looked up at the man opposite her; his mouth was twitching slightly, and his eyes did not meet hers. It was the same with the next. But the one after that was younger, and was shaking. Suddenly, they all exploded with laughter, some pounding their fists on the table. The younger man wagged a slim finger at the young woman, helpless with mirth.

"That was great, Kad!" snorted Untya, slapping her hand in a friendly way.

"Yeah, well done!" grinned Mad-Red, gesturing to a blonde barmaid to bring over a keg of ale. "You're good at something besides cooking! And I always said you was!" he continued quickly, aware of her face of mock severity.

Kadira smiled happily to herself, stretching luxuriantly like a feline. They had not been in a village for so long! And so to be in Lower Lyvilan, part of their capital city…she had never been so aware of the luxuries she had missed. She was intensely aware of Shakna, downing his ale, and Vine, hunched up against her. The latter pushed a tankard toward her, and filled it. "Drink up," he said in his silken voice, "Or you'll be too sober to sing later on. Or to hear Ghiron sing!"

At that unpleasant prospect she quickly raised her cup. The men started banging theirs on the rough wooden table, chanting, "Down in one! Down in one!"

Kadira put the cold edge to her lip, and gulped down the foaming liquid, only putting it down when the last drop of foam trickled down into her mouth. The cheers from her companions made her laugh again, and she pushed her tankard to Vine, noticing his mysterious smile as he filled it once more. Then she shrugged. Vine was always like that, mystifying and sensual. Not that she had one jot of attraction to him, but he was intriguing. If she hadn't been living as a servant and friend to the men for so long, she might have felt otherwise about them.

But now, here they were, in the peasants' district of the capital city of their land. She had gone with the men this far, though she had only really joined them to get to the person who had sent them on their task to destroy her village. She could not, would not bear hatred for them for doing it, for they had been pressurised, threatened and paid into doing it; it was not their malice that had killed her family. Their journey had led them here, and she was certain that the one she was seeking was close.

She was roused from her reverie by a loud conversation close by. With her eyes, she motioned for the others to pay attention. By the time the noisy group had gone, the mercenary band had heard enough to be intrigued.

"So, there's a chance of a job here? This is interesting," commented Sye, sipping his beer.

"Sounds like mighty powerful employer, too. Loadsa' gold, prob'ly," rumbled Desert, in his deep voice.

"We should find out more before we go for it, shouldn't we?" asked Shakna, the voice of reason. "They said something about a demonstration, tomorrow. We should go."

"Shakna's right," agreed Vine. When the others looked at him incredulously, for the two almost never agreed, he shrugged. "Doesn't seem like such a bad idea, does it? If it's gonna be lots of gold and little risk, then yeah! But if there's a couple of wrens and a bucket of trouble, then we find ourselves some other gig. Okay?"

This seemed logical enough, so the agreement was wholehearted and unanimous. Kadira sat back, her mind drifting off into a daze as she consumed her fifth pint. She struggled to keep awake, then wondered why. Soon the singing would start, and the betting, and the leering. Besides, she hadn't enough money to gamble now even if she had wanted to. She'd lost all the money donated from the lads on a bet on an unarmed combat. So thinking, she drifted off to sleep.

* * *

"Who's a lovely Fainy-wainy then? Aww, isn't she a likkle sweetie! And so cute, yes you are, yes you are!" The Royal Nursemaid to the baby Efaerin giggled, rocking the baby Kaji in the satin and mahogany cradle. The baby had woken up, peering with huge blue caricature-like eyes at the woman's creased but tender face. Her tiny mouth opened and closed, and she burbled happily, wriggling within her expensive bed.

On the wrong side of fifty, the nursemaid had looked after Destinariae, and also all the children of the Kai Tifiert. She was well past her prime, but had been kept on partly from kindness, partly from lack of a suitable and trustworthy replacement. She still knew how to look after a child, though one of her now older charges was contemptuous of her. Or at least had been, right up until her fat body had been found in the ornamental lake.

Thinking of Kajis going missing, she had seen something strange that morning. The Kaji Verda, wearing colours curious to her usually flamboyant taste, had passed by the far perimeter of the palace by herself. She had been without her usual palanquin, or her armed escort. What could the child be doing going out on her own in such dangerous times? It was safe here, in the palace, where you had both strong stone walls and strong, armed men to protect you.

But outside...she shivered. Without the protection of the palace, there was trouble. Only this morning she had heard of the death of Count Rhanno, a minor but nevertheless influential nobleman. And just the other week there'd been the death of that noble, the one who'd died in a hunting accident. The name eluded her now, but no doubt she'd remember it later.

The baby chattered on in her unidentifiable language, pausing every now and then to try and pull her embroidered sock off with her teeth. With a tender smile, the woman reached down and tucked Efaerin into her silk coverlet. The baby's cornflower-blue eyes began to close, but they suddenly jerked back open.

"What is it, my poppet? It's sleepy-time now!" cooed the nursemaid. A shadow fell over the pair. The baby chuckled as a gloved hand cudgelled her old nurse to death, and stared with innocent loving eyes at the pillow descending onto her tiny face.

*   *   *

Amidst the bustling peasants, a lone figure strode purposefully towards the busiest tavern. The

171

commoners had enough sense to keep out of the way, as any that jostled the grim man were glared at with a terrible stare that seemed to say, 'I'll remember *your* face'.

When he reached the large wooden building, Eskiros did not immediately enter. He was still stinging mentally from the contemptuous way in which his mistress had ordered him to gather more men for a demonstration. Why, he thought ironically, I could have just killed a few and got the others' attention for the great lady without her having to *exert* herself! But…yet, it might be interesting to see what she could really do. It might give him a clue to her identity. He had had no luck when researching the ladies of the court, or the Lords' daughters. He had a list of names, but no clue as to which she was. Well, he thought wryly, let's let her make the first move.

Entering the gloomily-lit tavern, Eskiros moved over to a group of likely looking men. They were swarthy, well-muscled guys who were talking in low voices. Probably mercenaries, Eskiros thought. Deciding his course of action even as he approached their table, Eskiros greeted them with a casual manner and a brisk, "I have a business proposition."

He was answered by a non-committal shrug, contradicted by the speed in which they produced an extra chair. He reversed the high-backed seat and sat down, resting his elbows carelessly on the back. "There's ample pay and simple enough work. What do you say?"

One of the mercenaries, a pinch-faced man with an officious manner, eyed him suspiciously. "Simple enough? What type of thing?"

Eskiros drummed his fingers lazily on the rough pine table. "Oh, just the run of the mill killings, some...gathering of information, no doubt, and...well, probably she'll want your full allegiance." As soon as he'd said it he cursed himself for his lack of foresight.

"She?" queried a black-bearded man, glancing amusedly at the others of the group. "We work for worthwhile causes, not for weak employers. Tell the *Lady*," he sneered the word, "That we're mercenaries, not pimps."

Eskiros stood up slowly, returning his chair to its original position. "Well, I'm sorry that you don't want to join us. And I'm equally sorry to have too tell the Mistress that she has been refused." He sighed dramatically. "I just hope there'll be some people left after she goes on her rampage. Last time she found the dissenters, their bodies were found the next day tied to stakes, and fleshless. You'll have to hope she's lost her keh-harande. She could also use her normal, non-metal whip..."

With worried glances the men ushered him to sit down again. Eskiros, smiling thinly, lounged indolently in his chair. He was back in the game.

* * *

The grey gelding cleared the ditch like a dream, and continued in an easy canter to the edge of the carefully trimmed green. Its shining hoofs flashed as they caught the sun, accenting the careful lifting of each foot. Its head was small and streamlined, held proudly upright despite a fully-grown rider's command, showing its fine pedigree. The long silvery mane and tail streamed back, tossing in the light breeze.

Maxirant brought his mount to a neat halt, wheeling the horse around to face the stables. Clucking his tongue, he brought it to a slow trot, and concentrated on moving himself in the saddle to avoid later aching. After an hour of riding his thigh muscles had knotted up, and he knew that he would need to be assisted in dismounting. Usually he could go on for longer, but he had needed to put the new horse through its paces, so a number of different riding styles had to be tried out. Including jumping, he remembered with a slight grimace, and rubbed his lower spine.

Pulling sharply on the reins, Maxirant slowed the beast to a walk, and smiled his thanks at Cemrin as the stablemaster stood by the gelding's head. A stable boy ran forward and helped the wealthy lord dismount, then went for the curry combs and brushes.

"So, my Lord, is he a fit replacement for Tasenai?" inquired Cemrin, stroking the horse's fine head gently.

Maxirant leaned against the side of the dappled grey. "Well, he lifts his feet adequately, actually, almost daintily, and he has a rhythmic, fluid funning motion. A bit too spirited, perhaps, but-"

The gelding whinnied and threw back its head, cutting Maxirant off in mid-speech. Cemrin, after quieting the animal with both hands, chuckled.

"He must have heard you, my lord Maxirant!" he smiled, watching his master's expression.

The muscular lord shook his head with a wry grin, then laughed too. "As I was trying to say, he's spirited, but that's not altogether a bad thing." He ran his hand through his riding-dishevelled hair, and smiled again. "Yes, Cemrin, I think he'll do very well." He patted the creature's neck, nodded to the stablemaster, and strode to the door.

"My lord," began Cemrin, and Maxirant turned back. "Will you want him readied for this afternoon?"

"This afternoon?" queried Maxirant with puzzlement.

"The Council of Lords," explained the older man.

A flicker of surprise registered of Maxirant's face, then disappeared as if it had never been. "No, thank you Cemrin, I will take the carriage. The white horses, if you please," he commanded before the man could ask, and left the stable block before he could be further detained.

He mounted the stairs quickly, pulling off his riding gloves briskly as he did so. Mentally he was furious. "Of course," he muttered to himself, slapping the gloves into his palm, "the Council meets this afternoon. How could I forget?" He threw open the door to his chamber, and threw the leather gloves down on the bed ill-temperedly. Looking about him, he noticed the absence of servants, and snarled aloud in frustration.

"Is there nobody in this Fate-damned household that can get me a change of clothing?" he roared, his handsome face reddening with infuriation.

At once a dozen servants flooded in through the door, some flocking around Maxirant to help remove his riding gear, and others leafing through the spacious wardrobe to rind a new set of robes. Seeing their actions, Maxirant groaned aloud in frustration, and brushed away the attending servants as if they were a swarm of pesky flies.

"No, you fools, my best robes! They were cleaned yesterday! Go, fetch them now!"

The servants instantly fled the scene, knowing from experience when their master needed a little time alone. They left in their wake a most disgruntled Lord of Eldron.

By all the Gods, he thought, sinking down onto the bed, I am surrounded by imbeciles! He clenched and unclenched his hands, feeling the tension begin to drain from him.

A timid knock at the door brought the temper straight back. "That had better be the arrival of my robes!" warned the lord, trying unsuccessfully to keep his voice level.

There was an audible gulp from behind the door, and then it creaked open. A male servant's head, face ashen with fear of punishment, popped through the gap.

"Your...your son, Lord Mathilane requests an audience with you, my Lord Maxirant." His voice quavered, and he bowed very low.

With an exasperated sigh through gritted teeth, Maxirant stood, wincing as the movement jarred his riding-fatigued muscles. What did the whelp want now?

"Very well, send him in. And tell those layabouts of lackeys to hurry up with my clean robes!"

The servant bowed in assent, and opened the carved door. "The young Lord Mathilane."

As his son entered, Maxirant again momentarily cursed Fate's cruel sense of humour that had taken the boy's mother from this life. The lad was the very image of his mother in facial structure, with dark blonde hair and long lashes. But he had a spoiled, pampered look about him, perhaps inherited from the other side of the family. He wore a silver chain tunic with a short scarlet cape, and a long sword in a scabbard at his waist that was meant to look threatening, but instead almost tripped Mathilane as he walked. All in all, Maxirant decided, the foolish, flamboyant boy looked as menacing as a cabbage.

Mathilane stared back at his father, seeing the lean, trained muscles, the richly embroidered undertunic, and the hawk-nosed profile. He also noticed the signs of his father's ill temper, but decided to proceed anyway.

"My Lord and father Maxirant, I come bearing a simple request," Mathilane announced with a sweeping bow.

"Whenever don't you?" Maxirant snorted, turning away from his son. Mathilane reached out to his father, and put a hand on his arm. Without speaking, Maxirant turned his head to stare down at the offending hand. It was immediately withdrawn.

Maxirant sighed. "Proceed if you must. What is it this time?"

Mathilane straightened up, then began. "It appears that a very close friend of mine is in some… financial trouble with some people he knows. I would very much like to aid him, but my purse is threadbare." He forced himself to breathe slowly, to ensure that he gave nothing away.

So, Maxirant mused, he's gambled again, and lost all his money. Or, he corrected, my money. And now he wants some more to gamble with and waste again, and has come here to lie and get it from me. I should really refuse, he thought, but there again, I need to keep on good terms with him. Having an heir might just be the deciding factor for a promotion. So I'd better humour him. The lord smiled. But that doesn't mean I can't make him feel guilty.

"Very well, he told his eagerly waiting son, "if your friend is in that dire need, you had better have the money. It touches my heart that you are so concerned about your dear companion, and only hope that some day you may accord me the same depth of love. Take five hundred eagles from the treasury. Now go, my son, for I must attend the Council of Lords."

Mathilane bowed very low, concealing a triumphant smile, and left the room.

* * *

The Kajarito guards bowed deeply as Destinariae strolled past, their uniforms bright in the resplendent sun. The armour they wore made them sweat in such intense heat, and the odour that reached the Kaji's nose was less than pleasant. She graciously forbore to mention it, passing them by with a slight incline of the head.

Ye Gods but it was hot today! The weather has never been so changeable, Destinariae thought exasperatedly. She had seen her stepmother lying half-dressed in the sun, with servants fanning her with broad leaves. A little too exotic for Destinariae's tastes, but that was Tifiert through and through. Her stepmother was still weeping for the death of her baby, Efaerin. The tiny body had been found just the other day, beside the still form of the ever faithful nursemaid. Destinariae had bowed her head on seeing Tifiert, and hurried on. None of her other sisters were out, but that was not surprising, considering the strict measures the Ka still insisted on for their safety. She was sure she had only been allowed to stroll through the small courtyard because she had pleaded so much. Well, it was small compared to the twelve square miles of palace gardens, anyway. And that was about the extent of her wanderings; her rooms, the Red Corridor, and the courtyard. The Ka had not shifted much on the point.

But...then there was the business about Verda. The beautiful Kaji had been missing for two days, and there was nobody that had caught a glimpse of her since one lunchtime beforehand. The Ka had been certain that Verda was still alive, as the previous murders had seen the bodies left where they had fallen, and no corpse had been found.

Verda, where are you, thought Destinariae. Surely you haven't been kidnapped? But...what was it you said to me, the day I found you in my room? *"I need some fresh air too"*...Verda, did you...run away?

Destinariae looked about her sharply as she heard a slight noise; then forced herself to breathe normally and think of something else. Yes, of course; the Ka's restrictions. She did not really see his point in keeping the Royal family locked up, even after Efaerin's death. At least they should be allowed to go about the palace unhindered, but it was just the rooms and the corridor immediately outside, and then only with a huge escort. Though the thought of there being an assassin that had access to the palace did make the atmosphere in the palace close, on edge. Destinariae shook her head and took a deep breath to try and reassure herself. *I certainly don't feel scared,* she reasoned, *for my escort are only at the gates at the side of the quadrant.* She could not see them at the moment, hidden as she was behind the large ornamental trees and ganfha-bushes.

Even in a light gown of flowing white, Destinariae was boiling hot. She tried fanning herself with her hand, but it did not make much difference. Indeed, that was partly why it felt so hot; the air was stifling, with not so much as a breath of wind. Destinariae glanced at a guard in black who was moving through the trees at the edge of the small park. She did not know how he could stand the heat. He seemed to be able to move quickly enough in it, even with a huge battle blade raised...it took her relaxed mind a moment before she realised that the 'guard' was running purposefully toward her with a sword! Gathering her skirts around her, she started to run through the dense tangle of vegetation, ducking and twisting around the foliage. Every time she looked back, the assassin was closer. Sobbing for breath, Destinariae tried to speed up, but her foot caught in a gnarled tree root and she fell heavily.

At once the assassin was standing over her, his sword descending to cleave through her neck. Destinariae rolled, and heard the swish as the blade narrowly missed her. But she had rolled right against the stone wall, and watched in dread as the killer stood over her once more. Why in Destiny's grace had she not screamed? She resisted the urge to close her eyes. She was a Kaji, and would face her death with honour!

But as the sword began its merciless descent, there was the sound of running footsteps. The assassin glanced around, then started to run away. Bursting through the trees, five Kajarito guards saw the murder attempt, and four branched off to chase the assassin, while the other helped a shaken Destinariae to her feet.

"Take me to my rooms," she gasped faintly, leaning heavily on her escort.

Chapter 10

"Well, here we are. Wonder when it's going to start?" mused Hound, glancing around the crowded square. All around the edges, groups of men were sitting at tables, drinking. It was mainly dark, due to the streetlights being blocked by the taverns that backed into the plaza. Only one thin beam of bright light filtered in through a narrow gap between two buildings.

The company moved to take the only spare table there. It was nearest to the light, so they could be seen quite easily. Kadira was quite worried about this. What if the others present noticed there was a woman there? She admitted her fears to the group.

"That's okay, Kad, you're wearing so many cloaks that no-one'll notice. And if they do, and have a problem with it, then we'll certainly have something to say to them!" Shakna punched his fist into his other palm emphatically. The others agreed with him loudly, their solid protectiveness reassuring Kadira.

Desert smiled in his esoteric way. "I strange to here too. Hope they not have problem with me, hey?!" The others laughed along, always careful to keep the easily irascible mercenary at his ease. They did not want to offend the dark-skinned warrior, knowing what he was capable of in a temper.

An auburn haired serving wench sauntered up, bearing a tray of drinks. As she was placing them in front of the group, Untya spoke, puzzled. "We didn't order any drinks," and he suddenly smiled roguishly, "though we'd be happy to relieve you of the heavy burden."

The woman smiled, tucking a stray lock of her hair behind her ear as she replied, "Mistress' orders that all the men were to drink themselves stupid. That means as many drinks as you want."

Mad Red grinned, his eyes running suggestively over the woman's ample curves. "Thank ye, my dear," he said with practised charm. "Now, know ye of a place in this fair city where my friends and I might...indulge ourselves?" He had a positively sinful twinkle in his eyes as he spoke, which make Kadira shudder as it once again shattered the illusion that her mind had taken to placing upon the others. Be calm, she thought, just because they know you're a friend and out of bounds doesn't mean they're not men. What do I expect of them, she reasoned, they're mercenaries after all. Though she noticed that Shakna already looked uneasy, nervous as he always was when the banter turned lecherous.

It seemed by the slight re-adjusting of skirt and twitch of lips that the wench understood Red's meaning and chose to stay quite deliberately to play the age-old game. "Indulge yourselves?" she asked innocently, acting the coy maid. Please, scoffed Kadira mentally, we can all see you're a whore.

Hound joined in, subtly diverting the woman's attention. "Yes, we have some...quite fine game cocks to train up. We'd place our bets that they could astound the local folk," he said with an easy smile, as those around him fought to keep their faces straight. Ghiron was choking with laughter behind his manic grin.

Untya smirked suddenly, showing stained teeth. "Know you of a place where they might...get a little exercise?"

The serving wench smiled suggestively with full, red lips. "In that case, you may be interested in an establishment run by some friends of mine. It's straight in front of you as you leave Runners' Street. Say that Doreyn sent you and you'll be very warmly welcomed, I'm sure." She paused to push her abundant hair back over one shoulder. "Say, are they particularly large game cocks?" she asked flirtatiously, smiling brazenly as she tilted her head towards the men.

Ghiron matched her enticing look eye for eye. "Yeah, I'd say," he replied, his grin threatening to take off the top of his head.

"Would you?" Vine slipped in the mocking question with an air of mild surprise. Beside him Kadira bit her lip within the shadow of her cowl, trying to muffle her laughter. The green-haired man continued, his sly jibe made all the harsher for the serious look on his handsome face. "I'd say they get excited very easily, then only pound away at the opponent for a minute or two before wilting!"

Kadira could hold herself silent no longer. "Whether the other's finished fighting or not!" she burst out, then pulled her hood further over her head as she choked with mirth.

Ghiron used the excuse of drinking ale to hide his extraordinarily embarrassed expression, while the other mercenaries threw their heads back and roared with laughter. Even Shakna's head had sunk down to the tabletop as he fought for breath, arms wrapped around his chest.

The wench ruffled Ghiron's hair with a merry laugh, and turned away with a swing of her hips. "Enjoy your meeting, gentlemen," she called, blowing them a kiss. The band fell upon the drinks like they'd been in the desert for a year.

As he sipped his foaming beer, Shakna started to receive a doubt at the back of his mind. The drinks were welcome, but something in the waitress' speech disturbed him. What had she said? *'Drink themselves stupid.'* As if they were meant to be stupid when...no, now he was just being too sceptical. It promised to be a good experience, something new that he could encounter. So why did he feel so uneasy?

Vine's mysterious smile crossed his face once more as Shakna spluttered through a mouthful of ale. The young man grinned sheepishly, the foamy liquid dripping from his chin.

"You're meant to drink it, Shakna, not inhale it!" chuckled Ghiron, patting the younger mercenary on the back. After coughing a few times, Shakna took another draught.

The others shook their heads in mock sympathy. It was better than the first time they had introduced ale to him, at least. He had taken a huge mouthful and then spat it out across the room, drenching a would-be employer. The dripping man had not been amused.

It was quite strange for a mercenary to react in this way. It really did not do their reputation any good, but fortunately Shakna was somewhat shielded from view by the other men congregating in the small square.

Mad Red looked about, then shrugged his broad shoulders at the others. "When's Sye getting here? I thought he'd have got here before us!"

As if on cue, Black Sye emerged from the crowd and seated himself next to the shadowy figure of Kadira, swathed in cloaks. "Sorry I'm a bit late. I got us some food, but the previous owner of it seemed to have some trouble with the notion that we've long given up the privilege of paying for things." He winced, rubbed his left arm, then produced a couple of roasted chickens from beneath his voluminous robes.

The rest of the group cheered, and passed the meal around the table, each one breaking off a section for his self. When the food reached Kadira, it passed right by her. She had no sooner turned to Vine to object than he whispered silkily, "If you removed your hands from your cloak they would be recognised straight away as a woman's." He held his own up to her shadowed face and drew a finger across her forehead lightly. "See the difference?" he pointed out, his green eyes dancing in the low light. He smoothed back his emerald hair in a slightly vain gesture, then picked up his chicken leg and tore off a strip. Lifting it to her hidden face, he held out the end for her to bite.

Kadira was startled by Vine's unusual chivalry, and a little put out at having to eat from his hand, but eagerly accepted the meat. She mumbled a thank you, and was rewarded by a wink and a curve of those sensual lips. The moment was interrupted by a pronounced silence. Every pair of eyes swivelled to the beam of light, into which a cloaked figure was stepping.

* * *

Lounging on a block of broken masonry, a woman surveyed the scene outside with a smile of satisfaction. There were many men outside, thieves and murderers, brigands and assassins; the scum of Lyvilan, and more were arriving by the minute. Eskiros has done well, she thought idly, as have I, buying that shipment of ale. They'll get so drunk that they'll do anything I tell them. Thinking of Eskiros, she mentally added, here the slimy devil is.

As he entered his mistress' presence, Eskiros bowed low. "Mistress," he began, still stooping as he waited for her to acknowledge him.

"Eskiros," she returned, slurring the name as if finding it hard to recall it to mind, and delighting in the quick flash of anger that passed over her assistant's face.

"They are assembled. Shall it begin?"

"You have done well, my aide," she congratulated him formally, for she needed his allegiance for the time being. As Eskiros suppressed a startled comment, she stood up, and started to walk to the nearby entrance illuminated by a shaft of light. "I'm ready. Bring them on!"

* * *

The assembled men fell eerily silent as the cloaked figure stepped lightly out onto the illuminated platform. "Men of Bakarn," rang out a harsh, feminine voice, "are you enjoying your drinks?"

The chorus of rowdy shouts was tumultuous, yet the audience fell silent again as the mysterious woman raised her hand. "I have called upon you for two reasons. Firstly, I need some simple jobs done, and some loyal underlings to carry out my little tasks."

As a wave of disgruntled muttering swept over the courtyard, but before it could intensify into pure discontent the woman continued, "My tasks require some easy jobs, ordering some others around, and of course lots of ale!"

This time the muttering had a brighter edge to it, and the air had definitely turned positive. But a group of men sitting amidst the throng stood up, and one called out in a sneering tone, "Who are you, woman, to try and order us around? We only work for the best, and you're far from that. Who the hell do you think you are, *your ladyship?*" His crew howled with derision, slapping him on the back.

The woman sprang off the platform, and the crowd parted before her as she flew through the now-silent masses to stand before the cynics. Before the leader had a chance to speak, she had produced a jewelled knife and plunged it into his chest. Two of his men, running forward, were amazed at the speed she produced her keh-harande, or steel whip, and dead before they had time to register her hand's expeditious movements. Another, charging at her, was brought down by a single lightning swish, and a few seconds later one more was decapitated. The remaining three rushed at her unprotected back as she sped back towards the platform. With a silent word she spun around, lifted her hand, and pointed at the attackers. All three burst into flame.

There was a short period of silence, while the knife was retrieved and passed up to her, and everyone fought to forget the sound of the men's agonized screams. She then spoke, her voice carrying a low undercurrent of malevolent threat as she faced her audience. "Who am I? I am the only one you'll ever need to work for. I will win, always, as you have just seen, with little real inconvenience. Either join me, or suffer the consequences." To emphasise her point, she ground the still smouldering pile of ashes into the ground with her booted foot.

She then went on, as if nothing had occurred, "Secondly, I have too much gold, and would like to make a present of it to the first two hundred volunteers to my campaign."

As she had well expected, the crowd erupted into frenzy, all trying to get to the front to give names and allegiance to Eskiros and Imcarr, standing at the front like bodyguards. She could see one dark-skinned man at the forefront of the throng, along with a darkly attractive man with green-dyed hair. A cloaked figure's cowl fell back, revealing a young woman. The Mistress grinned. Women were usually more useful than men, and better at surviving for longer. Men at the back pushed and jostled one another, and small fights broke out as everyone clamoured to join her. Someone somewhere in the mob started a chant, which swelled in intensity and volume as more and more took it up.

When she identified the word that they were frenziedly chanting, she grinned behind her thick veil. Her lips parted in ecstasy, she rejoiced in the power and raw energy of the masses that flowed from their chant into her, felt her magic swell and encompass her, and laughed breathlessly as she heard "QesAngared! QesAngared! QesAngared!"

Eskiros, smiling grimly to himself, translated the word in his head from the old language. He thought it very fitting that his murderous employer was named, 'Mistress of Blood!'

* * *

In a small forest glade, dappled sunlight made intricate patterns on the backs of two reclining forms. Kethar and Zakrivath were lazily draped over the verdant grass, warm in the morning sun. Kethar chuckled occasionally as a remark of his friend's reached him inside his head. The huge bird had spread his wings out to the fullest, to better warm them. They were far from the stubby monstrosities they had been three months ago; now they were well-proportioned, elegant, and gigantic. Actually, thought Kethar, surveying his friend proudly, they were much like the rest of Zak in those respects.

Actually, thinking on that point, Kethar realised that he was very rarely using 'Zaki' as one of his friend's names. It had felt right for the somewhat clumsy, comical chick, but it seemed too cute, too immature for the magnificent specimen that lay beside him. Kethar much preferred 'Zak', or the regal full name, Zakrivath. They seemed better suited to the mighty shikara.

Turning onto his back, Kethar basked in the warmth of the blazing sun. He made a little blissful sigh; now it was Zakrivath's turn to chuckle.

"You know, I never thought I'd be this happy," breathed Kethar, his black hair flopping across his eyes. The rest of the thick mane he had tied back with a leather thong; otherwise it got in his way.

I bet you never thought you'd be an outlaw, neither! replied Zak, taking his turn to survey his friend. The boy he had bonded to had grown as much as he himself had, though perhaps not in terms of size. He was tanned, fit and easygoing. His muscled back gleamed in the sunlight, and showed how well his training routine had been going. There were no marks of age upon his face, and the dark brown eyes were intelligent and full of life. The ample mouth was often stretched into a genuine grin, and the well-shaped nose was straight. The boy had become a man. *Yes,* Zak thought to himself as privately as he could, *I have the best soulmate ever.*

However much one of the partnership tried to hide their thoughts from one another, they were so closely Linked that it hardly ever worked. So Kethar smiled to himself at the feelings of love and simple satisfaction that emanated from the huge bird. He felt so amazed and gratified that this incredible creature could actually admire him…it was a great inspirer of confidence. But Zakrivath was right; Kethar had never thought he'd be an outlaw. They had raided the village of Siannorel so many times now, that they had fallen into an unconscious routine. It was time they made another raid, but they could not help but bask in the sun. There was no hope now of reconciliation with the village; even though they had only stolen in total about six or seven hawks worth of goods. In fact, the state of affairs was so bad that they had had to move their temporary shelter to three-quarters of the way up the huge mountain to avoid the villagers.

And we wouldn't have had to steal if they hadn't tried to kill us, he reminded both himself and Zak mentally. Otherwise I'd be drowning in guilt for having stolen goods. But even a bandit's life was richer than his previous one, before Zakrivath had chosen him. He shuddered. How empty those seemingly good days in Central Bakarn had been, now he looked back on them. He could not now imagine, did not even want to contemplate life without his friend.

Life in the forest was not all easy-going, though. Many vicious snakes, boars, and even a great cat had set upon them at first. But Zak had grown extremely skilled at using his deadly beak, and Kethar had been exercising thoroughly and practising a training routine of fights every day. He was the one that had brought down the wild boar.

All of a sudden he received a feeling of foreboding from the shikara. Instantly alert, he mentally questioned its origin. The answer came with a flicker of anxiety.

I sense something.

Signalling for Zak to follow him, Kethar climbed to the top of the grassy knoll at the edge of the clearing and craned his neck to see above the lush canopy of treetops. Walking quickly to him, Zak peered in the direction Kethar was struggling to see. Easily nine feet taller than his friend, the black bird could clearly see the large procession of armed men heading in their general direction.

The pair immediately grabbed all they could of their scant belongings and set off in the opposite direction. They made good progress, and Kethar authorised a quick break to see how the pursuers were faring. He sat down as Zak went to see how much time they had. He was not particularly worried about the hunters, but wondered what had suddenly spurred them to take offensive action against himself and Zakrivath. Then he shrugged. They were probably still scared of them, and more annoyed about the raiding.

He was abruptly roused from his contemplation by the return of his friend. The jolt of fear from the bird reached him just as the sight of the pursuers did. With an incredulous exclamation Kethar jumped to his feet and joined the still running Zak. No sooner than they had got a hundred yards from their resting spot then the chasers crashed through the undergrowth where Kethar had been sitting. As the pair ran, Kethar felt like a hunted hare, and the back of his neck itched as if expecting a spear or arrow at any moment. As they ran on up the side of the mountain, the men steadily closed the gap between them. Forced to run at Zakrivath's unsteady pace, Kethar was dismayed to see the large variety of weapons carried by the hunters.

They have bows, he mentally groaned to Zak. The bird was having trouble running, and Kethar realised that the pursuers would soon be on them. His own breath came in short gasps; the air was thinner here. Craning his head around yet again, he was horrified to notice that they were close enough that he could see their individual faces and features. Suddenly he bumped up against Zak, who had come to a dead halt. "Keep going! They're almost on us!" he wheezed, feeling that he had to stop for air. Then his exhausted eyes came to rest on a sight which made his blood run cold.

Not twenty paces from where they stood, the ground ended. They had run all the way up to the very summit of the mountain. They were higher even than the peak of Skyria. As he stood gasping for breath, his head hung in defeat, his arm was jerked by Zak. Throwing his arms around his friend, he found himself suddenly lifted into the air as Zakrivath stood up. Too weak to protest, he could only hang on as his friend thundered towards the sheer drop. As his talons cleared the edge, Zakrivath threw out his wings, and they soared out into the blue. Kethar swung his legs over Zak's neck to get a better grip, and laughed aloud in sheer thrill.

The valley lay below them like an enormous patchwork carpet, the wheat fields gleaming golden, the forests lush and leafy, and the meadows brilliant green. Jagged splinters of white rock protruded like teeth from the lower mountains, capturing Kethar's breath as he saw how high they were flying. Villages passed far below them, almost invisible from many miles above the ground. They soared so high that they glimpsed the sprawling city of Lyvilan as just a mere speck in the distance.

A strong beat of the powerful wings propelled them down, and they hurtled into a dive. Though his stomach twisted in exhilaration, Kethar's heart rose and sang with the sensation of harmony that engulfed him. Zak's wings closed, and their descent increased in speed, and after a mile down the shikara spread his huge wings to bring them once more soaring upwards.

The conflicting sensations of exhilaration and joy merged with Zakrivath's feeling of exultation in the wild thrill of flight, making Kethar suddenly feel quite poetic. But what words could describe the sense of fierce joy in soaring so high, the pride in Zakrivath's awesome figure, or the beauty of the earth that lay so very far below them? What words could show the incredible rush of adrenaline coursing strongly though his body, the glint of sunlight on sable wings, or the surges of wind that ruffled black hair and black feathers alike, and lifted you ever higher in the cerulean sky? Up here you could be the masters of the air, sharing the sky only with a few clumps of fluffy cloud, lower still than you, that refreshed you as you flew through. It was surreal, breathtaking, and absolutely fantastic.

As the immense wings beat the air strongly, Kethar felt the muscles under the smooth layer of feathers move underneath his legs, and shifted his thighs slightly so that with each movement he did not impede the great muscles. A leisurely flap brought them closer to the mountaintop from which they had launched themselves, and Zakrivath screeched in contempt at the wrathful band of men. Kethar whooped with derisive mirth when one of them fired an arrow. Its puny arc brought it only ten metres away from the bow that it had left.

Zak spread his wings wide suddenly, and they hung there, suspended in the sky with savage splendour. The sable bird screamed on high, and inside Kethar's head the feeling of exultation grew with his soulmate's words, fierce with pride. *I can fly! We are one! We can go anywhere we want, and we'll go everywhere! We are free as wind, the lords of the sky!*

They floated on the breeze, their love and dedication renewed in the glory of this new thrill, and their hearts were made firm and proud. Then with another fearsome scream that rent the air, they soared majestically into the sky.

* * *

"Repeat your knowledge to me, my son. I would like to see how well …how much you know." The old mage sits atop a broken head of a fallen column, and looks inquiringly at the albino boy in front of him. The boy has grown, he thinks to himself, in knowledge and stature, yet I do not think he knows what an exceptional pupil he is.

At the boy's hesitant stammer, he smiles encouragingly, and says, "This is not a test, Sirenthe. And if it was, it would be testing me, not you."

Heartened, Sirenthe begins. "The seven Gods, Eternity, Ashikra, Destiny, Chance, Luck, Fate, and Fortune, use a raw energy called magic to harness and control the elements of the world. Those of Royal blood have a small amount of magic of their own. A person may gain more magic by changing their name to one more like a God's. But the more successful they are at receiving the magic, the more dangerous it is for them. If it eventually gets to the point that the God has not enough magic to control His or Her element any more, the God is forced to combat the sorcerer." He pauses for a moment.

"Very good, Sirenthe. Do not continue with the teachings you learned from our first lesson, but rather our other lessons. Summarise." The elderly man coughs suddenly, and the boy helps him to regain his breath by supporting him. "Go on, boy."

The youth nods. "A God may use different ways to combat the sorcerer. They may send their divine creatures to kill them, for example the findaena, the urgroth, the mantifel, the nyaphim, the shikarath, the ishel, or the emathai. The God may also proselyte a human to carry out the task, rewarding them should the duty be properly executed. Lastly, the God may just use their element to destroy the sorcerer."

"Excellent. But what of our last lesson? You had many questions then. Let us see if you fully took it in."

"From what I understood, magic is also permitted to some others. There are the Tsumetai, the weapons masters. Each has a magic artefact that aids the Tsumetai in his work, and increases his deadliness and speed. The Tsumetai also needs to be able to use a little magic to be able to adapt their bodies to the artefact, as it is in some way inserted into their flesh."

The old mage smiles. "Well done, my son! You have indeed leaned well! Now what else did you remember of those who are permitted magic?"

Sirenthe smiles also, glowing with simple happiness at the old man's praise. How I love my master, he thinks.

"There are also the priests of the Gods, who train in the seven Orders. Those most trusted by the Gods are allowed more magic, and those are called mages, meaning 'Holy magic'. There are ten levels of the priests: firstly anmage, then eomage, trimage, tetramage, pentmage, hexmage, quramage, octmage, synmage, and then finally phinmage. There is one temple per Order, run by the Archmage. Each God may also choose one mage to be His or Her disciple, one that may do the God's work on the earth and receive a great amount of magic-" Sirenthe pauses, belatedly realising the fact that was staring him in the face.

"But that means that the Gods really trust you, as you know so much of magic! You must be a great man in religion; a disciple!" So saying, Sirenthe bows before his mentor.

Angrily, the old man pulls him upright. "You must not bow to me!" His voice is furious, but Sirenthe senses fear buried beneath; fear induced by his own act. "They," and he indicates upward, " are the only ones you should prostrate yourself before."

The old man turns his back on the youth, and it is clear that the lesson is at an end. Scared, for he has never before seen his tutor so irate, Sirenthe backs away. He has sensed a growing build-up of consternation through the months he has been here, and is increasingly worried about his preceptor. Thinking this, he decides to watch the old man carefully from now on, to try and discover what is bringing on the strange moods and inexplicable character change in his teacher and friend.

Chapter 11

The moonlight filtered between the bare trees, illuminating the small forest glade below. The air was still and silent, punctuated only by the lonely cry of an owl on his solitary hunt. The birds sat smugly in their nests, confident that they were well out of the reach of any predator. Rabbits and voles ran swiftly to their nests, then peered out, wary of any slight rustle or disturbance of the peace.

And they were right to be cautious. A dark shape, moving stealthily and lithely, moved out from the cover of the trees, and fluidly crossed over to the stream. A human watcher may have marvelled at the way that the female could walk so gracefully on four legs, or how alert and almost…feral the girl was.

However, the only watchers were the animals and the birds. They could smell a man-small, disguised among the musty odours that accompanied the creature. The sharper smelling amongst them could detect a certain subtle imperfection that their animal minds and memories could not fathom. So the watching creatures mentally catalogued the smell as 'man-but not-man'.

Man-but-not-man lapped greedily at the clear water. Her whole stance, even just while drinking, labelled her blatantly as a predator. And though she was human-shaped she had extremely acute hearing, and froze at each minute noise that punctuated the silence. As she drank, the watching creatures relaxed, and one bold buck hare made the mistake of hopping out into the open.

It was the last mistake that he ever made. In a flash, man-but-not-man held him by the throat. He kicked and squealed; with one smash from her paw-hand she broke his backbone. His limp body dropped to the ground, and man-but-not-man lowered her head to tear with ravening jaws at the pitiful carcass. The watching creatures cowered in terror, and not even when the beast had headed purposefully off in a different direction did they dare to venture abroad.

*   *   *

The fear consumed everything, its brooding presence a smothering blanket over her senses. But as she began to feel the rising panic in her waking brain, she opened her eyes, and winced as the daylight flooded into them. As her eyes grew more accustomed to the light, she opened them fully, and stretched out her legs languidly under the silken sheets. The richly furnished room was bathed in a soft light, and the gauze curtains cast a pinkish sheen over the four-poster bed.

There were no servants about to interrupt her, so she sat up, letting the lavender sheets fall from her body. Swinging her legs off the edge of the bouncy mattress, she stood up slowly and strolled sedately to the generous window. Through the gauze curtain she could see the gardens, smaller than the expansive palace ones she was used to, but just as beautiful. Abundant bright flowers of all species covered every surface except the neat paths. The magnolia bushes were blossoming, casting their creamy petals haphazardly about the gravelled path. Large weeping willow trees trailed their long green hair into clear pools, which occasionally glinted as lazy carp flicked their tails in an effort to seem active. Yes, she reflected, I love it here.

As she gazed out over the tranquil grounds, she was reminded suddenly of the situation she had left behind. It had been wonderful at the palace, and then everything had crumbled to nothing. Suddenly, the safe haven that she had enjoyed for so long was not safe. She had been left with relative imprisonment inside her own rooms, with her family being killed off, and her food being tasted for fear of poison! The dream had gone; the morning had come, and she had awoken. So to flee here had seemed the best option at the time, and she was now firmly convinced of that. Of course, she did feel slightly guilty at abandoning everyone, especially Destinariae, now the youngest Kaji. Actually, she thought with some shock, apart from Rieda she's the only Kaji left in the palace! But learning of Destinariae's excursions to the city had cheered her, and she had left the palace life for good.

Still, she was treated better here and she was safer. She was glad that the Ka had suggested it to her.

For his part, her lover had played his part well. He had acted so incessantly monotonous and boring, whenever attending Royal functions, that no one would dare suspect him of being anything but a dull, incapable, witless lord. He had told her of his conversation with one of the other lords, and how he had made the other believe he was in love with Destinariae to divert his attention.

Turning abruptly, she gazed at the figure still asleep in the four-poster bed. He was handsome as ever in rest, though sleep softened the somewhat hard lines around his mouth, and seemed to gentle it. Crossing the room once more, she gently fingered the face she had come to love. The sheet had slipped off his shoulder, exposing an expanse of tanned skin. With her other hand she caressed the smooth shoulder, and the sleeping man stirred. She quickly took her hands away, lest she scratch him if he moved. But his hand snaked out and grabbed hers, and his deep green eyes fixed on her own hazel ones with a look that said nothing about retreating.

"Verda," he whispered, his voice throbbing with deep emotion.

"Atisato," she replied with a loving smile, as she slid into his embrace.

* * *

As the small group of men travelled north, the sun was bright and glaring, and the temperature for the travellers grew steadily more unbearable. The other thing that really doesn't help, thought Shakna angrily, is this damned heavy black sash that we all have to wear. Still, I suppose it's better than wearing a heavy uniform, and we do need to be identified somehow. He pulled a small canteen of water from underneath his sash, remarking to Kadira as he did so, "It's useful for holding things, isn't it?"

Kadira smiled back at him, then took a long drink from her bottle. It always surprised her how enthusiastic and optimistic Shakna was; especially for a mercenary. Though, she corrected herself, they weren't actually mercenaries any more. They were all soldiers of QesAngared now, and had been named as 'Minions'. They were also the last group of Minions to be sent to Siannorel, where they were apparently to 'convert the villagers to their cause'. She could only presume that there would be some kind of forceful demonstration, and then they would take control of the village. She was not altogether happy with their new position, but she had been swept along in the tide of people, including her mercenary friends, who she had decided to follow. Besides, she was more likely to encounter the real killer of her family here. She thought she had seen him at the demonstration, but he had vanished into the crowd. So she would bide her time.

Similar groups of Minions had been despatched to other villages, like Mephra, Eredeth, and Thago, right out on the border between Bakarn and the Snowlands. She was relieved to have been sent to Siannorel, closest of the target villages to Lyvilan. Kadira especially hated long journeys, but travelling with Shakna was slightly more fun. The others of their one-time group had been sent to Thago.

Squinting into the blazing sun, she could just make out the shape of a large bird, soaring gracefully far in the distance. She was about to point it out to Shakna, for she knew his love of birds, when she was elbowed roughly and noticed that they had arrived.

* * *

Black, black, everything was black. To open her eyes was torture, to close them was to be again in darkness. How long she had remained in this state she did not know, but fevered dreams came and went so often that she imagined that she must be dead. But there was said to be no pain in the Shadowlands, so how could her leg hurt with such a blazing agony?

Torn between dreams and reality, Ionté had been carried in a sack on a wagon from Garoto to Siannorel. When the coarse sack was ripped off her, she shuddered in the sunlight, and screamed at the agony when she opened her eyes to the blinding light. Everything was blurry; people, voices, smells, her whole head felt like it was on fire. She was intensely aware of chains passing around her wrists and ankles. The roar of colours and sounds was so fierce that she slipped into a faint.

When she next opened her eyes, Ionté could see more clearly. Shaking her head, she tried to get rid of the fog that obscured her mind. The wall she was chained against was cold and unyielding, yet she leaned hard against it, thankful for its support. She could dimly hear somebody's voice, and it took her a few moments of thought before she could identify a few words.

"-will comply with our Mistress' wishes-"

Looking around, she saw with alarm that there was an open door, leading to a stage with a crowd gathered around. And they were all dark-skinned! Ionté had never seen Bakarnians before, except for the slaver that had captured her. To somebody who had lived among albinos, the tanned faces of the southerners were dark, and frightening. One stood at the door, and nodded to somebody outside as if receiving a signal.

"-show you that we will help-"

"-savage northerner to be burnt at-"

Ionté's mouth went very dry.

"Evening, you white alien bitch," sneered the guard at the door, coming forward and starting to release her chains from the wall.

"Please, were others...taken too?" she asked falteringly, staring with pleading eyes at the guard.

"Yeah, but you're the only one left. We did stop at other villages along the way, but we were savin' you 'till last." The man grinned evilly, and Ionté shut her eyes in fear.

She was dragged out onto the stage, and the yells and hisses of the crowd intensified as they saw her. Some threw rotting fruit and vegetables, some rocks; and Ionté cried out in pain as one hit her shoulder. The guard, however, was her unlikely saviour when he raised his voice to stop the crowd's actions, as he was also getting hit.

As Ionté turned her head, she saw with mind-numbing fear a large stout wooden log, standing upright in a nest of dry kindling. She wept in terror as they chained her to it, and as they piled firewood around her feet, her desperate, pain-filled eyes met those of a young brown-haired woman, standing at the back of the crowd. She was wearing a black sash.

"Stop!" The word was not shouted, but its tone of horrified sincerity cut sharply through the cheering around it. Everybody quietened, and turned to stare at the dark-haired woman that had spoken.

The stares of the hostile crowd were vicious, yet Kadira knew that she had to speak out. It was sickening to torture and murder this poor girl simply because she had a different skin and hair colour to them, and came from a different place. She didn't know quite what she was going to say, but opened her mouth anyway to stop what she knew was barbarous.

"This young woman has done nothing to hurt you, has she?" Kadira asked, gesturing toward the still weeping captive. "She hasn't killed your family, or kidnapped your children, or stolen your money, has she?"

Out of the corner of her eye she could see Shakna gesturing urgently for her to stop. This only convinced her more that she was doing what was right. She went on. "Look at her, chained to that log, she doesn't know what she's done to deserve this, and neither do I! If this is how you treat northerners, then no wonder they become savage! I'm not from Bakarn, but even I know that this is cold-blooded murder!"

"She's not a Bakarnian?" The words were from the mouths of villagers and Minions alike.

Then somebody else yelled, "Burn her too! Burn her too!"

The savage, stirred-up fury of the crowd bypassed all humane boundaries of sanity, and at once Kadira was being manhandled up to the stage, the crowd spitting on her and chanting, "Burn them! Burn them! Burn them!"

As she was roughly pushed through the contemptuous masses, she passed Shakna. Though not chanting or pushing her forward, he had not spoken out. Pulling forcefully back, she said through clenched teeth, "I was wrong about you. I thought you had a hint of compassion, a trace of morality left in you. But now I know you're just as inhuman as the rest of them. I hate you!" She spat into his face as she was again yanked forwards.

Though the black feathers on which he was sitting were quite cold from both their altitude and the late hour, the warm leather clothing that Kethar had stitched kept him just nicely warm. He revelled in the joy of flight as Zakrivath swooped to catch an up draught, and told his friend once again just how proud he was of him.

He then remembered what they were meant to be doing; they had to see what had prompted the recent attack from the villagers of Siannorel. The flight took less than a minute, and soon they were hovering above the village that they had raided so many times. Swooping closer, Zak relayed a few remarks to Kethar, his sight incredibly sharp even with the darkness all about them.

There are lots of strange people down there, some seem to be threatening people, looking as if they're going to set fire to some buildings. They aren't the usual villagers, either, but they seem to be working as a force. Oh, now they've stopped that, and are talking to the village people. Zakrivath obligingly gave a running commentary of what he could see, and Kethar struggled to work out what was going on.

'Are they wearing any uniforms?' he thought to his friend, wondering if the Kajarito had come to Siannorel.

Zak's reply was negative. *No, but they all seem to be wearing black sashes.*

'Black sashes? I don't know who they are, then."

Zakrivath wheeled in a leisurely way, his great wings shining in the moonlight. Suddenly he stopped and hovered, and Kethar felt his mind Link overcome with a feeling of hideous revulsion. As the great shikara beat his wings together furiously, Kethar noticed with astonishment the clouds swirl in dark floods of forbidding black, blue and purple, and felt a slight charge in the air as if a storm was building like the rage he could feel in his Link.

'Zak, what're they doing down there?' he mentally asked his soulmate, wondering what on earth could prompt this sick disgust.

209

Burning people! came the reply, and the mind voice was both aghast and shaking with fury. Similar feelings echoed throughout Kethar's mind, and with their joint feelings the pair knew exactly what to do.

Shakna wiped the spit from his eyes, and opened his mouth to tell Kadira that…but all he could see was the retreating back of his one-time friend. He would've spoken against it, but done it quietly to the other Minions, thinking they could help him, without causing a riot or more unnecessary deaths. Now she was going to be killed.

He was about to speak in protest, but then an ear-splitting screech rent the air. The villagers immediately forgot the threats of the occupying Minions, and ran for cover, yelling, "The demon has come!"

Turning his head he saw a black shape silhouetted against the full moon, with massive wings and fearsome beak. It screamed on high, and through the hostile skies a bolt of lightning lanced through, accompanied by an explosion of thunder. As Shakna watched, blood running like fire and ice through his veins, he saw the small black shape dropping vertically from the sky, getting larger every second, like a thunderbolt through the storm. It spread its wings before reaching the ground to swoop low over the heads of the panic-stricken crowd, who stampeded like panicked animals out of the square.

As it alighted on the cobbles, Shakna could see that it was an immense jet-black bird, with savage red eyes, tearing talons and hooked beak, and a wingspan that reached across the square. A sturdy-looking, black-haired man in black clothing jumped from high up on its neck, landing in a crouch before sprinting athletically up to the stage. Taking a small hand knife, the man sawed at Kadira's bindings while the bird severed the northerner's chains with one stroke of its vicious beak.

At this point, a group of seven Minions ran at the newcomers, weapons drawn. Helping both traumatised girls to their feet, the man was unable to do anything, but the bird moved with lightening speed to attack the leader.

A heartbeat later all seven lay dead upon the floor, their blood dampening the kindling while high above the lightning tore the sky with savage raking claws of light. The man helped the girls mount the broad back of the bird, and then leapt on too. The magnificent creature spread his wings, shrieked again, and launched itself into the wrath of the storm.

Chapter 12

The arena was immense, with high stone walls and row upon row of benches filled with cheering people. The number of spectators was so immense that many stood in the aisles or sat on the floor. The arena floor was circular, and was covered with fine sand. High walls surrounded the main 'stage' area, so the actual benches started quite a way up, for the spectators' safety. A heavy iron gate stood at one end of the arena floor, and at the other end, a wooden portcullis. Already there were 'sandmen' out with their sacks of sand and wood-shavings, covering up the pools of blood that had soaked in to the floor covering. Clowns and acrobats amused the audience while the new sand was sprinkled around, and people on the right wing of benches could see the men with loudspeaker funnels preparing to announce the next act. The reason for the huge crowds of people was that it was the Kaji Destinariae's birth-festival, and entrance to the amazing performance was free. As Destinariae was favoured for being the last daughter of the late Kai

Isete, it promised to be quite a show, and was already proving above expectations.

The next act was announced; and on came the horse acrobats. A dozen white horses came galloping into the ring, bedecked with streamers and plumed harnesses, and their tails plaited with brilliant ribbons. From their saddles, the riders performed somersaults and handstands, somehow balancing on the circling horses as they plunged and thundered around. The riders' costumes were as extravagant as the horses' own, and it was a marvel that the ribbons flapping in the horses' faces did not seem to distract them in the slightest. The audience gasped as a whole as a rider stood up on his horse's saddle, and balanced there for a whole lap of the wide ring. Then, with a final lap and a wave, the acrobats and their highly trained horses were gone. The crowd applauded crazily, and many emitted whistles and catcalls.

From her padded seat in the royal box, Destinariae applauded too, and smiled at her father. It was turning out to be a better birth-festival than she had hoped, for the joint funerals of her sisters had served to sombre the mood of all life in the usually extravagant capital city. However, though she had not asked for a main present, she was expecting to receive one anyway and was feeling slightly piqued that she had not.

Still, the entertainment had been brilliant so far, and she was looking forward to the mystery act, which she had been told was to be stunning. After seeing the horses, she was feeling slightly wistful, as when her horse costing thousands of eagles had died, she had not been permitted to have another large animal. She had thought it unfair at the time, and still harboured the same feelings, as the horse had died of lungworm, which was hardly *her* fault. Also, she had no servant, as Kethar had run away.

Kethar...Destinariae pictured his face, and to her dismay found it difficult to remember all the details. Has it really been that long, she asked herself sadly, remembering his devotion to her. She had taken him for granted. Well she had learned her lesson, and would never again take for granted the adulation of those who served her.

Focusing her mind back on the arena floor, the Kaji noticed that the announcers were walking back to their safe seats. She leant across to Rieda, sitting on her right, and asked, "What's next? What did they say?"

She was answered by a whispered, "The main spectacle, the fight of the wild man!"

Destinariae watched as a chained man was led out. His hair was long, dark, and matted, and his clothes, which she presumed had once been black robes, were in shreds. His mouth was moving, as if he was chanting something, or muttering to the guards who accompanied him. One of the guards said something to him, which she could not make anything of but notice the derisive tone, to which the prisoner snarled like a tiger and launched himself at the swaggering guard. The heavy metal chains brought him up short, and he strained at them, like a wretched, starving dog on a leash. The two convoys laughed, then fastened the ragged man's chains to a central post. They then sneered and taunted him, kicking him when he came forward and dashing back when he came too close. Finally one of the guards beckoned the announcers forward, and whispered information to them.

"This, my delightful audience, is a madman," started one, indicating the captive. "His captors have informed me that he is not only mad but...he worships false Gods!" A gasp of outrage greeted this astounding remark, and even Destinariae herself felt shocked. A couple of the audience hissed, more joined in, but were silenced by a wave of the proclaimer's arm.

He continued, "Yes, he prays to his fake Gods, he swears by them, he even has not heard of our own!" A hiss greeted each statement, especially the last. Revelling in his control of the spectators, the man went on, "And, if anyone defies his 'Gods' and tells him the truth of the world; that ours are the true Gods...he attacks whoever tells him!" The crowd went mad, screaming and shouting, throwing things at the madman, which quite often hit the guards and announcers, and yelling for an execution.

The man had not finished, though. He stood up on a raised platform, saluted the audience, bowed to the assembly in the royal box, and shouted above the din, "There should be no unbelievers, especially on this happy day. We shall execute him, in honour of the most beautiful Kaji Destinariae!" The roar from the crowd was deafening, and practically all were on their feet.

Destinariae was sickened. Time slowed for her, and she heard her own heartbeat throbbing in her ears. The noise of the bloodthirsty crowd, so distant now, was like bile at the back of her throat; their excitement for death made her feel ill with loathing. They were like hounds on a hunt, baying for the prisoner's blood. They were cheering for a man to be ripped apart in front of them, just because he had different beliefs to them. Why should they force their beliefs on him? He was obviously not mad, just a religious fanatic. And for them to excuse the murder as an act upon *her* behalf, in *her* name...suddenly, she could stand it no longer.

She rose from her seat; a million pairs of lips sealed themselves, and a million pairs of eyes stared at her. She was not to be deterred, and shouted in a nevertheless controlled voice that was heard by all present there that moment. "Look at yourselves! You call yourselves people, yet you are screaming for this man's blood! Is he really that different to yourselves? Does he really deserve to die in front of you all, torn apart for *entertainment?*" Her voice cracked on the word, but she turned with great dignity to face the Ka. "My lord Ka, give me his life as a gift."

Her father turned to look at her, and was both pleased and concerned by her request. She had put him on the spot, and he had to think quickly. He had no sincere wish for a murder in front of the cheering masses; had never had such a wish, in fact, but knew that a good ruler went by what his people wanted. If he were to let his daughter have her way, it would disappoint the public, and there may be more than a few seeds of dissent spread among his people. Not to mention the danger to himself, his wife and his daughters if there were a riot.

Yet he did feel great pride in his daughter at her great compassion, the strength that had made her speak out in front of all these people. Besides, why should he deny that this man's life should be saved? It would only be dangerous if the man stayed alive and free within their land, spreading a new religion...but if Destinariae were to keep him alive but out the way, it would be far better than having a public execution. Of course he could not let such a violent character within too close proximity of his daughter; but alive and imprisoned the man could be no harm. Plus, if he granted her this one's life, hopefully she would stop nagging him about having a new creature.

His mind made up, he nodded once to her. "I hereby judge that this man be granted his life, and that it may belong to my daughter, Kaji Destinariae.

The crowd erupted again. Some were pleased, or just singularly loyal to their monarchs, and others were openly incensed at the decision to let the man walk free. Between the two factions, fights were breaking out, and the Kajarito were called in. Fools, thought the Ka, they are not to know he will be imprisoned. He beckoned to the escort of Kajarito; now was the time to leave. He looked down at the ring as he turned to go; what he saw made his blood run cold. Destinariae was approaching the madman, and no one was near enough to stop her. The Ka swiftly ordered two units of officers to get to her, but saw they would not reach the arena floor for a few minutes, obstructed as they were by the hostile masses. He could only watch in frustrated desperation, and wait.

As she advanced towards the man, Destinariae could fully acknowledge the terrible punishments that must have been visited upon him. Her horrified gaze took in the new scars, scratches, and bruises on his face and arms, and the gashes upon his torso and legs. As he turned slightly, she witnessed horrendous welts on his bare back, brought about almost certainly by a keh-harande. At her next step forwards, he looked up at her, and what she saw filled her with pity. On his face was a multitude of cuts and swellings, and the dark eyes that bored into her own were sunken and weary. They nevertheless were the eyes of one who were prepared to fight to the last, as he had already borne the worst and had no fear left in him. She looked away, unnerved. As she did so he reached out a hand, and said in a strange but surprisingly gentle voice, "What they say...it not true. I just defend myself."

Destinariae gazed back, and saw in his eyes only honest truth. Though the man before her had been said to be a criminal, to be dangerous, she found herself believing him. His clothes were tattered, his mane of black hair continued for some way down his tanned shoulders, and his muscled torso bore the mark of many an ugly battle, but she warmed to his story, and said simply, "I believe you."

She reached out, and laid a hand on his arm. He flinched, and let out a low noise that sounded almost like a growl, then settled down again. Steeling herself, Destinariae then walked within the reach of his chains, but she was not attacked. Selecting a jagged bracelet from her arm, she began to saw through the top of the post to which the man was chained. The toothed edge cut through the soft wood like a knife through butter... well, a knife through steak really, she thought. Soon she had a fist sized chunk of wood in her palm, with which she could keep the pretence of having control of the captive. As she looked up, she realised that two squads of Kajarito were grouped nearby, and some were advancing, keeping a wary eye on the prisoner.

"Halt!" she commanded, her voice ringing out clearly over the assembled throng. The Kajarito, picked and trained especially in their ability to obey orders from the Royal Family, obeyed, but the brawlers did not. She nevertheless continued. "This man now belongs to the Royal family. I am now responsible for him; you heard my father the Ka. Nothing is to be said or done to him unless I will it. He will not escape; he will obey me, and me only. Now form up your positions!"

As the Kajarito assembled, she glanced sideways at the wild man, wanting to warn him to reinforce what she had said by not fighting or struggling. He seemed, however, to know what she was thinking, and at her slightest tug of his 'lead', he followed, meek as a palace greyhound. At this reassurance, the Kajarito continued as normal, but not until Destinariae had indicated the captive's original tormentors and whispered to the nearest squad, "Oh, and flog those men...oh...fifty lashes with the keh-harande, I think." Those who heard shuddered at this order, which would certainly bring the guards to a slow and agonising death. But some nodded; the Kaji rightly came down hard on bullies and torturers. Destinariae glanced sideways at the captive, and saw that he was smiling grimly. He had obviously heard the order. As she walked to her private carriage, she noticed two Kajarito trying to get her new servant to walk the gruelling six miles in the heat; she reprimanded them, and bade the man climb in before her. Hearing footsteps, she turned.

"Kaji Destinariae, what do you think you are doing?" The Ka's voice was tight with controlled fury, and his face was livid. "That...creature belongs in the prison, not in your carriage. And especially not alone with you! What have I said about the honour a lady of your heritage and bearing should always be mindful of?"

"My lord Ka, you said this man's life now belongs to me. I then wish him to be my servant, as I have been without a personal one since Kethar..." she broke off the sentence as the Ka interrupted. It would not do for the Kajarito to witness two of the Royals squabbling like children.

"Servant?" he snarled, eyes blazing. "You do not even know his name! You know nothing of his background...if nothing else, he could be an assassin!"

"Oh come now, my lord, had he wanted to kill me he's had plenty of opportunity since I came in reach of his chains. The fact is, when are you going to let me actually take responsibility myself?"

"I will let you have responsibility when you are responsible!" hissed the Ka. Then as if a veil was lifted from his sight, he looked properly at the young woman. The sight of her, ready to fight for her beliefs, blazing with anger, made him burst with admiration for her. She was his daughter, all right. One could see it in the proud stance, the resolute set of jaw, the defiant light in her brown eyes. With a sudden surge of fierce delight in his daughter he held up his hand to stop her retort.

"Enough, Destinariae. Seeing as you champion this man so devoutly I shall trust your judgement. He may be your servant, as long as he behaves himself. But," he raised a warning finger, his manner stern once more, "my Kajarito shall be watching. He makes one slip, and he will go straight back to the arena. I have antagonised enough today as it is, for your and his sakes." With a slight incline of his head to hide a smile, the Ka opened the carriage door for his daughter, waiting until she was seated inside before stepping back and allowing the coach to move off.

The journey was made in silence for a while, broken only by the occasional encouraging noises made by the coachman to his horses. Destinariae glanced at the man sitting opposite her. He seemed anything but worried, and he watched the scenery flash past with fascination. In the middle of one of her looks, he looked up at her, and grinned when he saw her staring. To hide her own embarrassment as much to break off the silence, she asked somewhat haughtily, "What name do you go by?"

The look in his eyes told her that he had seen her discomfiture. But instead of commenting on it, he just replied, "Marghaska." Before her brain had registered the name, he asked her, "What's yours?"

Destinariae was stunned into silence. This... this...commoner she had just saved the life of, he did not even know who she was? And then to ask in that impertinent tone and rude way as if *questioning* her? She opened her mouth to rebuke him, but he sat still, one eyebrow raised in question, still waiting for her answer, unaware that she had been offended.

Instead, she forced a smile, and said patiently, "I am Kaji Destinariae, third daughter of the Ka. I am well respected and obeyed in these lands, so none will dare harm you while I protect you. Marghaska," she said in a low tone, "if anybody so much as shouts at you, you tell me, and I will have them punished. Alright?"

Marghaska's eyes narrowed slightly, and she could tell that she, in turn, had offended him. He turned back to the window, and said with a hint of coldness, "I...I am grateful for your...intervention, but you find that I be no sneak. Can take care of myself." He spoke hesitantly, as if uneducated, but Destinariae knew that this could not be the case, as he had spoken some more formal words. If it wasn't that he was untaught, what was it? She racked her brains.

And who did he remind her of? That black hair, the tanned skin and penetrating stare...of course! Kethar! She mentally congratulated herself. Of course, it was strange that he should look like Kethar, when Kethar had the complexion of one from far away...that was it! She replayed it all out to herself in her head. Marghaska looked like Kethar, and Kethar looked like a foreigner, so Marghaska must be an immigrant, which meant he was unsure of the language. I must be losing my touch, thought Destinariae with some self-reproach, it took me far too long to work that out. She looked back at her new servant, who was peering with delight at the lush scenery flashing past the window, and found herself feeling guilty for her earlier airs of grandeur. It must have been really inhospitable, where he came from. He had the bearing of a commoner, a polite commoner of course, but still a peasant. He had, Destinariae considered, probably been made to work all his life, then escaped to see Bakarn, which had always been considered a land of glorious wealth and opportunity. And look what such misplaced hope brought him, the Kaji thought despairingly; he had been imprisoned, tortured, and sentenced to death because he believed something different. Destinariae almost cried as she thought of her own life of sumptuous luxury, with bowing, reverent servants at her beck and call; she felt a deep shame as she compared their situations.

They continued in silence for the rest of the passage. Neither was sorry when the uncomfortable journey came to an end, and the door was opened. Destinariae took Marghaska's chains in her hands, and led him out. She swept along the marble corridors and up the flight of carpeted steps that led to the Royal Quarters. Taking a left turn, she progressed up the narrower staircase to her own room, opposite Verda's abandoned chambers. Throwing open the door, and noting with some amusement the yelp from her pompous temporary servant, she entered.

"Would your highness care for some victuals?" asked the servant, rubbing his nose as he appeared from behind the door. He bent down and lit the fire, dropping the spent match onto the sea-blue hearthrug.

"No, Elwei, that will be all. You may go, and inform any comers that I am not to be disturbed. Oh, and you will no longer be my servant."

Elwei glanced at Marghaska, smirked, and said, "Not to be disturbed. I understand, highness. You have... your own things to do." With that he bowed condescendingly, and walked out of the door.

Destinariae sat herself down on her bed with a satisfying thump. Throwing the chains onto the floor by Marghaska's feet, she sighed in bliss as she kicked off her tight, high shoes. "Well, I hope you're thankful. I've wasted my largest present opportunity for a year on you, I've defended you from my father, I've saved your life, been smirked at, been insulted by you, and I just really hope you're worth it!"

At Marghaska's raised eyebrow, she returned crossly, "Oh honestly! I meant I hope you're going to be an asset rather than an encumbrance." Tiredness made her snappish, yet she regretted her words immediately.

Marghaska walked slowly over until he was standing right in front of her. To her shame, she gripped the edge of her robe in her hands, suddenly feeling the cold grip of fear. Had she done the right thing?

He just held her gaze, and went down on one knee. "I swear," he began softly, his eyes shining with the glare from the fire, "I always be true to the just cause, no matter who or number that fight me. If you are for truth, I will be with you."

She clasped his hands in hers, and nodded, her throat too tight to speak. Looking over at the cold, stone floor that she had originally designated was to be her new servant's bed, she appeared to reach a decision, and whispered huskily, "You can sleep on the rug, in front of the fire. He nodded his appreciation, kissed her hand, and stood up.

"I...can you not... the chains?" asked Marghaska, without much hope. At Destinariae's sympathetic shake of head, he grunted, and bowed. "Good evening, Mistress," he called softly, settling himself down on the fireside rug. He lay down on his side, placing his manacles carefully to the side. As Destinariae stepped into her lavish bathroom, she heard him say, "And thank you."

* * *

A new day had dawned in Bakarn, clear and beautiful as a summer day could be. Trees carried colourful flowers in their hair, and the sky was the deep sapphire of a mountain lake. The season had come early, when the Bakarnians expected the end of spring. A pensive, even melancholy calm had surrounded the city, neatly concealing the confusing welter of emotions harboured by its many citizens.

In the east wing of the palace, a select group of young women sat catching the last of the morning sun. They were sat in silence, bent over small, delicate pieces of embroidery. Looking at them, a stranger might not be able to tell at first on which the future of the country depended.

However, as their gaze travelled the young faces, they would perhaps detect a hint of authority, of serenity in the face of one. Then, perhaps, their eyes would wander down to the brocade gown, the gold adornments. Though perhaps her glorious hair would overshadow even those.

The watcher would be looking at the Kaji Rieda, the Kai-to-be. She was indulging in one of her favourite pastimes, one which she seldom had time for. Whilst her fingers worked industriously on the detailed pattern, her mind was just as busy. The heir to the throne was severely worried.

Such was her anxiety that she had commanded her ladies-in-waiting to silence; she needed to concentrate. The order had caused her to be the subject of many strange looks, but none would dare to question her. A good thing, she thought, for my future subjects must learn when to keep their silence.

Rieda sighed, and laid down the silken scarf she had been finishing. Four princesses of the royal line dead, maybe five. No matter how many lies her father wove for the greedy, power-hungry lords, this was not the work of nature, or of coincidence. The Kaji was sure that one, or probably two parties were involved in the almost certain assassinations.

Not that anybody had said anything about it. Indeed, some people were still claiming that Tioni was the only one who had been...she shuddered in distaste, hesitating to say the word even in her head...murdered. She could not ask the Ka or Kai about it either, as etiquette required one of them to bring the matter up first, in a delicate way.

Rieda's eyebrows creased in a faint frown, as she inwardly cried out against the unfairness. She was supposed to be the heir to the throne, yet nobody told her anything, nobody would talk to her properly. Until she was actually crowned Kai she had no more power than any of her other sisters. She was so concerned about the fate of her country...but that was melodramatic. Still, she needed to know what was going on. After all, she was going to be Kai one day.

Biting her lip, she thought about talking to one of her sisters. The one that was left, anyway. She shook her head, perplexed. Verda was gone, and she was the only one that Rieda could really talk to. With a sudden, cold shock, she realised that Destinariae was the only sibling she had left in the palace. I had six sisters, who I thought I was close to, she thought, mentally reeling, but it has taken me weeks to actually realise that they are gone.

Tired of doing nothing, the Kaji walked over to the window. Unconsciously her fists clenched...there must be something she could do! Turning her thoughts back to Destinariae, she briefly wondered why she was not that close with her. They were quite close in age. She shrugged it off; it was probably too late to do anything now anyway. Sighing once again, she returned to her seat, and took up her needlework. Grief constricted her throat, and she swallowed, remembering her baby sister Efaerin's happy gurgle, the way she smiled. Anger surged through her. How dare somebody do this to the Royal Family? To *my* family, Rieda thought furiously, struggling to keep vengeful, frightened tears from betraying her true feelings to the women she had almost forgotten about.

Then a sobering thought struck her, and her rage vanished. As the heir, she was the most likely target for assassination. Why had the others been killed first? They were not destined for the Imperial throne, so surely they were not threats to any would-be conqueror's plan. She thought it over logically, and the answer came to her quick mind as it always did. If she died then Verda would just take over, then Destinariae, and so on. The deaths of the younger Kajis meant that Rieda, and the throne, were becoming more and more vulnerable.

Rieda bit her lip as her needle ploughed feverishly through the silk. It was almost a good thing that Verda had left the palace, she mused; anywhere away from the Palace was probably safer than staying in the confining death-trap. Putting the needle aside, she cut off the thread with a small ivory knife. The safety of the Imperial Palace had turned into a killing ground. Everyone knew that the Royals were cooped up here, ready to be disposed off when the need arose. The perpetrator or perpetrators of these heinous crimes could just pick them off one by one at their leisure, confident that the Ka wouldn't chance moving the family anywhere.

Her thoughts moving swiftly now, she calculated with growing anxiety that as Verda was absent, and Rieda herself heavily guarded, Destinariae was obviously going to be the next victim. After all, her sister had survived assassination attempts already, but one could only be protected by sweet Lady Luck for so long. At this point she very nearly cried, but she pinched herself fiercely until the moment passed. She must be strong! Why, she cried despairingly inside her head, why this? Quickly, she regained her poise and followed her last train of thought. Her sister must be guarded, protected. Purposefully, she set her mind to the task, determined to keep her last family members alive. Now to tell the Ka, she thought with grim determination.

Reaching down, Rieda picked up her finished garment, realising that she had unconsciously been twisting and knotting it in her hands while she deliberated. Now she stared at it in blank horror.

The silken scarf had become a noose.

*   *   *

Hot ground. Tired limbs. Stench of humans. Clear smell of hated one. Claws worn down. Scent of river. Thirst. Hide self. Sound of hunt-bird, no danger. Smell of small furry, no danger. Area clear, go slowly to edge. Drink water. Cold. Muddy taste. No thirst, start running. Pick up scent. Still strong. No hunger. Ate water-buffalo before. Fat and juicy. Smell long slitherer; enemy. Stop running. Dead slitherer. Run again. Hunger. No food hunger; kill hunger.

*   *   *

Above the leafy expanse of Siannorel Forest, a dark shape flew elegantly, unencumbered even by three riders. Touching down on the forest floor, Zakrivath bent forward and lowered his wings to allow the two girls to climb off him. He jerked forward teasingly when it was Kethar's turn so that his rider fell off.

'Zak!' thought Kethar mock indignantly, trying not to laugh. He patted the soft head lovingly, and turned to face the others. No one spoke.

Ionté, still dazed from her near burning and dark people, and surprised more by their winged rescuers, was desperately trying not to cry from exhaustion, bewilderment, and aftermath of fear.

Kadira, angry with Shakna and grateful to those who were her salvation, was wondering whether to ask them their names or comfort and question Ionté.

Kethar, having doubts about whether he had made the right decision or had freed two murderers, was unsure if the girls knew each other and how they would react to himself and Zak.

Zakrivath was wondering why the three humans were not talking, and hoping that the two newcomers liked fish.

Suddenly they all burst out laughing, the only thing they could do with the mixed thoughts and emotions that were crowding their minds. Kethar mentally heard Zak's, *What is so funny?*, and this just made him laugh even harder.

When they had all quietened down, Kethar gestured for them all to sit down. "I'll start, shall I?" he asked jovially, trying to ignore Zakrivath's mental comments. "Let's do names first. I'm Kethar. And you are...?" he looked inquiringly at Kadira.

"I'm Kadira."

They both looked expectantly at the other.

"And I'm Ionté," she whispered shyly.

Kadira turned to the half-albino. "What a gorgeous name! It's so beautiful!"

As Ionté blushed her thanks, Kethar mentally remarked to Zak, 'Much like the rest of her then, isn't it?'

The shikara sent pleased thoughts back, commenting on how he thought she was very pretty.

Kethar intervened on Ionté's behalf. "I'm from Lyvilan. Kadira?"

She smiled wanly. "Kanako."

"However did you get here? Kanako is ages away, isn't it?"

"Stories later, Kethar," she smiled, waggling a finger at him. "Where are you from, Ionté?"

"Garoto." When the others turned still blank faces towards her, she added shyly, "It's...far north of here. It must be very far, since you all have..." Her soft voice trailed off. "I'm sorry," she mumbled, "I don't want to be rude, but you're all so...dark."

Kadira started talking to fill the silence. "We should really know one another's backgrounds." She wanted to say this quickly, to get it off her chest. "My family all died in a fire at my village. I've been travelling with a group of good-for-nothing bandits cum mercenaries for the past year, and have recently entered the service of a female criminal mastermind who is as nasty as they come. Okay, who's next?" she asked brightly, letting out a bright peal of laughter at the expressions on the faces of the other two.

Kethar swallowed his surprise at the bizarre story, and took his turn. "My family gave me away when I was a child to be a servant, I used to serve one of the Royal Family, and then I met Zakrivath, my best friend in all the world, who is that warm feathery thing you're leaning against."

It was Kethar's turn to laugh as Kadira, with a startled oath and an apology, whirled around. Seeing only a wall of black feathers, her gaze travelled up until she stared into the fierce golden eyes of Zakrivath. It pleased Kethar greatly that Kadira neither flinched nor screamed when looking up at a head, beak included, larger than herself.

"He's so magnificent!" she breathed, a slight tremble in her voice.

"He says, 'Thank you, and you are very pretty', Kadira, " said Kethar, chuckling slightly.

"He can understand me? He can talk?" asked Kadira, thrilled.

"Of course. With a head that size, he should be mentally equipped. We speak telepathically. In here, " he said, tapping his forehead at her quizzical expression. "You can touch him, if you want. He won't mind."

With a trembling hand, Kadira reached towards Zakrivath. He lowered his head with some difficulty, and ecstatic, she laid her hand on the soft feathers and laughed shakily. Suddenly she withdrew her arm, causing Zakrivath to back away slightly in alarm. "He talked to me! In my head! He told me to stroke slightly higher!"

Kethar shrugged. "You'd better do it then. But I warn you, do it for too long and he won't let you stop."

More confidently, Kadira stroked the soft ebony feathers. She laughed out loud at the sheer joy of it, and patted the colossal bird like Kethar had earlier.

I like this one, Zak remarked to his soulmate, *she strokes nicely.*

Remembering the other member of the group, Kadira turned to Ionté, sitting very still and staring wide-eyed at the shikara. Kadira touched her arm gently. "Do all your family live in Garoto? Are they all albinos too?"

To Kadira's guilty discomfort, Ionté burst into tears. "I don't know where they are now," she sobbed wildly, "but that awful man said that there'd been others killed along the way, in racial demonstrations."

As Kadira took her crying new friend off to comfort her, Kethar turned to his soulmate. 'Well, Zak, they seem nice enough, don't they?' he asked mentally.

Yes. I like them both. We also found out about some evil woman, a number of racial demonstrations, but…we still have to find out if they like fish!

*   *   *

From outside the expansive structure, only a faint murmuring was audible. The newly constructed concert hall stood unconcerned, its solid stone walls muffling the almost overwhelming noise inside. The Ka, closely followed by ten Kajarito, strode forwards to come before the large oaken doors. Two servants immediately sprang out, and pulled back the heavy doors by their gold-plated handles. As he slowly made his stately way into the view of the crowd, a hushed silence swept like a wave throughout the hall.

Smiling slightly to himself, the Ka made his steps measured, deliberate. It was important that he create the right impression. After all, this was the Kai Tifiert's Birthday, and the hall was his personal gift to her; everything had to be perfect. As he stopped at the Royal Box, the audience bowed, giving the effect of a ripple spreading gently across the surface of a pool. After he had assured himself of everybody's respect, he bade them rise with a wave of his jewel-bedecked hand. He then gracefully descended into his padded seat.

Settling himself comfortably, he glanced surreptitiously sideways at Destinariae, seated sedately on his left. Dressed in an azure blue robe, edged with ornate silver embroidery, she was elegant and lovely as always. Aware of his scrutiny, his sixteen year old daughter looked back at him, and her lush red lips twitched into a smile.

With a discreet wink he turned to Rieda, sitting on his right. Her face was pale but beautiful still, and it reflected the serenity that he was far from feeling. Although…was that a note of apprehension he detected from her constant hand wringing? No, it was probably just his anxious mind playing tricks. Rieda's slender figure was outlined in a long gown of shimmering white and gold, and her blonde head was garlanded with a coronet of open lilies. Her gaze was firmly fixed upon the square aperture on the stage that Tifiert was to ascend from.

It was an ingenious plan, the Ka mused, wrought by himself, Tifiert, and the Royal Carpenters. To make her birthday speech, officially opening her birthday present, the Kai was to be raised from under the stage on a moving platform, so she would apparently appear from nowhere. Even now he could see the rope that would raise the wooden scaffold. He hoped that it was not as obvious to the others in the audience.

The sculptors had done a good job on the interior, he noticed as his gaze wandered up to the cream and gold panels. The panels were separated by long interconnecting mahogany beams, wonderfully carved in the shape of flowers, fruit and leaves. His only grievance was that, as the carvings were not painted but left their natural rich brown, they looked to him unfinished. But then he shrugged, remembering Tifiert's insistence that the colourings be to her precise taste. If she was happy, and the people were happy, that was good enough for him.

A burst of enthusiastic applause greeted the fanfare of trumpets that announced the start of the evening's entertainment. "The Kai Tifiert!" proclaimed the Royal Herald.

There was a puzzled silence as no stately figure appeared through the velour curtains at the back of the stage. The Ka chuckled at their ignorance, and in anticipation of the evening to come. He saw the rope go taught and start to inch lazily upwards. He swallowed convulsively, unable to escape the tension that filled the massive expanse of the concert hall. The top of the Kai's head started to appear, and everyone exhaled loudly and started to applaud in appreciation of the clever stunt. Tifiert's face was pallid, but reflected a wonderful peace.

Only when she was half-way out of the orifice did the Ka notice the rope, twining like a sinuous serpent about her slender neck.

Chapter 13

In the palace, at a window overlooking the city, a young lady was sitting. Her mood was pensive, though her mind was not focusing on any particular events. This was surprising, as she had many to ponder on. She was contemplating the view before her. The city that seemed so colossal and overwhelming from inside seemed reduced and dormant, like an intricate model somehow brought to life. It would have, she supposed, the opposite effect from below. The palace must seem immense.

She shook her head gently, a wry smile upon her newly painted lips. A fine thing it was for a Kaji at this crucial period of time to have so much time on her hands. She was just idly pondering meaningless matters with no importance at all, whiling away the minutes and hours before the next report of a disaster. With a minute sigh, she turned away from the remarkable scene. As she moved around, the light from the open window caught on the surface of the

236

mirror, causing her to stop and gaze into its polished surface.

An almost flawless face stared back at her, mocking her with its ivory skin and perfect features. The chestnut brown eyes widened, sweeping the abundant lashes upward even as the full red mouth twitched in dissatisfaction. This, Destinariae supposed, was the reason for one of her most annoying problems. But now, with the numbers of Royal dead mounting and the seemingly imminent collapse of the once nine strong family, Rieda was attracting most of the suitors. Which was just as well, Destinariae reflected, brushing a lock of silky hair back behind her ear, as I'm running out of civil ways to say no.

The ripe mouth twitched into a taunting pout, and Destinariae's attention was once more drawn to the face in the mirror. But a bit of hardness around the eyes surprised her, and she raised her hands to run her fingers over the smooth skin. Then she shrugged, letting her arms fall to her sides. It was probably something to do with the stress of recent events.

Firmly, she drew her thoughts away from the drawbacks of life as a Kaji. It made her a little tense, and she needed to be calm at this period of time. With so much happening, she needed to be in top form, and prepared for anything. Life was moving so fast, now, with more excitement than she could have ever imagined. But she was not quite sure if she liked the kind of excitement she was getting.

She frowned, remembering the close assassination attempt. The indignity of it! Just when she had been mourning the deaths of her sisters, somebody had tried to kill her. And it was not so much that somebody had attempted to do it that stung, but that she had been almost helpless to defend herself. It had shaken her, how her safe haven had offered her no protection, and how she was ill prepared to deal with it. She had only just escaped, too. If those Kajarito guards had not come to investigate…she quickly switched her mind away from that train of thought.

Try as she might, Destinariae could focus on nothing but the morbid events of the recent past. To try and clear her mind, she determined to visit her grief-stricken father, to try and comfort him. She pushed open the hefty oak door, so much like all the others in the palace, and walked forward a few steps, letting her retinue fall into line around her. Strolling down the Red Corridor, with her hindering ladies-in-waiting and guards a few paces in front and behind, she made slow progress to her father's study. While she waited for the guards to announce her presence, her gaze focused briefly on the doors in front of her. At first the ornate carvings seemed only to be a swirling pattern of flowers and ribbons, but then an outline revealed itself to her.

When she recognised the creature, the tiger seemed to leap out from the tangle of vegetation, its tail knotting around the vines while wreaths of wildflowers cloaked its deadly, heavy paws. Its eyes stared out at her, huge and burning, from the undergrowth, intensely fierce and intelligent. How fitting, Destinariae thought, that it should adorn my father's door. He was like a great brooding cat himself, intellectual and elegant, but truly dangerous if the need arose. Then the pattern swung inward away from her and she walked quickly inside, hearing the murmur of the retinue cut off abruptly behind her with the bang of the doors.

The Ka ran to her, and embraced her tightly. She could feel his relief at her presence in the intensity of the hug, and knew how worried he must be. He held her tightly, knowing this was the one place his weakness would not be displayed to any others.

When at last they drew apart, she traced with her finger the deep sorrow lines that creased his ageing face. She was sure they had not been there a few weeks ago. There were small but noticeable creases at the top of his straight nose too, where he had been frowning too much. Even a lifetime of appearing hard and strong to the world could not help him hide his grief from her.

When she felt that he had composed himself, Destinariae asked softly, "What are you going to do?"

Her father slowly shook his balding head. "I... haven't been able to think properly for a while. There are so many scrolls coming in from those infuriating lords, asking me if I was taking another wife, if they could provide one of their daughters or nieces, if the Empire was really collapsing...it's just hard to breathe. Also, some scrolls come in that are bizarre, but are a total waste of my time. I feel swamped." He looked quizzically at her, as if measuring her up for something. "Here, take a look at this one."

He walked to his desk, and withdrew a short piece of parchment from an elaborately patterned draw. Holding it out to her, he paced back and forth as she read. When she put it down, he raised an eyebrow at her.

"Well, from what I understand from this, there seems to be some…demonic bird that's been raiding the villages...sorry, village of Siannorel. Lord Umbrador seems to think that the villagers are scared of it and some kind of…sorcerer or something that controls it." Destinariae looked up at her father, wondering if she had understood the civil, flattering, not very concise content.

His smile was interested. "What do you personally think of it?"

"I think it sounds like the poor villagers have seen some kind of shadow, and a clever thief has played on their fears while stealing from them. What do you think?"

The Ka chuckled at the pert question. "I think it's nice to have a change from reading about political problems, Tifiert."

Destinariae looked at him strangely. "I'm sorry?"

"I said, it's nice to have a change from reading political letters, Destinariae."

It's getting to him, Destinariae thought worriedly, all the stress is finally getting to him. Obviously he is still mourning Tifiert, and staying awake all night; every night is driving him mad. Smiling gently with a serenity she did not feel, she kissed him good-night and walked quickly out of the room. The ruler of the Bakarnian Empire watched her go, and his mind sank back down into its pit of turmoil.

*   *   *

The old man's thinning hair is as white as unbroken snow, yet the mind that lurks within is far from senile. The mentality that once belonged to a great, proud man is still the same as before, but hidden inside the aged shell of the mage's body.

As he watches Sirenthe work on his magical skills, the elderly man smiles somewhat sadly. The boy is coming along wonderfully, he thinks proudly. Sirenthe has learned more in his three months of teaching than he himself had in two years of studying. He watches as the albino's face turns beautifully serene and the pale lips move, forming the word, "Aerthen." At this word, from the bare patch of ground in front of the kneeling figure rises a slender flower, leaves extending from their crumpled state and buds bursting open to reveal delicate, pale petals. Sirenthe's face lights up, and he leans forward to inhale the sweet fragrance, delighting in the beauty of creation.

He does show great promise, does he not?

The old mage whirls around to hide his face from the boy. 'Master...I did not sense you.'

Erendiir, you must be getting old.

Catching the faint amusement in the God's tone, Erendiir feels a pang of sadness, but suppresses it as he has learned to do throughout his life. Cautiously, careful to play down the boy's talent, he answers, 'He is unlike anyone I have ever encountered. But I fear for his future, Master. I know how difficult it is to suppress the knowledge that you have leaned, when working so hard for it.'

You found it particularly hard, didn't you?

'If I had not, would I be your disciple?' he counters swiftly, catching the subtle sense of annoyance that tinges the God's reply and wincing as the mighty pressure on his mind swamps him with emotion amplified a million-fold.

Be cautious, Erendiir. There is a limit to my patience. I may yet seek a new disciple soon, for I have found a suitable candidate.

Erendiir feels his Master's focus sweep across to the kneeling albino, and cries out mentally, 'Do not take him, Master! He is strong, but has yet to learn self-discipline! If you take him, he may lose control of his powers!'

Or do you mean you will lose control of him?

'He will think that he has a chance to use his wondrous powers for good, and unleash them as he thinks will benefit others. On your side!'

Are you then saying that you are on the wrong side? But no, you will not lose him, for he made an oath to you, did he not? That Sirenthe would stay until his training was complete?

Erendiir's eyes are drawn back to the figure of his pupil, and he hears the word "Vitaal." Water flows from Sirenthe's outstretched fingertips, and flows into the earth around the stem of the pale plant.

'Yes, he made an oath, but though I am sure he will not break it I am not sure that I trust you not to help him find a loophole in it, Master!'

This is just because you are afraid. Afraid of being replaced as my disciple. Erendiir, your powers are great, much more so than his, but you are five hundred and eighty years old and he is sixteen! If he deposes you as my disciple, you will die.

'Please, Eternity, Master, do not take him for your disciple. For I do not want to see him go through what I had to. I would be happy to rest after these many long years, but I would stay for a thousand aeons more if it meant he was spared!"

I make no promises to you, Erendiir, except this; if you so much as align him against the Circle...then much more than your life and his will be forfeit.

* * *

Five days after the death of the Kai, the city was in mourning, by order of the Ka. The predominant colour was black. Black banners, black clothes, and even black ravens, which were released from high windows in the palace. Black flags flapped feebly from erect poles, helpless against the onrushing current of air. Indeed, the whole scene was gloomy, if a little monotonous. The Kajarito were in ceremonial regalia, which was, of course, black. A stranger might think that this was excessive, but the inhabitants of the city knew that the Ka mourned not only his wife, but also four of his daughters. For the most part, they were sympathetic. But the atmosphere mostly contained not sadness, but fear. With the weakening of the Royal family, Bakarn was ripe for invasion. So while the people of Lyvilan paid their respects, their minds dwelt on their own safety.

In the Royal Graveyard, the mighty ruler himself was seated on a bench, head in hands. The events of the past year, and the previous Kai's death, had taken their toll on the once proud and handsome man. Deep lines had appeared on his face where they had not been before, there were bags under his eyes from lack of sleep, and even when dressed in his impressive robes he had a haggard look about him. However, what had unnerved nobles and servants alike the most was the look of intense agony in his deeply sunken eyes.

He walked over to the elaborate gravestones of his beloved wives, thinking of Isete. Over sixteen years and he still missed her, heard her voice in his head. Still, he thought encouragingly, I've got Tifiert now. Hearing her call his name, he smiled fondly. Maybe she had thought up another of her ingenious schemes. Turning, his gaze found a grey headstone, and his face fell. The bold lettering imprinted itself in his mind, burning his eyes. Tears flowed for what seemed like the hundredth time as he read the coldly mocking words.

'*In memory of our beloved Kai Tifiert, cruelly taken from us in her twenty-ninth year, a devoted wife and mother. She will be lamented forever.*'

Down on his hands and knees, the grieving man wept as if his heart would break. This was, however, impossible, he thought, his sobs coming out as choked gasps. It was already wrenched in half.

When he had shed as many tears as his body would allow, the Ka rose unsteadily to his feet. Looking down at the place where he had knelt, he thought it mournfully fitting that the sombre lilies were watered by the salty droplets, symbolic of his grief.

Too overcome by sorrow to stare any longer at the stark gravestones, he walked shakily over to a nearby water fountain and stared at his reflection. A mainly brown face looked back, with bloodshot eyes and wet streaks where tears had left their damp tracks. Resolutely, he splashed his face with the ice-cold water, and walked more steadily back to the bench and sat down.

Before his coronation, the Ka had been known as the Kajo Turanis. It was strange, he often thought, how he was rarely ever called that now. Actually, since his wife died there was nobody who knew, or at least called him by his real name, except perhaps for the historian if he ever bothered to look at his dusty old records.

Drawing in a shuddering breath, Turanis walked over to the graves of his four dead children. There was also a blank one in case there was news of Verda's death. Though he knew her to be safe at Lord Atisato's, the stark stone monument's blank face helped the pretence. Is that all my family are to me, thought Turanis with a sudden urge of bitterness, objects to be manipulated in my plots? Staring at the gravestones again, he felt tears again begin to burn at the edges of his eyes. My poor, poor children, he thought sadly, so beautiful and so undeserving of their tragic fate. He sighed then, and turned his back on the unsettling scene.

His gaze fell upon the squad of Kajarito who waited loyally under the eaves, their faces void of any emotion. They suddenly realise I have feelings, Turanis thought. With a sudden shock, he recovered himself. What have I been doing, he wondered, shaking his greying head. I am the Ka, yet I was snivelling on the floor like any peasant woman. This is below me! And with that he strode towards the palace, signalling to the Kajarito to accompany him.

When he reached the Royal apartments, the Ka heard a small voice within his chamber. His heart hammering in his chest, he burst through the double doors and saw Chova, one of his favourite daughters. She smiled and walked towards him... but that was all wrong! Chova was dead...wasn't she? Her lower lip trembled. "Father?" she called, holding out her hands. With a start he saw that she was covered in blood. "Father, they have killed me!"

As he choked back a cry of horror, the wavering image disappeared.

Firmly, Turanis shook his head. You're deluding yourself, old man, he said to himself sternly despite his racing pulse, your wives are both dead and so is Chova. If you don't get a grip on yourself then you will slip into complete insanity! He shuddered, not daring to think what the results of *that* would be.

Once he was thinking as clearly as possible, he started to review the current situation regarding the assassinations. So well timed and fluidly executed were they that the Ka was starting to suspect one of the Lords- not one of the lesser ones, though. They had not got the intelligence or the ingenuity for such a criminal masterpiece. Perhaps the suave Lord Maxirant, for surely his high position had induced a craving for power. And he would have the money and resources to implement such a plot. The fairly young, wealthy lord had presented himself as a suitor for Rieda's hand. If he was to marry her, then kill off Turanis, Maxirant would be the new Ka.

But then, he reasoned, why kill the younger Kajis? Surely they would be no threat to him. Well, perhaps another lord...Atisato, for instance, was an intelligent and astute ruler. Maybe he had designs on the throne...

Yet...no. Atisato had given his support for years, and always paid his taxes on time. Unlike some others he could care to mention. Besides, the Lord was without an heir, so he would be in a more vulnerable position as Ka than he was at the moment. Added to this was the fact that he was sheltering Verda himself. Or had Turanis made a dreadful mistake, handing Verda over to him?

Maybe some other Lords had banded together in a united effort to overthrow him. He pondered this for a while, but again it produced a negative result. Those pathetic layabouts could barely stay in the presence of each other for more than a minute without regressing into spiteful bickering, let alone unite long enough to try to usurp the throne. No, he thought grimly to himself, it would have to be a man with the attributes of royalty to pull it off. Or, he thought with sudden inspiration, an extremely ambitious woman.

He searched his mind for possible candidates. It would have to be a woman with enough power to accomplish something of this scale, and she would have to be intelligent. But a woman would legally not be permitted to run the estate of a lord, so that narrowed the choice down considerably. Perhaps the sly Lady Diaran, wife of Lord Haruas of Odycum, who was rumoured to run an illegal trade of precious gems and information with anonymous customers in Garoa. Or perhaps Lady Poricala, the half-sister of the ancient Lord Thambar, who minded Thermone for the aged lord. She was a determined, middle aged woman, with the right breeding and leadership qualities that would be need by the usurper. And, he remembered with a cold shudder, Poricala's mother had been Turanis' own sister, Leicette; so she had Royal blood. Or maybe it was someone else; somebody, perhaps, from his past...

A powerful image flashed into his brain; a look of pure loathing, some twenty years or so ago. There had been one that hated, nay, despised him. A young Tsumetai...

The Ka's blood chilled suddenly, remembering a casual bow from a middle-aged man about a year ago. A dark-haired, powerfully built, well-dressed man who had introduced himself as the Tsumetai Viper...at the time he had had a fleeting idea that he knew him, but had dismissed it. Surely the battle-hardened Viper could not be the same young, overconfident man that had once served under Turanis in the early Kajarito all those years ago? Surely it could not be...Eskiros?

He would have to look into the matter immediately. Having an accomplished Tsumetai stalking him and his family changed everything. How far would Viper's revenge be taken? The Gods knew he had the skill and the wealth, being Tsumetai, to kill every last one on a whim. The thought made the Ka's mentality recoil in dread. Perhaps he should first talk to Rieda, ensure her safety and cooperation; she was more intelligent than he had realised, and may have ideas of her own as to the perpetrator of the deeds. And in a year's time, he might not even have her to talk to. He might be single and without an heir...he dragged his thoughts away from analysis of that terrible, but possible, situation. If only Tifiert was here, she would surely comfort him. As he pictured again the forbidding graves within his tortured mind, the scene altered, and he was then looking upon his own.

* * *

There is a bond between a torturer and his victim. A special bond formed of pain, malice, control, power, and enjoyment. The air is still and thick with tension; the hearts of both people beat strong together, and red blood stirs the senses; with its heavy metallic smell, and its wet, sweet flavour. Amongst the sweet screams and primal groans, the torturer's sinister art draws the human form through white-hot lines of fire to its agonised limit. The bodies of torturer and victim await a climax, where fear and agony are brought to the very edge...until pain is no longer the issue.

Blinded by the searing sting of the red-hot knife, the man convulsed, and then steadied again as the torturer advanced on him. The man's fear grew, and he squirmed in his bonds, watching the knife that the tormentor twirled idly in his fingers. The metal spun slowly, and the victim's eyes followed its every spin. The torturer came forward again, and took up another knife, the dulled blade and the shining one flicking about each other.

Transferring both knives to one hand, the heavy-set man casually twisted each weapon about his fingers. Faster and faster they whirled, capturing the eyes of the prisoner as he watched in terrified fascination. The man's awe suddenly tuned to agony as the dulled knife was sliced across his chest, opening yet another gash on his wounded skin. His sweating face contorted, and he clenched his teeth yet again, but it gave him no respite from the pain.

"Tell me of your master!" commanded the tormentor evenly. "I can make you experience a world of agony, but can keep you alive for...up to a week, if you persist in this annoying silence." He took the knife from his victim's flesh, and cleaned it upon a rag, before lifting the captive's foot and gesturing with the knife. "I can cut you up from the bottom up, so you can watch!" He sliced off the smallest toe, and pricked the next one with the knife-tip.

Thankfully, the man fainted, taking him far from his suffering for a moment. But he was awakened by the cool kiss of steel on his thigh. He looked with fear and hatred up into the face of his tormentor, and his bowels loosened in terror.

The face so close to his own was not leering, triumphant, and did not even seem to be relishing in the torture. Instead it was bland, and bored, and that somehow was more disturbing than enjoyment. "I can stop you doing that ever again, you know," he remonstrated mildly, pressing the knife against the prisoner's groin.

The man screamed at last, and the torturer smiled. Now he was getting somewhere. Humming softly to himself, he sliced some of the skin off the man's ribs. "Are you ready to talk now?" he asked, cracking his knuckles.

The man glared at him. " I will not betray my mistress! She will become the new Kai!"

The other smiled. This was the bit of the job that he liked. "Oh, so it's a woman you serve?"

The man fell silent, cursing his own stupidity. The other grinned; he would cause further discomfort by not revealing that he knew that piece of information already. But the grin faded. It was more information he wanted, for his investigations had not been extremely successful. He went on.

"I could always bring in the hounds. They would like a meal, the voracious beasts." At the man's look of vague incomprehension he sighed. They were all so similar; imbecilic, but loyal to the bone. "I see I am going to have to spell this out for you. Outside are

251

three ravenous hounds. They love meat, and blood. You are the nearest available pile of meat and blood." The man's face gained a look of sudden terrified comprehension.

The torturer nodded approvingly. "Ah, I see that you understand. They will eat you from the feet upwards. Hopefully you might still be alive when they get to your face." He stopped, and drew out a long metal pin from a supple leather sheath on the small table to the side. He poked it experimentally at the captive's ribs, and then pushed it between two of them, slowly enough to make his victim gasp with pain. He was very careful not to pierce any major organ. I could make this one last for days, he thought, and his eyes closed in pleasure as he withdrew the pin and felt rather than heard the agonised cry shudder through the man's frame. With a few breaths, unsteady with anticipation, Eskiros leaned in close, close enough to smell the sweat and blood and pain and fear, and whispered, "Scream for me." Then he plunged the pin sharply into the man's flesh. As the sobbing man screamed and arched his back in torturous agony, Eskiros' head lolled back in sweet pleasure, before straightening himself with a satisfied smile.

"I could remove your spleen, you know," he continued idly, wiggling the pin around. "You can live just fine without it. But, oh, what a shame! I seem to have run out of my anaesthetic! Never mind. Maybe I'll do that later." He left the pin in, and fetched a few small scalpels, and another five of the wickedly sharp pins. He took a pin in each hand, and closed his fists over them. Holding them in front of the prisoner's face, he asked playfully, "Right or left?"

The captive, knowing that refusal to play the deadly game could result in a worse torture, merely whispered, "Left."

"Wrong choice," grinned the other man, opening his fist. He displayed the pin he held there; one not straight like the others, but jagged, with sharp spikes protruding from it. The tortured man groaned, then screamed as the aforementioned pin was pushed into his body.

The other man cut at the skin with the scalpels, then left them embedded in the flesh. He was about to insert another jagged pin, when he noticed that his victim was unconscious. Swearing under his breath, he stood, and wiped his bloody hands on a rag before exiting the cell. He locked and bolted the door, and checked it securely.

He stood for a moment, closing his eyes and reliving the sweet screams of his victim. This was where true power lay. He raised his hands to his face and inhaled the heady scent of blood, and saw in his mind the man's arched back and his own words; "Scream for me." He realised with disturbed shock that he was more aroused by torture than he was by the best whores one could find in Lyvilan. Standing awkwardly for a moment, Eskiros struggled to regain control of his breathing.

Annoyed at how little information had been extracted from the one-time soldier, Eskiros then strode away down the underground corridors. He needed to know more information. He had got nowhere with his finding out about QesAngared. This man, he knew, was another of her agents, like himself, but less important.

How did she breed such loyalty in her soldiers? He had loyalty for none but himself. If he had some sense of honour, he would not have become a rogue Tsumetai.

He sighed, settling himself on a bench. Growing up under the near-impossible Tsumetai regime, the young Eskiros had learnt well and quickly, and had mastered the mortal weapons. He had trained under the finest of the Tsumetai- Shark, Falcon, Lioness, and of course his main mentor, Viper. He had been taught the code of the Tsumetai; to honour one's master, friend, enemy, and self. He knew that there were thirteen Tsumetai, no more, no less, and only when one was killed in combat with his predecessor could another take the place. But, though an expert swordsman, the youth had yet to master the magic arts of the Tsumetai. He could simply not access them. And so he did not have his own unique weapon, like the others did, so he had to remain content with being a superb human rather than a Tsumetai.

But how he had longed for his own weapon! He had seen the other young ones fight for and win their places; Falcon, Mole, Bat, and Butterfly, and he had congratulated them, but his heart had ached with envy for their new weapons. Falcon had his 'beak', a blade across the top of his head, fastened to the skin. Mole had his claws, fitted on gauntlets that came to his hands. Bat had his wings, which he could furl around himself to render him invisible in darkness. And Butterfly, his own beautiful Butterfly, had her poison spikes fitted. But he, Eskiros, had to stay behind as his old friends left in search of employment. They would be hired as infallible bodyguards, or as expert assassins.

Eskiros sighed, letting his hand fall to the belt of blades that he carried constantly. They had taken pity on him in the end, without magic, rank or his friends. After killing the old Viper on the floor of the Trial Arena, Eskiros had won his mentor's place. They had let him try the poison-teeth, but without any limited magic he could not successfully become accustomed to them. And so the new Viper had sworn his oaths as a Tsumetai and left in search of fame and fortune.

Ah, but those had been good days. The young Viper travelled afar, growing ever more experienced and proficient with weapons, but something had always held him back. Eskiros knew that, now. He had always been troubled with his failure of the Viper's teeth, and the knowledge of his failure haunted him continually, taunting, mocking, jeering. But Viper had seen his problem only as a lack of proper chance to prove himself, and so had entered service as one of the Kajarito.

He hissed to himself, remembering the hellish year he had spent spying in service to the Ka. Used to training under the Tsumetai, Viper had been whipped for disobeying orders, rather than praised for using his initiative. The Ka had overseen the orders of the Kajarito, and Eskiros, the Tsumetai Viper, had been ordered around by everyone. They did not know of his background; a Tsumetai would be unable to join the ranks of the Kajarito. He had especially hated the twenty year old captain, the Kajo who was in charge over fully half the Kajarito, as their main commander.

But he had paid them back. He had left the Ka's service, and had hunted down all the people who had ordered him around, flogged him, or ridiculed him in any way. Now they all lay dead, their corpses a tribute to his own greatness.

But there was one main enemy who still lived, apart from a few surviving Kajarito. One who had perhaps forgotten the young Kajarito Viper. But Viper had not forgotten him, oh no. That's why I joined QesAngared in the first place, Eskiros reminded himself. To get my revenge upon the Ka Turanis!

* * *

"Look out!" yelled Kethar as a dark shape glided in low over their heads, to settle like a swan on the flat pond. Looking towards the girls, he gave a great shout of laughter as he saw their scare. Ionté looked frankly bewildered, and Kadira was just angry as she realised the joke was on them. Still laughing, Kethar walked smartly to the edge of the large pond, and saluted playfully to Zakrivath as the black shikara paddled toward him. Turning his back on his friend, he grinned at the irate girls.

"C'mon, tell me that wasn't the least bit amusing! Your two faces! As if my Zaki would do anything to hurt you."

Suddenly a huge, dripping wing buffeted him from his feet, and pushed him into the pond. Rising to the surface, Kethar gaped at Zakrivath, who was primly settling himself in the dry grass at the side of the pond.

Of course your Zaki wouldn't do anything to hurt them, but it is pleasing to make you take a bath every now and again to quench that smell you give off!

Kadira squealed with laughter. "Your face! Honestly, Kethar, now *that* was funny!"

At Kethar's jokingly fierce scowl, Ionté joined the joke. Curtsying elegantly to Zakrivath, she put her hand to her mouth in mock surprise. "Oh, Kethar! You seem to be slightly damp! Maybe 'your Zaki' can help you dry off!"

Kethar, clambering up the bank, was suddenly drenched further by Zakrivath, shaking his bedraggled wings all over him. The girls screeched as the water soaked them too, and all three ran, laughing, to escape the shikara's justice. Kethar was the only one who heard the muttered, *Your Zaki, indeed. I might as well call you my Kethie-wethie.*

Drying off, the trio sat down together on the bank, Kethar leaning against his soulmate's sable chest-feathers. Kadira took off her sandal, and dangled her toe in the water. She sighed blissfully, then giggled as the others did exactly the same.

"Nobody's hungry, are they?" she asked, wanting to just lie back and relax. At the murmurs of dissent, she sighed again, and leaned back on the springy grass and rushes.

The late afternoon sun beat down on them as it continued its relentless journey toward the horizon. The sky was filled with golden clouds, and they all seemed to be...circling? As one, the watchers all sat up.

The golden clouds drew into a tight loop and circled above them, casting a ray of pure golden light down onto Kethar and Zakrivath. The humans shielded their eyes against the blinding glare, and heard a voice echo like almighty thunder from the skies.

I see the boy and his Shikara chick have grown. It is good.

Kethar stood defiantly upright, but still could not find the power of speech in the overwhelming presence of Destiny.

You are now man and Shikara. What a gift for the servant boy!

Kethar glared upwards, finding his voice at last. "Who are You calling servant boy?"
There was almost a chuckle from above.

Hold hard, little warrior. You forget yourself. You have a great gift in Zakrivath, have you not?

Kethar nodded sincerely. "That is very true. But what do You want of me? Why do You come to me like this?"

I have granted you a favour in your escape and gift, so you owe me a favour. To find the truth in my statement, only reflect on how many 'coincidences' happened for you to meet up with the newly hatched black Shikara Zakrivath. And if you are not still

convinced, think on how easy your escape was. Did it not occur to you that your fears of being recaptured were meaningless anyway?

Kethar nodded again, slowly. He did owe a debt to the God. "What favour do you ask?"

This time, there was no mistaking the laughter.

Not much, little mortal man. Only for you to save the planet.

Kethar gaped, incredulous. Before he could find any words to reply with, the God continued.

You have the means by which to defeat the evil one, the Mistress of Blood. She stands at the root of Bakarn.

Zakrivath intervened, and Kethar realised that he had not been aware of the Shikara's existence for the past two minutes.

The root of Bakarn. That could only be Lyvilan! exclaimed Zakrivath, his crest raised and wings unfurled, while his eyes gleamed red-gold with recognition of an enemy to fight.

The voice of Destiny now spoke only inside the minds of Kethar and Zakrivath.

You cannot do this alone. Find her and destroy her, before the Mistress of Blood becomes the Queen of Hell.

"Wait!" shouted Kethar, his hand outstretched towards the golden clouds that roiled in serene, silent splendour. Zakrivath shrieked to the very heavens as the sky churned back on itself, the clouds disappearing in a flash of light.

Dazed, the three humans sat down again. Silence reigned, and all three struggled to retain some semblance of proper thought.

Except Zakrivath.

Beating his immense wings, the black shikara stirred the entranced humans from their stupor as he screamed to the sky. *Then we will fly to Lyvilan!*

Some hours later, Kethar sat alone on a flat boulder. Zakrivath was away hunting, and the girls were talking quietly together as they made their separate beds. They had argued earlier, a proper argument of which they had never before seen the like. Kadira and Ionté had wanted to come to help Kethar, but he had feared for their safety, and so had wanted them to stay behind. The row had resulted in Kadira storming off, and Kethar sitting like he was now, silent and alone.

He had just decided to let the girls accompany him when a slender, pale hand clasped his own. He looked up into the ethereal features of Ionté. As usual his heart trembled at her divine beauty. She sat down on the grass opposite him, and squeezed his hand. They both turned their heads, and looked up at the night sky. The stars shone brightly against the black curve of the night, and filled them both with a gentle peace.

Ionté's voice came out of the darkness. "They seem so small, yet so much greater than us, don't they? They seem to say, we are beautiful, and you are not worthy, all at the same time. It makes you feel...so insignificant."

Kethar moved closer to her so that he could see the features of her celestial face. "If you feel like that, then just remember this. There will always be someone, somewhere, better than you. They may be more intelligent, more wealthy, or..." he lifted her chin with his free hand, "more beautiful. The stars may seem superior to us, but they are only the pins which fasten the cloak of night to the sky."

Ionté smiled back at him, then looked down quickly, tearing her head from the gentle cradle of his hand. "I...did not properly thank you for saving us." At his gesture, as if to shrug it off, she interrupted, her voice, quiet, but filled with passion. "No, let me speak. I was so...afraid, that day. I just wished that I could escape, pass out, die; anything to stop the awful torture that I was about to go through. I was going to die, die the death that I had always feared. Where I come from, fire is never underestimated, and though we had to use it to live we were always scared of it. I was terrified beyond belief; the crowds just looked on and called for my death, consumed by fire. I had given up all hope, as they made to light the kindling at my feet." She bit her lip and sobbed a little, one single tear trickling down one alabaster cheek as she remembered with terrible clarity that horrifying day. Then she looked up at him, and her voice strengthened.

"But then I saw something. A distant speck, travelling at an impossible speed from the heavens. It reared up high in the sky, blotting out the shining moon, its shadow huge as if it would come between me and the flames. That moment seemed to last forever, and I will never forget the majesty I felt humbled to witness. Then, looking hard through my tears, I made out two huge, black wings. And I thought, it has come for me, a black angel has come to save me from the terrible fire. And I knew joy."

She rose to kneel before him, and smiled that heart-wrenchingly pure smile at Kethar once more. "And so I say thank you. Thank you for the life you gave me, and thank you for the great joy that you brought me that day, and all days to come. You and your black angel."

Chapter 14

The midday sun sparkled on the still waters of the lake, causing her to look up. The reflections always seemed to her to be another world, parallel to her own, hidden beneath the mysterious crystal waters. Such things were, of course, pure moonshine, but it was nice to sit and daydream. It was so peaceful here, so soothing to trail one's fingers in the cool water, and watch the clouds go rolling past on the endless avenue of the cerulean sky.

A sudden splash made Destinariae look up. A heron catching his meal; nothing to worry about. A goldfish swam up and nibbled idly at her fingers. She removed them from the water and scattered some bread for the fishes to feed on. Immediately, a whole school of white, orange and golden carp came to feed, glints of pearl and bronze between the flourishing green rushes. Watching them, she dreamily wondered whether to bathe by the waterfall, or leave, as she should. As a compromise, she decided to stay for a while before returning to the palace.

Destinariae shifted on the grass so that her arm pillowed her head. Somewhere a bee buzzed indolently. The homely scent of mint and garden herbs filled the air. This corner of the Palace Gardens really did have a sense of timelessness, with its quiet calm and delicate fragrances that filled the air. High green hedges surrounded her on three sides, blocking her view of the Palace and giving her a sense of privacy. Butterflies, bees, even little fieldmice ran unchecked; all things to interest a bored mind. She hoped that the many gardeners didn't find out about the mice; they'd kill them all, poor things.

She thought back to the morning. She had helped Rieda put on the almost-finished wedding dress, and marvelled at how efficiently her sister's ladies-in-waiting had done the job. It was a beautiful dress, Destinariae thought dreamily, all close fitting white satin, studded with pearls, gold beads, and fringed with finest Jaharonian lace. The veil was stunning, with a new crown set with white gold and diamonds, and a gauzy, sleek veil hanging down in front and behind. She sighed. It must have cost the earth for the fabric alone.

She felt sorry for Rieda, though. Being forced into an abrupt marriage to stabilise the weakening Royalty wasn't everyone's idea of a dream wedding. But she also knew that Rieda would have to watch her back even more carefully until her marriage, for this was a ripe time for assassinations. The bridegroom, Lord Maxirant, would also have to be careful.

Not envious, are we, Destinariae? A sly voice issued from the back of her mind. No, she thought back sternly, marriage is the last thing I want. Women have so much power when they are single, and so many women didn't notice. And then they'd go and get married, and spend the rest of their lives having children and doing needlework. As if I'm envious of *that.*

But she couldn't help feeling a pang of sadness when she thought of Rieda, standing in front of the floor-length mirror, flawlessly beautiful in the spectacular gown. To deter herself from continuing in this train of thought, she sat up swiftly and called quietly, "Marghaska! Where are you?"

"Here, my lady," replied Marghaska, appearing behind her in the uncanny way he always did. Every time it startled her.

Hiding her surprise "I would like you to go to the stable and saddle my horse."

"Which one? The roan, or the bay?" he asked, his voice soft so as not to disturb the quiet tranquillity of the scene.

"Oh...the bay. Now, if you please, Marghaska."

He just looked at her for a moment, and then he was gone. She shivered. He had this strange knack of turning up silently just where he wasn't expected. He reminded her of some stealthy predator, a wolf, perhaps, or a prowling cat. But he had improved greatly from the state he had been in at the arena. He now spoke Bakarnian fluently, and sounded himself like a native. She shrugged, and stood up. Brushing off the leaves that had accumulated on her lap, she started the short walk to the stables.

It was only five minutes later that she reached her destination, her breath coming in easy bursts. Pushing open the rough wooden gate, she breathed in the bittersweet, musty odour made up of horses, leather saddles, and fresh hay. She surveyed the horses one by one. In the first large stable on the left, the mules and packhorses used for long journeys shuffled and snorted, awaiting their next task. The next stall housed her favourite riding horse, a pinkish roan, with white socked feet and a honey-coloured mane. She patted its neck, gently, and it whinnied. She liked horses; they were hard working, loyal, and could not plot, scheme, or murder, even though they had the power to kill with one hefty blow of their crushing hoofs. She gave the mare one last pat, and moved on to the next stall. Her father's favoured grey stood inside, a fine, sturdy white stallion, for indeed although she had been brought up properly to call them greys, the horse gleamed with the care that was fostered upon it. After all, thought Destinariae, he is worth more than all our other horses put together. And, she thought reflected with a twinge of jealousy, he is more handsome than the one my father gave me as a ceremonial horse.

She moved on again. The next stall housed her sister Rieda's favourite horse; a young bay, sweet-tempered and playful, for she was barely more than a filly. She passed by the rest of the Royal favourites, and came to the stalls that were for the horses of the guests. Nothing very remarkable stood inside; a chestnut mare, a silver-white colt and its dappled mother, and a tractable grey, suitable for a wealthy Lord. But as she made to continue to the next stall, Marghaska's voice warned her of the arrival of a young man. She stood facing the main door, not the small gate by which she had entered, but a large impressive archway with ceramic edging. Through it came the young Lord Anderring, son of the Lord Andrade.

Destinariae sighed inwardly; this overly persistent suitor seemed to be dogging her every move, and she found suitors tiresome. But the courtesy and honour of the Royal Family had to be upheld. Affecting a pleasant smile, she stepped lightly towards him, nodding to him as he bowed very low.

"Good morning, Lord Anderring. Have you been enjoying your stay here at the Palace?" She made sure to stress the start of 'Palace', to emphasise his luck in being invited along with his father.

"Yes, thank you, my Kaji." He was obviously trying to calm his voice, but the tremor of excitement that ran through it was duly noticed and catalogued in Destinariae's brain under 'reasons not to get involved with men'.

"I was hoping to find you…in fact, it is even better to find you here. I have brought a gift for you, a token by means to express my sincerity in seeking your favour." As he spoke, he led her gently towards four stalls at the back of the roomy complex. He walked with her past each one, commenting on the animal inside with, Destinariae noticed with some surprise, a good knowledge of horsemanship.

"This is my horse, Damor," said the young man as they passed a dark brown, sturdy-looking horse. "He was gelded recently, for with the new racing grey in we did not want his temperament to sour."

Destinariae nodded. It was a good name, translated from the old tongue as 'Thunder'. She smiled and nodded, noticing him blatantly expecting a reaction. They moved onto the next.

"This is a good mare we have brought as a gift to our regnant. She is young, but spirited, and though my father brought her for her looks, I say she has the makings of a racer." He moved aside to let her see the creature; she appraised it, and saw the truth in his statement. The horse had long, sturdy legs with shining hoofs. Her neck was long but slender and her head compact, ideal for racing. She nodded her approval. It was a fine animal.

Anderring suddenly spoke again, his voice slightly breathless. "Close your eyes, if you please, Kaji, to better see the surprise."

Close my eyes to better see? thought Destinariae, silently chuckling at the contradiction. He took her gently by the arm, and led her away from where she stood. His voice came again, by her ear, "Now look, Kaji Destinariae."

She opened her eyes. In front of her were two stalls. In one stood a huge black stallion, with rolling eyes and flashing hoofs, constantly snapping at the air and showing its teeth, or shaking its heavy mane. The stall that stood in front of her contained the most beautiful little horse. Its hair was a patchwork of brown and gold, with a white mane and tail. It had the kind of face that made one immediately wish to hug it, cosset it, and feed it sugar lumps every day. It whickered softly, and snorted.

"Oh!" Destinariae cried, speechless with delight. She turned a delighted face to Anderring. "Oh, thank you!" she cried again, and turned towards the horses. Running up to her new horse, she flung her arms around its neck.

"I'm glad you like her," sighed Anderring with relief, scuffing at the hay with his toe. "I brought the other to see if he could be tamed, for he will not…" he stopped abruptly upon seeing the horse that the Kaji embraced.

Destinariae was unaware of his astonishment. She had eyes only for the stallion that now neighed softly, letting her pat its head and fondle its coarse mane. The little mare in the next stall snickered, and hung its beautiful head. But the black stallion was placid at the Kaji's gentle touch. Anderring gaped, and staggered to the door. The sight was unnerving, no, eerily terrifying for one who had seen the now meek horse kick out a man's stomach, and bite out its sibling's throat at one week old. He croaked feebly, and then made his way ashen-faced from the stable.

Destinariae, noting the Lord's absence, called softly, "Marghaska?"

He appeared from the back of the stable, leading her bay gelding which was saddled and ready to ride. "Here, Kaji Destinariae."

She rubbed her new horse's soft nose. "Saddle this stallion instead, please. I will pace him, and see how he moves." She unfastened the catch on the half-door to the stallion's stall, and led the unresisting horse out by an arm over his slender neck. She waited while Marghaska brought over the rich-smelling saddle, and the horse rolled its eyes back and tried to snap at the newcomer. She soothed it with strokes and whispers until it stood, docile, only shifting its hoofs slightly as Marghaska adjusted the girths and stirrups and stood back, his hands cupped to help her mount. Stepping as lightly as possible on his hands, Destinariae mounted her horse, and settled her skirts at a modest angle.

"If you please, Marghaska, I would much like to be alone with my new creature, that he may get used to me. I will return within the hour. Please stay around here, so that my horse can be immediately rubbed down."

"Yes, Kaji. What will you call him?"

She paused, contemplating. "I think I shall call him…Sichan." And she rode slowly out of the door.

Marghaska stood still for a while after the Kaji had left. If he could remember the translation of the name…Sichan, Sichan…the name was similar to a word in his own language. Ah yes, that was it, 'exalted one'. A fine name for such a noble beast. He turned slowly, and walked to the bay gelding still standing aimlessly in the middle of the stable. He took its halter, noting its white-rimmed eyes, and led it back to its stall. He guided it inside, then slipped the simple bridle off its head. It shied away from him immediately. He carefully closed and latched the door, then returned the halter to the tack-room. Returning to the main stable, he noticed a new presence outside the door. Seeing no point in hiding, he stepped forward to meet the stranger who now stood in the open doorway.

"Hail, Marghaska," said the newcomer mockingly. The voice and posture were undoubtedly that of a woman, but the plain black robes gave no trace of identity. A thick veil swung down, covering everything except her eyes, which were hidden in the shadow of the cowled cloak she wore.

Marghaska inclined his head slightly. He could tell by the overbearing manner that this woman was of noble blood, and used to ordering people around, but he would not bow to someone that he did not know the name of.

Her laugh pealed out at his uncertainty. He looked up, surprised at the vaguely pretty sound. "Who are you, and what is your purpose here?" he said, his voice just short of a growl.

"Who am I? Why, I am none but myself. But I am known as QesAngared."

"And your purpose?" queried Marghaska, his mind racing. Destinariae might be in danger while this stranger stalled him. He tensed, ready to leave.

"Do not be in such a hurry to depart," she rebuked him, her voice showing a hint of a promise. She strolled casually towards him, a few smooth steps. When she stopped, five or so metres away from him, the promise still lingered in her voice. "I can give you something you desire. Something...you could use well."

"What do you know of my desires?" he asked harshly, the words ripping from his throat. His eyes narrowed warningly and a growl sounded low in his throat.

"I know something that you have never had, but seek desperately," she crooned, her hands undulating around each other in a way that made him shiver. "I can give you power beyond imagining."

He drew away, wary of the stranger. But if he could keep her talking, he reasoned, he could keep her away from his Mistress. When QesAngared's voice next came, it was strong yet caressing, as if talking to an old and trusted companion.

"If I make you this gift, will you use it to serve me? I sense greatness in you."

"I will not go to a stranger who talks nothing but fantasies and pretty promises," he warned, his face giving nothing away. He stood his ground, though his every sense warned him away, and the hairs on the back of his neck stood up despite the fact that there was no draught. He watched as the stranger's hands went inside her robe, and she drew out a crystal block containing a single golden feather. Its radiance was such that he had to narrow his eyes, and marvel at how the bright light had not shone through the woman's cloak.

QesAngared closed her eyes and hissed a few words between her teeth. The crystal's light seemed to pulsate like some primordial heartbeat, until QesAngared brought her hand up to point at Marghaska. Though she seemed unarmed, he could sense danger emanating from her gloved, pointing finger. He backed away slowly, but then her eyes snapped open as if he had struck her.

A sudden jolt of pain shot through Marghaska's head, and he winced sharply. Then his insides churned as if he was going to be sick, and all over his body came a feeling of extreme heat, as if it was bubbling and melting. He could not, would not scream, but a strangled gasp escaped his burning throat. He clawed desperately at himself, seeming to want to rip off his skin, and fell to his knees. Through the blinding courses of agony that inundated his shuddering form, he could hear only one noise; the mocking laughter of QesAngared.

Quite suddenly the pain ceased, and he fell forward to stand on all fours. His head still swam, but his vision was clear, and sharper than before. And his hearing! He could detect the voices of servants passing through the inner courtyard, the call of a frightened bird from the aviary, and the noise of Sichan's hoofs from the gardens, as loud as his own heartbeat. He tried to put his hand up to his face, to wipe away the sweat, but found that he could not. Looking down, he noticed with confusion that his hands were not hands, but black-furred paws. Tensing the muscles, he saw four razor sharp claws slide out like knives from their sheaths. He gasped in surprise; but the noise came out as a rasping purr.

"Do you like your gift?" asked a voice, complacent and amused.

Marghaska glanced up at QesAngared, having totally forgotten her presence in the light of his change of form. He snarled at her, and swiped out his paw at her stomach, for that was the height of his head. She leapt backwards, laughing yet again.

"Will you join me, Black Hunter?" Her voice was low and greedy.

In answer he snarled, a blood-chilling sound. She shivered slightly, then smiled as if the sensation pleased her. "I have ways of making you comply," she continued, unafraid. She held his glowing eyes with her own, and began chanting again. He felt himself drawn toward her like a moth to a flame, and felt all resistance drain out of him. It was an odd, if pleasant sensation. He sheathed his claws, and raised his paw to take that one, fateful step towards QesAngared.

And then Sichan kicked in the wall.

Everything happened at once. The cloaked woman's concentration broke, her eyes snapping away from his. Marghaska roared his defiance, and leapt for the back doorway that led to the cellars. And QesAngared stared after him, her face as black as the veil that hid it, before running to the shadows to skulk until danger passed.

*   *   *

Heat and blood, sweat and dust. Thirst. Hunger. Craving for blood. Craving for vengeance. Paws weary, one sore. People present; hide in shadow.

Beast-Khalla slid into the ditch, and eased her aching paw-hands for a second. She had not eaten for a week, and she needed food badly for energy. Sniffing at her paw-hand, she located the thorn that had been causing her discomfort and pulled it out with her teeth.

She then started to look around her. She sniffed; lies and treachery were rife here. The hated one' s scent lay like a fetid path on the ground, an easy trail to follow, despite being about a year old. Her burning lust for vengeance lit up the way he had taken in blood-red.

She turned her head slightly; there was movement over there. Two sentries patrolled a narrow stone bridge over a wide river. She crept stealthily down to the water's edge, and put a paw-hand in, withdrawing it sharply at the freezing temperature of the water. Too cold, too wide- swimming across would be impossible.

She slid noiselessly along the bank, occasionally stopping to ascertain whether or not her presence had been detected. When she was a fair distance from the bridge, she began to lope, until she realised that the river would continue for a long way. Although she was fairly sure that it would be the same in the other direction, she checked anyway, just to make sure there was no possibility of avoiding the bridge. As a general rule, she avoided humans, if she could help it. But this time she would have to kill. It was for the best really, she hadn't eaten in days...but no, she could smell human meat, and her mouth watered in anticipation.

She slunk closer to the bridge, bunched her muscles, and prepared to jump.

It had not been Captain Tansden's day. He'd had no lunch, lost an eagle and four hawks playing Void...oh, and received word that his wife had run off with his brother and his money, leaving his baby, he thought sourly. He kicked a stone across the bridge, hearing the faint clatter as the other duty guard kicked it too. But then from behind him he heard a different, terrible sound.

The steely click of talons on stone.

* * *

Heat and blood, sweat and dust. No thirst. No hunger. Taste of sweet man flesh. Running fast. Trail clear. Still a craving for blood. Still a craving for vengeance.

* * *

Destinariae leaned upon the marble rail, gazing out over the courtyard. She put her bare arm down, and shivered at the cool kiss of the stone against her bare skin. She stood on the balcony that surrounded the square, her violet dress blowing out behind her in the breeze that swirled gently around her.

Where could Marghaska have gone? When he had not appeared to help her unsaddle and groom Sichan, Destinariae had done the chore herself and scoured the palace for her servant. But there was no sign again. Why had he run off?

Suddenly, she heard a voice, raised in a familiar song.

"Rai antire vo yuntré es Ra geu-ty sen,
Yel kievon ta yuntré uth tiy anaren,
Rhan fal deis Rai ortire yar turiariel kye,
Ta maayl bey, ten sahr, mhan khitarevanai."

Destinariae smiled as she recognised the voice of Rieda. It was a beautiful, haunting song, with a plaintive melody line and lovely words, Destinariae mused. She remembered their old nurse singing it softly to her as she was put to bed as a child. It was sung in the old tongue, but to her the words sounded in Bakarnian.

> "I'm searching for answers so I can be free,
> The questions and answers all are part of me,
> I'll find what I'm seeking at dusk of the day,
> And that's when, my love, they will take me away."

Rieda's high, clear voice was perfectly suited to the tone and pitch of the song, and Destinariae found herself humming quietly along as she mentally translated the start of the next verse.

> "I can't see the future; forgotten the past,
> But I will endure it, my spirit will last..."

Leaning over the balcony, Destinariae spotted the Kai-to-be, strolling in a gown of shades of gold sat at the edge of the huge fountain, and sat looking down at her reflection. Like a cat with a looking glass, Destinariae thought amusedly. Then the third verse began. Rieda's lovely voice did full justice to it.

> "I'm living in darkness and longing for light,
> I may be beaten but I can still fight,

They tell me I'm not free, but I know my heart is true

And so, my love, I'll come searching for you."

The last note's echoes died away, and the watching Kaji turned to go just as Rieda started to sing the song over again. Then, suddenly, the beautiful music was cut off abruptly. Destinariae looked out over the railing, and saw her sister lying in the fountain, her golden robes stained with a dark crimson.

Polluting the water with the taint of murder.

Chapter 15

A narrow trail wound its way through the thick forest of tall trees, a thick rain of leaves falling with the blustering wind. Three travellers pushed through the heavy curtain of premature autumn leaves, sighing in relief at the short reprieves between each strong gust.

"Maybe we should take a short rest now," Kethar shouted back to the girls, "By the time we start again, the wind might have died down."

At the murmurs of assent that greeted his words reached his ears over the wind, he privately asked Zakrivath if he saw anything suitable. The shikara was only too happy to comply; he had been grumbling all day about staying overhead. Though Kethar and Zak knew differently, the girls thought that the wind was too strong for all three of them to ride upon Zakrivath and had refused all offers. Kethar grinned, knowing full well that the black shikara really wanted to make the best of the excellent flying wind, but was forced to stay overhead to watch for oncoming danger to the non-flying travellers. Zakrivath was still slightly irritated that the girls thought him incapable of carrying them in a high wind. Kethar had reassured him with his suspicion that it was not the shikara's strength that the girls thought was lacking, but their own courage at flying in such high winds.

If you carry on there is a suitable place, a clearing, with high trees surrounding to block the wind. It would be nice for you humans to rest your feet for a change, he coaxed, hinting that he could carry them.

Kethar deliberately missed the hidden meaning, apologising mentally. 'But we really do have to keep going as much as possible, you know, or we'll never get to Lyvilan in time. And you're a big strong bird, you can do this easily!'

That's what I've been trying to tell you! And I am not just a bird! I am a shikara!

Kethar had to smile at the pride in his soulmate's tone, because it reflected his own emotions. Zakrivath was definitely not just a bird. He was too incredible, massive, intelligent and generally amazing to be anything but what they knew him to be- a shikara.

Noticing that they were at the place Zak had mentioned, he called his other companions. "Over here!" he said, pointing to a small gap in the closely clustered trees.

After squeezing through the narrow opening, they saw a large open area devoid of trees. The wind abated almost immediately, prevented from entering the clearing by the wall of tall, broad trunks. A small, blackened mound in the middle suggested a bonfire of some sort. Zakrivath was already perched there, smugly waiting for them, upon a stout tree limb overhanging the glade. It creaked under the colossal shikara's weight.

Like it? he asked, his mental voice carrying an undercurrent of laughter.

Kadira sat down heavily, her breath escaping her in a great whoosh. "I am so glad we decided to stop. If we had gone on any longer I swear I would have dropped to the floor and never got up until you'd seen sense."

Kethar stared at her, not hearing anything else she said. The words sounded so familiar...for a second a forgotten memory flickered into the back of his head, and an image of a young blonde girl superimposed itself over Kadira's form, then flashed away before he could remember the details.

With a start, Kethar winked back into reality just in time to hear Kadira say, "We may as well have some food while we're here, to keep us going. It could save us some time later."

"I think that could be a good idea," agreed Ionté, trying desperately to smooth her windblown hair. She gave up. "I don't know about anyone else, but I'm quite hungry now. Kethar?"

I could force myself to eat something, hinted Zakrivath, his eyes glowing slightly red with hunger.

'Zaki, you know the others can't hear you,' Kethar said mentally. 'That is, unless you deign to speak with them'.

I would only do that as a matter of high importance, Zak reproved, slightly primly. He disliked the fledgling name Zaki now, except sometimes when used in affection by Kethar. *You are my rider and soulmate; so it is you that I speak with.*

Kethar felt surprised at this unexpected show of fierce possession, but it only mirrored how he felt subconsciously. Zak was his, as much as one could own a shikara, and he could not help feeling very slightly jealous when Zakrivath spoke to one of the girls inside their heads. But he had only done that twice; both times to Kadira.

To the waiting girls he said, "Yes, food sounds good! But not too much, or we'll be too bloated for any more vigorous walking today."

Zakrivath spread his great wings and dropped soundlessly to the earth. Ionté, standing nearby, ducked and ran out of the way of the shikara, knowing full well that one direct blow from one of the heavy wings could cripple her.

But she need not have worried. Annoyed that Ionté could think that he would ever accidentally or purposefully harm her, Zak raised his crest, giving a grating cry as he dropped low and beat his wings, showing his displeasure. Kethar rushed to the huge black head, and whispered soothing words while caressing the silver crest of feathers that stood defiantly upright. Slowly, the great bird folded his wings, lowered his fine crest, and his glowing red eyes faded back to their normal bright gold.

"I'm sorry...Kethar, I never meant to offend him," stammered Ionté.

"It would be better if you addressed him yourself," Kethar replied gently.

Ionté stepped out. She curtsied hesitantly, and apologised deferentially, "I am so sorry, Zakrivath. I did not mean to offend you in any way."

As the shikara nodded his head once, Ionté walked forward to tentatively caress Zakrivath's lowered head. She was starting to overcome her fear of the great bird, yet her face reflected awe whenever she got this close to him. And quite right too, Kethar thought, for the mere sight of the shikara should be enough to make anyone both awe-stricken and fearful, at the least. When Zakrivath was displeased, he looked magnificent. Terrible in wrath, but utterly magnificent.

Zak succumbed to the caress. He leaned into Ionté's pale hand.

She has come out of her shell, has she not? he commented to Kethar. *But her usually gentle temperament contrasts greatly with her pride in her partly albino blood. She has never quite accepted our liking of her, and sometimes takes it as hidden pity for her and her pale skin.*

Kethar did not reply. Zak's speech and eloquence had grown as much as he had physically, and the black shikara was now extremely perceptive concerning the thoughts and emotions of others. *I like her,* he affirmed. *And Kadira.*

Kadira took out some bread and cheese, and passed it around. After a good five hours of walking in a steady wind, they were all ready to eat. In fact, the food barely lasted five minutes.

"Kethar, does Zakrivath mind if I stroke him? I mean, I don't want to cause offence or anything."

Kadira, slightly jealous of Ionté having touched the magnificent shikara, spoke out.

"He doesn't mind at all! In fact, he'll like you better the more you stroke him. But he would prefer it if you talked to him. He can understand you," Kethar added casually, indulging in a wide smile. He was highly pleased that his friends accepted each other. In fact, he was struggling to keep from laughing as he saw Kadira's slight envy. Responding to his thoughts, Zakrivath spoke to him, his mental voice touched with amusement.

Kadira feels that, since I have spoken to her twice, she is far more popular with me than Ionté. She is mistaken. I do not show favouritism.

Kethar's thoughts, however, were on other matters. 'Don't you ever think it would be good to converse with your own kind? I mean, don't you feel alone sometimes?' He broached the subject hesitantly, in case it affected his friend strongly.

I will never be alone, Kethar, for as long as you and I are Linked. Anyway, it would not be of consequence, seeing as I am the last shikara. Zakrivath's mental voice held a combination of lonely pride and melancholy.

"Kethar, are you even listening? I've been talking to you for about the last five minutes and you haven't answered me once. *Say* something!" Ionté's voice, raised angrily, cut across the clearing. Her admiration of shikara and rider had not palled as far as Zakrivath was concerned, but the awe she had once felt for them both did not extend any more to Kethar, though it did help soothe her pride and prevent some arguments.

"What?" said Kethar, suddenly jolted out of his conversation. "I'm sorry, Ionté, I was a little pre-occupied."

"We noticed," Kadira sniffed, angry on behalf of her friend. Kethar was not usually inconsiderate.

Ionté turned her startling green gaze to Kadira, slightly perturbed by the irritation in her tone. She sighed sarcastically. "Don't worry, it wasn't even that important. I'm sure that whatever Kethar was thinking about was more important than what I was saying." She berated him facetiously, her voice sinking back into its mild calmness.

Kadira tutted under her breath. She liked Kethar immensely, but sometimes he totally ignored his surroundings, including his friends. Ionté said that he was probably talking to Zakrivath inside his head, but Kadira still thought it rude of him. Ionté, she thought, was too forgiving by half.

"What were you saying, Ionté? I apologise for ignoring you," he apologised gallantly.

She looked at him, honouring him with the full sweetness of her smile. "Don't worry about it. I was just asking about Zakrivath, you know, generally about him. He's so unique, and I..." she stuttered, then stopped with a faintly self-conscious smile. "I think I must be just overly curious. Any way, now that we're all finished eating we should probably get going. I don't know about the rest of you, but I feel much better already." She stood up and stretched gracefully, unwittingly showing off her slender body to its greatest advantage. She stopped, looking at the others for an agreement, but not before she had noticed

Kethar swiftly turn his head away, a faint tinge of red upon his face.

"Yes, you're right," Kadira nodded her assent. "We're losing time just sitting around doing nothing."

"Wait a minute!" Ionté suddenly looked anxiously at the black shikara, "What about Zakrivath? What's he going to eat? He must be very hungry."

A few seconds later Kethar smiled at her. "He thanks you for your concern, but he'll pick something up along the way." He turned so that he faced both of them. "I think it would be best if we headed towards Eredeth. I was born there, and my family still lives there as far as I know. We will be warmly received, given food and proper shelter. Also, it is just by the main route into Lyvilan." He looked questioningly at the girls.

"That sounds good, Kethar. Food and shelter may only be what we need to survive, but they'll be absolute luxuries." Kadira affirmed the plan. "I tell you, I'll be glad of a proper bed, and a bath!" She sighed rapturously, wrapping her arms around herself.

Ionté stepped forwards. "I agree too. It'll be really nice to meet your family, Kethar, and to stay with others. Although I hope they will not be prejudiced against me or Zakrivath."

Me too, the shikara agreed privately to his friend.

"Why should they be prejudiced against you?" asked Kethar, puzzled.

"Well, because of my, you know, well I'm..." Ionté's voice dropped to a whisper. "I'm not exactly the same as you," she finished lamely, when it seemed they were still waiting for her to finish.

"Why's that?" Kethar enquired with a slight laugh. "You have two legs, same as us, two arms, same as us, two eyes and ears, same as us, two..." he looked away for a second, embarrassed, "...same as Kadira...you're a human like the rest of us!"

For a second the girl looked like she was about to issue a scathing and outraged retort; then she looked thoughtful. "Yes..." she repeated contemplatively, almost as if she had forgotten the others were there, "I'm human like the rest of them." With a radiant smile, she shook herself out of her reverie and gestured to the edge of the glade. "Shall we?"

They all pressed to the edge of the clearing as Zakrivath suddenly launched himself into flight. Then they were on their way again.

The wind was as strong as ever, and this made the already unstable journey though the overgrown forest more perilous. Tree roots stuck up from the earth like the fingers of buried men, poisonous ivy draped at ankle height to seek contact with bare shin, and razor-edged vines looped from overhanging boughs, waiting to catch an unwitting traveller in their deadly green tourniquet.

To try and gain some speed, the travellers made their way to the edge of the wood, and continued on. The wind was stronger, as there were less trees to block it, but without the dangers of the thick undergrowth they made better progress. Kethar's eyes were constantly drawn upwards to the form of Zakrivath, watching the gigantic bird glide and soar with ease.

The black shikara rose steadily, until he was just a dark dot in the eyes of his three watchers. Suddenly, he folded his wings tight against his body, and hurtled downwards. The trio watched in thrilled delight, then lost sight of him as he entered the canopy of trees. They heard a muted bellow of a grazer, sharply cut off, then the triumphant savage scream of the shikara. Then all was silent, except for the noise of the wind.

After walking on for a few minutes more, they came across the scanty remains of Zakrivath's meal. Only a few hard bones were left, and the surrounding grass was dyed a sticky crimson. The girls looked slightly repulsed, but Kethar knew that Zakrivath had made the most of the meal. Nothing was wasted; the meat and entrails were for digestion, and the hair and bones would be used to grind up food in the stomach. Even so, Kethar knew that his huge friend would need at least another two to satisfy his appetite for the moment; the shikara had not eaten in two days.

The only thing that slightly disturbed him about his soulmate's feeding was the blood-lust, and hunger for the kill that passed through to Kethar from the emotions of Zakrivath. It filled him with a savage delight, and it seemed that he could almost taste the warm trickle of blood running down his own throat. Seeing the black form of Zakrivath rise again from a different area above the trees, Kethar watched grimly as his friend made the spectacular dive yet again, dropping like a stone from the sky.

A stone with blood-frenzy and a tearing beak!

* * *

The huge main square was overflowing with people. Not one of the uneven cobbles that blanketed the ground could be seen, such was the density of life. The aged dwellings and stalls seemed to be holding their breaths in, lest they crush the tremendous throng.

The old buildings and timber-framed shops that crowded the streets to and from the plaza were newly cleaned, and, judging by the many new pieces of timber that supported major beams, the townspeople had obviously made an attempt at strengthening their homes. Dilapidated barrels and crates served as window boxes, and bright flowers covered all possible surfaces, cascading down over their shabby containers like rainbows flooding from a dull sky.

Up ahead, its flushed stone towers rising gracefully upwards like a fairytale castle, stood the palace. Its slender spires and gracefully curving windows were adorned with coloured silks and garlands of costly exotic flowers, coldly mocking the humble decorations below.

All eyes were on the upper Grand Balcony, the extrusion of the castle that overlooked the market square, and from which the Ka could address his people. But it was his daughter who was to speak today. The townspeople waited expectantly, their banners waving, awaiting the last remaining Kaji. A small distance away, the Kaji Destinariae herself, along with the Ka and three squads of the Upper Kajarito, approached the scene from a different direction.

"Destinariae, I hope that you realise the importance of this speech," said the Ka, quietly pacing beside his daughter.

"Yes, I know," came the calm reply.

Turanis frowned, not reassured by her answer. "You must be careful in your speech. The recent... accidents have caused many to think that we of the Royal line are weakening. That must not be allowed to happen! You must secure their allegiance once more, Destinariae."

"I will do my best, my Lord Ka."

"May the Gods be with you."

Mounting the steep steps, careful not to tread on the hem of her new ceremonial gown, the young woman smiled, momentarily unnerved by the vast audience waiting in anticipation of her words. Once reaching the platform, Destinariae paused with the pretext of reclaiming her breath, whilst really surveying the extent of the multitude. She had not spoken publicly since the incident at the arena. But this was different; these people would hang on her every word. Surprisingly, she felt calm. To hold all of these people in thrall, that was to be enjoyed, not feared.

Suddenly aware that everybody was awaiting her speech, she smoothed down her many skirts and stepped forwards.

"The Kaji Destinariae!" the herald proclaimed. "Heir to the Bakarnian throne!"

With a regal wave, and a demure smile, Destinariae spoke. "Bakarnians," she proclaimed, clasping her hands together, "I come to you on this day with many emotions within me, and with many thoughts chasing around my head. One of these points I have to raise now. We have all been deeply saddened by the sudden deaths of the Royal Family," and here she raised her hands to her heart and bowed her head, "and the loss of them will be great to the kingdom." Her voiced throbbed poignantly, and many an eye glistened with sympathetic unshed tears for this gentle maiden's grief.

Destinariae continued. "I am not saying that I can fill the breach that has been left. But I am saying that I will strive at my utmost to follow the example that they laid before me." This got a cheer and a smatter of applause.

"I am not here to tell you of a new change in leadership which will not affect you. I am not here to speak about matters which have nothing to do with you, to waste your time before you can get back to the shops, trades and markets. I am here to set your minds at rest. As the heir to the throne of Bakarn, I am going to be there to help in hard times. I will feed you when you are hungry. I will clothe you when you are cold. I will shelter you when you are homeless. I will listen to my people!"

The roar of appreciation almost lifted her off her feet. She raised her hand sharply, and they quietened. Her head throbbing with the power she commanded, she went on in a strong, clear tone, spreading her hands wide. "I will bring order into chaos, light into the darkness, and make this kingdom great again! Who is with me?"

"We serve the Kaji Destinariae! Long may she reign!" came the deafening reply. She waved to them once more, then turned to face her father with elation lightening her step.

"Good enough, your Majesty?" she grinned, pleased with herself. If controlling a crowd and securing the respect and allegiance of almost one million people was not good enough, nothing would be.

The look her father gave her was just short of lethargic. "Good enough, I suppose. It seemed to do the job." Then he turned and beckoned over the Commander of the Upper Kajarito.

Destinariae watched them talking, quietly fuming. Good enough? He could not be bothered to do something himself, and then said that her great effort that 'did the job' better than he ever could was *good enough?* He never justified her achievements, not with praise, or even with body language. If he had winked at her or something afterwards, to show her that he was proud really, then that would have been acceptable, but...

Frustrated, she turned away, to where the crowd was starting to disperse. Then her anger abated slightly. Her father had not been the same these past weeks; he frequently could be seen mouthing silently to himself, talking when nobody else was present...screaming in his sleep. Even rooms away she could hear the frenzied, hoarse yelling, and his excuse when the Kajarito ran in with weapons drawn. Even the commoners whispered it now; they were living under the rule of a mad king.

Drawing her mind away She had not seen Marghaska since the day she had first rode Sichan;

his usual haunts were silent, his presence marked by its absence. She had looked for him, but could only presume that he had escaped. She had hoped that maybe he would be in the crowd; after all, she had been sure he had liked her. But there had been no sign. Still, looking for one man amongst a million was a near-impossible task, she reasoned.

A movement out of the corner of her eye distracted her, and she turned quickly. A member of the Kajarito approached her, and bowed.

"Your highness, there is a man who wishes to speak with you. Shall I admit him to your presence?"

"Yes, please do." She watched as the guard marched off, to return with five others and a young man of about twenty. She narrowed her eyes; he looked oddly familiar...but no, that was probably just her imagination. Beckoning him forwards, she watched him bow very low.

"Your highness, may I have leave to speak?" His voice was not very deep, more of a light tenor, and clear.

"Pray do, lest I become withered and ancient before I know the purpose of your presence." Her voice was lightly mocking, yet friendly so as not to cause offence.

He reddened slightly. "My Kaji, you could not look withered nor ancient if you were a thousand years old."

It was Destinariae's turn to blush. Struggling to retain her aloof demeanour she replied hastily, "Yes, well, that is neither here nor there. Please continue."

The young man stood upright once more, displaying his dark woollen tunic and leather sandals. Though his clothes were not fine, he wore them smartly, as if he at least took some care of his appearance. "Your highness, my name is Shakna. This has been my first visit to Lyvilan, and I have seen many varieties of people on my travels. Yet you seem to encompass the good that I have seen in all of them. I merely wished to shake you by the hand, that I might touch something so perfect and pure before I again witness the horrors of life. May I?"

Seeing the Kajarito about to step forward in protest, Destinariae beat them to it. She stepped forwards, and took the man's hand in her own. Squeezing it gently, she looked searchingly into his eyes. Brown and very trusting, they were the eyes of a dreamer, who would believe anything with proof enough. She gave his hand one final squeeze, and made to withdraw her own. But he grasped one, and drew it to his lips, where he placed a light kiss on it before letting go. She smiled, and bade him leave.

As he retreated she pulled back one of the guards. "See that that man gets a new pair of fine leather boots to replace his worn sandals. Here, take this," and she pressed two eagle pieces in to the man's hand. He bowed and left.

A good man, she thought, well aware of the troubles of life. Dreamers were so rare, and this one was rarer still. Firmly, she drew her mind away from the intriguing young man and walked toward her father, a slight smile still playing about her lips.

* * *

Shakna slipped off his old tattered shoe, and placed it on the ground next to him. Pulling off the other one, he laughed softly. The Kaji had been as kind as he had thought her, giving orders for him to have new footwear. He picked up one of the new long boots, sturdy and elegant, and pulled it onto his foot. It was padded inside, and he sighed in bliss as he felt how comfortable it was.

He had been right in his estimation of Destinariae. Many a nobleman would refuse to even speak with a commoner, let alone touch one. And she was a Kaji! She could have had him flogged for asking for her touch alone, not considering the kiss on her hand.

He sighed, lacing up the other boot. Her skin had been soft and smooth under his lips, her hand scented with rose-fragranced soaps. He placed his feet back on the ground and sighed.

Often he found himself thinking of Kadira. What had happened to her? Well, last time he saw her she had been rescued from a horrible death, but since then she had occupied his thoughts every day. He missed her innocent, yet enticing charm, and her fiery yet solitary nature. He had been so close to her, but had not realised it; now he knew that he had loved her. But now? Now he fretted over her safety as one would a relative. And they had not exactly parted in the best of tempers, Shakna reminded himself. He shivered, hearing on the wind a distorted parody of her malignant hiss, "*I hate you!*" If only I could see her again, he thought yearningly, I could explain everything; we could be friends as before. I will find her one day, he resolved determinedly, I will find her and make things alright.

Suddenly there was a scream from the alley over to his right. In the waning light he just made out the shadowy forms of street bandits attacking a small, cloaked figure. Drawing his short-sword, he unthinkingly charged down the cobbles and leapt into the fray. Two were holding the shrieking woman back against the wall, their bodies sickeningly close to her slender form. Another drew his sword as Shakna approached, snarling like a wild beast at the untimely interruption.

With a throaty roar the gang member raised his two-handed sword over his head for a skull-crushing blow. Swiftly Shakna darted in and plunged his blade into the broad chest. The man toppled backwards. Too easy, Shakna thought, but they know I am no amateur now. They will be careful. He turned to face the men and woman by the wall.

Shakna pushed his hair out of his eyes, watching as the one of the remaining men left the woman and walked cautiously towards him. He noticed the man was armed with a short-sword like himself. Ah, now this was fairer. Heartless rapist and assassin he may not be, but by the Gods, he was a swordsman!

Ducking a sweep of his opponent's blade, Shakna lunged for the other man's belly, but his sword was swept aside. Nimbly dodging another slash, he feinted to the right. When the larger man's sword swept across his body to meet empty space, Shakna pinned the arm against the attacker's body before hammering his own blade home in the broad chest. The man died with a grunt of surprise and pain.

Many thanks to the Gods, and the noble art of sword fighting, thought Shakna triumphantly. And a few nasty little tricks from my mercenary friends that you wouldn't find in any honourable school of swordsmanship!

He turned confidently to face the remaining man, unknowing of the faint, confident smile that lay upon his face. With a look at this self-assured smirk, the last attacker took his hands off the still-struggling woman and, with a dirty look at Shakna, loped off down the alleyway.

"Are you all right, my lady?" asked Shakna gently, reaching out to the woman still pressed against the wall.

One of the woman's arms moved up to her face, and threw back the heavy hood.

"Sweet Gods of light!" Shakna swore.

Destinariae smiled hesitantly; still shaken by the experience.

"What are you doing out here all alone at this time of night?" Shakna asked, more frightened now than he had been during the fight. Why, if he had not been there, she might have been raped, or worse, killed!

"I have to get out sometimes," she answered, her eyes on the floor.

"You could have been killed! What were you thinking of, you bloody idiot?" he cried exasperatedly. "You bloody idiot, your highness," he corrected, suddenly remembering who he was talking to.

Far from looking outraged, her face contorted into a lost, hopeless look. "I thought you may understand..." she whispered, looking straight at him. Then came the anger. "Of course you couldn't understand," she snapped. "You have the freedom to come and go as you please, you have learned to fight and defend yourself, you control your own future. What would you know of being trapped inside the palace, being kept penned up, waiting for the assassin that you know will someday come for you, waiting for the knife in the night, while people around know not and care not of your triumphs or of your fear of death..."

She broke off, her voice shaking with emotion, her eyes wide and shining in the moonlight. Shakna had never seen such eyes. He could see himself therein, amongst a billion shining stars...

Before he knew it, he had leaned forward and placed his lips on hers. Her eyes widened, then he felt her respond. It was not a kiss of passion, or of faked desire like those that he had received in the past, but a gentle, soft caress of the lips that he knew he would remember forever.

He finally pulled away and looked at her for a second. Then he looked away. "Sorry, your highness," he said huskily, and coughed gently. "You..."

"Yes?"

"You...had better be getting back to the palace," he finished, trying not to look at her disappointed expression. "It's not safe for you to be out here."

She laughed then; a little breathlessly. "As you've already proved," she said, tilting her head in the direction of the fallen men.

They started to walk along the alley until reaching the main street. Destinariae halted then.

"I know a secret way back to the palace from here; I will be fine alone from now on."

"Are you sure, my Kaji?" he persisted, fearful for her safety.

"Yes, I am." She looked searchingly at him for a moment, then stepped toward him slightly. "Thank you, Shakna. I will not forget." With a last smile she drew up her hood, and headed away in the direction of the palace which loomed up ahead.

Shakna watched her until she was out of sight. She would be safe now. The street was well-lit, and she passed several late-night traders who would be a deterrent for anyone considering attacking the solitary stranger.

He sighed, but his thoughts were far from melancholy. He had been right earlier; Destinariae seemed to encompass all that was good. She had even remembered his name, which had been mentioned only once some hours earlier. It was as if all the virtuous aspects of people had been siphoned into one person. But then he shivered; if there was one totally moral person, then by that same judgement there should be one totally evil person, too. Meeting him would be the last thing Shakna wanted.

Then he stiffened; what if he had already met that person? Only one person he could think of had never shown a sign of rectitude, and that was the employer for whom he worked.

QesAngared.

Thinking of her, he ground his teeth. He knew he was working for an evil woman, and knew also that he would rather work for a different lady. In his mind he compared the two; kind, compassionate Destinariae, completely unsuspecting of the plot to overthrow her, and wicked, butchering QesAngared, completely devoid of any trace of morality. They were complete opposites; one was a butchering monster, and the other an angel.

Shakna looked up. The sun had set, and he had to return to his Mistress. A cold chill settled in his mind, and he prepared with weary obedience to go. But though his mind coursed with hatred for QesAngared, his heart pulsed with love for Destinariae.

Chapter 16

Sitting in a garden, with one arm draped around a marble urn, he regarded his position. Knee deep in icy cold water, he was trying to decide about something. But when he tried to think directly of it, he could not remember what he was. He lowered himself further down into the water. It was still there, a niggling thought at the back of his mind, but when he reached for it again, it evaded him.

Frustrated, he started to withdraw his leg from the water. As he did so, the step beneath his remaining foot that he was standing on seemed to shudder and give way. In a panic he clutched at the marble urn, and was horrified when it came tumbling down with him. He landed with a thud; it landed with a crash. Before his eyes, the marble pieces burst into flames. The fire roared around him, puckering and blistering flesh that it touched. He knew that in a matter of seconds it would encircle him. With a speed born of desperation he launched himself through a gap in the flame wall. That leap to him went on for eternity, though in fact it was only a matter of seconds. He hung there, suspended, whilst the bright flames licked at his clothing and he screamed in agony.

A second later he collided with the surface of the water. Immediately the pain receded. With strong, powerful strokes he propelled himself through an opening at the bottom of the pool. A long tunnel stretched before him; he swam as fast as he could. After a while, he began to run out of air, with no sign of an exit. His lungs were bursting, yet he could see no end to the tunnel. In panic he swam faster. A stream of bubbles erupted from his mouth; still he swam on. Surely there would be somewhere to surface soon?

With joy he saw an opening above him and he swam up. The air on his face was like the divine breath of immortality, the air in his mouth tasted fresher than a breeze from snow-capped peaks. After regaining his normal breathing, he looked up.

A shining suit of armour was suspended in a block of slowly revolving crystal. In reverence he gazed at it. The sunlight bounced off the silver surface, reflecting and refracting through the crystal to burst in a rainbow, a multitude of colours in his eyes. With awe, he approached the rotating block. The armour was superbly crafted, anyone could see that, with a sleek silver shape and polished surface. The helm was also bright, shining with glory and light. Two long gold horns came out of the sides near the top, and curved gracefully upwards to end in keenly sharp points. The gauntlets were of the same metal, but with white-gold diamond shapes down the crest of the hand, at the base of the fingers. Altogether, it must have cost the earth to commission, but surely there was some magic woven into its steely fibres? Who could have made such a wonderful piece themselves? As he reached out a hand to claim it, he found himself falling backwards into water. No, he thought, I must have that armour, I must...His heart felt empty without the wondrous suit; his disappointment was so intense that he could have wept. He found again that he could not breathe, and sank back into the water.

With a start, Sirenthe sat up on his sleeping pallet. He tried to calm his breathing. It was a dream, the whole thing was a dream. But though he could not explain it, he knew instinctively that the armour was not. But it wasn't to be his, he thought wretchedly, no, not mine. He got out of bed and walked to the piece of broken glass that served as his mirror. He looked the same; tall, white haired, red eyed and youthful faced...plain clothed.

Then it struck him- in the mirror he could see something gleaming behind his reflection. He turned around, not daring to hope, and saw it. The armour! He ran up to it, noticing that there was now no crystal block to protect it, and lifted out the main section. Rather than being a breastplate or a mailshirt, it was one structure that...would not fit him. He once again felt the heavy press of despair, but bit it back. It would fit. He lowered it over him, and felt whole. As one being with the armour. It fitted him like a second skin. It was light, easy to move in, and surprisingly strong for something so weightless.

On impulse he threw a gauntlet at the pallet. A dent appeared in the surface, yet on inspection the metal of the gauntlet was unscathed. Fitting on the chain-boots, he reached longingly for the helmet. It felt awfully heavy in his hands. With trepidation he placed it on his head. It was so light, and not loose at all! He peered again into the looking glass. His red eyes and fair albino skin showed through the menacing slits in the great horned helm, making him appear a fearsome creature of legend. He laughed, and felt a surge of elation.

But common sense raised a hesitant point in his mind. Who would send him such a princely gift, and why? He had seen enough of life on his journey to realise that nobody gave without asking something for themselves. Well, whoever sent him the armour must want something quite important, or want it very badly. And somebody who could afford to send such a...unique and precious thing must be powerful indeed.

Yes, Sithe, we are indeed powerful.

He spun around as the voice, no, more like a collection of voices speaking at once, echoed magnificently around the ruined building. But nobody was in sight.

You are also correct in thinking that we ask a deed of you, Sithe.

With a shock, he realised that the voices were speaking inside his own head. Then, before he could wonder at that, a sword appeared in front of him, floating calmly in the cool air.

He knew at once that this was of similar substance to the armour which he wore, and of similar workmanship. The hilt was inlaid with sapphires and glistening ultramarines, and the pommel set with gold and silver runes reading in the old tongue; 'Iencein', or soul-sword. The blade was much more slender than a broadsword, and looked almost like a large elegant, yet deadly rapier. The flat of the blade was engraved with a cunningly impressed pattern that Sirenthe could not quite make sense of. Added to this, the whole sword shone with a bluish-white incandescence, and possessed his heart with a similar, aching, empty longing as he had experienced in his dream.

If you comply with our wishes, than this will be your prize, Sithe.

He opened his mouth to accept, but his gaze fell upon the frail, sleeping form of his friend and mentor. He had made a promise to stay until his training was finished, and he had been given no indication that this was the case. "Who are you?" he called, though he knew by the sick, empty feeling in his soul that he was inevitably bound to accept the tasks, "and why do you keep calling me that? Sirenthe is my name!"

This is the only way in which you can forfeit your oath to your tutor. Sirenthe made the vow, but Sithe would not have any ties to this person, and this

place. And after all, you would really be doing what Erendiir wants, for you obey him, and he serves us.

And then Sirenthe guessed who the entities that he spoke to were. Falling on his knees, he said quietly but fervently, "I am at your command, O divine Masters and Mistresses. I will do as you request. What task is to be laid upon me, what charge shall I undertake?"

There is a beast, dangerous beyond all measure, who is on the hunt. You must trail the predator, and ensure that it harms none.

"Surely slaying the beast would ensure that it was rendered harmless?"

No! The creature must live...for...we cannot sanction the killing of a living animal. But there is one who might encounter the beast. This must not be allowed to happen, for...the woman's own safety. Are we understood?

The sword glittered tantalisingly, and Sirenthe felt his mouth open and form words without bypassing his brain. "Yes, my Masters and Mistresses. I will follow the beast as you wish." He turned to the sleeping form of the elderly man. "I swear, by the Gods, that I will return to you to complete my training."

Then his brain intervened. "But how shall I follow a hunter on foot? I cannot move swiftly enough to keep up with it."

You will find people much more willing to help you with your quest. Coming up the track now is a horseman. He will find it much to his liking to trade his horse for your old boots. Then travel southwesterly. If you ride hard, you will catch up to the creature by nightfall.

As the sun shone down on the armoured rider on his new roan horse, galloping madly with bright hoofs flashing, the golden clouds above the derelict chapel rolled into themselves, and as they did one voice was heard.

I told you the sword would clinch it.

* * *

"Send word to my Minions. It will commence today."

"And will you be there in person, QesAngared?"

"I will be there to claim the power that is mine, by right and soon by name. I will...no, you will see later the true meaning of all this. For now, just go. I will see you at the Ka's afternoon stroll. And Eskiros?"

"QesAngared?"

"Ensure that the Minions are all loyal. Execute one if needs be. Actually, I had rather thought that Shakna needed convincing of his loyalty. See to it."

A rustle of silk, and Eskiros was gone. QesAngared looked back at her hands, and saw that they were trembling with feverish anticipation. She sang quietly, her voice echoing bizarrely through the stone cavern. The childlike rhyme sounded weirdly distorted and strangely sinister, making her shiver with fiendish delight.

> "Too long have I waited
> To sit on the throne,
> To claim all the glory that I should have known,
> The king shall be humbled,
> His soldiers will fall,
> And I will be Regnant, the Kai over all!"

* * *

Shakna was in a panic. He had no idea of the way to the Ka's private audience chamber, and he knew no one well enough for him to trust them of such an important message. There was less than three minutes until that inhuman cow QesAngared would make her move. One of the other Minions, Enikron, had tipped him off about Eskiros' orders to kill him, and he was thankful for that. But only then, stupidly late, had he realised the full extent of the plot. To kill the Ka to prevent a madman from ruling, maybe he could cope with that, but killing him to place that scheming, evil fiend on the Imperial throne was just totally against everything that he believed in. No good would come of such a ruler, he knew. He could already imagine the times to come with *her* on the throne. He shuddered, his mind screaming a premonitory image of bleak, mindless chaos at him. He had to warn the Ka. Even if the Ka was still declining as a result of the deaths of his wife and daughters, he would do it for the just, fair, Kaji Destinariae. She would make a fair and compassionate ruler. She was all they had left to believe in. And if she was killed, then they were all truly dead.

Shakna paused. He could go to her! But then he remembered that she had taken to walking with her estranged father. His stomach churned with fear. Then she, too, was at risk! Then he had a sudden flash of inspiration. He could go to the battlements and warn them as they strolled! He wheeled around sharply, and launched himself up the rough stone steps that led to the outer walls. If he could just reach them in time! As he ran he was thankful that there were no guards to hinder him. Then he realised what that must mean. The first stage of the operation had gone smoothly; the entire Kajarito had been wiped out. An overwhelming surge of despair rose in him, for he knew there was no-one to guard the Ka and the Kaji. Even worse, the soldiers now accompanying them were Minions! With a heart that felt like lead within him, he approached the wall and stepped onto the curved pathway atop it. From there he could see everything.

The Ka had been disappointed that his daughter was not to accompany him on his afternoon walk through the gardens. She had instead told him of her grief for the family, and that she would spend the day praying at the royal chapel. He understood, of course. He himself had not emerged from his chambers for two whole days after hearing of his wife's death. So he was alone. Alone, except for four guards who paid very close attention to him. He was moved by their loyalty, and stepped forward to speak to one.

"What is your name, man?" he asked in a friendly way.

The guard's gaze shifted to one of his fellows, then answered, "I am called... Captain Carver, my Lord. Are you feeling better this afternoon?"

The Ka smiled at him. "Yes, thank you for your kind concern. I can't remember seeing you about. Are you new?"

A flicker of amusement crossed the guard's face. "Yes, I suppose I am. Though I have ample experience, my Regnant."

The Ka had no time to wonder at the man's smirk, as the great Royal Clock boomed out three deep, melodious notes, and he turned toward the door. Instantly the guards formed up beside him, and he walked out into the gardens. As he walked his thoughts centred on his family. He unconsciously held back tears, his back straight with pride taught by punishment, but in his heart flowed a river of grief. His legs moved almost of their own accord, carrying him down to the Royal Graveyard. He stood at the foot of his wife's tombstone, and in his mind saw her laughing, scolding, loving...he could take no more. His strength had been shattered by the deaths, like an intricately wrought looking glass on stone, shards of himself lying scattered around. He heard the whispers of soldiers, servants and peasants alike; and he knew they were right in a way, for his whole world seemed...unreal. He hardly knew, or cared, what he was any more.

Yet something had stayed with him through the madness and grief, nourishing him, forcing him to carry on. It was the fact that he had to live for his daughter, the sole remnant of his once extensive family. Again his eyes misted with tears; again he held them back. And part of him wanted to go on living, too. He would find and execute the perpetrator of these deeds.

"Well, what a surprise. The Ka. How *charming* to find you here."

The Ka's head snapped up, and he saw a black-garbed figure standing not twenty paces away from him. He looked quickly to the guards, to get them to respond to the intruder, but they were standing upright, blades drawn, saluting the figure. He turned back in outrage. "Who the hell are you? A Lord? A Lord's thick son? Or just a passing piece of filth?"

"Silence!" snarled the stranger, making a incredible jump, soaring through the air to land at his side. A black-gloved hand snaked out, whipping the Ka's sword out of its oiled scabbard and holding it to his throat.

The Ka looked back, unafraid. "I should really flay the groundsman. He can't be doing his job properly, letting stinking trash into the gardens."

The stranger whispered a word. Instantly the air between them thickened, and the Ka felt pain as though a hand was reaching inside him and twisting his internal organs. He fell to the ground and vomited blood. He could see fear now, as plainly as he could see his own coming fate. He heard a malicious chuckle, and looked up in amazement. The stranger was a woman! Though he felt hideously weak, he struggled to his feet and looked her in the eye. He recoiled as fury and hatred blazed into him. Then he looked deeper, and realised the person standing over him held the same blend of sanity and madness in her soul. The stranger carried death in her eyes.

She looked down at the Ka. Although he had obviously met his match, and more, his face still carried that outlining of pride which marked him as of royal blood. She respected him for that. She was still going to kill him, but to hold on to your pride even whilst looking into the face of death is a fine thing to do.

She studied his face, noticing the frown lines that she was almost certain had not been there a year ago. He had aged beyond his years. But that was obviously due to the loss of his wife and daughters, and the fear that he must carry for himself. That was something she had never admired in him. He wore fear and grief on his shoulders, letting them get the better of him.

On the wrong side of forty, he had a plain face, slightly tanned from his tendency to sit in the graveyard for hours, and thick black eyebrows. He had fierce blue eyes, usually giving nothing away. Yet today they were starting to show fear through the cracks in his carefully oiled countenance.

"How does it feel to kneel before another, O mighty and powerful Ka?" she asked mockingly, contemptuously pushing him down again with a press of dark magic. Too weak to resist, he glared defiantly up at her and painfully turned his back on her to look upon yet more of the traitorous soldiers.

"Why do you not help your Ka? You have sworn to protect me, yet you stand by and watch while an impertinent stranger attacks me. Do your oaths mean nothing to you?"

Harshly pulling him back around to face her, the woman raked her eyes over his face, seeming almost to claw him like a raven's talons. He cringed away from her touch. "You have great audacity to speak so to my Minions."

She looked at them then, and her voice, wrought with haughty expectancy, lashed out at them. "Have you nothing to say for yourselves?"

The one whom the Ka had mistakenly thought to be the captain stepped out, his gaze fixed humbly on the woman's feet. "We have taken only one oath; to serve our Mistress, the rightful Kai."

The Ka fell back in shock, his mind reeling with the endless possibilities of this. "How long…"

The woman laughed cruelly. "Longer than you can have possibly suspected. My Minions have been replacing squads of your Kajarito for a while now." She began to pace, treading on the kneeling Ka's fingers as she walked back and forth. "I take no credit for the death of Isete. True, she would have been one of my targets, but I did not arrange for it to happen then. And it was so easy! A well-placed crossbowman was all it took, and she was dead! I almost laughed when I heard." She stopped pacing to kick the Ka in the chest, sending him reeling.

"I thought that, as you had three daughters, and had cherished Isete so, that you would remain solitary. But no, you married Tifiert." As if this angered her greatly, she stretched out her hands and let loose a bolt of jet-black lightning that engulfed the humbled

Ka in flickering tendrils of black light that spat sparks, making the fallen man writhe in agony. This seemed to cheer the stranger up, and she relinquished her hold upon him, then continued with her terrible story.

"Tioni's death was brilliant. The poison was so light it had to be applied in doses for four months. So drinking from the doctored liquid once, before or afterwards, would no more harm the drinker than any other drink would. Even a Damelin would find it difficult to distinguish a difference! But I had to be sure," she muttered, almost as an aside to herself. Shaking her head as if to dispel drunkenness she went on.

"Chova's, I admit, wasn't very imaginative. Actually, at first, I was content if she was only disabled. A physically stunted child could never ascend the throne. Paying a laundry-maid to push her down the stairs was very easy. But the fall actually broke her neck, so it went better than I had hoped. But Faitan's death I had to do myself. A swift push was all it took, and her fat body was as lifeless as a cushion."

"Stop!" yelled the Ka, his eyes watering. "Don't do this!"

The mystery woman looked down at him, and grinned behind her veil. "Oh? Does this hurt?" she asked in mock sympathy. The pained tears silently coursing down his cheeks gave her all the answer she needed. Good, she thought with a malignant smile, I will take everything away from him; his strength, his sanity, his Empire, and his life!

"So," she went on as if there had been no interruption, "where were we? Oh yes. The little baby Efaerin. Suffocation is always best for infants. Stops them bawling," she added matter-of-factly, as if commenting on the weather. "Tifiert's death, ah, now that was *inspired*. You had managed to cover up the seriousness of the other deaths, so I asked myself, what would cause the most distress? Then it hit me; you couldn't cover up a death in front of thousands of people! It would destabilise your position with the people you served, making Bakarn easier to take from you. And on her birthday, too! How perfect!" she added, almost laughing. She was about to torture him further with her magic when she noticed the Ka's face. It was evident that her words were causing him more anguish than any physical torture ever could. So she continued, savouring her triumph, and relishing in her adversary's grief.

"Rieda had to be disposed of quickly, before she could marry. A quick knife in the chest, not very original I'll admit, but it worked fine. And as for Verda..." the stranger clenched her fists, as if compelling herself not to scratch an itch. "Well, I am very close to locating her whereabouts, and when I do she will suffer for ever daring to think that she could escape my justice!"

The Ka craned his neck upwards, and mustered enough derision to say, "You haven't even found her yet? Some powerful ruler you must be!" He spat upon the ground at her feet, then curled back into a ball, awaiting the forthcoming torture. He was not kept waiting for long. Again black and silver lightning enveloped him, sending him into paroxysms of agony at the searing bolts of torture that pierced every inch of his being, as his nemesis' mad laughter echoed insanely around the graveyard. The pain flowed like boiling pitch through his body, like fiery whips flaying the flesh from his bones, sending him over the edge into raw, red terror. He did not hear himself scream, so immersed was he in the driving anguish of body, mind and soul. He sobbed when she released him; and his tears fell all the faster for he knew his spirit had been conquered at last. Through his pain and grief blurred vision he saw that he was cowering beside the gravestone of his first wife, Isete, and his shame was complete at betraying her line as he instinctively sought protection against the hard, unyielding stone.

There was a heavy silence, filling the air with a tense waiting, as though all the fates and destinies of the world led to and from this very moment, and the entire universe was listening.

"So now the moment is set for me to take my power. How does it feel to know you are doomed?" came the proud voice, filled with loathing.

Turanis looked up at her, seeing through his tears the triumph and insanity burn in her mad gaze. "You might kill me, but after Verda there is still another of my family to be reckoned with. You will never kill her!" shouted the Ka hoarsely, eyes blazing with all the contempt that his dying soul could muster. "She has everything, and you have nothing. You don't even have an identity, do you? Reveal yourself to me!"

"Your last remaining daughter? Yes, I will reckon with her very, very soon." The woman laughed, a hollow, mocking sound, malevolent to the core, and threw back her hood and veil.

The Ka Turanis collapsed, his last breath rising in his throat in shock as he at last looked upon the face of his tormentor. Eskiros, watching from behind the Minions, felt a terrible weight settle upon his mind like a dark shroud, the Minions in Kajarito uniforms fell grovelling on the ground, and Shakna threw himself from the top of the wall to meet death, knowing that there indeed was no hope for the future.

It was Destinariae.

Chapter 17

The passageway was pitch black, save for a pinprick of light at one end. The air was stale and musty, reeking of mould. From somewhere came the sound of water dripping steadily. The pale light of a lantern lit up only the five men who had entered the corridor, and the immediate ground before the leader. Their footsteps were muffled by the moss that covered the damp stone flooring.

"C'mon, Fraine, let's get out of here," whispered one of the men to the lantern bearer, his eyes flicking from side to side.

Fraine countered swiftly. "No, you know QesAngared wants every last corridor in the palace searched for intruders."

They continued in silence for a while. Then their footsteps became slightly louder as they walked through a flooded section of the passageway, and someone drew in their breath sharply as the cold water penetrated their badly-made boots.

"Oh, nobody will ever check if we patrolled this area," one of the Minions murmured. "It's not as if anyone comes down here anyway." He tugged on Fraine's sleeve nervously.

"Stop it!" hissed the last in the group scornfully. "You know why nobody ever comes down here? Because of the rumours, that's why!"

Fraine sighed loudly. "Look, Devarys, don't scare anyone with that monster nonsense again."

"Monster?" exclaimed another, and was shushed immediately.

Devarys continued energetically. "Yeah, monster. No patrol has ever returned from this area. They've just disappeared!" He waved his hands in an emphatic gesture. "One person says that he heard a scream. That's why there's been talk of a monster!" he finished, raising his voice triumphantly.

He was hastily shushed. "R, Ranalf's shaking!" jeered another voice not quite steadily, and was shushed by Ranalf especially.

"Am not, Wirghan!" replied Ranalf, laughing jerkily. "It's a load of old tripe, that monster story. I mean, we've been down here in this stinking place for ages, and we're...still...alive..." His rough voice trailed off.

Fraine turned around to face the others, his scarred face showing strained signs of irritation. "Look, there is no monster down here! Will you stop being such frightened, idiotic women about it! There is nothing to be afraid of, little girls. There is no need to tremble and fear for your lives because there is no

319

monster!" His voice rang around the underground passage, making the other Minions cringe.

Devarys seconded the opinion. "Look, Jienth's been quiet today, he's obviously not afraid. Right Jienth?" He questioned, looking for a bit of support.

No answer returned, and only the dripping of water was heard.

"He must have nodded off. Jienth?" queried Fraine.

There was still no reply. "He, he's gone!" stammered Wirghan, panicky sweat dripping down his pale brow.

"It's okay, we'll just stick close together, we'll find him," assured Devarys, with a confidence he did not feel. "When I call your name, say aye if you're here! Fraine!"

"Of course I'm here, dimwit! Get on with it!"

"Wirghan?"

"Aye!"

"Ranalf?"

Silence.

"Ranalf?" Devarys tried again.

Still silence prevailed.

"Stop being a prat, Ranalf, speak up!"

The three remaining Minions huddled together. Suddenly the lantern dimmed and then died. At the same time Fraine felt a displacement of air.

"What was that?" he whispered.

Nobody answered.

"Devarys?"

"Yeah, I'm here, but Wirghan's gone!" sounded Devarys' frantic voice.

"Look, Devarys, we have a better chance with our backs against the wall. Ready to move?" came Fraine's voice from the blackness, raised in fear. Without waiting for an answer, he shouted "Go!" and lunged for the wall.

"I'm here, Fraine! What now?" asked Devarys, his whole body trembling.

"Fraine?"

Devarys pressed his back to the slimy stone wall. His darting eyes tried to make out some form in the darkness, but he really could not see anything. Suddenly a match flickered, momentarily blinding him. When his eyes became accustomed to the glare he looked back.

A muscular, tall man stood holding the lantern. He was unshaven, and his long black hair grew like a mane across his head, neck, and shoulders. He wore nothing but a pair of torn trousers. His movements were graceful and athletic, yet there seemed something feral in the way he sniffed the air and shook his broad shoulders.

"Th...thanks, mate," stammered Devarys, using the wall to help him reach his feet. Then he looked around and saw the carnage. Fraine was lying opposite him, his belly slashed open, and his entrails spilling out. Wirghan's corpse was four or five feet away, blood pooling around the open tear at his throat. Of Ranalf's body there was no sign, but his head lay near Fraine's left boot. And Jienth lay where he had fallen in the polluted, stagnant water, his limbs almost severed from his body. Devarys shuddered, and then turned his attention back to the dark-haired man, who stood with his back to the survivor of the attacks.

"Thanks, friend," called Devarys again, wondering if the man had not heard him. When there was no reply, he asked, trying not to look at the carnage, "What is your name?"

"Marghaska," replied the stranger in a low, rough voice, as though he had forgotten how to speak. He turned slowly and looked at Devarys. The Minion's gaze was drawn to the man's eyes. They were bright gold, and glowed with inner fire.

"Oh, sweet Fortune," Devarys whispered, backing away. "Oh, Gods, no!" He looked down in panic as he stumbled over a severed arm, then a movement out of the corner of his eye made him raise his hands to protect himself as he saw Marghaska spring.

Time seemed to flow slowly for Devarys, the seconds stretched out so he could see every horrifying detail. In the air, sleek muscles swelled and torso deepened, the gleaming skin sprouting thick black hair. Marghaska's back curved, his shoulders extended and his outstretched fingers morphed into razor talons from heavy paws. His teeth lengthened and sharpened, his face shortening and growing forwards, and his hostile cry turned into a raging snarl issuing from a gaping red maw, studded with gleaming fangs.

The last sight Devarys had, as his body hit the ground beneath the rampant panther, was of the creature's eyes, reducing in size and glowing with furious hunger, as the pupils shrunk down to thin black slits. Mercifully he lost consciousness, seconds before the jaws tore into his flesh.

*   *   *

The forest ended at the crest of a hill, near the outskirts of the village of Eredeth. The lush green forest floor, abundant with flowering shrubs, continued beyond the fringe of waving trees, and for this reason the forest appeared unfinished. The lofty pines hung their heavy boughs in a verdant canopy but gave the feeling that, if they really tried, they could reach out still further.

The three travellers, wending their way through the maze of mossy trunks, came abruptly to the forest's edge. The black haired man continued to the crest of the hill. The fine-featured half albino girl stayed with the other, a curvy brunette. But both came running at the man's horrified exclamation, mingled with the shrill cry of the hovering shikara.

Kadira reached Kethar first, her chestnut hair mussed with her dash of speed. She clung to his arm in shock, just as Ionté reached them. The half albino's eyes widened, and her hands flew to her mouth as she gazed out over the seen below.

The village stood before them, if that's what one could call it. The buildings lay in piles of charred timber, strewn across the remains of other structures. Bodies littered the ground, burnt in some cases to the point of cremation. Bits of blackened wreckage had been flung all around, most unidentifiable as what they had once been. And a heavy coating of fine black ash covered everything there, like black icing on a black cake, giving the whole scene a feeling of terrible unreality.

Most disturbing, though, was the dreadful silence that hung suspended over the terrible place, like the gloomy clouds that even now were starting to give out a slight drizzle. It was a repulsive mockery of the forest, where one could walk almost not noticing the sights and sounds of thriving nature. These sounds were much emphasised by their absence.

Kethar's eyes burned with silver sorrow. He bowed his head in grief as silent, agonised tears dripped down his shaking face. Forcing back her own sadness, Kadira signalled to Ionté to come away and let him grieve in peace, but laid a hand gently on his arm to show her own sympathy. They retreated, leaving Kethar standing alone, weeping. And, far above it all, sable-feathered Zakrivath soared effortlessly; an angel of death.

* * *

The rider wearing a black sash drew up his horse at the gates in front of him. His mount whinnied, and tried to rear up, but the rider yanked sharply back on the reins, controlling the fatigued beast with force. He had ridden hard for several days, and the horse was close to collapsing. But it lifted its head and snorted at a lash of his riding cane.

"Upper or lower order?" came a voice from inside the gatehouse.

"Upper. I am of the Minions," replied the messenger, and after a few seconds the voice hailed him again.

"Passcode?"

Beating his mount back into submission, the rider called out, "Power brings Gods and kings trembling to their knees. Can you let me in now? This horse is going to drop at any second!"

The heavy gate creaked ponderously open. "Pass and be recognised, servant of QesAngared."

Touching his heels to the horse's flanks, the messenger rode in, and cantered down the avenue to the Palace. He jumped down from the beast's back, and handed the reins to one of the Rider-Minions. Striding forward, he came to the huge carved doors, and waited for confirmation of entry to reach his Mistress.

He did not have to wait long. The outer door swung open, and a squad of Minions faced him. "Who comes to the Kai QesAngared's court?" intoned one, stepping out to greet the messenger.

Though he was inwardly bored by the endless succession of formalities, the man replied. "I am Eratis the messenger, one of QesAngared's Minions. I bear news from the estates of the lords, and the villages in Central Bakarn." He raised his arms and allowed them to confiscate his weaponry, and succumbed to the search for any hidden dangers.

"Enter, Minion." They stood back to let him enter, and then formed up into a square formation around him. Then the inner door opened, and the small company stepped through into the court of QesAngared.

The huge room was divided into four by two intersecting aisles. In each of the four sections, huge numbers of Minions sat and talked, laughing and playing Void, and all the while keeping an eye to the figure at the head of the central aisle. The focus of their attention was a throne that rested upon a circular, raised dais. But this had not the stately magnificence of the late Ka or Kai's thrones; it was a black and gold, high backed chair, with tendrils of black curving up from the back. It was elegant in its own eerie way. But it was nothing to the figure sitting atop it.

QesAngared was clothed in a robe of gold, white, and black that swirled about her like wraithlike mist. Her skin, was pale and shimmering, and blended with the misty robes that she wore. Her face was neither young nor old looking, but it was mysteriously beautiful and expressionless. Her brown eyes radiated power and imperiousness, and atop her head a golden crown gleamed, studded with black agates and flawless rubies. Her raven hair cascaded down her back and shoulders, some tied into a heavy braid which was intertwined with ribbon and gold thread. Her legs were crossed, and she sat upright, one of her elegant hands lightly holding a stud at the end of one of the armrests on her throne. The other supported a slim rod, again of gold, like a sceptre. It was studded with large stones down its length, an emerald, a ruby, a sapphire, an onyx, an ultramarine, a diamond, and a topaz. Atop it sat a large raven, occasionally staring balefully at certain people about the court.

As the small party approached, the Kai of Bakarn fixed her gaze on the messenger. The Minion Captain stepped up to her, and all bowed. "Kai QesAngared, this messenger has j-"

"Silence, Tanjaron, and let the messenger himself speak." Her voice was stern and commanding, yet contemptuous also. She beckoned the messenger to come forward, which he immediately did.

"Your Majesty, I have scarce returned from my survey of the estates of the Bakarnian lords. You sent me on this mission almost two months ago, and I have the information you required of me."

QesAngared nodded, and signalled two servants to come forward with a silver tray bearing a goblet of red wine, and a roll filled with pigsmeat. Eratis ate and drank greedily, cramming food into his mouth and sopping wine. QesAngared looked on distastefully, and the raven flapped its iridescent wings in response to her annoyance.

Seeing his Mistress' displeasure, the messenger hastily ceased satisfying his hunger and thirst, and bowed again.

QesAngared sat forward on her chair, showing her impatience. "Out with it, then. What information did you procure?"

"I surveyed the feelings of the people as you particularly instructed. They grow ever more apprehensive, and their mistrust of their lords grows deeper each passing day."

"Is that it?" QesAngared exploded, a fiery gleam of madness bursting out from her cold and superior mask. "That's all you discovered in close to three months?" The raven beat its wings and cawed loudly, and QesAngared's fingers twitched convulsively, a warning to all that she was about to act.

"No, Majesty, I have other news!" gabbled Eratis, knowing he was inches away from incurring the Kai's wrath.

QesAngared sat back in her throne, soothing the raven on her sceptre. "Amenis, you may decide his fate later. Hush now," she crooned. Then she turned back to face the messenger. "Tell me the news, then," she asked, her voice dripping honey.

Eratis passed a trembling hand over his sweat soaked brow. " The people are unhappy with the deaths of the Royal Family, milady. They are uncertain of whether to support their lords, you, or neither, for they think that the lords are all under your thumb. They believe that you killed both Destinariae and the late Ka, and do not trust you. The Minions have secured all Central Bakarn, using the special demonstrations that you ordered. Eight villages that did not succumb, including the slave breeders', were burnt to the ground. And the squad you sent to the Snowlands have returned, and used all their captives in the demonstrations."

QesAngared smiled. Eratis, taking this as a good omen, smiled back. Quick as lightning Amenis lashed out with a talon, and Eratis sat back with a gasping scream of pain, his hands over the gaping socket where his eye had once rested.

Ignoring the terrible screams, the Kai beckoned to a Minion, and waited for a small side table to be brought forward. She looked around at the Minions, and then grinned wolfishly as she took out the nine large cards. The Minions cheered sycophantically, and craned their necks to see, or shoved amongst themselves for a better view.

"Amenis shall decide your fate. You should have returned far earlier, with more information. All that you have told me I already knew. Amenis!" QesAngared summoned the raven, and it hopped forward to grasp the ridge on the table. Eratis watched in fascinated terror, his hands trembling so much he had to clench them into fists. Amenis cocked his head, then decisively jabbed his heavy beak at one of the cards in front of him. QesAngared lifted it, and Eratis gibbered something under his breath. The heavy gothic script said plainly; **Death**.

"Oh dear," crooned the Kai, in mock sympathy. "Amenis has foretold death!"

The Minions cheered, and Eratis closed his eye. Then suddenly he turned and started to run to the door, the sound of his footsteps echoing all about the hall. He was speedily intercepted by a squad of Minions, who brought him, struggling and sobbing, to the foot of the throne.

QesAngared leaned down, a maniacal lilt in her voice. "Take him away," she spat, " and execute him as you see fit."

Another cheer went up, and the Minions by the former one of their number stood the man up. Then he suddenly raised a snarling face and yelled raggedly, "Wait, *woman!*"

With a lazy gesture, the Kai of Bakarn halted the group. Eratis spoke again, a wild look on his face. "This is fun, isn't it? You enjoy this, don't you? It's disgusting. You used to be a sweet little princess. Look

329

at your face, the sweet girl's face turned monster. Are you just playing tough, *Destinariae*? Or is it all just a game? People's lives and deaths are just a game to you, aren't they?"

A forbidding silence fell. QesAngared sat upright, her deep, dark eyes cold. "It is a game," she said vibrantly, "and you know what, Eratis?" she leaned forward. "You lose." And she gestured for the condemned man to be taken away, a look of pure malice on her beautiful face.

Before the assembled multitude could react, QesAngared called briskly, "Your attention, my Minions. After that peculiar episode, there seems to be some confusion regarding my identity."

A chorus of affirmative grunts confirmed this, then subsided as the Kai resumed talking.

"You have known me as two different women: Destinariae and QesAngared. QesAngared is a name you gave me, a name that was as many of your names, I suspect; untrue, and for show. Yet it was in respect that you named me the Mistress of Blood, a respect due your Mistress. Destinariae was the name the late Kai Isete gave me, as every parent has a right to give a birth-name to their offspring. But Destinariae, the little princess," QesAngared spat distastefully, "was just a mask I could put on when it suited me. She was my informant, my body to assume inside the palace, where I would not be questioned or captured. When I had the chance to kill, I took over, and used the princess' body for a few minutes, before retreating back into her consciousness. I could not be there all the time," she reasoned, waving her gloved hand idly, "for I could let nothing of my real character remain to mar the sweet girl's charade, that could be noticed and used to capture me."

"But now I don't need her any more," she smiled strangely, a reckless light burning in her soulless eyes. "I never have to be the little girl again. And today, you have the honour...no," she corrected almost to herself, "men like you have none...the privilege of attending as I give myself a name."

She turned to the raven, busy preening its wing, and it fixed one baleful eye upon her.

"Amenis, my dear friend," she said lovingly, "tell me the omens of my nametaking." She gestured to the cards that still lay in front of her, then proclaimed, arms wide, "Let the Taraht cards show my glorious reign to come!"

Amenis did not hesitate, but hopped straight to the ledge, finding a claw hold easily in the rough wood. His head swung left and right quickly, as though many silent voices were shouting advice to him. Suddenly he shrieked, and jabbed his beak at a card. The Kai turned it over slowly, anticipation written across her face, then cried out in triumph, holding the card up for all to see.

"It is a good omen! This is the Taraht card of the Reckoning! It is a confirmation of my taking rule, and reckoning with the contenders in line!"

Amenis' head jerked round and he blinked slowly at her with tilted head, until loyalty reaffirmed itself. He took wing, and cawed loudly before re-settling himself on the sceptre. His Mistress carefully stowed the cards beneath her flowing robe, and turned back to her intent audience.

"Now we have read the omens, I can create for myself a new name. It will be a name that grants me not just the power of both my old titles, but also access to a greater, far stronger force." Her voice throbbed with excitement, mirroring the stirrings in the Minions.

Tanjaron glanced around, seeing their rapturous faces, and thought, they're hooked. After the plan is successful the employer needs to reassure them that they've done the right thing, and should continue to serve and fear her. Look at them. They know they're on the winning side. She's a damned good talker. But listening to his mistress' fervent words, and seeing the zealous light in her face, he realised she was truly showing her emotions, and his mind was cleared of thoughts as anticipation took hold. He gazed raptly at her as she rose to her feet, took up the sceptre in both hands, and plunged in down into the oaken floor.

QesAngared let go of the tall golden staff, and placed the tips of her fingers together for an invocation, letting her hands rise up to her chest. Servants, evidently recognising the signal, scurried forward to light the tall candlesticks. One placed a lighted taper in the Kai's hand.

Her voice, when it came, was calm, but trembled every now and then with suppressed emotion.

"In the name of Chance, the earth, and all the power of the forest, the strength in the land and the hardness of the rock, I invoke your power and bind your strength to mine." She gently touched the taper to the incense in the first of the holders swinging slightly above her. A ribbon of green light began to gently spiral around her, and the emerald on top of the staff flared.

"In the name of Fortune, the water, and all the power of the ocean, the might of the waves and the glory of the depths, I invoke your power and bind your strength to mine." She lit the second burner, and inhaled the sweet, musk fragrance as blue lights joined the circling green one. On the staff, the sapphire blazed into being.

"In the name of Luck, the fire, and all the power of the flames, the hunger of the blaze and the infinite inferno, I invoke your power and bind your strength to mine." She breathed heavily, noticing the ruby flare, and felt the power tremble in the air around her. She knew there was much more to contain, but she knew the preparation was right. The Gods and their elements had to be named, and she had to call upon the powers of her own strength to link herself directly into the heart of the incantation. Weaving the magic around her, she continued.

"In the name of Ashikra, the air, and all the power of the wind, the force of the storm and the death in the lightning, I invoke your power and bind your strength to mine." The topaz flared amongst the purest gold in which it was set, which seemed dim and shadowed next to the glory of the shining jewel.

"In the name of Fate, the ice, and all the power of the blizzard, the frozen force of the glacier and the crushing iceberg, I invoke your power and bind your strength to mine." She was oblivious of everything else except containing the power, and her eyes were closed as she stood amongst the radiant different coloured strands of pure light, twisting a robe of rainbow about her shuddering figure. Still she went on, as the diamond blazed incandescent white.

"In the name of Eternity, the future, and all the power of what is to be, the weaving of the infinite and the everlasting, I invoke your power and bind your strength to mine." The staff was shuddering much like her body, the ultramarine joining its fellow gems as it shone and added its blaze to the swirling vortex of colours. Now she shook with the effort, her hands clenching and unclenching, with only her willpower to keep the tremendous powers she had invoked in check.

"And in the name of Destiny, time, and all the power you can claim for yourself, the reliability in your soul and the strength within, I invoke your power and bind your strength to mine!" With a blaze of black light the onyx flared into life; adding its brooding darkness to the cloud of magic surrounding her. Her lips trembling with the raw magic she embodied, QesAngared gasped out four words.

"*Ten...tylencharr...Destinae!*" she cried, then repeated in modern tongue, "My...name...is... Destinae!"

She looked breathtakingly magnificent, colours flashing around her, her robes and hair flying out like in a wind, her white-knuckled hands pressed together and shaking. With a final, superhuman effort, knowing she had mere seconds to seal the spell without unleashing the power she controlled in a random burst of destruction, she screamed, "*Karela!*"

Suddenly all the seven energies boomed outwards in a circle, the impact throwing Minions flat on the floor. Before they reached the walls the colours arched gracefully away and soared back like seven streaking arrows towards the waiting figure. Her eyes snapped open, her spine arched back and she shrieked upwards as she contained the raw energy. There was silence as they hit her, then a massive thunderclap sounded a moment later, as if delayed by the sheer momentum of the forging of destiny.

For a second QesAngared did not move, but stood and trembled, her eyes wide and glazed. Then her eyelids closed, and her lips moved gently, although no sound could be heard. Those who could lip-read were puzzled, for the words formed by her lips were in the old language, and could not be discerned. Then, as her voice grew gradually louder, the language changed into hissed words that they could understand all too well.

"You lie there, neither dead or alive; banished from mortal existence. You remember when you were created and called into the world of men; a land of boundless horizons, small weak beings of flesh to serve you, and limitless prey for your consumption and amusement. Then you were tossed aside, into a place of darkness and fire, where your bodies were imprisoned, your hearts stilled, your sibilant song muted. No more can you run, hunt, or feel the air on you scales.

Her voice grew stronger, filling the hall with echoes, and an almost greasy feeling entered the air, as boundaries between worlds collided and were held in place by the briefly enhanced powers of Destinae's mind.

"But you can return to the place of light. Follow the pathway my mind has created. Bend your souls unto my will; bind your spirits to my cause. I will not cast you aside. I am your new Mistress. I am Destinae. Serve me, and once again be alive. Fear me, and once again be great!"

Before the last echoes had died away, there was an almighty cracking noise. A monstrous, jagged split appeared in the thick stone floor, and the building began to shake. Those nearest the widening chasm shrank back from the ferocious heat that emanated from the yawning gulf, and as huge, red-black flames blazed up two rows of Minions screamed as they were burned alive.

But there was not one face that did not blanch in mind-unhinging terror as the first of the urgroth levered its hideous bulk over the edge of the maw.

It shook itself free of black dust and rock debris, and stretched up to its full height. It stood over eighteen feet tall, with scaly, black-green hide, enormous yellowing teeth, flat, reptilian features, and strips of raw flesh hanging from its grey clawed hands. Other similar primordial looking monsters heaved themselves over the edge, and when the shuddering finally pulled the crack to little more than a fingernail wide, a full twenty of these flesh-eating, poison-toothed, reptilian nightmares stood facing their new Mistress.

The Kai stood up slowly, grasping her sceptre, and gestured for the first urgroth in line, that had been the first to arrive, to step forward. She stood on her raised dais, inches away from those terrible jaws, staring into those flat unblinking eyes.

Her voice came sharply, not quite masking the tone of weary satisfaction underneath. "I am your Mistress now. You will obey me, and only me. I am Destinae!"

The urgroth opened its mouth. "We hear and obey, Miztresss," replied the lizard in a rasping, inhuman voice, its forked tongue flickering out between the fearsome yellow teeth.

Destinae smiled thinly, then beckoned to one of the Minion Guards. "Fetch Eratis from the cells. I would like him to meet my new subjects."

Eratis was led in, blood streaking down his face from his ruined eye as he struggled wildly against his bonds. But upon seeing the Urgroth, all movement drained from his limbs even as colour drained from his face. He was chained to the floor before the throne.

"Eratis!" called Destinae, in a light mocking tone, "I'd like you to get aquainted with my new allies. Eratis, my urgroth. Urgroth..." she smiled cruelly, an insane flicker in those pitiless eyes, "...lunch!"

*   *   *

At the door to his bedchamber, a man waited in tense anxiety. He wrung his hands in frustration every now and then, as he paced backwards and forwards in front of the door. Each time a servant came from or went into the room, he blocked their way bodily and quickly asked in a strained voice, "Any news?" The answer he received was always negative, and he bit back his distress every time.

He did not, would not notice the rich hangings and ornamental sconces on the wall next to him, but instead just wore down the hand-woven rug with his constant pacing. Lunch forgotten, he had stood waiting outside the beech-wood door for five hours, but had not yet heard any news of what was happening behind the closed portal.

A movement from down the corridor made him look up. Aramil, his head servant, appeared bearing a tray of light rolls and goose liver pate. He turned away. He could not face eating at this most important time. With a wave of his hand, he dismissed the waiting servant.

But Aramil was not to be dismissed so easily. "Calm yourself, Lord. It will be fine, do not worry."

"How do you know that?" Atisato demanded, pushing his hands through his abundant coppery hair. "How can you stand there, and say that? Have you received word from anyone? Have the Gods told you?"

Aramil did not lose his nerve in the face of his master's rare temper, as he knew the stress that the tense Lord was undergoing. Though he had said many things in the past, either to redeem himself in his Master's eyes, or to placate the Lord, he could not lie to him now.

"The Kaji Verda is strong, Lord. Stronger than most women, methinks. She has not shown weakness before, or at least we of your serving staff have not noticed a sign of it."

For a moment Atisato's face lit up slightly, but then it had returned to the brooding, shut face he had worn before. Aramil continued desperately, loyalty and fondness to his kind master warming him to his theme as he went on.

"She did not blanch when the birthing-woman said it was to be a difficult pregnancy, or show fear when she was told there was more than one. True, it is her first birth, but you will not lose them all. You will likely get a son, an heir, like you've yearned for in the past."

Atisato turned to his head servant. His face was haggard with worry but his eyes were alight, and burned with a desperate sincerity. "Listen to me. Verda is my first wife, and more important to me than anything else, except perhaps a strong heir. If I lose her, and the babes..." he suddenly broke off, and resumed pacing.

The bedroom door opened, and a female healer came out. Atisato immediately sprang forward, his eyes beseeching. Before he could force the first syllable out of his mouth she spoke.

"Lord, she's lost a lot of blood, but she's asking for you, and you alone. If you please," and she held the door open for him to enter. He cared not for her doubtful tone, blatantly disapproving of her mistress' request, but darted in.

As the healers and birthing-women inside saw Lord Atisato, they quickly vacated the room. But Atisato's eyes were on no-one but his beloved Verda. In a flash he was kneeling by her side, regardless of the bloody cloths that littered the floor. The agony of childbirth had marked her face, but sweaty and bloody as it was, she had never looked more beautiful. He kissed her forehead lightly.

"Where...the babes? Please, give them to me," she panted, looking at him with unnaturally bright, fey blue eyes. He glanced at what he had first taken to be a pile of sheets, but on closer inspection turned out to be three tiny babes. He carefully handed each one to her, noting the frailness of each as he handled it.

"Look, Atisato," she smiled weakly, cradling them against her chest, "we have three beautiful daughters. What...shall we call them?"

"For this little redhead...Verpaythe?"

She nodded and pointed to a baby with blondee wisps upon her tiny head. "Verbethe?"

Atisato nearly laughed, regardless of the tears that were beginning to fall from his eyes. "And little brunette Vershesa."

Verda smiled tenderly up at him, tears beginning to roll down her cheeks. "Love, it's them or me. I can't survive for much longer, unless the babes die. And they can't live if I live." At his horrified expression, she started sobbing again. "I know, it's...it's terrible, but it's something to do with the, the magic of those with Royal Blood. If I'd only...known I would have triplets..." she paused, and her sobbing breaths quietened. "But no. I am honoured to have brought them into the world, and I'd do it again."

Suddenly her eyes unfocused, and he could tell that she was no longer talking to him. Though no sound was coming out of her moving mouth, he could just about make out the words.

"I have made my decision, O divine entities. I will descend into the Shadowlands. On the condition that Verpaythe, Verbethe, and Vershesa grow up to be powerful, and prosperous."

Verda's eyes refocused for a few seconds. She looked lovingly up at Atisato, reaching painfully up to caress his wet cheek as she felt the sting of his bitter tears fall like a fresh spring shower on her face. It brought her back to that day they had met in the gardens, under the hazy shade of the weeping willow, by the serene, still lake. She felt the cool breeze, the dew-beaded grass beneath her feet, and the gentle kiss of cool rain on her cheeks. And there he was, as she had first seen him, handsome, lordly, and yet surprisingly gentle. He looked wonderingly at her as if she was a divine goddess, his smile soft and warm, and she saw the love in his eyes. He walked slowly up to her and said nothing, but put his hand out, a searching question written plainly on his face. With a dreamy smile, she took his hand, and he led her away under the trees.

Chapter 18

The full moon shimmered in the night sky, its ghostly pallor casting an eerie light over the scene before her. Fine silk tapestries adorned the walls, their vibrant colours dimmed in the low light. Casting her gaze over to the bed, she noticed as if for the first time the intricate gold embroidery on the delicate fabric. A single feather floated down onto the satin coverlet on the bed, by the pillow from which it had escaped. Gold leaf and gold enamel ornamented the dark chestnut wood of the late Kai's desk. The jewelled necklaces carelessly strewn across it sparkled despite the weak moonlight. A flask and goblet of the finest crystal graced the delicately carved table. Royalty, it seemed, deserved nothing but the best.

Sitting wearily down in the padded velvet chair, the Kai of Bakarn surveyed herself in the elegant looking glass opposite her. Her full lips, perfect as always, were twisted into a speculative smile, her pale cheeks not showing any wrinkle. Her small nose seemed to be carved from the alabaster that made up her skin. Long, silky black hair tumbled down over one shoulder, greatly contrasting with the delicate face. It seemed as though she was Destinariae once again, innocently beautiful and pure.

Leaning closer to the mirror, she looked at her eyes. They stared right back at her, round, dark, and so deep that you could almost lose yourself in them. There lay the only sign that the innocent girl had gone, replaced by a soulless murderer. The eyes winked slowly at her, great gaping sockets, and she looked upon the glass with horror and repulsion. Her skin was pale and ghostly, her mouth a jagged red slash in the centre of the face. And while Destinae clapped a hand to her own mouth in terror, the face in the mirror stayed constant, leering, mocking. It *knew*. The ghastly black holes where the eyes should have been seemed to be calling to her, pulling her in, she was being summoned by that gaping red maw and pitiless holes of oblivion. Then the face changed, and Chova looked out at her with eyes beseeching and tear-filled.

"Destinariae, you should be careful..." her worried voice crooned a warning, as her face blossomed blood and jagged cuts. Her voice faded as the face changed to that of Tioni. Tioni's soft voice was troubled, and she looked in desperate concern out of the mirror.

"My dear sister, why do you look upon me with such revulsion?" Her mouth stretched obscenely wide, and writhing black maggots crawled out from the back of her throat.

The image flowed into the face of Faitan. The scowling, rounded face was sulky, the eyes accusing.

"Don't think you can get off so easy, we won't let you!" sneered the dark-haired little girl, her red face suddenly paling and bloating, the accusing eyes frightened and sad.

The face changed again. Now Efaerin stared curiously at her as if to try and see who she was, then her face creased and she wailed despairingly, her skin turning black and her tiny tongue lolling out.

And then Tifiert pursed her pretty mouth in disdain. "The guilt will eat you slowly, not like the quick snap that was my death. You will pay, *daughter!*" Her head jerked sharply, then became blue-tinged, and her skin stripped away, exposing the raw flesh beneath.

Rieda's serene countenance formed, her clear blue eyes full of bewilderment. "Why, Destinariae? Power corrupts, but you must have been born corrupted. We will not leave you alone, but we will return again and again to torment you. Is the rule of a terrified land, and dark visions of insanity, really worth the price you paid?" Her golden hair slowly became dirty blood-red, yet her eyes remained open and staring until...

Verda's tranquil face appeared then, her eyes sad and filled with pain. "You drove me away to my death, Destinariae. Me, who loved you most of all our sisters! Yet my children will have far more power than you..." her voiced warped as her face became blood smeared and lined with agony. "Look behind me," she said hoarsely as blood bubbled from her mouth, and gestured at a grey, throbbing mass behind her. As she spoke, the gathering enlarged and started to emit a humming noise. "Those are the souls of all the people who have died through your evil. They will be watching, and waiting, sister, and when you die they will scorn the very Void to find you!" Behind her the grey mass became distinguishable as a swarm of souls, whispering dire threats of vengeance and desolation as they hovered menacingly.

Verda's face morphed, until finally Turanis looked sternly upon the panting and dishevelled form of his daughter, lying on the floor with tears streaming down her face.

"You killed us, Destinariae. Killed all of us. All my beautiful daughters. Yes, even yourself. You betrayed the good Kaji for evil QesAngared. It will drive you mad, eventually, and then after your death, people will curse your tainted life, and then forget all your macabre accomplishments. Nobody will remember you. All you will have created is chaos. You have murdered us all, but have damned only yourself." And with that, the vision was gone, leaving the Kai of Bakarn rocking backwards and forwards, crying alone with her arms around her knees.

After several minutes, Destinae stood, steadying herself on the back of the chair. She sat upon the bed, being careful not to look in the mirror. Wiping the moisture from her cheeks and chin, the young woman sniffed, then firmly strengthened her resolve. It was a daydream, she told herself, nothing but a silly dream. But even then she would not turn to face the looking glass.

Walking quickly to the door, Destinae opened it and peered out. The two urgroth guarding it hissed, then bowed their heads to her. "Yess, Miztresss?" they asked sibilantly, their forked tongues flickering in and out of the teeth studded caverns of their mouths.

"Nothing, my urgroth. Just ensure nobody enters. Kill if you must, but spare Eskiros if the fool dares to disturb me." She slammed the door shut once more. Returning to the bed, she half-turned towards the window, then looked sharply away as her eyes fell upon the shining mirror.

What was it the dreams had been telling her? To watch out, that was for certain. But she remembered the face of the late Ka Turanis, and recalled his words, '*Nobody will remember you.*' It stung deep in her chest to think upon that point. All she had accomplished, all she had slaved and schemed and waited for would be as nothing in the minds of people in the future. She would be forgotten when she died.

And it might even be soon. Calling the urgroth had been a huge mistake, she realised that now. Yes, the huge flesh-eating lizards were more loyal and efficient than Minions, and served well when she needed to make examples of people. But she had further provoked Destiny. The state of affairs might hopefully have passed almost unnoticed by the God, but now Destiny's own guardians, Her prized pets had been summoned by a mortal, there was little Destinae could do to absolve herself.

And nothing of my rule will be left, she thought, her father's words echoing through her head time and time again. My name shall be cursed, and then forgotten.

Unless…

Destinae stood quickly, and swept to the door in a flurry of black and white cloth. Beckoning her urgroth to escort her, she made her way quickly to her private chapel. Motioning for her lizard-like guards to wait outside the stone door, she stepped quickly up to the altar. Taking a bowl of incense oil, she scattered drops of the sweet liquid around the heavy cloth that adorned the shrine, muttering incantations all the while. Amenis dropped form the rafters to alight upon her shoulder, screeching an enquiry.

She lit the candles, muttering insanely to herself and the raven, "I will create an heir, so that one will live to remember me and take their place upon the throne. And I have sworn never to take a man to my bed, for he will sully it, defile it. So I can create a child with my magic, and place it within my womb."

The Kai paused, as if struck by a sudden thought. "Yes!" she hissed, exultation in her voice as she placed her hands together for the incantation. "Because it will be of Royal blood, it will be permitted magic anyway. And it will have been created of magic so it will be all-powerful! And," she closed her eyes, breathing heavily, "I will call it by one of the Gods' names. They cannot harm a child! My heir will be seated on the throne of the world, and all shall bow to him!"

She paused again in her tirade, re-opening her eyes. Her voice slowed until it was more contemplative, and she raised her hands above her head, letting magic begin to pool into a sphere above them. "But then, a boy would be impure, and would need to take a mortal wife to ensure the line would succeed. Therefore," she decided resolutely, the raw magic collecting between her hands, "I will make it a girl, and she can carry on the line like I have. My descendants will survive until the end of the world," she vowed darkly, the energy flooding painfully down her arms, "and one day, my last and greatest child will conquer even the Gods!"

The magic swirled around her, cloaking her in colour, pain and majesty. Her arms shook and fingers stretched like claws while she struggled to contain the raw forces balanced within her. As the pain reached its zenith, she shrieked, "I shall never be forgotten!"

* * *

Zakrivath alighted carefully in the deserted square, his talons making a steely echo as they clacked loudly on the cobblestones. Allowing his three passengers to disembark, he slithered and slipped about, the awkward surface under his feet new and disturbing. He asked Kethar mentally for reassurance, then took off from a short run.

Kethar watched his friend soar effortlessly, and his pride and love for the shikara was renewed once more. Tearing his eyes with difficulty from the black spot in the heavens, he turned to the others and shrugged.

"Zak says it looks deserted," he relayed, keeping his friend's other comments to himself, "except for the remaining soldiers. Apparently," and he cast his eyes upwards before continuing, "if we stay away from the barracks we'll be all right."

Ionté stepped forwards, her arms folded firmly. "So," she commanded, her voice ringing, "what happens now?" She turned her slight figure to Kadira, but knew ultimately what Kethar would say.

"We've got to split up," explained the dark-haired man, his voice quivering slightly with suppressed emotion, "you know what I have to do. I'm sure that there's plenty for you to do here, so don't even think about trying to come after me."

By the time he had finished, Kadira had a mutinous look on her face, and Kethar knew that they still had a long debate on their hands. Both women had their hands on their hips, and were glaring fiercely. He sighed, looking at them with pleading eyes. However it was, he knew by now all too well, pointless to argue with two women. Or more precisely, against two women.

"Don't make this harder for me than it already is. I don't like it either, but I can't risk your lives too! Kadira, stop glaring! The answer is no."

Kadira stepped forwards, her eyes blazing. "We want to help you! Besides, Destiny said you can't do it alone."

"All right, how did you know She said..." began Kethar. Then, his eyes flicked upwards for a second. "Fine," he exploded," if that feathered idiot wants to jeopardise the lives of my closest friends, so be it. But I will not allow you to come!" He turned away from them, trying to block out Zakrivath's distress and anger at his own hostility.

He felt a gentle hand on his arm, and turned his head slowly. Ionté looked at him in concern, her piercing green eyes like two flawless emeralds. As usual the sight of her face made it hard for him to think clearly.

"Don't be angry. We just can't let you go off alone as much as you can't let us go with you. Besides, what if you need help? Zakrivath is too large to enter the palace."

He turned fully around, and gripped Ionté's shoulder with one hand and Kadira's with the other. "You do understand, right? I love you two so much, and if anything happened to you I think I'd...die of guilt. Once I lost..." his voice dropped to almost a whisper with long-suppressed grief, "I lost...two good friends. I just couldn't live with losing you two now!"

"But you love Zakrivath, and he's coming with you!" blurted out Kadira, shaking off his hand.

Kethar turned away again, saying over his shoulder, "Yeah, well Zak can take care of himself."

"And we can't? What do you think we are, some simple village girls who scream when a mouse runs past? Honestly, Kethar," Kadira's voice softened from the snarl, "we thought you thought more of us than that." And with a frosty yet poignant look at him, she turned to the shaking girl beside her. "Come on, Ionté, we're not needed here." Before Ionté was led away, Kethar caught one guilty glimpse of the beautiful girl's face, tears coursing down her ivory cheeks. Zakrivath landed nearby, his wings beating strongly. The women stopped by the shikara, and talked to him, giving him one final stroke before disappearing behind a ruined house.

Kethar, we should go. Soon, added the shikara, with a hint of some unidentifiable emotion in his mental voice. Kethar nodded, and crossed the square to stand at the side of his soulmate. *They don't really hate you*, assured Zakrivath, reading his Linked friend's thoughts, *they are just worried about you. They love you. We all do, despite your criticism of us all. Kadira told me that they would spread the seeds of doubt and dissension among the troops, so that they would hopefully continue leaving QesAngared's service. Ionté said to take good care of you, and to make sure that you come to no harm. As if I need to be told such a thing,* he muttered indignantly, flapping his wings in annoyance at the thought that he would not always protect his rider. *There again,* he mused sardonically, *I am just a feathered idiot, I suppose.*

"Oh, Zak," said Kethar lovingly, leaning against his friend's wing, "I'm so glad I have you to go with me. And I'm sorry I insulted you, I'm just confused at the moment."

I told you I would always be there for you, replied the shikara, and Kethar received feelings through their link of the ultimate truest, overwhelming love. He looked up at his partner, noticing how much Zakrivath had grown since the arrival of the girls, and smiled proudly. Zak leant down so that Kethar could caress his head.

Looking into the huge golden eye nearest to him, Kethar ran his fingers through the soft, downy feathers at the base of the shikara's massive, hooked beak. He let his hand glide upwards over the ebony feathers until his fingertips separated out the silver fore-feathers of Zakrivath's magnificent crest, lying down in a shining mane down his head and neck. Kethar had to smile; he could no longer reach up to the

351

prominent, longer feathers of the crest. The immense size of his friend saw to that.

They stood there together, trying to put forward feelings of confidence and happiness, but both feeling the inner turmoil that roiled beneath the surface. The embrace lasted for a second longer, and then wordlessly Kethar leapt up onto the extended wing and sat in his usual place astride Zakrivath's broad, feathered back. With hardly a preliminary run, the black shikara leapt into the sky. Before they could even begin to mount an attack, they both had a lot of thinking to do. Saving the planet would just have to wait.

* * *

Kadira turned to Ionté. "I feel so guilty just sitting here doing nothing, while Kethar goes alone to face QesAngared. W-"

"No, with Zakrivath," chipped in Ionté, clasping her hands.

Cut off in mid flow, Kadira stared stupidly at her albino friend. "What?" she asked, her tanned brow wrinkling as she frowned.

"He's not alone, he's with Zakrivath," repeated Ionté patiently. She pushed her hand back through her white-blonde hair, causing it to fall prettily over one shoulder.

Kadira dismissed the point with a wave of her hand. "Well yes, but even so he's vulnerable. We should do something!" She punched her left fist in her outstretched palm emphatically.

Ionté looked florid. "Kadira, you're not going to do anything...drastic, are you?" She nibbled her lip pensively. It was easy to be the timid, led one while Kadira was dominant and outgoing.

"No, of course I'm not gonna do anything drastic. *We* are!"

"Oh dear," murmured Ionté, "I was afraid of that." She turned to her friend, eyes beseeching. "He'll manage, won't he?"

"Oh come on. QesAngared has hundreds of Minions to do her bidding. We can help to even the odds!"

"How?" In that one word, Ionté showed that she had been convinced.

"Well, politely put, we could...inhume them!" suggested Kadira, her eyes glittering with excitement.

Ionté flatly refused the notion. "Hey, you don't always have to spill blood. There's more than one method of getting people out of the way." She noticed how Kadira's mind always jumped straight to the most violent solutions. There again, she had spent a lot of her time with a group of men who dealt in violence by trade.

"Well, what do you think we should do then?" demanded the brunette, standing up in her exasperation.

Ionté beckoned her closer, and outlined her plan.

A hushed silence fell. Everyone looked at Enikron, waiting for him to make his move. He studied their faces, then through down his cards.

"Double Void beats your hand, Phantra, and eight comets win me the game."

There were some sighs, some mutterings, but the pile of coins and tokens was pushed across the table towards Enikron. He gathered them up quickly, lest some disappear before he could count them. Pushing them quickly into his already half-full bag of winnings, he grinned in a vague manner, stunned by his good fortune. And a fortune he must have won!

Amongst the reluctant congratulations of the other players, Enikron heard the voice of Arakiao, his one-time 'business partner'.

"Yeah, well played Enikron. Good game. But I wish I'd won, 'cos I think in the days ahead I could use it." His hoarse tones sounded regretful. He was backed by a murmur of agreement. Arakiao spoke again, encouraged by the support. "I tell you, I think we're about to find ourselves out of a job!"

Phantra shrugged, obviously unimpressed by Arakiao's words. "Our Mistress seems to have it all going for her, though. Things aren't as bad as you're trying to make out."

"No, you idiot, Arakiao's right," Enikron declared scornfully. "It might look all blue skies at the moment, but soon enough the storm's gonna be upon us. Destinae's weak now, pregnant, scared, and insane, and mark my words, the Gods aren't gonna stand for what she's done. Destiny needs to make her move sooner or later. And I reckon it's gonna be sooner." He scratched his chin, noting the wiry stubble with surprise. "I mean, creating new life's got to use a huge load of magic, let alone summoning the hell-spawned urgroth!"

One of the other Minions stepped in, his face obscured by his bulky hood. "Don't even mention those flesh-eating monsters!" he warned with an expressive shudder in his light, tenor voice. "It makes my skin crawl just thinkin' about 'em." His tone became bolder. "And with 'em, it seems like Destinae don't even need us any more. We might not even get paid!" In the clamour that followed, he pulled his cowl further over his shadowed face, and disappeared back into the crowd.

Phantra shook his head, excavating the dirt from under a fingernail. "Oh, come off it, we're steady and safe here for ages yet."

"Don't bet on it," announced a voice with a mordant laugh, and a dark clothed woman leapt gracefully from amidst the crowd onto the playing table.

Phantra jumped up. "Who the heck are you, woman?" he snarled, glaring pugnaciously up at her.

"Don't you recognise me?" demanded the newcomer angrily, "when I am a Minion like yourself?"

"Not like us," called another moronic voice, "you're a woman!"

"So is Destinae, you male chauvinistic blockhead," retorted the brunette with more than a trace of fierce feminist pride, "and I don't see you taking her to task about it!" She paced up and down the length of the table, talking to the whole gathering. "I'm Kadira, one of the handmaidens of Destinae, and so I rank the whole lot of you. And if you want any proof," she shouted, to quell the rising hubbub, "then talk to Shakna!"

"Oh yeah, talkin' to corpses is really one of my favourite activities!"

Kadira stopped dead in her tracks. "What?" she hissed sharply.

Phantra grinned savagely, punctuating his words with sharp emphasis on all the consonants, mimicking her comparatively refined voice. "Well, Shakna's not really alive enough for me to be holding any lengthy conversations with him!" He shot her a glance filled with withering scorn.

Kadira paled visibly, and swayed ominously. "No..." she whispered under her breath. The derision of the crowd blurred with her memories of Shakna, of their final parting, of all the things she wanted now so much to say but could not ever tell him. Tears filled her eyes, threatening to spill across the tanned skin of her cheek.

The hooded urgroth-fearing Minion pushed through the crowd and jumped up beside the stricken girl. The heavy cowl fell back in the sudden movement to reveal the angelic features of Ionté, to a chorus of whistles and cheers by the Minions as they beheld her beauty.

"Kadira, be strong. We almost have them!" came the soft but firm whisper from between those pale lips. Two slender white hands shook Kadira's shoulders.

Kadira stared at her half-albino friend blankly for a second, then made a sound that was half sob, half sigh. Stepping forward once more, she rasped, "So be it," in a voice that was steeled to the point of being emotionless. Then as she turned to address the crowd once more, the passion, vigour, and vibrancy shone back through her words.

"I left here with the Minion squad seven, bound for Siannorel, and was content to be a servant of Destinae. But then the God Destiny Herself appeared to me, and showed me the future. She said that the time for reckoning was at hand. Soon she will destroy the magic-stealer Destinae, and anyone who stands to protect her. She sent me here to deliver a message to all of you; if you leave now, and forget completely everything about ever serving Destinae, then your wretched lives will be spared."

"How do we know that you're telling the truth?" queried Arakiao, uncertainty clouding his tone.

Kadira could almost have laughed at the offered opportunity. "Because She said that She would send a sign. She sends a gigantic black demon to kill Destinae, and it comes at any moment!" She glanced upwards at the open sky, hoping that Kethar would make his move, but nothing came. Come on, Kethar, she thought desperately. Where are you, Zakrivath? Beside her, Ionté gestured frantically to her to stall for time.

"Look," Kadira cried, improvising greatly, "your so called Mistress will not come to your aid! Like he said," she pointed, "him with the big bag of cash, Destinae is pregnant, weak, and mad, cowering alone in her castle while you're left out here in this place!" she gestured contemptuously with her arms to the less than satisfactory temporary barracks, and some of the Minions agreed loudly with her. "She used you to claim her throne, and then discarded you when she had what she wanted. Well, I say you do the same to her! Why sacrifice your life claiming allegiance to a doomed weakling? Just go! Go now!" She raised her face and arms skyward, just in time to see the huge, forbidding shape of Zakrivath swoop low over the courtyard. The shikara was eerily silent; no battle cries nor shrieks sounded in the still air, but as the enormous shadow swept across the courtyard, chilling everyone packed there, the soft, ghostly beats of those massive wings seemed thunderously loud, making the heart jump in the chest. Nice timing, Kethar, Kadira thought to herself.

The Minions literally fell over each other in their haste to leave the place. They screamed and yelled, pushing and barging others out of the way, leaving in their wake a scene of empty mayhem and two women. One had a look of triumphant delight written upon her face, but the other, for all her desperate impassioned speech, was sobbing like a broken hearted little child.

* * *

As the weary traveller reined his horse into the yard, a dozen or so eager stable-hands ran forward to help. Dismounting, the armoured horseman tossed the reins negligently to one of the lads, who immediately wheeled the tired mount round and walked it inside the stable.

Several innkeepers, all anxious for him to stay at their lodgings, immediately accosted the traveller.

He nodded wearily to one of them, and was rapidly led to a large timber-framed building with freshly filled window boxes. He followed the bustling man up some rickety stairs to a small room, complete with a neat bed, table, and stool. He smiled briefly to the nervously hovering man, who sighed audibly in relief at the guest's favour, and scurried out of the room like a frightened mouse.

Sitting down at the table, a plate of cold meats, bread, and cheese was placed in front of the newcomer. He waved away the servants after tossing a few bronze coins in their direction. They left hurriedly, after scrabbling about for the money.

Once he was alone, the traveller removed his tall, horned helmet, and ate ravenously, tearing into the hunk of bread and filling his mouse with the slightly stale cheese. It was his first good meal in four suns, and he left little but a few crumbs on the plate.

When he had finished his meal he sat back, and ran a hand through his long white hair thoughtfully before crossing over to the door. Making sure it was securely bolted, he removed his armour piece by piece, and polished each separate part. Though it did not make hardly any difference, for the gleaming suit always looked pristine, it was a necessary exercise for part of his consciousness. As he rubbed the oily rag up and down his gauntlet, he felt charged with energy, self-confidence and power. But that was the feeling he always had when close to his armour. He picked up the helmet, admiring as if for the first time the dark slits for the eyes, and the gracefully curving golden horns that made him look like a shining demon when he wore the wondrous suit.

He chuckled humourlessly. The Gods had been right, though he had not doubted them once. Everybody he met seemed to be overpowered with a zealous, burning desire to assist him. Why, he doubted they would even mind if he didn't pay! Although he always did, to reassure himself that he was not anybody special, and that this way of life would someday come to an end. He liked to think that it was all because of the compulsion that the Gods had filled the armour with, not because of his terrible and demonic appearance. Then he shrugged. If not the appearance of the armour, people on his travels had always been afraid of his white hair, pale skin, and red eyes. All people were scared of things or people strange to them, he mused, then smiled as he heard the echo of his mentor's teachings. All people...but not Erendiir, who had welcomed him with open arms. Not Erendiir, who he had betrayed. He forced himself away from the painful yet poignant thoughts of the old disciple. There will be time enough for that later, he told himself harshly.

Sitting down on the small bed, the albino considered his situation scrupulously. He had followed the beast for many suns, and had learnt its habits closely. It had found a deserted cave just before the sun rose, and he knew that it would sleep until dusk before continuing. That meant he had a chance to get some sleep; a luxury he had missed somewhat in the past days.

He lay down on his side, dragging the coarse mountain-goat hair blanket over him. Though the bed was lumpy to the point of being mountainous, and being neat had been its only good attribute until he had sat on it, it was infinitely comfortable compared to the cloak on stone floor that he had endured for several months. The thought still brought a pang of sadness, but he suppressed it with difficulty. He had not relinquished his oath to the mage, but changed his identity, so the promises that remained to bind Sirenthe were ineffectual when applied to him. Though a small, honest part of him screamed out against the twist of the truth, he suppressed it. To acknowledge that he had become what Erendiir had hated would be his undoing. *I have sworn*, he thought desperately, *to return to him, to explain and to finish my training.*

But as he looked down at the forbidding, horned helm, a steely, expressionless voice captured his mind for a moment. *You are Sithe Ren*, he heard the metallic tone echo around his head, *not the young, naïve, inexperienced Sirenthe; that part of your life is behind you forever.*

Easy as it would be to agree to what he assumed was his own thoughts, the albino could not help questioning the end word. Forever? *I thought this was temporary*, he questioned himself, putting the headpiece on the bedside table.

We shall see.

Snuggling down further into the folds of linen, the albino pushed that train of thought away. Soon dusk would come, and he would have to resume his vigil over the beast. The thought wearied him further, so he shut his blood-red eyes and drifted into the embrace of sleep.

The silver helm's empty eye slits watched him.

Chapter 19

Eskiros ran swiftly through the maze of corridors below the palace, cursing under his breath. Every now and then he would look behind him, as if to check if anyone was following, then fix his eyes again on the dank passageway before him. It was only human instinct that kept him going in the right direction, as another feeling all but wiped out the map inside his head.

Fear.

For once in his life, Eskiros was afraid. As the top swordsman of his class, he had long passed the knowledge of how to feel the sensation. Or so he thought.

He had no use for QesAngared now; indeed, he was leaving her to her own fate. After all, she would not be able to come after him when she was dead. She would not be able to escape, being burdened and weakened by pregnancy. If she did, then woe betide her. Destiny would challenge and kill her, if Her flesh eating urgroth did not get there first. The pull of their real Mistress' power would bring the creatures back to the God's influence straight away...not that some might not find staying in the mortal realms more appealing than returning to the Shadowlands.

He shook his head, feeling something akin to pity, but nowhere near as strong. QesAngared had given all of it up for the baby. Eskiros was shocked, for a number of reasons. If he had had the same power, influence, and rank that she had given up, he would enjoy it to the full. When he was dead, either a worthy successor would have been found by lies and trickery, or by evil and battles. He would not waste his life raising a child, who would probably just grab the reins of power and evil by murdering its parents. He was also bewildered, as he had no idea that she had enough human emotions left in her to want and look after a child. That was another bizarre thing. How had the inhuman bitch conceived a child, with only herself and her magic? It was unnatural, and unnerving. Ye Gods, he thought, when all the women can do that, there will be no need for men on the planet!

The passageways that he ran through were cold and dark, and he was thankful that he was not hindered by guards. QesAngared's Minions had fled, each finding better, safer tasks and employers to occupy their time. A pregnant, weak Mistress, falling from power, with the life expectancy of a Minion who shouted "Oi! Stupid little lizard!" at an urgroth, was no use to them. The dark empire had been disbanded; the fear was dissipating. But he, Eskiros, would withdraw far away, and claim the power and wealth that was rightfully his. Then he would return, and the forgotten Bakarnian throne would also be his.

As he ran, his bloodshot eyes began to make out a tiny pinprick of light, enlarging by the second. With a yell of triumph, he sprinted towards it, revelling in the knowledge that he would soon escape. He clambered out of the doorway, feeling the wind on his bare shoulders. Far below, he could see the harbour, and a small boat moored close to the jetty. He began to trot down the steep steps, and then noticed a dark shape streaking across the land. He stopped, stunned. Nothing on earth could run that quickly, that gracefully! It also stopped, and moved what Eskiros took to be its head. With a start, he realised it was looking straight at him. It screamed, a wild, eerie ululation, reminding him of a hunting wolf. It started to run, even faster than it had before. This made his shivering legs unfreeze, and he began to jump down the steps, taking them three or four at a time.

*   *   *

Beast-Khalla sprinted across the plain, her front and back foot-paws pounding the hard-packed earth. Every now and then she would stop, lower her nose, and start to run again, satisfied that she was indeed getting ever closer to her quarry. In the distance a vast building with balconies, towers, and elegant masonry loomed, and she could sense humans on a hill further on and to her right. But the main scent that filled her lungs was the essence of the sea. With her sharp hearing, she picked up the sounds of the humans' conversation. Of course, with her God-sent insanity, she made nothing of it, except unconsciously realised that they were female, and continued onwards. She became aware of the presence of fear, and stopped. Her head lifted, and swivelled until she could fasten her hungry eyes on a lone figure, dressed in black. He was standing on a flight of steps, leading down to a long wooden structure with a boat tied to the end. Even with her bestial ignorance, she realised that it was a possible source of escape that the hated one might use. She had to block the way!

Beast-Khalla howled her wild cry to the heavens. She started to run, intent on her purpose, and was wolfishly pleased when the enemy resumed running. Her eyes narrowed into burning, bloody slits. It was always more...interesting, when they ran.

* * *

Ionté sat on the side of a grassy hill, the sun warming her pale skin and casting a golden sheen onto it. Beside her, Kadira shifted upon her elbows, and propped herself up, the better to view the sea. As she did so she tilted her head, and her dark brown hair fell from its elegant position to its usual waterfall down her back. Ionté envied her, with her tanned skin and brown eyes. Looking at herself, with her skinny body and almost white skin, it was hard for her to imagine that she would ever be loved again. I'm a freak, she thought despairingly, a stranger who will never fit in.

"I hope Kethar's alright. I can't believe I let him go on his own." said Kadira worriedly, chewing on a lock of her dark hair.

"You've said that about a hundred times today," replied Ionté a with a little chuckle, although she thought cattily, *you* let him go on his own? Oh, I get it. It's you and Kethar, and I'm just a person who hangs around because she doesn't have any other friends. Just because you have your heart set on Kethar means that nobody else in the world possibly could. It must have come as a shock to Kadira, she realised, that she was not the top woman any more. Travelling with the mercenaries, she must had got used to being longed-for and idolised, mainly because she had been the only female present, Ionté thought snidely. Now there's someone else, albeit an albino, prettier than her, she just can't face that she might have competition.

I've seen the way you look at him she thought jealously, staring over at her brown-haired friend, wishing she had the courage to say her grievances out loud. Why is it, she thought angrily, when Kethar can talk easily and smoothly to Kadira, laughing and joking, that when speaking to me he is faltering, never laughs, and looks uncomfortable? It's because of my appearance, she decided, her heart a burning stone, he doesn't want to mention that my skin is hideous to him. Still, she mused slightly less heatedly, she could hardly blame her friend Kadira for that, though she still hoped...well, not to win Kethar, but for nobody else to have him.

Looks like I'm just as silly as Kadira, she thought to herself, her pale lips twitching. To apologise she said simply, "I know he'll be okay, if Zakrivath is with him. We got rid of the Minions, so he won't have to worry about them. We'll see him later, to celebrate the victory. Don't you worry." She squeezed Kadira's shoulder and winked at her.

Kadira smiled her thanks, having also seen the ugly mark of jealousy coiled like a sleeping cobra behind Ionté's shy guise. She looked at her friend, and sighed. How could one so tall, so fair and beautiful, with such pale, flawless skin and emerald green eyes, consider herself an ugly, despised beast? It had always been a mystery to Kadira that her friend had been so, well, blind concerning her own appearance. She knew Kethar was overawed by Ionté, and was slightly envious, but if nothing else she was glad that Kethar regarded her, Kadira, as a good friend whom he could laugh and joke with.

But, she realised, that's not enough any more. She thought of Kethar, of his broad shoulders, tanned skin, impressive physique and furious strength. His ruffled black hair, deep brown eyes either flashing with rage or warm with love and laughter, generous, expressive mouth, and endless kindness and sense of humour. His bond with Zakrivath, the devotion in his gaze as he laid a firm hand on those gleaming black feathers, his fierce pride in his soulmate. She imagined those strong arms holding her, supporting her, touching her...

He has nothing in common with Ionté, Kadira thought treacherously. He just likes her for her beauty. Though I would give anything for Kethar to look at me in the same way he looks at Ionté, not that she could ever see it. The thought of Kethar's wasted affection made her want to cry. I know he'll be happier with me, she reasoned, blinking back her tears. We have fun. And in the future, Ionté's beauty will fade, but the times Kethar and I would have together as partners would be magical. If it comes to a choice, I will make sure that of the limited comparisons he could make, mine will be the winning ones. After all, it's not as if either of us have any kind of external benefit; we've both lost their families, homes, and every fine dress or coin they had once owned. Yes, if Kethar had to choose one of them, she would do everything to make sure that he would choose her. She would console Ionté afterwards, remain the very best of friends of course, but Kethar would be hers.

Poor Kethar, Kadira thought with a smile, he has no idea of my plans for his future. But he will be mine. She laughed out loud at the joy of the idea. Ionté looked at her, not guessing the reason behind the laugh, but a giggle soon escaped her too. Quite soon, they were both rolling on the grass in fits of laughter. They stayed on their backs for a while after they had stopped laughing, looking up at the small wisps of cloud that adorned the sapphire blue arc of sky.

Some minutes later, they were back to their original pensive silence, though both now were feeling slightly drained. Indeed, Kadira was now contemplating her dead family. The fire had consumed everything, her parents, her home, and her possessions. She had seen her twin sister, alone in a circle of flames, and had tried to reach her, but a heavy black beam had fallen across her dear sibling and prevented Kadira from reaching her. She knew that her two cousins were visiting her house at the moment that the fire started, and had seen their blackened bodies. Alone in her grief, she had wandered the plains, keeping no track of time or distance, and after a confused blur of events, had ended up here, on a hill in Bakarn.

Ionté stood carefully, and walked to the tree that spread a cooling shade not far from where Kadira lay. She reached out, and plucked an apple from a low branch that threatened to fall to the ground. Returning to her friend, she sat down again and offered the dark haired girl a bite of the fruit. When the offer was declined, the half-albino took a small bite. She had picked the apple at just the right time, she decided, noting its sweet flavour and crunchy, moist, texture.

A movement to her right startled her; she turned, and saw a perky-eyed sparrow watching her, its brown tail flicking quickly up and down. She smiled gently at it, then broke off a small piece of her apple and offered it to the cheeky bird. It cocked its brown head at her, skipped towards her, then back, as if trying to make up its mind. After a second of tail wagging, it suddenly darted forwards and seized the offering. Spreading its tiny wings, the sparrow fluttered off. Before she turned back to Kadira, Ionté just heard a voice say, 'Thanks, miss, that was just the job!'

How odd, thought Ionté to herself, it must be the sun getting to me. She shook her head in despair at her overactive imagination. She reached over and tapped Kadira on the shoulder. But before she could speak, her friend butted in.

"Did you just say something to me, Ionté? I'm sure I heard someone." She saw the look on Ionté's face, which vanished instantly. "You know, you don't have to call me miss. You're probably more important than me anyway." She grinned easily, shifting position.

Ionté shook her head, smiling warily. "No, I didn't talk to you. I didn't hear anything anyway," she remarked, with a hidden smirk at Kadira's crestfallen expression, which must have been a little like her own when doubting her sanity a few moments earlier. To resolve the situation, she changed the subject.

"I say, it's glorious weather, isn't it? Quite different to where I'm from. Actually, it was rarely that we ever saw the sun there. What about you?"

Kadira paused before answering. "The weather was always like this in Kana...what are you staring at?"

Ionté pointed, her voice rich with excitement. "There! A rider, in silver. Why, look at the speed he's going!"

Kadira followed the line of her arm, then something below the thundering hoofs of the horse caught her eye. She looked down at the pebbled pathway, and her heart skipped a beat. She looked wildly at the worried Ionté, then back at the dark streaking shape, and choked out in a whisper, "It... can't be...not..." But she had already incredulously realised who the dark shape streaking across the ground was, and started to run to intercept the one she had least thought to be here.

Behind her she heard Ionté call, "Who? Who do you see?"

Kadira shouted back, tears flowing freely down her cheeks. "My sister! Khalla! Oh by the Gods,

Khalla!" She ran down the hill, still calling her sister's name.

Ionté stared at the horseman, who by now had reached a point at which she could see him clearly, started to shout something. She was incapable of focusing on his speech when his colourings were like hers. He was an albino! Not a tainted one, like her, but a pure blood like back home! She saw the urgent look in his red eyes just as her brain translated the sound of his speech; he was screaming, "No! Don't let her, stop her, she's heading for the beast!" She tried to reply, to say that everything was actually fine, but his gaze disturbed her. When he reached her, he vaulted off his horse, and ran to the crest of the hill. What he saw made him close his eyes in recognition of failure. Kadira was too far to be stopped, or to hear them if they were to shout. The two white skinned folk could only stand, and watch.

* * *

Beast-Khalla ran like the wind, the scent of her prey strong in her nostrils. The thrill of the chase overwhelmed her, sending adrenaline pumping to her brain. Though her sight was firmly centred on the hated one, a blur in the corner of her vision appeared and moved swiftly towards her. Through her head rush she could dimly hear the human shouting a familiar word, over and over again. Though her speed and agility were great, she could not help but collide with the running person. The woman picked herself up and threw her arms around her. Beast-Khalla disentangled her head, and snarled in frustration as she saw the hated killer run along the jetty. The woman had prevented her from reaching her lifelong enemy, she must be an enemy too! Rage enveloped her, and she scythed her claws through the human's chest, noting with satisfaction the sweet smell of blood. The dark-haired woman's body fell to the ground after the second swipe. Beast-Khalla looked to the jetty, and to her intense anger and disappointment saw a small boat, already surrounded by cold, terrible water. She raised her head and screamed, again and again, venting her fury. He had escaped, her prey, the one she had been chasing for so long! Her main enemy had slipped through her claws!

When she ceased howling, she sat, and started to sniff at the carcass. If it was a relative of the killer, she would eat its heart, and gain some small satisfaction that way. With one paw-hand, she turned the body over, and started to remember. Realisation flooded through her mind, filling her with a terrible, overwhelming grief and despair. She sank down, not registering the changes in her body as well as her mind, threw herself across the body of her beloved sister, and wept.

Chapter 20

Zakrivath continued to circle around the topmost spire of the palace while he and Kethar planned their attack.

'Of course, the whole thing depends on where she is!' snarled Kethar mentally in frustration, annoyed at not thinking about that previously.

I can sense her, replied Zakrivath, tilting his wings to bring them round again. *She is alone.*

'Where about, Zak? Can you land me nearby?'

Wait, sent the shikara, an odd shrill spark in his mental tone. Then suddenly Kethar was swamped with feelings of hatred and violence though their Link, and struggled to keep his balance on the shining black feathers as he flapped his wings furiously. *She has protectors!*

'Shh, shh Zak! What protectors are these?' he soothed, sending loving reassurances to calm the black shikara.

Urgroth, came the hissed reply. *She has summoned our deadliest foes to guard her!* He did not have to wait for

Kethar to ask, but immediately explained, *I remember...I remember fighting, being born knowing I had to fight. Only now do I see my ancient enemy!*

'How many are there?' asked Kethar, apprehensive at the thought of anything that could worry his immense, fierce friend. 'Can we get past them?'

There are two, replied the shikara. *And no, they stand outside the only entrance to the room where the evil one lies. I must fight them.*

'We must, you mean', corrected Kethar faithfully, 'I'm with you!'

No, Zakrivath replied, and Kethar was stunned. His Link had never forcefully disagreed with him before. *No, you must go on, to face the dark one. I am sure of this! Besides,* he added with a crafty, amused tone, *I can't fit through the door.*

With a stroke of the soft feathers, Kethar set back his shoulders and breathed deeply. 'Take us in then, Zak.'

Angling his wings back, their tips folded under, Zakrivath dropped into a low dive, aiming straight towards a small courtyard. He swerved breathtakingly close to avoid spires, balconies and gargoyles, trusting in his rider to hold himself tightly on. His breath held tightly in, Kethar tensed on the great neck as it seemed they were going to clip the edge of the roof. With a fearsome shriek, the black shikara hurtled like a thunderbolt, talons first, into one of two colossal urgroth.

Throwing himself from his friend's neck in time to avoid a huge scaled claw, Kethar landed in a crouch and sprinted towards the small door set in the red wall, pausing only to look back at his friend when he reached it. Zakrivath was rolling in a heap of dusty grey-green scales, flashing claws, tearing jaws, and blood-streaked black feathers, as he fought for time to let Kethar get in. He screamed with agony as the poison teeth met in his leg. *Go,* he shrieked, *go now!* He rose high above the hissing urgroth, beating his wings in their faces as his heavy black beak fell like a great sharpened maul, and his talons reached for vulnerable eyes. Then a thick mailed tail whirled through the air, knocking the perilous shikara to the ground, where the lizards at once dived on him. With a last, desperate glance back at his Link, Kethar burst through the door and drew his long-knife, slamming the heavy wooden bar down to lock the door against intruders. Then, trying to block out Zakrivath's agony and savagery, he turned.

Contrary to his expectations, a neat and orderly room met his gaze, with fine hangings and rich ornamentation decorating the walls. At the opposite end, in a padded purple chair, sat a young woman of about seventeen years of age. Her silky black hair reached down to her dilated belly, and her lovely gown was stained. Kethar gaped in amazement at his one-time mistress, and recovered himself as the lady looked up. Her eyes seemed to focus on him, and she held up a hand, as if to warn him away.

"If you are here to kill me, you will fail. They all do, all who try to stand against me." Her voice was different to how he remembered it; somehow wearier, and harsher.

Kethar approached her, trembling, and knelt down as he had always used to; at her feet. "My lady, it's me, it's Kethar." He smiled reassuringly, his danger and anguish forgotten as a dreamy feeling entered his head. "You are in no danger from me, my Lady. I will protect you from harm." He kept his eyes locked on her face, hardly daring to believe it was her. Just seeing her again brought it all back, his hopeless love for her, and the safe, same old way it used to be. Had always been. He was back with his beloved Mistress, and he was happy. The past year had been a dream, that was all. And yet, why was there a blade unsheathed in his hand? "I am so sorry about this, your highness," he said, indicating the stained long-knife.

"Your Majesty," she corrected, looking unconcerned by the weapon.

"Ye...I'm sorry?" he questioned, looking at her oddly. His dreamy, vague mood flickered for a moment.

"Not your highness, your Majesty," she repeated impatiently. At his blank look she grinned, and snapped her fingers. "I am the Kai Destinae!"

Kethar fell back as the padded chair she was sitting on suddenly rose, and huge black and gold tendrils forced themselves upwards. The wall behind her began to bubble and warp, becoming dark and grimy, covered with torturous implements of pain. He whirled around, a gasp ripping from his throat, as the illusion vanished and he saw the sprays of dried blood up the walls, the rotting, yellow skeletons, and the smoke-blackened, blood spattered altar.

The enormity of realisation hit Kethar so hard that he was incredulous. "But...but I am here to kill the evil one!

The young woman's eyes widened with the pain of a contraction, yet she still answered in a proud voice, filled with contempt and a hint of insanity. "Evil? Who are you to talk of evil? And where is this darkness you see? I have created a perfect empire, where the chaos is so balanced that it becomes order. My urgroth are instantly obeyed, and they serve the greater good; me! I see no darkness, only light, and power."

Shaking his head dazedly, his world turned inside out, Kethar could only repeat in a whisper, "You? You are the... the Mistress of Blood, the Queen of Hell?"

"I am indeed called by many QesAngared, wielder of power. But hell? Your views are different to mine, yet I do not object to you harbouring those different thoughts. You say you are here to kill me, yet I do not call you evil."

Kethar's head began to throb agonisingly; he gritted his teeth against it. He had to prove there was a mistake somewhere. It was all just another kind of illusion. "But I was sent by the Gods! You cannot go against the divine beings, the holy entities, and say you are doing what is good, and right!" The pounding spark in his head increased, as if battle drums boomed throughout his skull.

"Hearken to me, fool," her voice was low and mocking, with a low undercurrent of patronisation. "There is no good, and there is no evil. There is, and has only ever been, opposing sides. To themselves, they are pure and true, and their enemies are evil, and malevolent. To the other side, they are working for a just cause, and their foes are vile and dark. It is not good against evil, but people against people. And the sooner you learn that, my pure-minded adversary, the sooner you will learn that we are all damned." With her last words, she unleashed a bolt of black lightning, and it hit Kethar in the chest. He fell back, choking on his own blood, and she grinned viciously, shouting as she raised her hands to summon more magic, "But you are destined to see hell more early than I!"

Kethar received the second bolt in his calf, and felt rather than heard Zakrivath's cry of agony reverberate through him as he fell to the ground. He felt angry, scared and foolish, and this gave way to wrath. His skull ached and it was hard to think, yet he faced a terrible choice. He had been sent to kill her...yet she was a woman! Though Destiny had told him that the Mistress of Blood was female, nothing on earth could have prepared him for this. He could not kill an unarmed human, especially a female and her unborn child! It was an unforgivable crime! How could the Gods sanction such an unspeakable deed? Even a mercenary wouldn't do such a thing, to kill a young, pregnant woman. Especially Destinariae, who he had loved, who he still loved. Surely the sweet lady that he had served could not be capable of this? Surely it was not of her own free will? He had to try and call her back; he knew she was not responsible for her actions. He scrambled painfully to his feet, trying to ignore the hammering in his head.

"Kaji Destinariae," he began, then leapt to the side to avoid a lightning bolt. He dodged behind a red-splashed pillar as a series of explosions followed his limping feet. "Listen to me, Destinariae," he said again, hearing her hiss at the sound of her one-time name. "This isn't you thinking, and doing these terrible deeds. Come to the light, Destinariae. Follow the sound of my voice." A warning premonition made his neck prickle, and he sprinted painfully away from the column as it blasted outwards in a shower of mortar and falling masonry. He dodged once again as the head of the column smashed a crater in the place he had previously been standing. He saw her unleash another bolt of lightning, and rolled behind the abominable altar, despising himself for having to seek protection behind it. But by her snarl of rage, he realised that she would not attack and risk destroying it.

"I know you can hear me," he called out hoarsely, coughing dust. "You can get the evil one out of your body, I know you can do it! Believe you can, and you will be able to! Come on, Destinariae, let me help you end this!"

A peal of silvery laughter rang through the air. Kethar stood slowly, daring to hope. No murderer could have a laugh like that!

Then Destinae's voice came again, malicious, insane, and scathing. "I'm afraid Destinariae can't talk to you right now, little servant boy. No amount of calling can make her 'come to the light'. You think I am taken over by an evil spirit? How laughable! How pathetic! The sweet Kaji Destinariae was nothing but an act, an innocent mask I put on to conceal my identity. This is who I truly am." Quick as the lightning she released, she shot the black energy towards him where he stood, horrified. It struck him on the hip as he turned to deflect it, and he crumpled in agony onto the altar. In his agony of mind and body he could only watch his one-time mistress. However, she had not finished gloating.

"Your Gods," she spat, "are not all you think they are. Yes, they picked you to come and deal with me. But do you think this makes you more special, more unique? Let me tell you this. If some other boy with an inferiority complex and an ego to be boosted came along, they'd have just as easily played on his pride, and made him arrogant and petty like you. Yes, you were just there at the right time. The Gods don't see us as individuals, as people in their own right, but as little insects, all the same, crawling around on *their* planet. If the Gods have to crush a couple of thousand for their own purposes, they don't care, it's not their primary concern. Yet you think they are good, and divine beings. Yet if I have to remove just a couple of people to get a greater power on the throne, that, to your way of thinking, makes me evil!"

While she was talking, Kethar had been slowly reaching out to touch his fallen knife, the movement hidden by his travelling cape. If he could just disable her, distract her, cause her a little pain, maybe the dark power that infested her would leave. Maybe he wouldn't have to actually kill her. He had seen in the past slaves who were hallucinating, who were believed to be inhabited by evil spirits bringing the visions. Some of their blood was let, for apparently the demon lived in it, and they had recovered fully. If he could only draw blood...

Suddenly he pounced, but the wounds in his leg and chest slowed him, so his knife plunged down her shin. As he hit the floor again, the pain was so intense he wept a little.

Destinae hissed at him sharply, first in pain, then in a kind of malevolent snigger. "I see your thoughts, fool. You still believe I am not myself. Well, I shall have to cause you enough pain that you will not doubt who I really am." With glowing eyes she reached in a small jewelled pouch hanging at her side, and drew out a glorious crystal, blazing with colour and light. "We can't have you trying that again. Now, into what shall we transform you?" she smirked, playing with the extraordinary item. Directly to Kethar she added in a bizarrely conversational tone, "It doesn't really matter. It will hurt beyond all types of torture anyway. It would have to be something weak and defenceless... how about a locust or cricket, so my faithful Amenis could devour you? No, even better, a ram, so I could skin you and make a lovely blanket for the baby." Then she added to herself in a dire growl, "That's if that accursed cat doesn't get you first."

She noticed Kethar struggling to rise. "Well, maybe I'll just have to kill you. Don't worry though, I wouldn't be so heartless as to deprive you of your daily dose of pain."

Kethar stared at her, despair written all over his face. She was truly insane, the way her mood switched backwards and forwards, and how she turned to scan the whole room with bright, fearful eyes. If he was lucky, he would merely die.

Suddenly she looked straight at him. "Do you hear that?" she asked, her voice shaky. When he did not answer she asked again, quickly, "Do you hear that noise?"

He only stared at her, his fear exposed across his face.

She looked around, her arms wrapped protectively around her belly. "They're humming, they're whispering to me," she cried, rocking backwards and forwards. "I can hear them, the swarm of souls, ah! Ah! I can hear them whispering to me!" her head twitched from side to side apprehensively, looking deep into the corners of the terrible room. Suddenly she leaned forward, her finger stabbing at the shadows as she called evilly, "I see you! Skulking there, watching me. You always hated me, envied me! You didn't want me to be happy!" Then her voice reduced to a frightened snivel. "I didn't mean it, I didn't mean to do it, sister, why do you look so at me? Mother, please! Don't tell father! I didn't do it!"

Kethar stared at her, sadness and pity rising within him as he beheld her terrible madness. He looked at the beautiful murderess that had ruined her life, that was crying out in an unhinged plea to the darkness.

"Be still! Be still! I cannot see you unless you stay still. I know you're there…watching, like you always have done. Go away! Help me! Your speech gives you away by your lack of it. I hate you, I tell you there is nothing here for you! Why can't you go away and leave me in peace? Don't you understand how I loathe the very sight of you? I can't see you now…are you hiding from me? Where are you? Help me to see. Please? I need you! Where are you?"

Then her eyes focused again, and fixed themselves on Kethar. He was shocked to see that they had turned black from rim to rim, as if there was nothing but empty, soulless oblivion beneath. "I will kill him, yes, one more gift for the darkness will make all my fears and visions go away. One more death, and I can sleep in peace without these terrible dreams. Just one more…"

Lightning collected between her hands, so much that he felt he was surely going to die. It flooded around her, surrounding her with razor edged magic spitting black sparks. As she was about to unleash the magic upon him, she suddenly shrieked as an agonising contraction gripped her.

Now you must choose, came a voice in Kethar's agonised mind. Do you kill her and end her reign of terror, or does she kill you? Do you serve the Gods by committing the unpardonable murder of a woman and child?

No, he thought with tears streaking down his cheeks, as his head felt like it would split apart with the pressure. Even if it means she lives, and kills others, to commit such a hideous crime would be going against all that is good. By giving my own life, I shall make my stand on the side of light! Through the red mists of Kethar's pain, he saw the lightning collect even more strongly as a result of Destinae's torture. He saw her struggle to regain her grip, and then gasp for breath, bringing her hands down to point at Kethar. He looked into her contorted face and shook as he tried not to close his eyes in fear. As he shrank back, waiting for the inevitable blow, there was an explosion from behind him. Turning back to look, Kethar found the weight on his mind suddenly lifted, as the rear wall exploded in a fountain of glass, dust and plaster. Destinae's head snapped to the side, and she saw Zakrivath, shrieking with wrath and anguish, beating his wings as the sunlight streamed in around his gargantuan, wounded figure, banishing the darkness.

Time seemed to move sluggishly for all three for that moment. Kethar's heart soared in his chest with recognition of his winged rescuer. His soulmate had never looked so proud, so beautiful, and yet so powerful, flinging his head back to scream like a black angel fallen from heaven. His body was coated in grey dust, dark blood running down the once shining black feathers, but he was the epitome of savage splendour as he soared down the room like an avenging demon.

Kethar turned back to Destinae, saw the expression on her face with panic, and shouted a frenzied warning just as the magic left the Mistress' hands and blazed towards Zakrivath. The magic enveloped the shikara, and the scream intensified to an ear-splitting pitch. His sable body, clothed in writhing lightning, charged across the remaining distance, and hit Destinae. The lightning enveloped them both, highlighting the ebony beak as it struck once. Just once.

And then it was over.

"Zakrivath?" asked a weary voice, and Kethar struggled upright. Then he saw the bundle of limp dark feathers. His wings a black shroud, the shikara lay in a bed of carnage. "Oh by the Gods, Zak!" He ran across awkwardly, and collapsed by the side of his ever-loyal friend. Stroking the soft cheek, he wept unashamedly, and the feathers beneath his shaking fingers became wet with grief.

Suddenly, as if the tears revived him, Zakrivath raised one mighty wing. Kethar rocked back on his knees, incredulous. The other massive wing rose from the plaster, showering Kethar with dust and rubble. As he looked on, awe-stricken, the shikara flapped his wings, and rose from the bed of disarray in which he had fallen.

There was no mental communication between them, but Kethar inexplicably knew what he had to do. He vaulted onto Zakrivath's ebony back as the huge bird paced over to the gaping aperture where the wall had once been. Feeling the bunching of powerful muscles under the smooth feathers, he tensed; and the shikara leapt into the sky. With immense wings fully outstretched, Zakrivath soared away from the destruction. He soared away from the bodies of two dead urgroth and the evil, finally beaten, Destinae. He soared away from the abandoned palace, high into the cloudless sky. The almighty wings beat the air strongly, and in the rush of wind Kethar experienced an overwhelming surge of pride. The linked minds shared the exultation, and the overpowering sense of devotion to each other flowed anew. Climbing ever higher in the cerulean sky, man and beast flew as one. By now Lyvilan was small and insignificant, so high they were. Feeling Zakrivath exult in his power, Kethar laughed in exhilaration, and Zakrivath shrieked a challenge to the heavens.

As they hung there, suspended in the air, a shaft of pure golden sunlight fell upon them. Across that land Destiny's voice was heard, and Kethar thrilled with the sensation in his blood the God's voice created.

I thank you for the great deeds you have done this day. You have completed your undertaking. You are now truly as mighty as the first shikara.

And with these words a colossal black shikara, outlined in golden light, appeared in the sky beside them. Zakrivath bowed his head in recognition of Zar. Fate spoke then, with a voice as intense as the first, but touched with dry amusement.

You have performed a great service to us all. Gods and men will be ever reminded of this great thing you have done for us.

And now there was a thunder of voices, all speaking as one. But most discernible amongst them was the voice of Ashikra.

We have conferred between us, and you are to be as the first. You are as Zar was. And you will found the new generation of the shikarath. Even now the new eggs in Skyria we have created are waiting. Find

them soulmates, and they will help you. Like you, they will grow quickly, and then we shall no more interfere in mortal matters. The shikarath are ever a fighting race, and they must fight to save honour, gain rank and protect the people. Even now the stray urgroth are multiplying. Fare thee well, Kethar and Zakrivath.

And as the Gods receded back into the heavens, the mighty Zar stretched out his wing and blessed Zakrivath. The rumble of the first shikara's voice was audible to all, though it was to Zakrivath that he spoke. 'I am Zar, first of the shikarath. You are my disciple, and you will bow to none!'

As the outline of the gargantuan shikara faded into the golden sky, Zakrivath raised his wings in a reverential salute. Kethar stood high upon his soulmate's back, and his shout mingled with the scream of triumph from Zakrivath. The glowing sunlight illuminated them from behind as they seemed almost to blot out the fiery orb, and the shadow they cast was multiplied into enormity. The ground, so far below them, was bathed in breathtaking light, and it seemed as though the very earth itself was in tribute to the shikara who soared on high like a black angel.

Epilogue

A young woman sat, sobbing over a maimed corpse. As Khalla wept, she did not see the movement behind her, though she heard a sound through her heightened senses. Though her own shape and mind had been returned to her, she still had her amazing senses and instincts.

But even these could not let her see the jet black panther walk up behind her, or see what happened to it as it neared her shaking form. All she knew, as she turned to bury her face in the chest of the black haired man that had just appeared as if from nowhere, was her own terrible grief.

* * *

Though there was still snow on the outside of the sheer mountain, the network of caverns was tepid. The five crazily rocking eggs jiggled fiercely, almost falling over. The ten people standing around in a loose ring watched nervously, each glancing more than once at the enormous form of Zakrivath, standing watchful and proud at the opening of the huge chamber.

All of a sudden the largest egg seemed to shiver; then burst open. A fiery coloured chick stumbled forth from the broken shell fragments, and immediately attacked all people to get between him and a sturdy, golden-haired lad who came forward in tense excitement for his soulmate. Three other eggs were opening; one hatched a glittering gold, one a stormy grey chick, and the other a brown one. While the brown chose a pretty strawberry-blonde partner, and the grey found an brown-haired man, the gold moved unerringly to a tall man with red eyes, who stood towards the entrance to the cavern, a horned helmet under his arm. The lucky four moved off with their new-found soulmates, and left a handful of envy-stricken candidates on the sandy rock. As the last egg broke open, all moved with groping arms for the beautiful creamy-white chick that staggered free of the broken egg. All but one, that is. And it was for this person that the chick made her way. The girl raised brilliant green eyes to meet the shining ones of the shikara, and smiled in sheer joy as she Linked.

I am Vecinae, Ionté!

* * *

In a once-proud room, littered with rubble, something stirred. The torn black wall hangings swayed in the gentle breeze from the ruined wall, and the overturned, black throne that lay on its side by the wall seemed diminished, less evil in the soft golden light. There was a sudden gasp from a figure lying flat on the floor, and a flutter of wings as a large raven fluttered in to land at the head of the dying woman.

Destinae looked down at her new baby, watching its tiny eyelids raise for the first time. She had felt the huge surge of released energy as the baby had been born, and knew that the birth of an only half mortal child must have set free a huge amount of magic into the world. It did not cry, though. Instead, it sneezed abruptly...and changed shape. The woman looked down at the kitten in her arms. It kept changing then, so Destinae was holding a squirrel, a mouse, a starling, a snake...the changes were so bright and frequent that Destinae's closing eyes had to look away. The eye-blistering shifting continued, until the dying woman had a sudden idea.

"Amenis," she said hoarsely, coughing up blood, and beckoned the raven forwards. Upon seeing the bird, the new baby stopped in the form of a small raven, and cocked her tiny head to look up at the larger bird standing above her.

"Amenis, take her away. Raise her as you would your own. She will know what to do, when she reaches her full growth." She released the small raven onto the debris-strewn floor, and whispered softly, "Remember me, my love, and remember who you are."

As the two shining black birds leapt from the nest of destruction into the air, Destinae sank back, her task complete as she watched them grow smaller in her dimming vision. As her chest rose for the last time, she said with her final breath, "I name you...Eternitae!"

* * *

The sun shone brightly down on the sleeping man, warming him despite the cold sea wind. The gentle rocking movements of the boat roused him, and he woke. Opening his eyes slowly, Eskiros tasted the sweet flavour of freedom in the air, and smiled in deep satisfaction. He would sail across the Anleian Sea, and find another job. He'd get rich, and travel more, maybe buy a Title and set up his own lands...the world was open to him now, and life had never tasted so sweet.

As he tried to sit up, he felt something cold and hard press against his throat. He tried to lift his hand to investigate, and then someone nearby said, "Don't even think about it."

At once his blood ran cold at the close proximity of the voice. But when he dared to look up at his captor, he almost laughed bitterly at himself for his lack of instinct.

The sandy haired boy looked arrogantly back at him, his deep green eyes smug with self-satisfaction. "Caught you napping, did I?" he smirked, regarding his captive with mock-pity as he held the sabre against the man's throat.

Eskiros lay still, knowing how capricious youngsters could be.

The youth continued, his gleaming eyes never leaving Eskiros' dark, brooding ones. "You're Eskiros, I presume?" At the man's nod he added almost as an aside to himself, "Well, you look just like Khalla described."

Khalla. The name cut like an icy dagger through Eskiros' heart. She had survived? And...oh, by Eternity, she was that thing that was chasing him! He screwed up his eyes, uncaring of the boy's contemptuous glance. Khalla. He still couldn't believe it. She had seemed so weak, so young and trusting, and had welcomed him into her village, her home...and her bed. He had held true to something, at least; he had taught her some fighting moves, but not nearly enough to get her into the Palace of the Tsumetai.

"I can see that yew know who I'm talkin' about. So, I'm gonna tell yew a little story. A story about an arrogant guy who thought 'e could take, and take, and give back only death. Listen up, Eskiros, for I wanna see yew *squirm*."

* * *

He must be disposed of. If he had access to the land across the ocean, who knows what power he could muster?

And the boy with him could be the one to do it. He is full of pent-up emotion already, so we only need to make a spark to light the fire.

But who will do it?

I am with only enough energy to control the air.

Holding the icecaps in place takes all of my magic.

My element drains me also.

Chance, you have done little other than your basic duties. It should be you.

I have the most energy of you all, yet not enough for an Influence. The oceans could flood the land if I was to use too much.

We have none spare. It must be you.

*   *   *

The sun that shone lazily upon the small boat was partly obscured by fluffy clouds. The rest of the sky was clear and blue, but there was a forceful breeze which Eskiros was not quite happy with. As he sat motionless, the cold edge of the blade pressing against his throat, the boat's other occupant continued with his story. The words took the man's mind back to a better time, when he had been the greatest of men, not the poor servant of some haughty murderess, and he swallowed at the unearthed and jagged memories, wincing as the blade nicked his throat.

As he stared at the sandy haired boy opposite him, he marvelled at how the escape had dulled his senses. Otherwise it would not be him being held at sword point. He studied the lad's hate-filled face, seeing a semblance of his own boyhood feelings, somehow softened by the gentle green eyes and abundant freckles.

But even as his gaze raked the youthful face, a shadow fell across the little boat. Glancing upwards, Eskiros frowned. The sky was now almost totally obscured by a thick blanket of grey pregnant clouds, dark and foreboding. He almost shook his head, remembering the knife just in time. This was surely the work of Gods, for no clouds could move that fast!

The boy appeared to notice the ominous weather, for he glanced upwards, and a touch of fear momentarily passed across his face. But just as he tossed his mop of hair back, the rain started to fall. It was no gentle smattering of refreshing droplets; this was a pitiless, driving storm. Within seconds the two were drenched, and Eskiros gritted his teeth against the torrent of pelting raindrops that tore into his skin and sodden clothing. The harsh, stinging wind rose in a gale and wrenched the little craft to the side, almost knocking them down. Waves the size of palaces rose and fell, tossing the miraculously upright vessel and catching it.

As the furious ocean played cruelly with the helpless craft, the sandy-haired boy advanced towards Eskiros, gripping the wooden rail for balance. Too late Eskiros saw the hardness in the lad's eyes- and then he stared stupidly at the dirty sabre handle seeming to grow out of his chest. As he fell backwards over the low rail into the heaving ocean, his hands caught the edge of the boat. The dying man was pulled down into the relentless waves, and with his last grip the vessel overturned. Even as they struggled for life, the man, the boy, and the boat were swallowed by the contemptuous waters.

When the sun sank low in the azure sky, the surface of the ocean shone as if inlaid with a billion glittering diamonds. The now placid surface was calm and still, punctuated only by a flock of elegant diving birds. Beneath the glistening waves, two bodies lay side by side, their blank eyes forever open as they gazed far beyond the ethereal moon, the mute witness to the deaths. And, out on the lonely waters, a song was heard that only the dead could hear. A single, beautiful, haunting refrain.

The song of an angel.

THE END

Character names, their pronunciations, and a brief summary

Quick note: 'ah' sounds to be said quickly, like the vowel sound in 'rat', whereas 'ar' sounds are long, like in 'after'.

In all cases, 'th' is said like 'think', rather than the sound of 'they'.

Each bit of word between hyphens is a syllable. Stress to be put on the emboldened syllable.

Amenis	(Ar-men-iss)	Destinae/QesAngared's intelligent raven
Anderring	(And-air-ring)	Destinariae's suitor, the son of Lord Andrade
Andrade	(An-drayde)	The wealthy lord of Gianesa
Arakiao	(A-rah-kee-ow)	A minion, friend of Enikron
Aramil	(Ah-rah-mill)	Lord Atisato of Rhaleon's head steward
Araquin	(Ah-rah-quin)	Khalla's childhood friend
Aryss	(Ah-riss)	Lord Maxirant's dead lover
Atisato	(At-iz-ar-toe)	The lord of Rhaleon, lover of Kaji Verda
Bheffor	(Beh-for)	Kethar's boisterous friend
Black Sye	(Black S-eye)	The leader of Shakna's mercenary group
Cemrin	(Sem-rin)	Lord Maxirant of Eldron's stablemaster
Chova	(Choe-ver)	A Kaji, one of Tifiert's daughters
Desert	(as written)	Black-skinned mercenary from Garoa
Destinae	(Dess-tin-ay)	The name that QesAngared gives herself
Destinariae	(Dess-tin-ar-ree-ey)	A Kaji, the youngest child of the late Kai Isete

Devarys	(Deh-var-riss)	A Minion of QesAngared
Dyrebus	(Dy-ree-buss)	A middle-aged albino at Ionté's village
Efaerin	(Eh-fair-rin)	A Kaji, the baby daughter of Tifiert
Elwei	(Ell-wy)	Temporary servant of Destinariae
Enikron	(Eh-nik-ron)	A Minion
Eratis	(Eh-rar-tis)	A Minion, messenger of QesAngared
Erendiir	(Eh-ren-deer)	Sithe's mentor, the Wanderer, Eternity's disciple
Eskiros	(Ess-kih-ross)	Rogue Tsumetai, Viper, working for QesAngared
Eternitae	(E-ter-ni-tey)	Half-human, half-magic daughter of Destinae
Faitan	(Fay-tan)	A Kaji, the second-youngest child of Kai Tifiert
Fraine	(Frayn)	A Minion
Ghiron	(Geer-ron)	Mercenary, brother of Black Sye
Hound	(as written)	Mercenary, talks to canines
Hurai	(Heur-ry)	A blacksmith from Khalla's village
Imcarr	(Im-car)	Jailer working for QesAngared
Ionté	(Eye-on-tey)	A half-albino from Garoto, in the Snowlands
Isete	(Iz-et)	The first wife and Kai of the Ka Turanis
Jienth	(Jee-enth)	A Minion
Kadira	(Kah-deer-rah)	Khalla's sister, presumed dead, from Kanako
Kethar	(Keh-thar)	Soulmate of Zakrivath, once a servant
Khalla	(Kah-lah)	Kadira's sister, from Kanako
Kieso	(Kee-ay-so)	A young albino at Ionté's village

Luellor	(Loo-el-lor)	A traitor to QesAngared
Macharra	(Mah-char-rah)	A pony herder from Garoto
Mad Red	(as written)	Mercenary, from Cular
Marghaska	(Mar-gass-kah)	A foreigner, becomes Destinariae's servant
Mathilane	(Math-il-lane)	Lord Maxirant's illegitimate son
Maxirant	(Max-ih-ront)	The Lord of Eldron
Mocrin	(Mock-rin)	An executed supposed murderer
Naraia	(Nah-ray-ah)	Khalla's old nurse
One-eyed Em	(as written)	Mercenary, branded
Onguet	(On-gew-et)	The bankrupt lord of Cyllnar
Ontua	(On-teu-ah)	The son of Lord Onguet
Opias	(O-pee-as)	A pretty girl from the slave village
Phantra	(Fan-trah)	A Minion
Poricala	(Poh-rih-car-lah)	Lord Thambar's ambitious half-sister
Pravar	(Prah-var)	Shoy's real name, a child bandit
QesAngared	(Kess'-Ang-gar-red)	A power-hungry, magic-wielding woman
Ranalf	(as written)	A Minion
Rhanno	(Ran-noe)	A Count
Rieda	(Ree-ay-dah)	The eldest Kaji, heir to the Imperial Throne
Sanniah	(San-nee-ah)	Kethar's friend
Shakna	(Shak-nah)	A young mercenary
Shoy	(as written)	A young boy who befriends Khalla (see Pravar)
Sindarre	(Sin-dar)	Ionté's mother
Sirenthe	(Sih-renth)	An albino youth seeking knowledge
Sithe Ren	(Scythe Ren)	The changed name of Sirenthe
Tanjaron	(Tan-jah-ron)	A Minion Captain
Tansden	(as written)	One of Maxirant's captains
Thambar	(as written)	The ageing lord of Thermone
Theyron	(as written)	Sirenthe's father

Tifiert	(Tiff-ee-urt)	The Kai after Isete
Tioni	(Tee-own-ee)	A Kaji, the oldest child of Tifiert
Toria	(Tor-ree-ah)	Khalla's childhood friend
Turanis	(Tuer-raa-niss)	The Ka of Bakarn
Untya	(Unt-yah)	Mercenary, one-time partner of Black Sye
Verda	(Vur-dah)	A Kaji, Destinariae's beautiful older sister
Verpaythe	(Ver-payth)	Verda and Atisato's red-haired baby daughter
Verbethe	(Ver-beth)	Verda and Atisato's blonde baby daughter
Vershesa	(Ver-shee-sah)	Verda and Atisato's dark haired baby daughter
Vine	(as written)	Mercenary, green haired and cunning
Wirghan	(Wur- gan)	A minion
Yaelon	(Yay-lon)	Khalla's childhood friend
Zakrivath	(Zak-rih-vath)	The black shikara, soulmate of Kethar

Terms of Interest:

Damelin-   potions specialists who excelled in healing, poison-making, and dabbling slightly in earth magic mainly to increase the power of their herbal mixtures.

Gijau-   a board game of strategic warfare played amongst the nobility. Often games can last days, or weeks.

Ka, Kai, Kajo, Kaji-   Ranks similar to King, Queen, Prince, and Princess. Can also be used as suffixes to imply rank amongst a group e.g. shikarakai (shikara-queen), Tsumetai-ka (king of the Tsumetai) or Kajaritoka (leader of the Kajarito).

Kajarito-   the soldiers comprising the national army, trained in loyalty to the Royal family.

Keh-harande-   a whip made of intersecting rings of steel

Skyria-   the fabled home of the mythical shikarath, a huge snow-covered mountain near Lyvilan

Taraht cards-   cards with different words and pictures upon them, used to forecast the future. Traditionally read by ravens.

Tsumetai-   weapon masters, named after animals, trained for years in a secret base. Kill their mentors to assume ranks, before emerging into the world do as

they please, usually being hired as
bodyguards or assassins

Gods and their Creatures:

Ashikra –
Shikara(th)

God of air and the skies

Chance –
Nyaphim

Goddess of the earth and nature

Destiny –
Urgoth

Goddess of time and the seasons

Eternity –
Emathai

God of the future and infinity

Fate –
Mantifel

God of ice

Fortune –
Isha/ Ishel (pl)

Goddess of water and the oceans

Luck –
Findaena

Goddess of fire

The Royal Family:

Ka Turanis
Kai Tifiert
Kaji Rieda
Kaji Verda
Kaji Destinariae
Kaji Tioni
Kaji Chova
Kaji Faitan
Kaji Efaerin

Festivals:

Midwinter festival-   the poor always suffer the most through winter, trying to ration their food to last and this day is when they celebrate being together by breaking their fast and feasting.

Spring Equinox-   the festival celebrated by Bakarnians to mark the start of the New Year. All shops and businesses are closed, and nobody works.

Autumn Equinox-   similar to the spring Equinox, Bakarnians celebrate a profitable Harvest and summer.

<u>Languages:</u>

Bakarnian modern tongue
The old language
Garoan

<u>Countries:</u>

Bakarn-   An empire run by the Royal family, bordered by the Anleian Ocean, Jaharon, Kanako, Cular, Garoa, and the Snowlands

Cular -   A generally cold country south of the Snowlands, north of Kanako, and north-west of Bakarn

Garoa-   A huge, hot, desert land to the south of Bakarn

Jaharon-	A cold, stormy marshland area south of the Snowlands, north-east of Bakarn, and north of the Anleian Ocean
Kanako-	A large, dry, mostly plains country south of Cular, north of Garoa, and west of Bakarn. The Kanakoan desert lies within.
The Snowlands-	A land of snow and ice north of Bakarn, inhabited by albinos who live in small, desolate villages.
The Anleian Ocean-	The ocean to the east of Bakarn; translated from the old language as the 'one-sided' ocean because nobody has yet been able to find what lies on the other shore.

Towns/Villages:

Darea-	a village in the Snowlands, near to Garoto
Eredeth-	the slave village, with tax-free housing so long as every first-born child is sent to be a labourer for the Crown.
Garoto-	Ionté's village in the Snowlands
Lyvilan-	the capital city of Bakarn, where the Royal family live.
Mephra-	a town renowned for its carpentry
Siannorel-	the village that Kethar and Zakrivath are thrown out of, that they raid

Character names, their pronunciations, and a brief summary

Thago-   the last Bakanian village, little more
than a hovel, before the Frozen Pass into
the Snowlands

Treulle-   a village in the Snowlands, near the
Frozen Pass to Bakarn

About the Author

Charlotte Lester was born during a tornado in October 1987. She has been reading fantasy since she was six, and writing it for almost as long. She finished 'Black Angel' at 14, and is now immersed in the completion of two other novels. Though fantasy is her true love, she has devised the plots for over 50 books, films and screenplays of various genres.

Charlotte enjoys reading, writing, acting, being sarcastic, invading popular places with equally insane friends, playing her black sax, and seduction by piano; she does not enjoy working, being serious, physical exertion, spontaneous combustion, or getting up before 2 p.m. She would reveal whereabouts she lived in England, but is afraid the men in white coats will finally find her.

Printed in the United Kingdom
by Lightning Source UK Ltd.
101753UKS00001B/37-123